PREGNANT WITH THE BOSS'S BABY

BY
SUE MacKAY

REUNITED WITH HIS RUNAWAY DOC

BY
LUCY CLARK

MILLS &
BOON

Sue MacKay lives with her husband in New Zealand's beautiful Marlborough Sounds, with the water on her doorstep and the birds and the trees at her back door. It is the perfect setting to indulge her passions of entertaining friends by cooking them sumptuous meals, drinking fabulous wine, going for hill walks or kayaking around the bay—and, of course, writing stories.

Lucy Clark loves movies. She loves binge-watching box sets of TV shows. She loves reading and she loves to bake. Writing is such an integral part of Lucy's inner being that she often dreams in Technicolor®, waking up in the morning and frantically trying to write down as much as she can remember. You can find Lucy on Facebook and Twitter. Stop by and say g'day!

PREGNANT WITH THE BOSS'S BABY

BY
SUE MacKAY

Published in Great Britain 2017
By Mills & Boon, an imprint of HarperCollins*Publishers*
1 London Bridge Street, London, SE1 9GF

© 2017 Sue MacKay

ISBN: 978-0-263-92653-8

Our policy is to use papers that are natural, renewable and recyclable
products and made from wood grown in sustainable forests. The logging
and manufacturing processes conform to the legal environmental
regulations of the country of origin.

Printed and bound in Spain
by CPI, Barcelona

Dear Reader,

I can't imagine having to work all week with a gorgeous man I love and not wanting him to have an inkling of my feelings. The tension would be huge. Throw in a pregnancy and it would be more than awkward!

For Tamara the choice is taken out of her hands—and the shock to Conor is massive. But working together actually helps them resolve some of their issues. Of course nothing's straightforward, and I've enjoyed throwing obstacles in their way...

You'll also briefly meet Kelli and Mac in this story. To see how their romance unfolds look out for my next book in the coming months.

Happy reading!

Sue MacKay

suemackay.co.nz
sue.mackay56@yahoo.com

Books by Sue MacKay

Mills & Boon Medical Romance

Reunited...in Paris!
A December to Remember
Breaking All Their Rules
Dr White's Baby Wish
The Army Doc's Baby Bombshell
Resisting Her Army Doc Rival

Visit the Author Profile page
at millsandboon.co.uk for more titles.

CHAPTER ONE

'THAT WAS TOO close for comfort.' Nurse Tamara Washington watched the paediatric intensive care team wheel their tiny patient towards the lift and PICC.

'Every parent's worst nightmare,' Conor agreed as he dropped onto a chair at the emergency department's work centre. 'At one point I didn't think we'd get him back.'

The baby had stopped breathing while being examined to find what was causing his dangerously high temperature.

'But you did. We did.' Sometimes it astonished her that they were able to revive someone so young and small. Always it shook her up. Today... Today it had been hard to hold her emotions in. Too close, too frightening. What-ifs played in her head as she stared at the man typing in notes on the baby's file. He needed to know.

'Have I grown a wart on the back of my head?' Conor asked in that Irish lilt that tightened her toes, and a whole lot of other areas of her body.

'Can you spare me a few minutes at the end of the day?' Tamara's chest clenched as her reluctant question came out. A few minutes that would change Dr Maguire's quiet, easy life for ever. No matter which path he took in response to the lightning bolt she had to deliver.

'Sure.' He tossed her a negligent eyebrows-raised

glance. 'What's bugging you? More stuff about med school?' He'd been more than patient with her over the application, and must think she was a pain in his gorgeous backside with her continual, often repetitive questions.

Tamara glanced around Auckland Central Hospital's ED, the place in which she felt most at home, and definitely most confident. This was where she knew her stuff.

'That's me. Crossing the "t"s and dotting the "i"s before I finally push "send".' Not even a reputed university had been going to get the better of her. These days she checked *everything*, over and over.

'Those "t"s and "i"s will be so crossed and dotted they'll be unrecognisable.' Conor gave her one of his dynamic, tummy-tingling smiles.

Except her stomach was far too tense to tingle. 'Today's the day I finish with it.' Literally. Trash-bin finish. Training to become a doctor was the dream she'd been working towards all year. The dream she was so invested in had turned to dust over a thin blue line on a plastic stick. Two test kits, different brands, same result. No argument.

Tamara's left hand pressed, oh, so gently on her unhappy tummy while her teeth worried her bottom lip. At least her mouth was better occupied doing that than spewing out any of the thoughts mashing her up on the inside. This being in charge of her life was full of pitfalls, all of them deep and dangerous. It was *her* life, right? Sometimes she wondered.

Conor cut through her worry. 'As long as the shift doesn't run over too much, let's go to the local for a drink and food.'

'No.' Nausea swamped Tamara at the thought of greasy pub food. As for alcohol, forget that for a while.

Sweat saturated the folds of her baggy scrubs. Since the first tweak of nausea on waking last Friday morning she'd been in a terrible state, gutted at the abrupt about-turn in her well-laid-out, Tamara-controlled plans. Of course she'd fought the obvious, denied the deepening despair, knowing she'd lost another round in life's plans for her.

'Why not?' Conor looked bemused.

He hadn't spent the weekend fighting the inevitable. No, that started for him later today. 'Can we stick to your office?' So you can vent in private. 'I won't take up much of your time. Promise.'

His kingfisher-blue eyes widened briefly. 'This *is* about your application for university?' As head of this emergency department, Conor had backed her all the way when she'd decided to start studying extramurally with the goal of entering med school next year.

'For the absolute last time.' No doubt there.

'Right, my office when we're done with headaches and broken bones.'

His thick brogue wrapped around her, softening her heart when it needed to be steel, making her feel all mushy about him despite not wanting to feel anything for him. A sexy man with a whole lot more going for him, he was hard to ignore. They'd shared one night in his bed—with devastating consequences. No denying the tingle in her thighs and lower belly whenever he turned all Irish on her, though. But that was about the sex they'd shared. He'd been hot, and imaginative, and very, very good. Phew, her cheeks were warming at the memories. Of the sex. Nothing else. Sometimes she still pinched herself to make sure she hadn't imagined it. Now she had the evidence. No more pinches.

The strident sound of the buzzer from the ambulance bay curtailed any further discussion as Conor leapt up from the chair. 'Here's our guy.' A car-versus-truck victim. Possible flail chest injury.

Hurrying after the only man Tamara had been intimate with in years, her gaze automatically scanned Conor's longish black hair at the back of his neck, remembering how she'd run her fingers through the glossy waves. That had been then. Today was a whole new ball game. Learning she was carrying his baby was going to knock Conor off his impeccable stride.

Tamara heard the paramedic begin to give Conor her report on their latest stat one patient, and pulled on her professional face, straightened her back into its now usual, though false, don't-fool-with-me, ramrod-straight line and pushed aside any thoughts not related to work.

'Impact to the chest from the steering wheel, suspected broken ribs and perforated lungs.'

Conor interrupted the woman. 'Tamara, take over debrief. I'm getting this guy into Resus and the radiology technician onto him now.' Calm belied the urgency of Conor's statement; the only giveaway to his concern a thickening of that mouth-watering drawl. He was already rushing the stretcher towards Resus, a second ambulance officer with him moving as fast.

Time was running out if their man had a flail chest. With broken ribs tearing holes in the lungs on every breath, the guy would simply run out of oxygen in very little time.

'How long since the accident happened?' she demanded of the paramedic, worried about the man's chances of survival.

'Approximately fifteen minutes ago. Just around the corner on Grafton Road. We were already on the road, heading to another accident, when the call came through. It was a load-and-go the moment we figured out what might be his major injury.'

'Good on you for not hanging around, checking him out.' Seemed something was on their patient's side. 'What else have you got?'

As the paramedic listed the other injuries Jimmy Crowe had sustained, Tamara couldn't help sighing with relief. She was going to be busy for the next hour, so her mind would stay shut down on everything else.

'Tamara, we need oxygen happening,' Conor called as she ran into Resus. 'ASAP.'

'Onto it.' Tamara shoved the paperwork into another nurse's hands. 'Kelli, can you read these obs out to Conor?' Reaching for the gas, she mentally crossed her fingers they weren't too late and that some oxygen would do its job.

She and Kelli worked in unison with Conor to get Jimmy's bleeding and breathing under some sort of control. A cannula was slid into the left arm to allow for essential fluids to enter the man's bloodstream.

Michael, a registrar, joined them. 'A steering-wheel injury?'

Conor nodded. 'Yes.'

Tamara wiped blood from the man's mouth. 'This could back up the lung-damage theory.'

'Stand back, everyone,' the radiology tech called from behind his portable unit. *Whizz, click, whizz.* Angles were changed, more images taken. Even before he'd finished Conor demanded, 'What've we got?'

'Give me a minute.'

'We haven't got a minute.'

Tamara understood Conor's impatience. Their patient's life depended on what the X-rays showed.

The images appeared almost immediately on the screen and Conor studied them with the intensity of a specialist determined not to lose his patient. 'Fractures to the right side of his rib cage but no ribs pushed in at the front. There's some displacement at the front, and two ribs have broken off the sternum, but they're not causing further damage to the lungs.'

From beside him Tamara also peered at the images. The tightness in her shoulders did not ease. 'I think our man's very lucky.'

'On count one, yes. But from my observations so far there's probably a skull fracture, likewise with the right elbow, where, going by the amount of blood leakage, the artery is torn, plus internal injuries to deal with.' Conor had already called for someone to get onto the lab to come and take a blood sample for cross-match. He turned to the guy from Radiology. 'I need pictures of his pelvis and arms while you're at it. Flick them all straight through to the radiologist.'

'No problem.'

'His spleen's damaged,' Conor reported later after a call from the radiology department. 'Wonder what caused that? And the other injuries below the ribs,' he pondered aloud as he snatched up the phone again. 'I'm getting the surgical team on standby up to speed.'

'The corner of the other vehicle must've pushed the side of the car inwards,' Tamara commented.

'How's that oxygen flow?' Conor demanded as he held the phone to his ear. 'What's his sat level?'

Everyone worked quickly and thoroughly, doing their damnedest to save the man's life. When they finally stepped away to let the orderly take Jimmy to Theatre, where surgeons were scrubbed and waiting, Tamara felt exhaustion roll through her. 'That was crazy.' But what they were used to. Except she didn't usually feel so tired afterwards.

Tiredness *and* nausea. Not normal for her. But they were for pregnancy. The towel she was unfolding dropped to the floor. It was so unfair it was incomprehensible. Oh, like life hadn't been inconsiderate before? Hadn't blown up in her face in the past?

On the far side of the room Conor was talking through a yawn. 'I hate impact injuries. They're often extreme and messy, let alone hard to stabilise.' Why was he tired? Had a busy weekend between the sheets, had he?

A twinge of regret tightened her already tight stomach. Jealousy didn't suit her, and was irrelevant as they were only friends and colleagues. Conor liked the ladies, nothing new there. She'd been quick to walk away after that fantastic night in his bed, being wary of any more involvement with him. Even then her heart had sent her a warning: *Beware, Conor's dangerous to your determination to remain single*.

She watched him rubbing his lower back as he stretched up onto his toes, swivelling his neck left then right. His gaze caught hers as he continued, 'Vehicles of all kinds are so damned dangerous.'

Her breath hitched in her throat as she locked eyes with him. A look like this one had led to her predicament. A night on the town with colleagues and *kapow!* One of those lingering, across-heads-of-people-dancing looks and she'd known they'd have to connect up. And reciprocal knowledge had been blinking out at her from Conor's eyes. No denying something had to happen between them. And it had. Her mouth watered at the memories of the hottest night she'd ever experienced. And he was looking at her like that now. Her gut tightened. It would be so easy to follow through on the promise in those eyes.

Problem. They were at work. It wasn't happening again. She was about to turn his world upside down. How many more reasons did she need?

'Hello, Tamara. Anyone home?' Conor waved at her, stopping those distracting thoughts. Not that he looked any more comfortable than she was.

What had they been talking about? Vehicles and danger. 'Enough to put me off driving.' Tamara dragged her eyes forward, away from the promise, avoiding that toned body, and focused on the bed she needed to strip. The muscles his scrubs were hiding were lean and strong and sexy.

She'd been rambling on about driving when she didn't own a car. That eye-lock had a lot to answer for. 'Being bowled off my bike would be a bigger mess, I reckon.' The bike on her back porch that had a thick layer of dust covering it and spiders' nests between the spokes of the wheels sitting on flat tyres.

'You ever going to ride that thing again?' Kelli asked with a hint of amusement from the other side of the bed.

Not in the foreseeable future. Her hand touched her tummy before she realised where she was and jerked it away. People around here had eyes in the back of their skulls. 'I doubt it. I'm such a wimp. Since that day I rode into a grass-covered ditch and got tossed into the field, I keep thinking about splatting onto the road.' She shivered. The media had been chasing her for a comment on her ex's latest crime that had been exposed. It was lucky she'd got away with three stitches in her arm where a broken bottle hidden in the grass had sliced her. 'I know a warning when I see one.'

Not with Conor, she hadn't. His easy manner and take-me-or-leave-me attitude had added to the compelling physical need he'd stirred up within her over that dance floor. He'd been the first man since Peter. The first kiss, first sex, first sleepover. Sort of like getting back in the saddle, only more frightening because she'd understood how hard the fall could be.

At least with Conor it had only been about the great sex, and one night had not led to others. In fact, he'd seemed relieved when she'd leapt out of bed the following morning, hauled on her clothes, and declared, thanks, but got to go. He hadn't seen the fear of wanting more from him that she'd struggled to hold at bay until she'd got away. The fear made harder to hide when he'd done an about-face and invited her to breakfast at a classy café near his apartment. Almost as if her rejection had piqued his interest. When, in desperation, she'd declined, he'd insisted on walking her to the bus stop. All part of his charm, and utterly dangerous in its temptation.

'Incoming severe asthma attack,' the triage nurse called as she slammed the phone back in place. 'ETA ten minutes.'

'No rest for the wicked.' Conor grinned. 'Or even the slightly bad.'

'We can't complain that the day's dragging,' Tamara retorted. Her day was taking for ever to tick by, yet at the same time three o'clock was charging at her full speed. How would Conor react? Would he storm out, shouting that she was a liar or a con artist? Or would he pat her on the head and say good luck and goodbye?

'What is up with you today? You're very distracted.' Conor studied her from his six-foot-plus height. 'Come to think of it, you're looking peaky.'

'I'm fine,' she snapped, and headed to a cubicle where she could hear a middle-aged woman with a suspected broken ankle groaning. Peaky? Right. Of course she was peaky. She'd tossed up her breakfast that morning, hadn't she? At least it'd happened before she left home and not on the bus, or, worse, not here where some nosy parker would notice quicker than wildfire ignited dry tinder and come up with the wrong cause. Or the right one.

'Tamara, I want you on the asthma with me,' Conor called after her.

'No problem,' she lied. *Ask someone else.*

'In a better mood.'

Tamara nearly leapt into the air. She hadn't heard him coming closer. 'Don't sneak up on me,' she growled as her heart thumped loud enough for the whole department to hear.

'Whoa.' His hands were up, palms towards her. 'Maybe you need to take a quick coffee break. Get some caffeine into your system. Something's got your knickers in a twist and it's not a good look in ED.'

He was right. When wasn't he? On a long, raggedy indrawn suck of air she managed, 'Sorry. I had a restless night. Seems it's catching up with me.' As if she could have slept when the truth had been leaching into her mind, pushing aside her dreams, taunting her. No wonder her head was beginning to pound like there was a band of bongo drummers in there. She never did well on less than eight hours' sleep. Something she'd planned on getting used to once she started her medical training.

Now she was readjusting, learning the new phrase— once she became a mother.

'Your mood anything to do with what you want to talk to me about?'

Too shrewd for your own good, Dr Maguire.

'No. Yes. Sort of.'

'Bring me a coffee when you get yours, will you?'

In other words, she wasn't getting away without a caffeine fix. Sorry, baby. Don't take any on board, or you'll be buzzing all afternoon. 'Three sugars?' She arched an eyebrow at him.

'For you, not me.' He flipped a smile in her direction before reaching for another patient form, that earlier tiredness now tugging at his mouth.

Damn that smile. It could undo all her resolve to be firm with him. 'Looks like you need the caffeine more than I do,' Tamara muttered as she headed for the kitchenette. Tea for her. It might be less aggressive on her system. See, getting used to there being a baby growing inside.

Her knees gave out on her and she buckled against the wall as very real fear overcame her. Her dream was going up in smoke before she'd even pushed 'send' on that application. Becoming a mother was not part of the plan, had only been a remote, 'not likely to happen in this lifetime' kind of dream. But not any more. Not in her current situation. How was she going to cope? It wasn't as though she'd had a good role model in her mother. While Dad had been the steady influence, Mum had always been a little off kilter, doing things without thought to time or place or other people. Like hopping on a flight to Melbourne for the fashion show and not telling Dad where she was until she'd landed. Dad had shrugged, said that's your mother for you, and taken her out to dinner at a five-star restaurant. She'd been six at the time. Which parent would she follow? She knew which one she wanted to be like, but wasn't sure of her capabilities.

'Tamara? What's going on?'

Conor could be so nosy. She shuffled her body up the wall until she stood upright, not quite ramrod straight, and eyeballed him. 'Having a wee kip on the way to get those drinks.'

'You think you should be at work? You're not exactly on form today.'

'Have I made any mistakes? Looked incapable of doing my job?'

'Not yet.' Conor studied her for a long moment. No heated connection going on now. 'Take thirty. Get something to eat to go with that coffee.' Her face must've given her away because his hand went up, palm out. 'No argument.'

When he took her arm and led her into the tiny space that was the staff kitchenette she had no choice other than to go with him. Putting up a fight was a waste of time and energy that was best saved for other more important issues.

'Here.' Conor removed a brown paper bag from a cupboard and placed it on the bench. 'Cheese scone from the café. Get it down you.' Then he reached for the coffee.

A warning rose from her tense gut. No way. Food would have to wait. 'Th-thanks. Tea for me.' And this was the woman who had taken control of her life and refused to let anyone or anything tip her off track again? Tamara reached for the bag, tore it open and broke off a tiny corner of the scone. *Shut up, stomach. Whose side are you on, anyway?* And she popped the morsel into her mouth and chewed. And chewed. Swallowed. *Take that.* She took another small bite, and locked eyes with Conor. 'Just what I needed,' she agreed around a wave of relief that her stomach was supporting her. However briefly. For now she was back on track.

'I'll hand that asthma over to one of the junior doctors, then we'll take our drinks to my office and have that talk you asked for.'

'What? Now?' She tipped sideways, grabbed at the bench. 'It can wait.' *I'm not ready.*

'Something's up and it's affecting you. Best we sort it and get on with the day. Finish making those drinks, will you?' Conor shot out the door, leaving her shaking.

On autopilot she spooned coffee into one mug, dropped

a tea bag into another, added sugar and boiling water to both. Stirred. *It's too late to do a runner. Time to face the facts.*

'Ready? Good.' Conor swooped back into the small space, picked up both full mugs in one hand and took her elbow in the other. 'Let's go.'

And then they were there, Conor's office door clicking shut behind her, and the air all hot and heavy. Tamara sank onto the closest chair, gripped her hands between her knees and stared at the floor. She should've dug into the back of her wardrobe and found something half-decent to wear for this, instead of looking like the frump she hid behind. But then he'd have known something was up.

She heard the mugs being placed on the desk, Conor's chair being pulled out, his knee clicking as he sat down. She felt his eyes on her, his bewilderment boring into her. Her skin chilled, and the moisture evaporated from her mouth.

Slowly lifting her head, she nearly leapt up and ran. There was so much concern radiating out at her from across the desk it undermined all the lessons on men she'd learned from her ex. Could Conor care about her that much?

'Start at the beginning.' Conor's soft voice flowed over her, tightening already tight muscles and jangling nerve endings.

There was no beginning. No ending. Only the facts. Her spine couldn't straighten to ramrod straight. Her tongue felt too big for her mouth. Her heart squeezed in on itself so hard pain shot out in all directions. 'I'm pregnant.'

He rocked backwards in his chair, those beautiful eyes widening with disbelief. Or was it shock? She couldn't read him clearly. Gone was the open-faced, cheerful, friendly man everyone adored.

Might as well go for broke, put it all out there. In a strangled whisper, she told him, 'You're the baby's father.'

Then she waited for the axe to fall. And waited and waited. The silence was stifling. The walls came closer, squeezing the heavy air around her, suffocating her.

Say something, Conor.

CHAPTER TWO

'I'M PREGNANT.' The words ricocheted from wall to wall.

Conor slammed back in his seat as all the air in his lungs spewed into the room. The silence was deafening. As if everyone in the hospital was holding their collective breath.

'You're the baby's father.'

Tell me this isn't true. But Tamara looked certain. Apprehensive, but definitely sure. There was no colour in her cheeks, no warmth in her eyes, and her hands were rubbing her arms like they were cold. 'You can't be. I used condoms.' Rule number one: when indulging in sex, use protection. No exceptions.

'I am, and you did.'

No, no, no. He leapt to his feet, an oath spilling across his lips. 'You're saying one was faulty?' He saw his disbelief drill into her, wanted to regret his words, but couldn't quite. She mustn't be pregnant. Not with *his* child.

Tamara pulled back, her eyes locked on him. 'Faulty, torn in use, I have no idea. I only know that I haven't had a period since that weekend, and there was a blue line on the test stick.' She gulped. 'On both sticks.'

'Making certain, were you? Crossing the "t"s and dotting the "i"s?' So like Tamara, he'd laugh if there was anything humorous about this. A chill was spreading through him. She wasn't lying. It wasn't a sick joke. Not that she'd ever do that. It was just that… It was impossible to believe.

Because he didn't want to. He'd been running from getting involved for the last fourteen years. Hell, he'd come all the way down to New Zealand to keep the yearning for love and family at bay. To stand alone, not get close to anyone. Showed how much he knew. Seemed life had always been going to catch up with him, regardless of what he did.

'There's a lot at stake.' There was a quiver in Tamara's voice that rattled him.

And pricked his heart. *Don't go there*. He wasn't available. Conor opened up to the chill ramping through him, let it into his voice box. 'Sure is. When did you do the tests?'

'Friday. Then Saturday.'

Conor felt his face tighten, worked at softening his facial muscles. Failed. 'You could've said something sooner. You've got my phone number.' Genuine anger was moving in, heating his cheeks, deflecting the chill.

'I could have, yes.' Tamara swallowed, started again. 'But I didn't want to believe it. Telling you makes it irrefutably real.'

'You were in denial.' That he could understand. About where he was right now.

'Totally. I have—' *Gasp*. Her hands clenched tight on her elbows. 'I *had* plans, and being pregnant is upending everything. Again. I've worked so hard to be in charge of my future.'

What did she mean by again? And being in charge of herself? Wasn't everybody? 'You don't want the baby?' he snapped. How did that make him feel? Relieved? Not at all. Really? Who the hell knew? Not him. He charged for the door, reached for the handle to haul it open. Stopped. Spun around to face her, rose up and down on his toes as he waited for her reply to his telling question.

'I never said that,' she said sharply. 'Or implied it.'

'Just checking.' *Sounding like a heel, boyo.* Now, there was a surprise. His head was full to the brim with questions, denials, longings, anger—every blasted emotion under the sun. Name it, it was there. 'I don't know you well enough to read your mind.'

Tamara fixed him with a glare. 'Then take this on board. I won't be going to university next year after all, and I so wanted to become a doctor. Instead I'm having a baby. Then I'm going to be a mother, something I know next to nothing about.' She stared at him, imploring him to understand. 'I don't want to be like my mother. She believed nannies were put on earth so she could go to charity meetings and play mediocre golf.'

The bitterness colouring those words was almost tangible and Conor wanted to wipe it away, make her feel better. So he remained by the door. Start doing that and who knew what would happen next. They had a lot to get through over the coming weeks and any out-of-the-ordinary moves like that would only turn everything murky. He had to be aloof, separate. 'I'd have said she did a great job with you.' There, honest but uninvolved.

Tamara snarled, 'Don't talk about something you know nothing about.'

Ouch. He'd hit a painful point, for sure. 'Fair enough.' He strode back to his chair, dropped into it and banged his feet on the desktop. His hands gripped together under his chin as he studied Tamara. Looking for what? He wasn't sure.

'There's nothing fair about any of this,' she retorted.

He couldn't agree more. But what he said was, 'You have no idea.'

'About what?' she asked in a rare belligerent tone.

'I can't have children.'

'Wrong. You are having one next year. In April, I reckon. It's no one else's.'

'I am not accusing you of lying to me, Tamara.'

She lurched, as though stabbed by pain. Her hands clenched even tighter. But she kept her head high and those cocoa-coloured eyes fixed on him. 'Then I don't understand.'

'I can't have children. It's as simple as that.'

Someone knocking on the door had Conor hauling his feet off the table quick fast. 'Go away. I'm busy,' he yelled in frustration.

They both held their breaths until it became apparent whoever was out there had taken his advice.

Tamara asked quietly, 'You can't? Or won't?'

Back to the elephant. She knew next to nothing about him, and he wasn't about to let his tongue go crazy filling in the gaps. Though there was one detail he'd have to reveal. His feet hit the floor in an instant, and his head spun as he came upright. Not now. Not today.

'Conor?' Not so quiet.

'Either way, it makes no difference.'

Tamara's eyes narrowed. 'If there are things I need to know for my baby's sake then tell me.'

He moved away from the desk abruptly, his chair flung back against the wall. His hands went to his hips, held tight. 'All my adult life I've actively avoided this exact moment. Yet here it is, staring me down.' Commitment with a capital C.

'Don't you like children? You're always amazing with them in the department, teasing and fun, easing their distress. I wouldn't have believed you were faking it.' She paused, and when he didn't answer she continued. 'We need to talk, about a lot of things. Seems you've got issues. Which means I do too. I need to know what they are, Conor. For our child's sake, if nothing else.'

'What I need right now is some air. This office is stuffy. I'll see you back at work shortly.' Pulling the door open, he stepped right up against Michael's extended hand.

'I was about to knock,' the registrar muttered, dropping his hand quickly. 'We've got a situation and you're both needed. Urgently.'

'I'm on my break.' Conor hauled the brakes on his motor mouth, breathed deep. 'Sorry, start again. What situation?'

I need to get away from here, from Tamara and the distress in those serious eyes. I need to work out what's just happened. Have I spent fourteen years being deliberately solo for nothing?

He felt movement beside him, heard Tamara ask, in a voice that didn't sound a lot stronger than his, 'What is it, Michael?'

'I've just got off the phone from Ambulance Headquarters. All hell's about to break out. There's been an accident involving a busload of children.'

Saved by the phone. Conor started down the corridor towards the centre of the department, and swore. He didn't really wish harm on those kids so he could avoid facing up to Tamara's news. News that at the moment had to go on hold. 'Continue.'

'A school bus has rolled off the motorway on-ramp in Newmarket. There are many serious casualties.' The registrar's voice slowed, dropped an octave. 'And some fatalities.'

Conor saw the precise moment the reality of what he'd

reported to them hit Michael. The guy's eyes widened, and his body sagged a little. Something like his own re-action to Tamara's news. Laying a hand on his shoulder, he said, 'Okay, get everyone together and I'll outline how we go about this.'

'They're all waiting for you and Tamara at the desk.' Michael's voice cracked. 'This is huge.'

'We'll manage by breaking it down into components.' Conor was already busy drawing up a mental list of peo-ple to call, jobs to do, equipment to check over. The mo-ment he stood in front of his team he wasted no time. 'Firstly, no one's going home at three.' The clock showed two thirty-five. He glanced at Tamara, who'd moved in beside Kelli.

Horror and despair for what they would shortly be dealing with filled her eyes. All of the previous distress about their own personal situation had been shoved aside. He nodded at her. Very impressive. She'd been ahead of him.

A tall, blond-haired man stepped into the area. 'What's up?'

'Mac.' Conor nodded at the head of the evening shift as he joined them. 'We're about to receive multiple stat one junior patients from a bus accident.' He quickly added the few details he had. 'You should take over right from the start. It's going to be your roster.'

Mac shook his head. 'No, you carry on, get things roll-ing. Your team's all here, mine is yet to arrive.'

It made sense, and in some ways Conor was pleased. He preferred leading from the front, but that also meant there was a very long night ahead. He turned to Michael. 'When can we expect the first patient?' Patient, not child. It helped him keep his distance a little bit. But only until the first victim arrived. Then his heart would break for the child and his or her family. Every time he had to tell a parent bad news he saw his mother, distraught, inconsolable as she kissed his brother goodbye before the funeral.

Michael's voice came through. 'Coms couldn't tell me times or numbers. She said it's absolute chaos out there. Because we're closest we get the first, most urgent cases, then they'll start feeding out to other hospitals.'

'First we need to clear as many beds as we can. Michael, what've we got?'

'One lad about to have his arm put in plaster. A woman with unidentified head pain awaiting lab results. There are also two stat five patients in the waiting room.'

'Kelli, take the boy, get him fixed up and on his way home. Michael, see if the general ward can accommodate the head-pain patient and let them follow up on her blood results as they come in.'

'Onto it.'

'Tamara.' When had she come to stand next to him? Like she was offering support? He should've felt her there, but he wasn't used to looking to someone else for comfort or sharing. He looked into that steady dark gaze and knew he was glad she was with him. For now they were on the same page, despite the chasm yawning between them. A baby. Longing unfurled slowly deep inside. Family. The thing he'd denied himself for life. Even when he'd desperately wanted one. Was this the universe's way of saying he was wrong?

An elbow nudging his arm reminded him of what he was meant to be thinking about. Nothing to do with babies. 'Right, Tamara.'

'What do you want me to do?' she asked, clearly weighing up all that had to be done before their first little patient came through those wide doors from the ambulance bays.

'In the waiting room, those stat fives. Send the man with the possible sprained ankle straight to Radiology. I'll let them know he's coming and why the hurry.'

'Right.' She made to move away.

She was obviously not as distracted as he was, then. This woman was the ultimate professional, hiding behind that impenetrable façade, letting nothing personal affect her work. He'd only once seen her mask come down completely. *Whoa. Do not go there.* 'Wait. The man with a constant bleeding nose can go over the way to the emergency doctors' clinic.'

'He's going to love that,' Tamara muttered as she reached to pick up the patient notes.

'Explain the situation. He'll get just as good care there, and certainly a lot quicker. Tell Reception to send people to medical centres where possible after the triage nurse has assessed them. Once those kids start arriving no one else is going to get a look in unless they're stat one.'

'Give me the easy job, why don't you?' There was no acid in her retort. Maybe it wasn't a retort, considering the lift of those full lips into something resembling a tentative smile. A Tamara smile—rarely given, and never over-eager—was something to hold onto.

Warmth flooded him because of that smile. Warmth that only Tamara seemed capable of giving him at a deeper level than just fun and enjoyment. He found her a smile in return, and drank in her surprise. Hopefully she didn't know how she affected him when he wasn't being careful, which around her was becoming more and more difficult. Hence why he'd applied for a job in Sydney, hopefully starting next month.

Staff from the next shift were wandering in one at a time. A low hum of whispers told the newcomers what they were about to deal with. Conor looked at Mac, who said, 'Pretty much everyone's here so carry on. You've started the process.'

Facing the eager faces, Conor told the nurses and registrars, 'All of you, double check we're ready and prepared for every eventuality. You know what to do. Treat this as you would any stat one coming through the door, but know there's going to be a seemingly endless stream. It will come to an end, I assure you, but there'll be moments when you doubt that.' He paused to let his words sink in, then said, 'I'll be on the phone, putting people around the hospital on standby, but interrupt me if you find there's a problem anywhere. There are going to be double ups amongst you but, believe me, you will all be required.'

Mac took over allocating jobs while Conor punched in the direct dial number for the theatre manager. 'Sister, we have a situation.' He quickly brought her up to speed and then left her to get on with cancelling surgeries and getting theatres prepared for the influx due any moment.

Theatres, done. Running through a mental list of who he had to notify, he punched in the next number. Radiology, then surgeons and other specialists, blood bank.

'Everyone's busy so I can take some of those calls.' Mac stood in front of him, phone in hand. 'Who's next?'

'Orthopaedics.'

Together they worked systematically through the list, the whole time Conor watching the minutes ticking by, feeling the tension building in himself and the department as the doors from the ambulance bay remained firmly shut. He slammed the phone down on his final call. 'Come on. Where are these kids? The odds aren't great if they don't get here *now.*'

Mac shook his head. 'We're organised, ready and waiting. But, yeah, where the hell are those children?'

The buzzer screamed, cutting through the air, sounding louder and more urgent than normal. Instant silence fell across the department and every head turned towards those doors.

Conor drew a breath. 'Okay, everyone, good luck. I know you'll do your damnedest.' And then some.

As he took a step his gaze slid from the doors to Tamara. She was pale, but ramrod straight, and her nod in his direction was assured. Then she was moving to let in their first patient, and Conor was right beside her.

'Jamie Johnson, eight years old, severe concussion.'

Then the flood started.

'Carole Miller, facial injuries, nine years old.'

'Toby Crawford, eight years old, unconscious, suspected skull fracture, internal injuries.'

Once it began the line of trauma victims was continuous and the severity of the cases presenting mind-numbing. A brief gap ninety minutes in gave everyone time to nearly catch up before the second wave of children arrived. These kids were in worse condition than the initial ones because they'd taken longer to be extricated from the wreckage that had once been a bus.

'We need blood here.' Tamara was beckoning to the lab technician to take a sample for cross-match from her patient prior to his surgery for a severed foot.

'And here,' Kelli called from the next resus unit, where a tiny lad with a broken kneecap and torn artery lay whimpering in a fog of morphine.

Conor called to Tamara, 'Get the orthopaedic surgeon in here.'

The phone was at her ear immediately as she hadn't put it down from her last urgent call. For a brief moment they locked eyes and he felt a surge of adrenalin. It was like she was his other half. The calm, self-assured nurse who now had him under control and as calm as she was. The woman carrying his baby. Conor's gut clenched. Baby. Child. Accidents. Death and destruction. Forget calm. What if something like this happened to their child? What—?

'Here.' Tamara shoved the phone at him and instantly replaced his hands with hers on their small patient's leg to continue pressing on a pad staunching the blood flow that had restarted while they'd been investigating his injuries.

Conor swallowed down the fear and said into the phone, 'Kay, we've got a lad whose left foot has been severed.' As he rattled off details he refused to think about how the loss of a foot would affect a young child. Instead he concentrated on Tamara as she bent over the boy, whispering sweet nothings to him even when there wasn't a chance in hell the boy heard a word. This was Tamara at her best. Calming.

That night in his bed she'd been the antithesis of calm.

Conor slammed the phone back on the hook. *Concentrate, man.* He called, 'Orderly,' and returned to the lad's side. 'Obs? How's that oxygen flow?'

Mam, how did you survive watching Sebastian die?

Conor's heart stopped. Slashing his forearm across his eyes, he stared at the boy before him. Life was so unfair. But he wasn't going to let this kid die.

Bright lights flashed in the department, temporarily blinding Conor. 'What the…?'

'Get out of here,' Tamara snarled. 'Conor,' she yelled. 'We need Security. Yesterday.'

Conor blinked, saw rage fill Tamara's face, her eyes, as she stalked past him towards a man pointing a camera in the direction of their patient.

'The media?' *Tell me I'm wrong.* 'How the hell did

you get in here?' he demanded of the man, anger now running in his veins too.

'Like they always do, by pushing people aside as if they have a right to.' Tamara was shaking.

He placed a hand on her shoulder. 'Ignore him. Our patient needs us.' Where were those security guys?

The camera flashed again, and Tamara stepped away from it, her face contorted with a mix of anger and hopelessness. Then two guys in uniform were hauling the cameraman away none too gently.

Conor turned Tamara back to their case. 'Don't think about it. Save it for later. You're needed with our lad at the moment.'

Her body shuddered as she drew a breath, and she slapped the back of her glove-covered hand across her cheeks. 'They have no respect for anyone.'

'Tam, focus now.'

'Don't call me Tam,' she snapped, but at least her spine straightened and all her focus returned to where it was meant to be.

He worked with Tamara, stabilising and checking blood flow, oxygen, getting the boy ready for surgery. Then his patient was gone, onto the next phase of being put back together, though for the boy that would be a long process.

Tamara's eyes were chilly and giving nothing away as she stretched her back, pushing her breasts up. His mouth dried. Then he recalled some comments made about her when he'd first started here. Something about how the media were always waiting to pounce if she so much as breathed out of order. She had history with them, but he'd never asked what it was about, figuring it was none of his business.

Now he wanted to take them all down in a bloody thrashing for upsetting Tamara.

A little girl arrived before them.

'Nine years old, suspected fractures to both arms and legs, and possibly ribs.' A nurse from the nightshift read the details as Conor nodded to the X-ray tech.

The thrashing would have to wait.

As would thinking about that baby.

The hours disappeared in a haze of anguish and despair. Children came through ED, some staying longer than others before moving on to Theatre, or, for the lucky ones, to the children's ward with plaster casts or multitudes of stitches.

Finally, 'We're all done.' Mac appeared from the adjoining resus unit, looking like he'd been living a nightmare for hours. Which he had. They all had.

It was over. Air leaked from Conor like a puncture as the tension that had been with him from the moment Michael had told them what they were in for softened. 'I didn't know they could fit so many children on one bus.' The exhaustion that'd been beating him up earlier in the afternoon returned at full throttle. 'Glad that's done.' Except there were parents throughout the hospital dealing with their worst nightmares.

Parents. Closing his eyes, he rubbed them with his thumbs, and was confronted with an image of Mam letting herself in through the front door, shoulders drooped, knees buckling. Those laughing eyes he'd looked for on waking every morning of his four short years had been dulled with pain and anguish. Her arms had shaken as she'd clung to him. He hadn't recognised her voice as she'd croaked, 'Sebastian and Daddy are in heaven, my love.' And there had begun the rest of his life.

'I've never dealt with anything like it.' Mac rolled his neck left then right.

'What?'

'Go home, Conor. Get a beer in you and hit the sack.'

Looking around, Conor couldn't find Tamara. He stumbled. 'Where is everyone?'

Tam, did you cope? Really? Behind that mask, are you okay?

Mac was muttering, 'I sent day shift home half an hour ago. They were shattered after already working a shift, and I figured my team could handle the remainder of cases. Not that they're in much better shape.'

'It's going to be a long night for them.' What was left of it.

Mac gave him a rueful smile. 'You sure knew how to cope with the situation.'

'For all the wrong reasons, unfortunately.' The wall clock read nine twenty. He wouldn't have been surprised if it was after midnight. As it was, he'd be back on duty all too soon. With that thought his mind filled with the urgent need to get out of there while he could still walk. 'I'm gone.'

Home. A shower. Bed.

Tamara.

Now that you're coming down from the high we've all been on for endless hours, are you looking all peaky and worried again?

She'd be beyond exhausted now that she had pregnancy to contend with as well.

I hope you're all right. That my baby is doing okay.

CHAPTER THREE

TAMARA HUDDLED AGAINST the bench in her kitchen, waiting for the toaster to pop. Wet hair hung down her back. Blow-drying it would take energy she didn't have. Tomorrow it would stick out in all directions but right now she didn't care. All she wanted was to eat something fast before slipping between the clean sheets she'd put on the bed that morning. To fall asleep and forget all the horrors of the day.

Those poor little kids, broken, in agony, some damaged for ever. The parents' distress had been equally harrowing. Not something she'd have considered from a parent's perspective until that thin blue line had entered her life. Never before had she seen such despair, so much shock, all at once.

The day the fraud squad had turned up at her family home had been shocking, but in a very different way; certainly not life-threatening, only life-changing. Back then, the press she had been used to, following her around to photograph her latest outfit or hairstyle, or who she'd dined with and where, had turned on her. Painted her the same black shade as Peter. From that day on she and the media had come to a mutual understanding. They disliked each other; a far cry from the fawning she'd grown up knowing and enjoying. These days, loath to attract attention of any kind, she no longer wore supermodel clothes or spent a fortune on make-up and hair. Nowadays she hid behind dull and duller.

A sigh escaped. What a day. And she'd thought telling Conor about their baby had been difficult. It had been a breeze compared to what those poor parents were dealing with.

Ding-dong. The doorbell was loud in the quiet space.

Her neck cricked painfully when her head snapped up. Who was here at this hour? She didn't have visitors at any hour. Staring at her bedraggled reflection in the microwave door, she hoped whoever was out there would take the hint and go away.

Ding-dong.

Pulling the belt of her bathrobe tight, she took another moment to stare at the image gleaming back at her. Whoever it was, they'd soon take a hike when they saw her looking like something hauled out of a dumpster.

Ding-dong.

Persistent. 'Yes, yes, I'm coming,' she muttered as she gave in. Opening the front door, a gasp escaped her. 'Conor.' Might have known, considering the persistence aspect.

'Did you check to see who was out here before you opened the door?' he growled.

She hadn't given it a thought. 'Hang on.' She made to close the door and peek through the eye-hole just to wind Conor up. How else to deal with him when she could barely remember her own name?

He was too quick for her, splaying his hand on the door to keep it open. 'Can I come in?'

Don't tell me we're going to discuss our baby now.

She'd be at a huge disadvantage, her brain only functioning on low. Yet she stepped back, breathed him in as he passed. Her body succumbed to the scent of man with an overlay of antiseptic. 'You've come straight from the hospital?' she finally managed.

'I wanted to make sure you'd got home all right and was coping with what went down in ED today.'

Of course she was. And wasn't. 'There'll probably be some nightmares, but I'm fine.' He cared enough to check on her? When he had to be feeling as shattered as she did? Raising her eyes to his, she found concern and something she couldn't interpret fixed on her. 'Thank you,' she whispered around the lump suddenly clogging her throat. When was the last time a man—anyone, for that matter—had shown her such care? No one since her father had become ill with the dementia that had taken him from her. Not even Peter had managed to pull on a mask that had suggested he'd been genuinely concerned for her any time. One of the lesser reasons he was now her ex. 'Thanks,' she repeated.

'Come here.' Conor wrapped her up in a strong yet gentle hug, held her against his warm length and lowered his chin to the top of her wet head. 'It's been a huge day.'

Tamara's arms lifted to his waist without any input from her brain. She snuggled her face into his chest. 'Massive,' she agreed.

'You were amazing with your little patients. So caring, understanding, unflappable. I've worked with a lot of nurses and you are one of the best.' A large, warm hand ran soft, soothing circles over her back. Slowly, slowly, the tension ebbed away, leaving her feeling comfortable with Conor.

Seriously? Oh, boy. That made her feel so good. 'I could say the same back to you.' And mean it as much as she believed he meant it.

'So...' Conor hesitated. 'You're okay now you've come

down off the high brought on by the adrenalin rush today cranked up?'

'I'm shattered so I don't want to discuss our baby and how we're going to deal with this situation tonight. I don't believe I can be as focused as I need to be for that.' Conor holding her like this made her feel as though she could tell him anything, open up to him, explain how she hoped their future—their baby's future—would unfold. And probably give too much of herself away.

'I came around to make sure you were all right. I also needed to hear you mention the pregnancy again. It's been a blur from the moment Michael knocked on my office door.'

Leaning back in his arms, she gazed up at him. 'We are going to have a baby.'

'Right.' Those blue eyes locked on hers, and this time the electricity that often flowed between them was quiet. More of an accepting, compliant force. But he'd have his own agenda. Everyone did. While talking about her training to become a doctor, he'd mentioned his plans for the coming years, starting with an application he'd sent in for a position in an emergency department in Sydney Hospital.

Had he heard whether he'd got the job? She tensed. Where would that leave her and the baby? Free to raise her child as she chose? Or would he demand she follow him across the Tasman? If Conor turned out to be as manipulative as Peter had then she wished him to Siberia. Neither would she be following. Her exhausted muscles contracted some more. There was a lot to learn about this man before she could begin to make any plans for her and baby's future.

'Easy does it,' Conor murmured above her. 'Relax.

We can put off in-depth and meaningful conversations for another day.'

Sure thing. She tried to pull out of those compelling arms. Conor simply tightened his hold, keeping her spread against him. Giving in, she went with the moment, absorbed his strength, his warmth, him.

Who knew how long they stood there, holding one another? All Tamara understood was that she didn't want to move ever again. She'd temporarily found her safe place in Conor's arms, and to pull away would sever whatever had brought them together. To move apart would bring back all the doubts and questions, would waken her up to the reality that she didn't know her baby's father well enough to put their needs in his hands. Or to trust him to do what was right for her. At the moment she was beyond leaving his arms, no matter what the consequences.

Finally Conor lifted his head and tilted it back to look down into her eyes. 'I've ordered Thai. It should arrive any minute. I had to make sure you ate something more than a piece of toast.'

'How'd you know that's what I'd have?'

'It was a guess. Might know you better than you think.' He smiled, a slow cautious lifting of those clever lips. 'Can I take a shower before we eat?'

'Help yourself.' Or should she be kicking him out? She was still edgy about him being here.

Conor dropped his arms. 'Thanks, Tam.'

'Don't call me Tam.' It was an automatic response. She didn't deserve her dad's pet name any more.

His eyes widened but all he asked was, 'Where's the bathroom?'

'In the interests of saving you what little energy you've probably got left, follow me.' As if her flat needed a map. 'Here. Help yourself to towels under the basin. I'll pull on some proper clothes and warm the oven for the Thai so you don't have to rush.'

Conor ran his knuckles lightly over her cheek. 'Stay like you are. I'm only here for a short while and you'll be wanting to head to bed as soon as I've gone.'

Bed and Conor in the same thought should've cranked up her desire levels. They didn't. Right now she was all out of anything but the need to eat and sleep. And by the exhaustion rippling off Conor he wasn't any keener to get naked with her either. 'Okay.' Anyway, something as intimate as sex wasn't happening while they were grappling with this new situation. She couldn't afford to let him under her radar. The more caring and concerned he was for her the more worried she was he might want to take something from her.

Ding-dong. Her doorbell didn't ring as often in a week as it had tonight.

'I'll get that. Take your time. There's plenty of hot water.' She closed the bathroom door before Conor said anything that could possibly change her mind and start to stir up her hormones. If he began peeling his clothes off in front of her, well… Risky, given how comfortable she was feeling with him. Almost as if she'd take a step off the edge to follow him. Almost. Went to show the state of her brain. Messy. Chaotic. In need of sleep.

'This green curry is delicious,' Tamara told Conor twenty minutes later as they lounged in her sitting room, laden plates on their knees. Hardly fine dining but very cosy. Her mother would have kittens if she saw her daughter like this in front of a man, especially as she was wearing a bathrobe that had seen better days a long time ago.

But you walked away from me, Mum, so your opinion doesn't count.

'I wasn't sure if you liked spicy food so I went with middling chilli.'

'It's yummy.' Her taste buds were in overdrive and even her unreliable stomach was happy, though usually it was used to hot curry.

'Glad you like it.' Conor shuffled further back in the armchair he'd snagged earlier, pretending he wasn't yawning and all the while looking exhausted.

Then she thought of the cosy factor and the happiness retreated a step. Doing cosy with Conor when they had massive issues lying between them did not make sense. Even without the baby, cosy wasn't an option for her. Cosy would suck her in and leave her wide open for Conor to make everything go his way. At the moment she knew so little about him. Being sexually attracted to him didn't mean anything in this situation. She needed to get up to speed, and fast. Like checking the legal process for keeping her baby in New Zealand if he wanted to take it home to Ireland any time. Forewarned was forearmed. Protecting herself. Something she hadn't known to do with Peter. 'When you're not at work, what do you do with your time?'

His head tipped back and he blinked. Not expecting any questions? 'I run quite a lot, do the occasional half-marathon. Socialise, go fishing with Mac, visit places within easy driving distance.'

'Playing the tourist? I can't see you following the umbrella-waving guide and listening to a taped explanation about the geysers in Rotorua or the Hole in the Rock up north.'

His alluring mouth lifted in a wry smile. 'I am a visitor to this country. I might be working but I also want to see some of the sights. There's so much that's stunning. I could spend months just travelling the length and breadth of both islands.'

'Why do you want to go to Australia, then?' Or would that now be on hold?

Conor sat up straighter, stared at some place behind her. 'It's time to move on. Staying in one place too long often leads to complications.' Definitely holding back. 'Okay, make that it *was* time to move on. Everything's up in the air since your announcement. Apart from becoming a father.'

'You intend returning home some time?' Would he expect her to follow wherever he decided to go? Did she want to?

'Dublin is where I grew up, where all my family live. Dublin is who I am—what I am.' Was it her imagination or had his accent thickened?

'If that's how you feel, why leave in the first place?' What would it be like to live in Dublin? There was nothing to keep her in Auckland. On a positive note, there'd be no interfering television crews to bug her in Ireland.

He'd been yawning when she'd asked that question, but instantly his mouth slammed shut. The relaxed mood had gone in a blink.

When he didn't answer she gave him a break and changed the subject. 'Maybe you should stop running if it makes you so tired.'

'Never.' One word, spoken firmly, quietly, but full of *don't go there*.

It was all too much. They were going round in circles, and she didn't have the energy to try to figure it all out. Her eyes were itchy with tiredness, her head heavy and her body past ready for sleep. So she let it go. A voice in the back of her head was saying, *Look what happened last time you didn't ask the questions*. Not that she'd have got the right answers from Peter. Worry fired up. She bit down on it. Not tonight. 'You want a hot drink before you go home?'

He shook his head, the tightness in his shoulders easing again. 'You're right. I need to head away, give you some space. I've seen you're okay.' But he made no effort to move. 'It'll be time to get up and go to work soon enough.'

'Do you have to remind me?' Tamara hauled herself upright. 'I'm having some camomile tea.'

Conor's eyes locked on hers, causing her to hesitate.

Here we go. He's going to say something about the baby, and what we're going to do about it.

Her defences were rising and she made ready to protect herself.

'Thanks for this interlude.'

Thanks in full Irish lilt was not like thanks in Kiwi-speak. It came with warmth and intrigue and passion. It sent funny tingly sensations down her legs, along her arms. It said things she was certain Conor did not intend. And she had not expected. 'I didn't do anything.'

'Exactly. You could've started in on me about the baby, but instead you've been quiet and thoughtful.'

'I'm tired too.' Her breath stopped in her throat as she waited for the other shoe to fall.

'Exhaustion's puffing off you in clouds. It already was earlier in ED, which is why I had to make sure you'd got home safely and were looking after yourself.' Those lips twitched. 'After bad days at work I usually pace back and forth across my tiny apartment for hours on end. Tonight I don't feel wired, just shattered, yet okay with knowing I did everything I could for those kids, that I couldn't have done any more.'

'You're an amazing emergency specialist, always going the extra distance for your patients.'

Surprise lifted his thick eyebrows. 'But I never stop questioning myself, wondering what else I could've done. It's why I became an ED specialist in the first place. To save people.' Conor's hands tensed, his whole body winding tight. His mouth was flat as he dragged in air, then expelled it immediately. Those sunny summer eyes turned darker than an Auckland overcast day.

There was something else going on in his head that she had no line to.

Conor needed a hug.

Like that would solve anything. More likely he'd push her away. Wise man. Shoving her hands deep into the pockets of her robe, she turned for the kitchen and that tea, trying to ignore the painful squeeze her heart was giving.

They'd once shared a great night together that she'd enjoyed more than she'd have thought possible. Probably because she'd wanted nothing else from him than some fun. But that was it. End of. Except there was now a baby lying between them. There was no room for her heart to have its say.

Listening to her inner voice would undo all the effort she'd made over the last two years to get back on track. It'd also take more courage than she possessed, and would mean a breakdown of all the strictures she'd placed on herself to keep safe.

'Tamara.' Conor leaned against the doorjamb, watching her watch the kettle. He inhaled, sighed out the breath. 'Thanks. Again.'

'No problem.' Please go. Before she said something she regretted.

In a low, rolling version of that bone-melting accent

Conor said, 'Don't be afraid to show me your true feelings or thoughts.'

Slowly turning, she stared at him, her heart now
clunking heavily against her ribs. 'I'm not,' she muttered, and had to suffer the disbelief in his eyes. Fair
cop. 'Okay, I've learned that showing my feelings about
anything usually has severe repercussions.' When his
mouth opened to spill words—a question?—she rushed
in to cut him off. 'Not tonight.' Probably never. 'We're
both in need of sleep, not long, convoluted conversations.'

Damn, but her head hurt. A steady throb pounded behind her eyes, matching her heart. There was only one
cure. Bed. Alone. So she needed to drink her tea to help
obtain that oblivion, and see Conor out the front door before hitting the sack. Not necessarily in that order either.

Why was the water taking for ever to boil?

Conor's eyelids were weighed down as he tried to open
his eyes. 'Where the hell am I?'

He scoped the room, semi-lit from the hallway light,
saw the cream leather armchairs and sighed. Tamara's
place. Now he could feel that leather beneath his backside
where he was sprawled along the matching couch. With a
blanket covering him. When had Tamara put that there?
Had to be her. There'd been no thought of him staying
when they'd finished their meal and dumped the plates
in the sink. No, he hadn't even done that much tidying
up. She'd gone to make herself tea and he couldn't remember another thing after that. Except the ease with
which he'd shifted from the chair to the couch and laid
his head on a cushion.

The ease that had settled over him almost the moment he'd walked through Tamara's front door, despite

his misgivings about coming here when they had a massive problem to deal with.

Careful. He'd be taking risks soon. Risks he'd spent the last fourteen years fighting. Risks that had had him finally fleeing Ireland and family and heart-aching despair. He couldn't imagine falling in love and getting married, having children. Children who might inherit his cardiac problem. A wife who could find herself bringing up their children alone because the big one had got him.

Conor sat up. Threw the blanket aside. Falling in love would mean breaking the rules that ran his life, kept everyone safe. So it wasn't happening.

A vision of Tamara looking gorgeous in her thick, faded navy-coloured robe with her dark blonde hair gone wild from her shower. Part of his brain had been functioning correctly when it had kept him from following through on the desire that had kicked up at the sight of her. It would've been the worst move possible, and there'd have been no thanks from Tam.

Don't call her that. The shortened version of Tamara disturbed her, for reasons he knew nothing about. And wanted to know. No, he mustn't. Knowing meant caring, meant sharing. But to him she was Tam. He just had to keep that to himself.

Time he was out of there. He needed to go home to his randomly put-together collection of furniture that was more practical than inviting; a home that spoke of moving on, not settling down.

Nothing like this warm and welcoming nest created with what he suspected were top-of-the-range furnishings. Not that he knew a lot about these things but this home seemed classy. That sideboard made of polished wood that he didn't recognise was stunning in its simplicity. In fact, everything was understated in a grand way. Was this why she didn't have a lot of spare money to go to university with? A shopaholic gone wild? If so, only when it came to her home. No money was wasted on clothes.

Who are you, Tamara Washington?

Deep down he knew he was never going to find out. His teeth ground as he leapt up to stretch the kinks from his body. He wanted to learn everything about her. Which would bring a load of problems best left well alone. It'd be easy to search on the web, but he didn't feel comfortable with that. That'd be a shallow act, and if Tamara couldn't find it in herself to tell him then best he left it alone.

A carved black clock with a gold face that had to be many decades old chimed once. Picking up his shoes, he made for the front door. Was Tamara all right? Sound asleep? Or was being overtired keeping her wide awake? He turned the other way.

At her bedroom door Conor stumbled. His lungs stalled and his heart slowed. Curled up on her side, her hands tucked under her chin, Tamara was sound asleep—and more beautiful than ever. Gone was that wariness with which she regarded the world, replaced with a gentleness and relief he'd not seen before. Relief because she was hiding from the world? Because she believed no one could get to her while she slept? Didn't she know she was at her most vulnerable when comatose?

His heart hammered in his chest. Excited or afraid? Didn't matter. He had to go home for what was left of the night. All it would take was to haul his tail down the hall and out the door to his car.

But he wasn't that strong. 'What's your history, Tam?' he whispered as he leaned down to lift an errant curl from her forehead. She approached people as though they were about to take something from her. Everyone except patients. They only needed what she was prepared to give.

As Conor reached to switch off the bedside lamp, she stirred. He held his breath, wishing her asleep. They both needed to get some hours' slumber before facing another day in the department.

Her eyes opened slowly. 'Conor?' His name slipped over her lips like melted chocolate, tantalising his taste buds and sending longing for more through his body, straight to his manhood.

'Yes, it's me,' he whispered. 'Go back to sleep.'

Before I can't control myself and haul you into my arms to kiss you senseless.

Because he wouldn't want to stop at kissing.

She snuggled her pillow around her neck. It was an innocent move and it stabbed him deeply.

And had him aiming for the front door.

Everything he'd been denying himself for many years was coming back to taunt him.

And those reasons weren't holding up as strongly as they usually did.

Get out of here. Fast.

CHAPTER FOUR

TAMARA WOKE SLOWLY, fighting her way through a haze. That had been the best sleep she'd had in weeks. No nightmares. No tears. Just plain old sleep.

Unwinding her body from its curled-up state, she pushed a foot across the bed, seeking Conor. Came up with empty space. Like why wouldn't she? Conor had not stayed the night.

For one, she hadn't wanted him to.

For two, he wouldn't have wanted to.

Three, she'd have been setting herself up for a crash.

Disappointment struck. She liked Conor Maguire. More than liked him. Charming, superb in bed, top-notch ED specialist, lots of fun at appropriate times. Hardly a résumé for the position of dad and partner in raising their child. But that shoe could fit her foot too. Her mother hadn't exactly set her up for this role.

So, like Conor or not, she had to keep him at a distance. At least until they'd had a serious talk about the baby. Several serious talks in which baby came first every time. Which meant keeping her heart uninvolved. Trusting that particular organ had once before led to monumental trouble with huge consequences affecting more people than herself. She would never subject her child to anything close to the destruction that falling in love with Peter had yielded.

'Your mummy's going to fight for everything you need, baby.' Her hands slid across her stomach, gently trying to feel the wee dot growing in there. As if. Hard to believe that something so small could create so much havoc.

Her stomach rolled uncomfortably. The first warning.

On the bedside table her phone rang. The screen read Conor. This early? Before work? Couldn't be good. 'Hello?'

'Just checking you were awake. Not sure if you set the alarm before you dropped into unconsciousness last night.' That Irishness surrounded her, warmed her, and tightened her stomach further.

'I didn't, but it seems I woke at my usual time anyway.' Her feet swung over the edge of the bed.

'You want me to pick you up this morning?'

That was getting too friendly. Her stomach lurched, another warning it wasn't going to play nice for much longer. 'I'll catch the bus as per normal. See you later.'

But he hadn't finished. 'Thought we could do breakfast at the Grafton Café, talk a bit about things so the day won't be too rocky, if you get my gist.'

No, no, no. Rolling her head from side to side, she dug deep to control her roiling stomach. 'I've got a couple of things to do before I leave for work.' Like throw up, for one. 'I'll see you there.'

'You can't avoid me, Tamara.' A thread of annoyance tightened that brogue.

'I'm not. It's just I don't do so well with breakfast at the moment. See you at work.' Got to run. 'Bye.' She threw herself out of bed and down the short hall to the bathroom. That had been far too close.

* * *

Tamara rushed into the department a little before seven thirty, knowing she looked dishevelled. 'Sorry I'm late,' she gasped as she struggled to get her breath back after running from the bus stop.

'Where have you been?' Conor asked. 'I was getting worried.'

'You don't need to keep track of me all the time because of—' *Quiet*. Lots of ears around here. 'I got busy with things and lost track of time.'

'You're never late.' A furrow formed between his eyes. 'You've been crying.'

Not *crying* crying. 'Soap in my eyes.' Her life had done an abrupt turn. Of course there'd be the occasional tear.

Conor's delectable lips didn't look so tempting when they pressed together tightly. Neither were his eyes the light, sparkling blue of a kingfisher any more. He ground out, 'Try again.'

The ambulance bay buzzer saved her from answering. 'I'll get that.' She raced away before someone else could take the case and leave her to deal with Conor's questions.

'Morning.' Kelli bounced alongside her. 'Did I sleep well last night, or what? The only good thing to come out of that bus accident.'

'I had the best sleep in for ever,' Tamara agreed. Not that she'd felt that flash since baby had had its say first thing.

'Conor's got a glare going on this morning.' Kelli nodded back at the department hub. 'Any idea what's brought that on?'

Tamara blanched, and tripped over her own feet. 'Why ask me?'

'Just wondering if something's going on between the two of you.'

'You've got an overactive imagination, Kelli Watts.'

'You're overreacting to a simple statement, Tamara Washington.' Kelli grinned. 'The man's hot, and you're single.'

'I'm still getting over my last mistake,' Tamara snapped.

Kelli's hands went up in submission. 'I'm sorry for teasing you, but sometimes you need to let go of the past enough to have some fun at least. Who better to get back in the saddle with than a gorgeous Irish doctor who's not hanging around for ever?'

Couldn't argue with that. So she didn't. But Kelli still had to be shut down in a hurry. Just knowing all about what had gone down with Peter didn't give her the right to interfere. 'The thing is, I don't want to get back in the saddle. That leads to complications and I've had my share of those.'

And I have another, bigger one under my waistband right now.

'You know what, girlfriend? Not all men are devious, manipulative, nasty pieces of work like your ex.' Kelli's words were followed with a quick hug.

'Yet you avoid Mac like the plague.' Tamara was certain her friend was halfway to being in love with the night-shift specialist.

'Low blow.' Kelli stepped back. 'But you're forgiven since you are very wrong.'

They reached the ambulance line. 'Who's this?' Tamara asked the ambulance officer standing with the stretcher.

'Cassandra Wright, thirty-three. The car she was a passenger in was involved in a nose-to-tail car accident on the southern motorway,' they were told. 'The driver's in a second ambulance about to arrive.'

'Hello, Cassandra. I'm Tamara, and this is Kelli. We're nurses. I hear you had an argument with the windscreen.'

The woman was wearing a neck brace, and blood covered most of her face from abrasions to her forehead and chin. 'Stupid of me not to put my seat belt on.'

Definitely. 'We'll take you through to ED so one of the doctors can examine you,' Tamara told her. 'Have you got a headache?'

'A blinder,' Cassandra acknowledged.

'Any numbness, pins and needles?'

'No.' She shook her head, then winced. 'Ouch. I can turn my head either way. That's got to be good.'

'We'll be cautious until the doctor's seen you.' The neck brace was standard with any head injuries, and hopefully it wouldn't be needed for much longer.

In a cubicle it was all hands to the blanket as they transferred Cassandra onto a bed. Then Tamara began attaching leads from the heart monitor to the pads already stuck on the woman's chest. 'We're off to a busy start.' At least that'd keep Conor from slipping under her skin and turning her into a nervous wreck.

'Welcome to the A team, Cassandra.' Conor strode in, taking up space and air in the cubicle. 'After yesterday we can handle anything,' he said in a quiet aside to Tamara and Kelli.

The buzzer went again. 'That'll be Cassandra's friend,' Tamara muttered. 'I'll bring her in.' Kelli could work with Conor and she'd go with another doctor. Fingers crossed. She needed distance from Conor while coming to terms with his new role in her life.

Tamara reached her next patient, grateful for the distraction. She was told, 'Suspected concussion, fractured left wrist, and upper arm pain where she hit the steering wheel. Obs are good.'

From then on they were busy, but after yesterday no one was complaining about the steady stream of patients with mid-level urgency.

At five past ten Tamara looked up from typing obs into a patient's file on the computer and said to Kelli, 'Take a break while you can.' Having got over its morning petulance, her stomach was rumbling with hunger.

Conor leaned over the counter. 'I shouted Danish pastries for everyone. After yesterday we deserve a treat.'

'I'm out of here.' Kelli grinned and headed away as the desk phone rang.

'That's good of you,' Tamara sighed as her stomach sat up to attention. 'I love Danish pastries.'

'I've noticed.' Conor dropped some ambulance patient notes into the 'finished' basket.

He hadn't bought them especially for her, had he? She studied him and got a shrug in return. 'Thanks. I—' The phone continued ringing. 'I'll be there in a minute.' Hopefully.

The first tummy-tightening smile of the day appeared. 'I'll save you two.'

By the time Tamara had dealt with the haematology tech about a CBC result the department was quiet. As was the crammed kitchen space when she walked in.

'Tamara.' Kelli was at her side, her voice troubled.

'What?' Her antenna was up and rotating as she looked around at the faces of her colleagues watching her.

'Same old, same old,' one of them muttered, and drank from her mug.

'What's happened?'

Conor stepped in front of her and reached for her elbow. 'Bring your coffee to my office.'

Her stomach dived, right to the floor. The idea of food was suddenly abhorrent. When Conor tugged her gently she stood strong, kept both feet planted firmly on the floor. 'Tell me.' Why did this sensation swamping her feel so familiar? She dropped her gaze to the table.

Newspaper headlines screamed out at her.

Heiress Making Good for Her Misdemeanours?

Beneath that was a colour photo of Tamara and Conor in Resus One, working on their wee patient's foot—or where his foot had once been.

Nurse Tamara Washington and Dr Conor Maguire in the emergency department, working to save the children involved in yesterday's horrendous bus accident on the motorway.

'Will this never go away? Why won't they let me get on with my life?' She slapped her hands on her hips in an attempt to stop the shaking. 'Then again, why am I even surprised? They're never going to let me live my pathetic little life in peace.' Of course the media weren't going to drop anything about the rich young woman who'd tantalised them for years and now sold papers and turned on TVs just by living. Every time this happened it was another slap across her face, saying *See, this is what happens when you get involved with wicked men.*

'Breathe, Tam.' Conor spoke quietly beside her.

She hadn't been aware she'd stopped. Apparently her lungs had given up the ghost. If only her brain could follow. At least until her rage died down to a disgruntled angst. About the middle of next year.

Angry tears slid down her face. Frustration made her

clench her hands so her fingers were bruising her hips. 'I hope something's been done to beef up security. No reporters should've got in here.'

Conor nodded. 'I've talked to the CEO. It won't happen again.'

'Hope he realises they're persistent by nature.'

'You know all about that?' Conor asked. He knew little or nothing about her past, and she'd liked it that way. Could be why she'd allowed herself to get closer to him than she did anyone else. Except Kelli, but she'd been there for her the whole way through.

'Sit down before you fall down.' Conor pulled a chair from the table and took her elbow to direct her.

One step and that blasted newspaper got all her attention. Her hands were shaking so badly she couldn't pick it up so she pressed them to the table, either side of the evil missive, and stared at the words.

'Don't read it, Tamara. You know what they're saying. It's old hat.' Kelli made to remove the paper.

Tamara slapped one hand bang in the centre, anchoring the paper on the table. Old habits forced her to read everything the media wrote or said about her. A tear splashed onto the newsprint.

'Here.' Conor passed over a handful of tissues before putting his hand back on her shoulder, his thumb immediately going into soothing mode by rubbing circles over her. He must've read this and now had more knowledge than she cared for.

'Guess you had to find out sometime,' she snapped. Longing for normal hit her. The need to lean back against Conor without having to consider the ramifications was very strong. But history kept her still. She'd be fooling herself. Nothing was right, and didn't look like becoming so in the near future. Whenever a reporter wrote yet another sensational article about her she folded, let them walk all over her with their comments. Some were kind, but no better with their fawning comments about the girl who'd been sucked in by the fraudulent lawyer than those who said she was as guilty for making it easy for Peter to get away with her father's fortune, and hurting others along the way. She slashed at her wet cheeks with the tissues.

You have a baby growing inside you.

The truth sideswiped her, shoved everything else to the back of her skull, settled the turmoil back into the smouldering anger which she drew on to redirect her thoughts.

She had to toughen up. This was no longer just about her. These people mustn't be allowed to hurt her any more, because they'd be affecting her child.

Glancing around, she saw only Conor and Kelli left in the room. The low murmurings outside the door indicated everyone else must've stepped outside the kitchenette to give her space. At least they knew the score. 'I presume someone's already filled you in on my past.' She nodded at her baby's father.

'Not at all, and if this morning's reaction is anything to go by I don't think anyone's bothered except for how it affects you.' His fingers were gentle on her shoulder. 'The media can't destroy you if you don't let them, Tam.'

She jerked sideways, away from that warmth. 'Don't call me Tam.' Now the tears were a flood. 'Dad called me that. My wonderful dad.' She stabbed the headline glaring up at her. 'I let him down so badly that I don't deserve to be called Tam.'

'That's a lie,' Kelli growled. 'You weren't the first person Peter ripped off, and I bet when he gets out of jail, you won't be the last. He fooled your father first, remember?'

Tamara gasped. 'Kelli.' Where had her supportive friend gone?

'It's true, and it's about time you acknowledged that instead of taking all the blame. As in really accepted it deep down. Conor's right. Stop letting these guys hurt you.' The words were harsh but Kelli's smile was kind. 'Only thinking of you, girlfriend.' That knowing glint from earlier was back in her eyes as she glanced at Conor. 'I'll go and cover for you while you get your mojo back.'

If only it was that simple. But, yes, she could no longer sit around sulking, or dreaming up ways to kill off every reporter walking the country. 'Thanks, Kells.' Then she turned to the man who deserved an explanation. He hadn't disappeared out the door; neither did he look starved for the gossip. He only appeared concerned—for her.

'Have you read any of that?' Tamara nodded at the article.

'Didn't finish the first paragraph. I can't stand idle nastiness. You're not that person he's written about, Tamara. Nor has anyone around here told me anything. I suppose they all think it old hat and don't need to bring me up to speed. If I'm going to learn what it's all about I'd prefer you told me.'

'You don't think I'll paint a dishonest picture about being the victim to keep you onside?'

'No.'

'You have no idea, and yet...' He didn't understand the gift he'd given her. Warmth swamped her, right down to her toes.

Conor was spooning coffee into a fresh mug, and now he hesitated. Turning to look her in the eye, he seemed to be searching for something. And she really needed him to find it. Whatever it was. They had a baby to think about.

Even her own future was waving at her. The next few minutes were going to have a lasting effect on how that went once Conor knew about her past mistakes.

Sinking onto a chair, she turned the paper over. As Conor had said, she could tell the story without the innuendo and nastiness. Propping her elbows on the table and her chin in her hands, she began. 'I grew up in a wealthy family. Dad started an engineering company when he was twenty-one, and went from strength to strength, making a fortune. Timing was everything, and he'd hit it bang on. I had the life of a princess, and I certainly took on that role very well.'

Conor placed a mug in front of her. 'Get some of that in you.'

Liquid didn't slop on the table when she picked it up. It had to be Conor's calming influence because her body wasn't feeling completely out of kilter as normally happened when she talked about her beloved father. 'Dad wanted me to join the company but I was determined to become a nurse. If I hadn't been in such a hurry to prove I could do anything I chose, I might've figured out that I really wanted to study medicine and become a doctor.' But that was another story, and irrelevant. She was avoiding the real screw-up in the room. A mouthful of coffee and she put the mug down. 'Peter Gillespie was the company lawyer, a hotshot man who charmed everyone. Including me. I fell hook, line and sinker. We got engaged, but the wedding kept being postponed for one reason or another. Mum wasn't happy with the venue or Peter wanted to invite someone who wouldn't be able to attend on that date. Then Dad was diagnosed with dementia.'

More tissues appeared in her line of vision. 'Take it slowly.'

'I haven't talked about this for so long I should be

rusty, but the words are always there, banked up in the back of my skull ready to spill any time I press the button.'

'How old were you when you got engaged?'

'Twenty-three. Old enough to know better.' Her sigh was bitter. 'But, then, I was used to people falling into line with me. Peter seemed to be following the same path. He was a lot older than I was. I liked that.' His age had lent itself to his authenticity. Yep, she'd been naïve.

Conor sat opposite her, not staring at her as though she was a nutcase, or avidly hanging onto every word and waiting for the dirty details.

If she wanted to fall in love, here was the perfect man. But she didn't, so no go. 'I was twenty-five when Dad's dementia became apparent, and a year later he was beyond running his company.'

'Fast, then. Or had he been hiding it?'

'A bit of both, not that anyone can conceal having dementia. But he was clever at covering his errors until— until he couldn't any more.' She scratched at a mark on the table as some of the heartbreaking memories rose before her. 'Fast was best. I'd have hated for him to take years of slowly diminishing before us. Watching him was hard enough anyway.'

Conor's hand covered hers, gentle and caring. There was no need for words. He understood her pain.

But would he understand the worst? Pulling her hand free, she leaned back to put space between them. Being strong, right? 'I, along with the lawyer and head accountant, had been given power of attorney over Dad's companies and personal assets.'

See where I'm going with this?

'I gave up my hospital job to nurse Dad, and when that became too much we brought in other nurses to help me.

The mental aspects of looking after him were appalling, but seeing my once fit and active father turn into a small, wizened man was equally heartbreaking.'

'You were distraught, unable to cope with anything else.' The guy got it on every level. Scary. Didn't mean she could trust him yet.

'Peter seized his opportunity. He already oversaw all business decisions, but he kindly read documents and affirmed their content so I only had to sign them. He invested company money, made policy decisions. All to give me more time with Dad, you understand. The accountant wasn't any less helpful either. Between them they were well qualified to run the business, whereas I was too easy to fool.' She held the mug, rolled it back and forth in her hands, staring into the murky brown liquid like she might finally find some answers in there, yet knew she was deceiving herself. 'I let them steal everything from us. I let them.'

'It must've been difficult, dealing with your dad's situation and keeping tabs on a huge business, which, as you said yourself, you weren't qualified to do. Did you have grounds to doubt Peter's loyalty to your father? To you?'

'None. No one did. He was always so willing to help, to be there whenever Dad asked for him, even when Dad couldn't remember who he was half the time. Right up until the end, Peter would turn up every morning to have the business meeting they'd spent years having, despite Dad not comprehending a word.'

'How did you find out what he'd done?' Still nothing but concern and care radiated out at her from across the table. Scary or compelling?

Tamara dropped her gaze from Conor, afraid of the hope he'd started waking up inside her. Instead, she stared at the tabletop, focusing on that awful day that had culminated in ruin, seeing everything, including Peter's smug face, as clearly as if it had happened yesterday, today even. How had she been so stupid not to see what he was doing? How?

'Tam?'

'Don't,' she whispered.

'You're Tam to me, and nothing you've told me will change that.'

Hadn't he heard everything she'd said? Or not understood it fully? Finish the story, get back to work. Work where all her colleagues would be watching her, even when it was old news to most of them. An ache encompassed her. She'd had enough of that, didn't want another round of feeling like a fruit loop. 'We'd been home from Dad's funeral less than an hour when the fraud squad arrived and all hell broke loose.' Flashing cameras, shouted questions, pushy reporters trying to get in her face.

'The media had a field day, huh?' His expression still hadn't changed.

Maybe she did have another friend in this world. 'They'd been at the funeral, and followed the procession to the cemetery, then on to our home afterwards. All my supposed friends had plenty to gossip about, and appeared to be very knowledgeable on things they couldn't have had a clue about. Even my mother talked about me.' Her voice faded away to a strangled whisper. 'I was to blame, you see. I let Peter sign the papers that shifted funds offshore into bank accounts that did not have Washington Enterprises in their name.'

'Your mother didn't have signing rights?' Conor asked.

'Now, there's the irony. Dad knew she'd be forever signing papers without a clue what they were about. As long as there was enough money in her accounts to keep up with the lifestyle she adored then everything was fine in her world. Besides…' She hesitated, suddenly feeling disloyal to her mother, a woman who'd not often shown her any loyalty most of her life. But Conor needed to know who he was getting involved with for his child's sake. 'Mum is a bit of a loose cannon, never stops to think of the consequences of anything she wants to do.'

'Where is she now?'

'Living with a distant relative in a small town in Australia.'

Conor rose and came around to her, held out his hands to haul her to her feet. His hug was gentle and reassuring. He wasn't about to trash her for her past. If only she could truly trust him she might risk falling under his spell. Might. But, no, there was too much at stake. They hadn't even begun sorting out the future for their child.

'You want to take the rest of the day off?' he asked, still holding her close.

Yes. Home seemed like the perfect place to be right now. Close the curtains, turn on the TV, though not the news channel, and pull a blanket up to her ears. But she'd done that too often. Straightening out of his arms, she eyeballed him. 'I'm not leaving before the end of the shift.'

'Go, you.' His smile pinged her right in the tummy. 'I've got your back all the way.'

Unease slipped in. 'Why, Conor?'

He looked taken aback at the question. He was certainly thinking about it. 'I just do, that's why.'

She nodded. The best answer in the world. He was accepting her for who she was, despite not knowing her too well. When was the last time that had happened? Yet she still didn't fully trust him. Because of Peter.

Another reason could be that her world was righting itself. Then her stomach cramped, reminding her of the baby. She was fooling herself. And Conor.

CHAPTER FIVE

'TOO MANY PATIENTS for a Tuesday afternoon,' Conor muttered under his breath as yet another yawn pulled out of him. 'Tuesdays are meant to be slow. Tuesdays following the Monday we had yesterday at any rate.'

A woman burst into the cubicle. 'Mum, what happened? I told you to come and live with us but, no, you want to be independent and this is what happens.' She bent down to plant a loud kiss on his patient's cheek.

'Hello, dear. I had a fall, that's all. It would've happened wherever I was.' Mrs Gowan was beaming at her daughter.

'Yes, but then I'd have been able to help you.' The daughter tugged a chair up to the bed and reached for her mother's hand.

Tamara was watching them with something like envy in her expression. Something else in her background he had yet to learn about. She'd said her mother had dumped on her with the media, but why?

Another yawn ripped out of him. Damn, he hadn't been this tired since he'd been in nappies. A red flag went up. He hadn't been like this for fourteen years. Since his heart attack.

Shock rocked him back on his heels. Was this a precursor to another cardiac incident? His head spun. No way.

'All normal there.' On the other side of the bed Tamara unwrapped the BP cuff from Meredith Gowan's arm.

After that jolt over the newspaper article Tamara was coping well. He'd kept her at his side, brought her into all his cases, stared down any staff member who gave her a questioning look. Not that many had. It seemed most of them knew the story and didn't need to rehash the details.

'Dr Maguire.' Tamara spoke firmly. 'Mrs Gowan?' She nodded at their patient. Definitely not one for schmoozing over him despite that hot night they'd had in bed. Instead, she kept him on his toes, and for some perverse reason that made him worry he might fail her. He was good at looking out for people, just as long as he didn't get involved.

Ah, hello? You're having a baby together. Whether you want to or not. Is that not involvement?

A sudden, clenching ache gripped him in the chest. Panic unfurled, ramped through him, sending fingers of shock expanding throughout his chest, his gut.

Tamara appeared in front of him. 'Are you all right? Should I get Michael to take over here?' Her voice was filled with nothing but concern. For him.

'I'm fine.' His chest tightened further.

I am not having a heart attack. I know what that feels like and it's not this.

Nodding abruptly at Tamara, he dropped his gaze to his patient. Away from those all-seeing eyes still focused on him. 'This fall you had today? Run through what happened. I know you've told the triage nurse but I'd like to hear it myself.' Mrs Gowan might add something previously overlooked. Concentrating hard on the answers could keep the growing tightness in his chest at bay, help him calm down.

'I was coming down the steps from the laundry to the

porch and next thing I know I'm on my back, staring up at the sky, Doc.'

'Did you trip over something? Slip on the step?' The pain was not abating.

'I don't remember anything like that. One minute I was upright, the next I wasn't.'

At least Mrs Gowan had been conscious when it had happened to her. 'Can you recall any dizziness?' Conor asked as he rubbed his temples. Talk about feeling off balance. And he was the doctor. Leaning his thigh against the bed, he blindly studied the page in his hand while listening to his patient with all the attentiveness he could muster.

'Conor?' Tamara remained near him, that concern now reflected in her eyes.

He flicked his gaze in her direction for a quick fix to hang onto and clashed with a serious enquiry on Tamara's face.

'I'm getting Michael.'

Not what Conor wanted to hear. 'Stay with your patient.' His chest wall gave a squeeze, reminding him of what he was trying to ignore. *Think like a doctor, man.* Not a useless twit who panics at the slightest twinge. Get someone, Tamara, to check his pulse, put him on the monitor for a heart reading. But then everyone would know his dirty little secret.

The air whipped around Tamara as she stomped to the head of the bed.

I'm light-headed and my chest's tight, the panic's rising, but otherwise I'm good to go.

'Mrs Gowan…' He tapped her notes. 'This says you haven't had any headaches recently, no unusual chest discomfort.'

'Nothing, Doc.'

Tamara had some serious questions for him. He knew how her gaze could shine with wicked delight and hot anticipation, and how the brown shade could sparkle like hot chocolate. He'd seen fun and laughter twinkle in Tamara's eyes for the first time that night two months ago. He'd also seen despair and sadness dull them at work when she thought no one was watching. There were many layers to this woman. Layers he wanted to probe and learn about, to peel back and reveal her depths. Now she was watching him like a hungry falcon.

Crack. His chest tightened. While his head lightened. He did not want Tamara knowing about this. She'd draw him in, get too close, want to fix him. They were going to be parents together. He couldn't. Not when at any moment a heart attack might take him out of the picture, like it had Dad and his brother.

'Are we transferring Mrs Gowan to the medical ward?' Tamara knew damned well they weren't until they had some answers to what'd happened to her. She was hitting him over the head with a sharp reminder to focus on his work. Strange how quickly things turned around. A short time ago he'd been helping her to pull herself together.

Conor swayed on his feet and fought the need to reach out for the bed to steady himself. He also ignored the way Tamara looked at him. Like he shouldn't be here. 'Right. I'll arrange some blood tests before we go any further.' He disappeared through the curtains without another word. Not the usual friendly, 'take as long as you want' Dr Maguire, but 'I need to sit down before I fall down' Dr Maguire.

He diverted directly into the next cubicle and stopped by the bed.

My chest's too tight.

Those old memories of chest pain crashed through his mind.

My breathing's all over the place.

He knew how to calm down by drawing long, slow breaths into his lungs, huffing them straight back out. Knew the muscles holding his chest would eventually let go their fierce grip.

I am not having a heart attack.

This was a panic attack. Simple as that. He knew those. Hadn't had one for over a year. The tightness in his chest muscles wasn't easing off. What if he was wrong? What if he deserted his child before it made its appearance?

'Conor?' Tamara stood in front of him, reaching for his arms. 'Tell me what's going on,' she demanded.

Lifting his head far too fast, he growled, 'Can't a man have a moment to himself around here?' He should've taken his time straightening up before answering her. Should've. Didn't. Swaying, he grabbed for something to hold onto. Unfortunately, Tamara was the first stable thing within reach. Thing? Sorry. Nothing *thing*-like about her with all those curves she kept hidden under layers of baggy clothes.

'Sit down.' She tried to shove him onto the bed.

He pushed her hands away. 'I'm fine,' he ground out through a wave of panic. Not pain.

'And I'm a monkey's backside.' She did those retorts so well. They could burn a man if he wasn't careful.

'I can honestly say I don't agree with you about that.' Focusing on annoying Tamara might help distract from the panic building relentlessly.

Her mouth flattened into a warning.

Quick, defuse her. 'I'm overtired.'

'So you said.' Her brows came together into a dangerous frown. 'I'm not buying it.'

Faster, man. Or next she'll have the whole crew in here. 'I ran in the Auckland marathon on Saturday.' The frown didn't soften. She was seeing right through his attempts to divert her, something she was obviously better at than him. 'Throw in that busload of broken children and your news, it's hardly surprising I'm a bit wobbly on my feet.'

At last. No more frown. Instead, those luscious lips that had once played havoc on his feverish skin were tight and uncompromising, while hurt stabbed at him from those eyes he couldn't forget. Hurt and...? Disappointment. No, distrust. Like he'd let her down big time. Over what? Try not being honest with her. Right, like he'd tell her about his family history of cardiac problems right here, now. Going to have to sometime, though. That baby might already be in trouble.

'Right.' She snatched the patient notes out of his hand. 'What blood tests did you want done on Mrs Gowan?'

'CBC, electrolytes, LFTs. And a CRP.'

'Right,' she repeated, and stalked off, those shoulders almost meeting in the middle of her back and her chin shoved forward.

He could've added how he hadn't slept much in weeks for thinking about her and that amazing body she never showcased in fitted clothes.

What was with her frumpy style of dress anyway? Surely that had nothing to do with what her ex had done? Most females would kill for a figure like Tamara's. He hadn't expected it and could still feel the wonder he'd known as he'd undressed her before caressing her from top to toe. And back again. It had been like unwrapping a gift he had asked for and finding something far more exciting. That, and how she'd reacted with blatant enjoyment to his lovemaking.

Sex. He did not make love. He had sex with willing women and said goodbye in the morning. No fault with that. He was saving a potential partner and any children they might have from a life-load of worry and fear.

Got that wrong, hadn't he?

Slam. The clouds in Conor's skull thickened, his muscles tightened. Breathe in, out. In, out. Still no pain. Not a heart attack. Relief flooded his tense body to loosen the tautness, push the fog in his head aside. Thank goodness for something. Stretching his arms high, he rolled his head in a circle to loosen the tension in his neck until finally he felt capable of functioning as a doctor again.

Blasted panic attacks. No accounting for when they made an appearance.

'You all right?' Kelli asked when he returned to the counter, where Tamara was fiercely intent on entering details in a patient's file on the computer.

'Absolutely.' A quick glance at the wall clock. Thirty minutes to go and he'd be out of there. Straight home, no stopping at the supermarket for food that would sit in the fridge until he threw it out next week. No, he'd put his feet up, chuck on a CD and order in something to eat. Probably fall asleep and wake up in the morning all stiff and achy. But at least his heart would be ticking along perfectly. The last traces of that panic that'd been overwhelming him had evaporated.

Twenty-nine minutes to go.

You and Tamara need to talk.

Double damn.

Conor snatched up the top file of waiting patients and stalked off to the waiting room. 'Jason Grove?'

Twenty-eight minutes to go.

* * *

Tamara pressed 'talk' on her phone and held it to her ear.

'Hello?' came the voice she'd known all her life.

Surprising how her mother hadn't put her name in her phone by now just so as she didn't have to answer her calls. 'Hi, Mum. Don't hang up. Please. I've got something—' *Click.* 'Important to tell you.' She stared at the far wall of her lounge. No surprise there. Shouldn't have bothered trying. But seeing Mrs Gowan so happy when her daughter had raced into ED that afternoon, she'd wanted to talk to her own mother right there and then. Wanted to connect, to share about the baby, to be a family again.

Tamara slammed the phone onto the armrest of the recliner and stared off into nowhere. Her favourite place when everything was going pear-shaped.

Please, talk to me one day, Mum. I want to hear you say my name again. Could even do with one of your whacky hugs right about now. I know I screwed up but I don't think all the blame was mine.

Huh? That was new. Of course it had been her fault. She'd been the one to trust Peter. Not the only one, as Kelli had pointed out. Dad had too, long before her.

Conor hadn't freaked out or blamed her. He'd listened to her story and carried on like she wasn't a complete waste of space. Was that why she'd tried to contact her mum tonight? Because he'd stirred up some hope inside her? Dangerous stuff. Especially when it came to her mother.

Ding-dong. That blasted doorbell sure was getting a workout this week. Tamara chose to ignore it. Note to self: take batteries out when whoever was out there had gone.

She could understand Conor's exhaustion. If indeed

that was all that had tipped him off his feet earlier—and the jury was still out on that. Fatigue dripped off her, leaving her body barely able to drag itself around the flat. There was no energy left in the tank to entertain a visitor.

If Kelli had come bearing wine and food for a girls' night of chatting then sorry, but she wasn't coming in. Tamara huffed a sigh. Drinking was out these days with a baby under her belt. Not that she'd ever indulged much.

Ding-dong.

If it was Conor then tonight she wasn't able to face him and the endless questions he'd have about where she was with planning the future for her and baby. Especially when he hadn't been forthcoming about that episode in ED knocking him sideways. They both had to be upfront, not just her. Hell, Conor had spent the remainder of the shift barking at just about everyone who moved, while sending her strange looks that had explained absolutely nothing. And reminded her not to trust him too quickly.

Ding-dong.

'Go away.'

Her phone pinged. Conor.

I know you're in there, Tamara.

Ding-dong.

The door hit the wall when she tugged it open. 'Not tonight, Conor. You had your space, now I want mine.'

The guy just walked on in, like he hadn't heard a word she'd said. 'Not happening.'

Guess he had heard then. 'Excuse me? You think you can walk all over me as you choose?' Like Peter had. She growled, 'Don't walk away like that.' The words were strong but her voice lacked real grit. Damn, this toughening up wasn't as easy as she'd hoped.

Conor spun back to face her, hands on hips like earlier in the day. 'I am not walking all over you. What I am doing is making certain you understand I will be a part of this, that I will always support you. I will not be shoved away.'

'I don't remember shoving you anywhere.' She *had* tried to push him onto the bed when he'd been having his moment in ED.

'Just so you're fully aware. After what you told me today about your ex I want you to know I stand at your side.'

She'd take her time over that, assimilate more about him and how he reacted to situations and other people. 'Right. Message received loud and clear. Now can you go?'

'We have things to discuss, and I for one do not believe in putting them off.'

'Oh, really?'

Conor swallowed hard. 'Yes, really. Delay only leads to worry and more problems.' He stared at her, as though waiting for her to fold. 'We already left talking about the baby last night.'

He had a valid point. Unfortunately. But she wasn't folding. Shoving her chin out, Tamara said, 'Fair enough. But be warned, I'm shattered and will kick you out the moment I need to go to bed.' Like about now. Oh, and make that go to bed *alone*. Two in her bed would require energy and trust and knowing where they were headed with baby. Which led right back to what Conor had said as he'd walked in.

'I hear you. Not everything is going to go my way.'

'You're onto it.' This new her, the stronger version, the less trusting type, seemed to be working. Amazing what pregnancy did to a girl. If she had to be a mother, then she'd give it her all to be the best.

Closing the door, she headed for the lounge and the big recliner to curl up in. Comfortable was the only way to go.

She didn't make it that far. As she stepped past him Conor caught her hands gently, shook her softly. 'Look at me, Tamara.'

Then she'd be lost. He'd be able to demand anything.

No, he wouldn't. Less trusting until you know more about him, remember? Charm doesn't cut it when dealing with major decisions.

The gaze she met was serious, with tenderness hovering at the edges. Her mouth dried. Why hadn't she met Conor before Peter? Her life might've been so different. Now all she could do was put her baby first. 'Yes?'

'How are you keeping? You hinted at morning sickness when I phoned early. Other physical discomforts?'

Knock me down with a feather.

He was doing *nice* to perfection. A ruse? She stared at him, delved into that gaze, searched for lies. Got only honesty. She didn't think she was wrong. Not with Conor. Or was that more wishful thinking on her part? She'd go with it for now, see where it led. 'Like I said, I don't do breakfast any more. It has a habit of regurgitating.'

'Hence those big morning teas you've started indulging in this week.'

Tamara nodded. 'I get a bit tired. Otherwise all's good.' She made to pull her hands free. His hold was compelling and she didn't want to throw herself at him, needed space between them.

Conor had other ideas. His hands tightened around hers. 'You won't have been to a midwife or your GP yet.'

'Give me time. I've only known since Friday and the first hurdle was to let you know.'

'Hurdle?' Hurt crossed his eyes. 'I'm an obstacle in all of this?' Now her hands were free, dropped like hot coals as he stepped back from her.

'Wrong choice of word.' When he continued to stare at her, she hurried to explain, though not a hundred per-cent sure what her problem was. There were too many of them. Sigh. 'I'm getting my head around the fact I'm pregnant. I still have no clue what you're thinking about becoming a parent.'

'Not good enough, Tamara. It was always going to be a shock for me, which I'm supposing it was for you, but you're coming through it, as I will.'

She moved past him, dropped into her chair. 'I'm going to be completely honest, though you might not like what I say.'

'Can it be any worse than what you've already hit me with?' He took the chair opposite but didn't relax back into it, sat instead with his elbows on his knees, his chin in his hands.

'Any worse? I get that an unplanned pregnancy is the last thing most of us want, but it's not the end of the world,' she snapped. 'I want this baby now that I have it growing inside me.'

It was true. *It was true.* Her hand spread across her stomach. She hadn't allowed herself to believe that one day she'd be a parent, yet it was happening. *Oh, my.*

'I'm going to do everything possible to look out for this baby.'

'You're days ahead of me, but I do not want to get rid of it, if that's what you were implying.'

So much for thinking they were starting to get along quite well. They didn't understand each other at all. 'I wasn't.' Silence crept into the room as she strung her thoughts into a cohesive statement. She had one shot at explaining herself. Finally, 'I told you about my past and what Peter did. What I didn't go into was the screw-up I became afterwards, and mostly still am. I used to trust everyone, now I trust no one. Hence all that dithering about my med school application.' She locked her eyes on his. 'Do I trust you to do the right thing by our child? Absolutely.' She paused, swallowed hard.

Damn you, Peter. You ruined everything for me. But, then, you wouldn't give a toss, would you?

'I hear a "but"…'

Again silence reigned. Until she gathered up her courage and told him the truth. 'I am afraid of what you might want to do regarding our child. Will you try to take him from me? Go back to Ireland with him? I'm going with calling the baby him for now as I hate saying it.'

Conor's face was tightening, his eyes darkening dangerously, but he refrained from uttering a word.

So she continued, digging a bigger hole. 'Do I trust you to do the right thing by me? I…' Swallowing the bile building up in her mouth, she tried again. 'Honestly? I want to. I want to believe *in* you, but I don't believe in my judgement.' She sank back, huddled in on herself, becoming small and tense. No sign of her new, stronger backbone, but, then, she had managed to put the truth out there so she had to get points for that. Didn't she?

'Firstly, I will never take the baby away from you.' Conor ground out the words through clenched teeth. 'Just so you know,' he added with as much anger as she'd ever seen in him.

'Thank you.' Did she trust him on that score? Yes, she thought she did. 'I didn't really think you would, but as I said I have trouble believing everything first time up.'

Any relief was short-lived. 'Whether I return to Ireland with my child—and you—is something I cannot say yet. But you should know I've always intended returning home at some stage. For good.'

'Is that non-negotiable?'

Conor nodded. 'I thought it was. But that was before the baby announcement. Of course it'd now be up for discussion.' He paused. 'Could you ever consider moving to Ireland?'

'Since I've been intent on hiding away these past two years I hadn't thought about moving anywhere, but I'll put Ireland on the list of changes to be contemplated.' Why not up sticks and head to the northern hemisphere? As Kelli had pointed out, she had nothing to stay here for. Even better, no one in Ireland would know her history, would chase her with cameras or ask for comments on everything from fraud to investment funds. A move out of New Zealand could work in her favour. 'You never fully explained what brought you Down Under.'

'I wanted a change.'

'From what?'

'My family.' What wasn't he telling her?

'Thought you adored them.'

Conor leapt to his feet, stared around the lounge and sank back down. 'I do. All of them. But it's like happy families, all my sisters married and producing delightful little offspring. I was overwhelmed.'

'You're not telling me everything.' See? Knew not to trust him completely.

'Whether I return home or decide to stay in New Zealand or move to Australia, I won't shirk my responsibilities, Tamara.' A non-answer if ever she'd heard one.

It didn't bode well for trusting him completely. 'Being a parent isn't all about responsibilities. Where's the enjoyment factor, the loving and caring without always being serious?' Where had that come from? No idea, but now that she'd voiced it she knew it was true. Already she was sticking up for her child, like a good mum should.

Hear that, Mum?

Maybe Conor understood the truth because his mouth suddenly softened enough for a smile to appear. A self-deprecating one, but she'd take it as a good sign, a thawing of the chill filling the room and making her skin uncomfortable.

Then he threw another curve ball, and she was back at the beginning. 'What are you hoping for from me? Apart from being there for our...' He choked. 'Our child.' Reality was sinking in deeper and deeper. It was there in his eyes, face, and the way his hands tightened around themselves.

'I hadn't got very far with that. Nor with what I'm going to do about work. Obviously university is a no go.'

'You can always do that later.'

Her eyes did a roll. 'Sure. And spend all those hours studying or training you warned me about away from my child? Never.'

'You're not in this alone.'

Good to know. 'Expand on that if you can.'

'I can't give you specifics yet. Like you, it's still too new to have all the answers, but know that if I'm going to be a dad then I want a full-time role in my child's life.' At last Conor leant back in his recliner, looking more at ease than he had since walking through her door. As though reality was finally falling into line. 'Obviously that means helping you with whatever you decide to do.'

Truly? She ran the words through her mind again and again, searching for the hidden agenda. Nothing waved at her. Either Conor was very good at hiding his true thoughts or… Or he meant what he'd said. 'I've been quite happy living on my own. I adore my job and can adjust to not becoming a doctor. Having a child when I never thought it possible is a far better option anyway.' An opportunity to fill some of those empty spaces within her. Some of those spaces could be for Conor too.

No, they could not.

'You said quite happy. Not good enough, Tamara. You deserve better, lots better.' Then he slammed his hand through that wonderful long hair, shiny black locks weaving between his fingers.

And her fingers stretched, like she needed to feel that hair on her skin. Instead she growled, 'It isn't the life I'd planned on, and while that's not too bad, how I arrived at all this is.'

Apart from that night with you.

'You're letting one man wreck your life. Not to mention tarring the rest of us with the same brush. Not every male is intent on robbing you, or lying to you. Especially not me.'

She had to know. Now, before any further discussion led to decisions regarding their child's future. 'Care to explain what was going on with you in ED this afternoon?' If he couldn't be honest about that then what chance did they have of making this work?

Conor swore. 'Guess I walked into that one.' He unfurled his long body from the chair in one rapid movement and then stopped to stare down at her as if he had no idea where to go from here.

Tamara held his gaze, afraid that if she looked away it would be the end of everything…that he'd find a reason to walk out and send her money once a week via the internet. Honestly? She didn't quite believe that. He was honourable and had said he'd be with her all the way, but history was a hard taskmaster, making her so damned cautious it hurt.

Conor did a lap of the lounge before returning to his chair and locking fierce eyes on her. 'I was having a panic attack.'

She waited. Any questions might shut him down again.

The sound of the building creaking in the cooler night air was loud in the silent room.

And she waited.

'I had a heart attack when I was twenty-two.'

Tamara's jaw dropped. 'You what?' So much for no more questions. They spilled out. 'Twenty-two? But why? You're lean and fit. That's very young for a heart problem.' Seriously? Of course seriously. This wasn't something he'd joke about.

'Family genes have a lot to do with these things.'

Gulp. What? 'You've got an inherited heart disease?' And she'd thought the worst had been thrown at her already. Shoving her feet to the floor, she sat forward, her hands gripped together between her knees as she waited for his next grenade. And fought the flapping in her stomach. This could not be as bad as it sounded. Huh? Hadn't she learned anything? Life threw grenades at her all the time. What was one more?

'I don't know,' Conor told her.

'But you will be all right? Won't you?' Please. For baby's sake he had to stay around. For her sake. Gulp. Truly? Was she prepared to accept Conor's place in her life as her child's father if it meant he'd never go away? Probably the second biggest mistake of her life but, yes, he had to stay. And not only for the baby. She wanted him there because—because she liked him far too much. Then the truth slammed her.

What if her baby had a heart problem?

CHAPTER SIX

CONOR WATCHED TAMARA closely, but couldn't fault her reaction to his announcement. Nothing but shock and concern in those brown eyes. But she hadn't heard the worst. 'My dad died when I was four.'

Those knees pressed her hands tighter but he'd already seen the tremors roll through her. 'But you're onto it, right? You're not going to die early.'

Conor studied her face, the face that more and more he looked out for first thing in the morning as he logged on in the department. There was something about Tamara he couldn't go past that kept him returning to talk to her and working to raise one of her heart-tugging smiles. Smiles that didn't happen often enough. Hell, she was the only woman in a long time he'd gone to bed with and wanted to repeat the experience. Hence his application for that position in Sydney. He was meant to be a solitary man.

'Yeah, I'm onto it, and I don't intend clocking out early. But there's always that "what if?" factor hovering in the back of my head. Some days, like today when my body was strained from running the marathon and working so hard yesterday, my mind gets in a mess and I freak out, thinking every muscle twinge is a cardiac arrest in progress.'

Had the real issue sunk in yet? Or was Tamara deliberately ignoring it? Somehow he doubted it. She liked honesty and being up front. No doubt a result of what had happened to her in the past.

'What condition have you got?' she asked in a high-pitched squeak.

Conor still wanted to avoid talking about what had kept him single most of his adult life, but he owed Tamara because of their baby. 'Nothing that the cardiologists have been able to put a label on. That's why I can't be sure it is hereditary. But Dad and I both having heart attacks—I'm not prepared to gamble with that information.'

'That must be hard. If you know what you've got it'd be easier to face it down. Or so I'd have thought.'

Got it in one. He smiled; a smile he hoped went some way to lightening the anguish beginning to creep into her eyes as she considered their child might also have a cardiology problem. 'I've learned to live with it by keeping fit, my cholesterol low and my BP normal. Mostly I get on with life without too much interference from the back of my brain, but occasionally it goes haywire. The specialists say my chances of another malfunction are less than most other people's out there because I've got everything under control.'

'Heck, Conor, how do you manage to get up and move, run those marathons even, with that hanging over you?'

By remembering the anguish in Mam's face at Sebastian and Dad's funeral. One funeral, two coffins, two goodbyes. Half the family gone. 'Some things just have to be done, and for me it's running endless kilometres. Don't know what I'll do when the body doesn't want to pound the pavement any more.'

'Take up go-go dancing.' Tamara flicked him an uneasy glance, like she didn't want any more bad news yet had to find out. 'So. Our baby. What are the chances our child will have a heart problem? Is there any way we can find out or do we have to wait until a cardiac event happens?'

She'd got to the crux of the matter. The reason why he'd determined never to have children in the first place. 'I didn't explain properly. My brother didn't die of a heart attack but as the result of being in the car Dad was driving when he had his. The car went over the bridge onto the rocks thirty feet below.'

'That's a rough deal,' she gasped. 'Your poor mother. And you. How did you cope? Hell, Conor, I'm burbling. I don't know what to say. It's awful.'

'Yes, it is. So you'll understand when I said I couldn't have children. There's no way I wanted that happening to my family again.'

'I get that completely. But now you are going to be a dad so we have to talk about our child's medical future.'

He tapped his fingers on the arms of the recliner he sat in. 'It will be a wait-and-see approach for now. Who knows? Medical knowledge is progressing all the time so things could change. But I'll have junior checked by a cardiologist from the moment he's born.' Now he was going with the male thing. 'Or before if it's thought necessary.'

'*We* will.'

'Sorry.' He wasn't used to factoring someone else into his decision-making.

Her hands splayed across her belly. 'We've got knowledge on our side.'

Conor reached for her hands. They were cold and shaky. 'I'll talk to one of the cardiologists in the next couple of weeks. One step at a time, eh?' And he'd keep his fingers crossed all the while that nothing ever went wrong for junior.

'*You'll* talk to someone? Excuse me, buster, but I am as much a part of this as you.'

Conor winced. He'd done it again. 'This is as tricky for me to negotiate as it is for you to take in.'

Tamara nodded as her hands tightened around his. 'I get that.' She gulped. 'I'm afraid.'

His chest felt as though it'd been slammed. Tamara afraid? 'Why?'

Her eyes widened. 'Can I do this?'

'You? Tamara, you'll be amazing.'

'I always wanted children, to have the kind of warm, loving family I grew up in.' Another gulp. 'Until Peter, that is. I got him so wrong. How can I—or you—trust me with a baby? To steer a child through to adulthood? I'm not qualified. I make dreadful decisions.' The words were tumbling out as though she had to say all this fast in case she froze.

Yep, that man had a lot to answer for. This kind, wonderful woman was a blithering wreck behind the confident nurse's façade. 'You're better than that. Don't let him continue winning.'

'I'm trying not to.' Her bottom lip trembled, reminding him of a little girl he'd treated a couple of days ago with a greenstick fracture to her ulna. Only it was Tamara's confidence that was fractured here. And, he suspected, her heart.

He'd have to nurture her, show she was capable of giving love and receiving it back. Huh? Love had nothing to do with their situation. Or did it? He'd been intending to leave Auckland to get away from her, and that hadn't been because he couldn't stand her. But to do that meant getting close. Not happening. 'You don't need qualifications to be a parent, just love and patience and understanding. Kindness. Sympathy. You've got the lot, Tamara.' Conor stood up to pull her to her feet so he could wrap her in a hug. 'Take that determination you had for applying to med school into this new scenario. You can do whatever you want if you don't let the past shackle you.' Definitely do as he said, not as he did.

Her head nodded against his chest. 'I know. Some of the time.'

She fitted so well in his arms, against his length, as though made to be there. Which had nothing to do with their predicament. Or maybe everything to do with it, considering how babies were made. A deep breath in fed his senses with hints of spring and had him softening further into her, holding her tighter, closer. 'You've got me with you on this.'

Tamara shivered, and tension crept into her arms. Too much?

Then his own words whacked him around the skull. He'd just made a commitment he hadn't thought through. So withdraw it. No way. That wasn't how he operated. He did not walk away when life got tough.

You left Ireland when you couldn't face your sisters' happiness, knowing you couldn't join them in family life.

His fingers dragged through his hair. Okay, so what? He wasn't leaving Tamara to face raising the baby on her own. Neither would he ever desert his child. Hell, now he was going to be a dad he should be looking forward to embracing the whole deal.

She told him, 'We'll keep a fierce watch over our child.'

Conor slowly let his arm fall away and stepped back. 'I don't want to repeat what happened to my brother.'

Those sweet, generous arms were back around him, and this time he was the one being pulled close. 'Conor, you're tormenting yourself over something you can't control. I understand that's why you've opted not to have a family but that's changed.' The words were whispered against his throat and were followed with a feather-light kiss. Then Tamara stood still, holding him, letting him hold her, as they absorbed strength and comfort from each other. At least he hoped he was giving Tamara as good as she gave him, because it felt right, and she needed good as much as he did.

Finally, as though there'd been a signal, they stepped apart and sat down in their respective chairs. Conor watched Tam closely, glad to see nothing to suggest she wanted him gone, out of the picture because of his history. He risked, 'We'll sort all this out but no more tonight. We're both exhausted.' He still needed to get his head around the fact he was going to be a dad. And then there were decisions to make. Only that morning he'd had an email from Sydney about a second interview for the job—this time face to face. The job he'd been excited about and still wanted.

'At least I'm not on my own.' Relief warred with worry in that brown gaze fixed on him.

Hopefully Tam would move to Australia with him if he got the job. That would solve everything about how to jointly raise their child. 'You've told no one else you're pregnant? Not even Kelli?' When she shook her head he asked, 'What about your mother?'

Her face tightened, and she sat up straighter. 'We don't communicate.'

'At all?' Didn't sound like there were many people in Tamara's life to support her.

'I tried tonight. She hung up the moment I said hello. That's how it works with us.'

'Because of what happened with your fiancé?'

Her nod was sharp. 'Mum was so hurt by it all.'

As her daughter had been. Conor smiled into that worried face and changed the subject to something lighter. They'd had more than enough doom and gloom for one night. 'Have you eaten?'

A blush crept up her cheeks. 'Ah, no. I could go for a pizza delivery right now. All I had today were those pastries for lunch.'

Yes. Her eyes were lightening, the mud shade beginning to sparkle just a little bit, reminding him of cocoa this time. He hadn't realised how much he'd needed to see that twinkle and how special it was when it happened.

'Your propensity for takeout food's interesting. Going to feed baby on Indian curries before he's twelve months old?' More than once he'd seen her hoeing into a korma at lunchtime in the department.

'If it's good enough for Indians to bring their children up on spicy food, it's got to work for mine.' Now the sparkle was at full wattage.

On the inside he was melting, giving in to the wonderful sensations suggesting he might've found his soul mate. Suggesting he might not turn tail and hide from happiness. 'You should bottle that look.'

'What?' Puzzlement tipped her mouth awry, and he just had to lean over to kiss her. To seal the day with a kiss? To show her they were on the same page? Two kisses. They hadn't even started sorting all the obstacles in front of them. Three.

As his lips brushed hers again he felt her pushing closer, and deepening the kiss was a natural follow-up. Afraid she'd tip onto the floor, he grabbed her and lifted her onto his thighs. She was acting as if she wanted more, despite all her misgivings. Because she had plenty, that was obvious. Well, he was going to do all he could to see her through some of them, to banish or work them out of her system. She deserved someone on her side. Someone to bat for her, to hold her when the going got too tough. Someone who still had to figure out what had been dropped on him, and changed his world for ever. Right now he had no energy for thinking.

If you had to get stuck in the pregnancy situation then you couldn't have picked a better, more gorgeous woman to be there with.

Conor straightened. Whoa! Where had that come from?

'What's wrong?' Tamara asked as she tipped back against him, her fingers tracing her lips where he'd been placing those kisses.

Kisses he'd love to follow up on. To turn away from their problems and lose themselves in each other. But nothing would've changed, might even be harder to work through if they did that. Could have him aiming for the moon, and not only working to make everything okay for their baby. Hauling the brakes on his libido, he answered her question. 'Nothing, absolutely nothing.'

Disbelief filled her eyes. 'What are you on, buster?'

'Adrenalin.'

Another aspect of Tamara filled his mind as he looked across at her. Laughing, sexy, fun Tamara letting her hair down with him as they made love. And they'd made a baby apparently. The tension in his stomach turned to goo. He was going to be a dad. The decision had been taken away from him and now he had to go with it. Could go with it and imagine the excitement. Let it in.

I want to go with it.

'I'm going to be a father.' The love winding through him was beyond description. For so long he'd refused to contemplate becoming a parent and now it was happening regardless. So, yes, he was starting to see it for the wonderful opportunity it was. Not that he was foolish enough to believe the worry wouldn't be huge, hold him down at times, but Tamara had been right to point out there was more to becoming a parent than the apprehension.

'Weren't we talking about food?' Her practical question knocked him back into the here and now of finishing their day on a normal note.

'Yes, and I'm starving.'

'I can't wait for a pizza delivery. There's some steak and things to make a salad in the fridge.'

'Let's hit it.' He hadn't had dinner either, having been too wound up and needing to have everything out with Tamara to think about eating. 'I'll cook the steak. I don't do a bad job.'

'Go for it. There's a barbecue at the back door, though I'm not sure if it works. I've never used it. Hardly seemed worth the effort for one small piece of meat.'

'What's the alternative?'

'A heavy pan on the element.'

'That'll do.'

In the kitchen Tamara was opening cupboards, lifting out a pan, plates, salad bowl. All top-of-the-range equipment.

'You have excellent taste in furnishings and utilities,' he noted as he opened the fridge to find the steak.

'They came from my parents' home. I helped myself to enough to furnish this place before the courts placed a "to be sold" order on everything. But even then I think I'd have got away with going back for extras if I'd wanted. The receivers were more than kind to me after they heard what had happened. They didn't believe I deserved to be thrown out in the street on my butt with absolutely nothing but the shoes I was wearing. By then they'd had time to study the business affairs and follow the money trail.'

Placing the steak on the bench, he went in search of cooking oil in the pantry. Go for serious or fun? 'I'm trying to get around the vision of you sitting naked in the street wearing only a pair of shoes. It's quite a sight, believe me.'

'The neighbours mightn't have approved.' Tamara's laughter filled the room, pulled them together in a cosy, let's-be-normal kind of way.

Except it wasn't normal for him. He didn't share his kitchen with anyone. Or his lounge or bedroom. Tamara had been the only woman he'd taken back there.

'Bet they would. You forget I've seen that butt and it's quite something.' Not that he wanted to share the experience with anyone else. Didn't want another man knocking on Tamara's door anytime. Down, boy. Keep to the cosy and cook the steak.

'Tell me more about your family.' Tamara was chopping a red onion at a frenzied rate that had no consistency behind it.

Fearing for her fingers, Conor placed his hand on her wrist. 'Stop, woman. You're going to do yourself an injury at that rate.' He tugged the knife free and began systematically dicing the onion. 'What else do you want sliced?'

'All of these.' She placed tomatoes, cucumber, capsicum, a carrot and celery on the bench before digging through the vegetable bin again.

'The steak's on hold while I do this.'

'You worry too much. I've been chopping vegetables for years and still got all ten digits.'

He turned to her question about his family. 'I've got four half-sisters and they're all bonkers. I adore them, and wouldn't swap them for a saner variety.'

'That's cool. Are their kids normal or—' she made finger quotes '—"bonkers"?'

'Still up for debate. The brothers-in-law are leaning towards bonkers, but they're not fazed either way. The kids' ages range from two to seven. They're so much fun. So cute and crazy.' Oh, hell. The chopping stopped as he stared across the kitchen at Tamara. 'I—we—are going to be adding to the Maguire brood. There're going to be five grandkids for Mum to spoil.'

Tamara stilled, a pair of kitchen tongs in one hand, some mushrooms in the other. 'Is that all right?' Caution laced her question.

'It's more than all right. It's— It's wonderful.' It really was.

As long as baby's heart is fine.

Conor shivered. Go away. Let me enjoy the moment.

'It *is* going to be all right.' Tamara stood in front of him, her hands on his upper arms. 'We're in this together.'

'But—'

'But tonight we're going to share a meal, acknowledge we're going to be parents and just take in the wonder of that. There's plenty of time to worry about what might or might not happen.' She shook him gently. 'Okay?'

'That's how I want to play it, if only this pesky little voice in my head would leave me alone.' He was getting to share parts of him he'd never told anyone about. Not a good sign for his independence.

Tamara wagged a finger between them. 'Pesky little voice, go annoy someone else. Tonight is ours. Not yours.'

Laughter began deep in his belly and rolled up and out between them. What a tonic she was. If he had to have anyone onside if things went bad then Tamara was who he wanted, needed. 'How do you like your steak?'

* * *

Tamara placed her empty dinner plate on the floor beside her chair and watched Conor as he finished his meal. Letting him kiss her had been wrong. Kissing him back worse. But there hadn't been a stop-go man in her lounge, flipping his sign back and forth. Just her and Conor. Tired, and temporarily at ease with each other, needing to keep the truce running for as long as possible, she had to ignore the flare of need that kiss had evoked. The need that refused to die down even though they'd stopped kissing ages ago.

Why had Conor ended the kiss? His withdrawal had been gentle, but had left her depleted when everything sensible in her head—okay, not a lot—had shouted at her, *Don't do it*! She had so much to lose. More than ever before. Yet her body had craved him, her mouth devoured his taste, her arms desperate to be wound around him, holding him. She'd made a baby with this man. Her body remembered every little detail, every spin of desire, every heightened sensation, the exquisite release of that night.

She wanted it again. Needed to connect with him in a deep, intimate way that showed they had made a baby together, that this was real. That it wasn't another lie thrown at her by people she'd trusted.

Already she was beginning to believe, really believe deep inside that Conor meant every word he'd said so far about being there for her, not against her. Giving in too easily? Because she desperately wanted a man at her side to go through her pregnancy and the years to follow with? A man? Any man? No. Conor. If there was going to be someone at her side then Conor was the only man she'd consider. But they had hardly touched base on the issues ahead. That's when her burgeoning belief in him might step back.

'You're awfully quiet over there,' the man making her brain do somersaults said. 'Should I be worrying about something?' Conor looked so relaxed and at ease her own tension lightened somewhat.

'No.' Yes. He'd have a fit if he knew what she'd been thinking. 'Just putting the day into perspective.' Some of it, anyway. The tantalising part, the warm sizzle component of a long day fraught with landmines.

Conor hauled himself out of the recliner. 'I'm off home so you get some shut-eye.'

'That's probably best.' Unfortunately. She followed him to the front door, her heart getting heavier with every step, lonelier with every breath.

With his hand on the doorknob Conor hesitated. 'Goodnight, Tam.'

She sucked a breath, bit down on the automatic 'Don't', and whispered, 'Conor.'

He shifted his hand to her neck to gently pull her closer to his face, his mouth hovering above hers. His other arm went around her waist, brought her against his wide chest. Then he was kissing her. Again. And she was sagging with relief. And firing up with desire. 'Hold me tighter.'

Her lower body pressed in against him, felt his reaction behind his zip. Her hips rocked forward. Conor froze. Great. His head was at odds with his body. Of course he didn't want her. She'd made another mistake. She pulled away. 'Sorry. I got that wrong.'

'Tam, I have no idea what's right or wrong at the moment. I only know I want to be with you tonight. I understand it's asking a lot, considering what's lying between us. But tonight…' He lifted his shoulders. 'Tonight I want to remember what was so good between us last time, and forget everything else for a few hours.'

Was that so bad? It was what she wanted too. 'Stay.'

Tamara touched his chin, his cheek and then traced his lips. 'Stay.'

Feed the heat devouring me...feel the wetness waiting for you.

Before she could blink he'd swung her up into his arms and was heading for her bedroom.

At the door he hesitated. 'You're sure?' He was holding his breath. If she changed her mind she knew he'd leave.

She placed her lips on his neck, right beneath his ear at a sensitive spot she'd discovered last time with him. Her tongue licked and teased his skin. A deep shudder racked him, and he responded by placing her on her feet and sliding his hands under her blouse and up to her breasts. A flick of his thumbs across her nipples and her desire level shot from simmer to boiling. Once had never been enough with Conor.

With their mouths joined they somehow shucked out of their clothes, breaking contact only to haul shirts over their heads. Then they were on the bed, sprawled across each other, hands touching, teasing, awakening deep needs.

'This is one hell of a way to say yes,' he croaked as his knee slid between her thighs and nudged her wide. His eyes were hazy with lust and the same need that was scalding her on the inside.

Tamara opened up to Conor, exposing herself completely, letting his body join hers, his gaze see right into her. To see her truth, fears and hopes. Hopes she hadn't allowed herself for so long.

Her fingers pushed through his hair, tension growing in the fingertips that pummelled his skull. Her breasts ached with need and she throbbed at her core. Then Conor slid into her, and wiped away the day, the problems and the worry. Left her mindless and replete.

CHAPTER SEVEN

'WHO'S THE NEW man in Tamara Washington's life? No one's saying but at Auckland Central Hospital—'

Tamara slammed the clock radio so hard it spun off the bedside table. 'Shut up,' she cried.

'Hey, take it easy.' Conor sat up beside her and draped an arm over her shoulder. 'You're letting them win.'

'Don't you get it? The new man? That's you they're talking about.' How did the reporters know Conor had anything to do with her? Even *she* didn't think they were an item, baby excepted. Another hot night excepted... 'They've been hanging around my flat again.' Bitterness spilled into her mouth. What would the reporters have to say when her baby bump became apparent?

That arm on her shoulders increased its pressure as Conor shuffled closer. 'You think reporters saw me arrive here last night? Hung around to see if I left?'

'That's how it works in my life.' Damn them all to hell and back. 'This round started with that photo of us working with the children in ED. I'm sorry. I totally get it if you only want to meet at work or with the shift guys when we go to the pub after hours.' Conor didn't deserve her mistakes being played out in his life.

Before she knew what Conor was doing she was on her back with him above her, his elbows framing her, his hands holding her head gently. 'We're going to ignore them. I won't hide away because some reporters have nothing better to do with their time. They'll get bored with me soon enough.' His mouth covered hers, preventing her from retorting that they hadn't forgotten her in years, and she wasn't half as exciting as Conor.

As Conor's kiss deepened she gave in to the warmth that expanded through her chilled body; forgot everything but the man delivering it. Spreading her hands across his chest, she absorbed his strength through her palms, and understood she was safe when she was with Conor. When she rubbed a finger across his nipple he groaned, long and low, and she wanted more. The whole deal. Making love in the morning was different from any other time. It came with sleep-lazy bodies waking up to a new day together, with promise for more, with a languidness that wasn't there at the end of a busy day.

Conor touched her thighs, nudged her legs wide, and then she wasn't languid any more.

'We're going to be late for work,' she murmured as she grasped him in her hand.

'I can do fast.' He chuckled and immediately proved his point. What's more, he was very good at it.

When they walked into work Tamara knew she shouldn't be smiling like she'd had chocolate for breakfast. Face it, she hadn't had anything for breakfast.

Not true. She'd had Conor.

Conor and chocolate. Hmm.

Chocolate. Food. Yikes. Stomach not happy. 'Excuse me.' She dashed away, leaving Kelli, who'd just joined them, staring after her.

'What's going on?' Kelli asked as she followed her to

the bathroom. 'Why didn't you stay home if you were feeling…?' Her voice trailed away. 'Oh. I get it.'

Tamara closed her ears to that sound of astonished comprehension in her friend's voice. She had an annoying stomach to deal with first.

Then Conor was there. 'Need anything, Tamara?'

Yes, to be left in peace for a moment. 'I'm fine.'

'You reckon?' Kelli squeaked.

'It's normal,' Conor grunted.

'Will you both go away?' Tamara called through the door. 'This isn't exactly fun to be sharing with the pair of you.' But it seemed her stomach had decided to behave, probably more interested in the conversation than heaving. Out at the basin she splashed cold water over her face.

'Here.' Conor blotted up the trickles from her chin and cheeks with a hand towel.

While Kelli gaped at him, then her, then back at Conor. 'I think I've missed something. I know I said you should let your hair down, Tamara, but it seems your knickers were what came down.' Then her face split into a big grin. 'Go, girlfriend.' Then the grin vanished. 'Are you all right? Is Conor doing the right thing by you?'

As Conor spun to face her friend Tamara stepped between them. 'All's good, Kelli. Promise. I'm sorry I haven't told you anything but it's been a bit tricky.'

'I take it this news is not up for grabs out in the department.'

'No.'

'Not yet,' muttered Conor.

'Then we'd better get out of here before people start asking dumb questions.' Kelli led the way from the tiny room.

Yeah, Kelli was the greatest friend she had, and could

ever wish for. Of course she was the only one. But she'd just been delivered news that'd have her reeling and yet there'd been no criticism, or any hurt feelings about not having been told earlier. Tamara slipped her arm around her waist. 'You're the best.'

Kelli returned the gesture. 'You bet.' Then her face clouded. 'How are you really? Getting back in the saddle is one thing, but a baby? With a guy you hardly know outside work?'

The happiness evaporated. 'I'm all over the place about it,' she muttered. 'I believe Conor when he says he's on my side, and then the past springs up and I'm afraid of what he can do to me.'

'You're not ready for this.'

Tamara huffed out a lungful of despair. 'Tell me something I don't know.' How could she have spent last night making love with Conor when they hadn't got anywhere with working out plans for the future? She'd given in to her physical needs too easily. Given in to Conor too easily. Hadn't found the strength to say no. Hard to do when her body was screaming for him to take her. 'Guess I haven't changed half as much as I'd hoped.'

'We'll talk later.' Kelli gave her a lopsided smile and tipped her head in warning towards the group waiting in the middle of ED for handover from the night shift.

Talk later. Hadn't she heard those words earlier today from Conor? Seemed her immediate future was going to be filled with talking. About her baby, Conor, the future. Time to lay out what she hoped for, not sit back and see what Conor would offer. This time she had to fight for the needs of her baby, not fold, or let anyone else determine how the next year, years were going to play out. Doing that would only prove she hadn't learnt a thing. And that she wasn't fit to be a mother. Not happening. Her vertebrae clicked as she lifted her head high.

I have changed. I am strong. I will not let any man dictate the rest of my life.

She had to learn to trust herself first, and then everything might fall into place more easily with Conor.

'Two car accidents during the night.' The day began. 'There's still one patient from the second incident here under observation with severe concussion but no other injuries.'

'Kelli, he's yours.' Conor nodded.

'Cubicle seven. Fifty-six-year-old female, fell down the stairs around midnight. Concussion, broken arm, bruising to her face and upper body.' Nothing major enough to still be here.

'What's the problem?' Conor asked.

The registrar leading handover said, 'Her husband doesn't believe his wife drinks, yet her bloods showed a very high reading. He blames the lab for the results.'

'Had he been out for the evening and not known?' Tamara asked as she focused on work and nothing else.

'Nope. Her liver tests were abnormal. I'd suggest that's from a high and sustained alcohol intake.'

'So the husband's playing ostrich,' Conor noted.

The registrar added, 'I'm concerned about sending her home.'

'I'll talk to Social Services when their offices open.' Conor looked around, caught her eye. 'Tamara, I want you on this one.'

'Not a problem.'

It was like any other day in ED. But for Tamara it *was* different. Everywhere she went Conor was there, whether it was him or his voice through the curtains or his laughter as he chatted with other staff. Once she even smelt his spicy aftershave when she entered a cubicle he'd just vacated. Her body wouldn't settle down, as though her hormones had got a taste for Conor that had to be fed at regular intervals. Sure made working beside him awkward. And thrilling. This time Conor was responsible for her inability to eat, not baby.

The buzzer sounded.

'Tamara, can you take that?' Conor nudged her out of her reverie as he walked past, flicking her one of those smiles she adored.

And, yes, cranked up the desire level. 'Sure.' The man could ask her to do anything when he smiled like that. He oozed charm.

Charm? As in used to getting his own way? Was this all just a ruse to soften her up before he explained how he was going to deal with her and their baby? Tamara shivered, rubbed her hands up and down her arms. Please, not that. One Peter in her life was one too many.

No. Conor was nothing like her ex. Conor was genuinely kind, caring, honourable. Gorgeous, sexy. Oh, and sexy.

But… What if she was wrong? What if he was laying out plans for her already?

No. He wouldn't. He'd told her so.

'Peter Gillespie is a hard-working man with your and my interests at heart. He'll always look out for you and Washington Engineering.'

So had said her father as he'd pushed documents in front of her to sign that would give her control over the company and its finances once he knew his mind was going because of the dementia.

'He'll explain everything to you before you sign any papers. You can trust him completely.'

Yeah, Dad, thanks for that.

Yeah, Dad, I miss you like it all happened yesterday.
Tonight she'd look into the laws covering a mother's rights. Only being a responsible parent.

In the end Conor had to let the woman with alcohol issues go home. There were no grounds for keeping her in ED, and no other ward would take her. Alcoholism, a broken arm and an unkind husband were not reasons for admittance.

He'd forwarded the details to the woman's GP with his concerns and to Social Services after talking to them. Then he got on with the day, treating a steady stream of patients coming through the doors.

For the last hour Tamara seemed intent on avoiding him, swapping from cases he was on as often as possible. Too often for his liking. Seemed that morning's cosy mood had gone, replaced by apprehension and long, questioning looks that didn't give him confidence in their upcoming discussions.

Conor had seen her yawning far too often. The pregnancy was taking its toll. Nothing to do with a very physical night, of course. He winced. Tam had been more than willing to make love last night. And this morning. Yet now she was treating him like she would a white-tailed spider.

An ache stabbed him under the ribs. Unfair. But he had to be patient. Give her time and space to get used to him in the role of father to her baby and hopefully someone she would learn to rely on in the coming weeks and years. To love him? Seriously? No, that was going too far. He couldn't ask more of her than he was prepared to give. Love meant sharing their lives, losing his freedom to do as he pleased, always having to check with Tamara before doing things he normally just went and did. He wasn't sure he knew how to do that. Or wanted to. But the baby was going to give him a few lessons along the way.

'You know you're going to be on the news tonight?' Tamara nudged him during one quiet interlude.

That's why Tamara couldn't let go enough to trust him completely. The past was still in her face, refusing to go away. He replied, 'If that's all people have got to make their day, they're the ones with problems, not me.'

As reporters jostled for position in front of them when they'd walked down her path to his car that morning, his rare temper had leapt to the fore. At least he'd managed to hang onto it. One look at the resignation in Tamara's face and he'd known not to react, not give the media what they wanted. Ignoring every one of them, he'd been rewarded with Tamara holding her head high like she didn't care about what they'd write. 'We did all right this morning.'

'You haven't thought it through. Everyone here's going to start talking about us.'

'Then let's fix that. We'll announce it ourselves.'

'Announce what?' she gasped, the colour draining from her cheeks. 'The baby?'

'Why not? You won't be able to hide it for much longer. Personally I'd prefer for it to be out in the open.'

'I'm not ready for that,' she snapped. 'I've only just told you, and we—we haven't planned anything yet.' Tamara pulled that frightened look away from him but left him with a sense of having betrayed her somehow.

Guess he had. He hadn't asked her how she felt about telling others. 'Hey.' He stepped close.

A hand went up between them in the universal stop sign. 'I can't believe you'd suggest such a thing.'

Now what? *Think, man.* What was behind this? Tamara was rattled big time. Calm her down, get her back on her feet so she can face her colleagues without going into another meltdown. 'Fair enough. We won't mention the baby yet. But we can say we've spent some time together and are continuing to do so. Sounds a bit like a press release from the rich and famous.' Hell. That's what she was used to, had had to put up with before. 'I'll reword that.'

That thick blonde braid swung across her back from shoulder to shoulder. 'They'll understand.' She headed for the ambulance bay, though there'd been no sign of a patient arriving.

Conor followed, reluctant to let her go on a bad note. 'Since we've got lots to discuss, want to do it over a meal tonight?' As in a real date.

Hope warred with resignation across her face when she turned to look at him. 'I don't think so.'

'With what's ahead we should be getting to know each other better.' Next he'd be down on his knees, begging her to spend time with him. Only went to show how his thinking had changed since hearing about the baby. 'Say yes. We've got to eat anyway.'

'We've spent the last two evenings together and haven't got around to the big issues. Why would tonight be any different?'

'We won't have had an eventful day to use up all our energy?' *Tempting fate, buster.* He continued when she wasn't forthcoming with a reply. 'Are you changing your mind about my role in our baby's life?'

Guilt flickered. 'I don't know exactly what your role's going to be.'

Got you. 'Then we need to go out to dinner and talk. Before we get much further along the track.' Try asking, not pushing. 'Please?'

One eyebrow rose, but she only stared at him.

'Have you tried that new Indian restaurant on K Road?'

'Low blow, Dr Maguire.'

'Did it work?'

A shrug. Then a tiny, reluctant smile full of caution. 'What time are you picking me up?'

She didn't trust him. Despite everything he'd said. Despite showing her with his lovemaking. It was going to take time. And that sucked.

Could she want more from him? The boundaries he'd lived with were coming down because of a baby. His baby. And because of this amazing woman who'd first tipped his world a little bit sideways, and was now following up with a big shove just by revealing more about herself. He wanted to support her, stand by her and deal with the past, and not just for the baby's sake. As long as he could do it without losing his heart, without giving up that solitude he'd struggled to maintain. The solitude that kept him safe. And which had begun cracking wide open these past few days. And since he no longer needed to push Tamara away. Conor shivered. Hell, did he want the whole deal after all?

I'm not falling in love with Tamara.

No, he wasn't. Spending more time with her had grown on him, and not to discuss nappies and baby formula. Was that love? Creeping in to bang him around the skull now that he had no excuse to keep his distance? He was going to be a parent regardless of his family history so why not pursue the other half of that picture? The mother of his child. Tam. The woman who'd had him aiming to move to another country because she'd woven a spell around him when he hadn't thought it possible.

Because it still wasn't. Or was it? Spending time together might resolve some of the dread lurking in his head. Might displace the fear of hurting Tamara if his family history roared into life and left her alone with their child.

* * *

'I'll have the lamb dhansak.' Tamara looked up at the waitress. 'Hot.'

The only way to eat curry. She shrugged out of her faded denim jacket and dropped it on the back of her chair. It had seen too many wears, the threads barely holding together at the elbows. But, hey, it matched her scuffed ballet shoes.

'Butter chicken, mild, for me,' Conor ordered, before asking her, 'You don't worry all that chilli might upset junior?'

'He'll probably come out with a taste for spices, which would be great.'

'Where does this enjoyment of Indian food come from?'

'I had a friend at school, Savita, and I spent many weekends at her house.' Until Sav's family had packed up and moved to Melbourne for family reasons. 'At first I wouldn't eat anything except naan bread but Mrs Kesry was very patient and drip-fed me spicy food, increasing the chilli slowly, until the day came when I could eat whatever Savita ate.'

'You'll need to be as patient with me.'

'We're going to spend that much time together?' Did she want to? Absolutely. When she wasn't feeling un-certain about him she wanted nothing more than to be with Conor. They'd spent three nights in a row together and were still on friendly terms. Had to be a good start.

'We're going to be parents. Don't they have a lot to discuss and share and enjoy together?'

'You're giving back my comments from yesterday.' She liked that. They were on the same page for tonight. 'Right, curry training starts now.'

'You're not going to change my order?'

'I have the power.' She laughed. It felt good to laugh. Something she did more often when around Conor. He was good for her. When she wasn't doubting herself.

'Please, please, don't be harsh on me. I'll tell junior in years to come how cruel his mother can be.'

Junior. *His* mother. Tamara folded her hands in her lap and took a big breath. 'Do you want to find out if junior is a boy? I should be seeing the midwife anyway and he's going to suggest a scan.'

'He? A male midwife?' Conor's eyelids were doing some rapid movements.

'You didn't know there's such a creature?' she teased.

'Yes, of course I do. Just hadn't considered it.' He shifted in his chair.

'So I'll make an appointment with *him*?'

'If it's a boy, you're going to be outnumbered right from the start.'

'That's a yes, then.' Tamara tapped in a reminder on her phone. Not that she was likely to forget but best to cover all contingencies.

'Are you intending to continue living in the flat once the baby is born?'

So he wasn't offering to set up home with her. 'I don't have anywhere else to go. Besides, I like it there. It's not flash or big but I'm comfortable.' There wasn't money to rent a house. The money she'd put aside for next year at university would be used for her current level of rent, and all the other things to buy, such as a cot, pram and change table, a car that would be safe for a baby. That was only the beginning. She had no doubt the list would be endless over the coming years.

'Fair enough.' Conor sipped his water, looking distinctly uncomfortable.

'What?' Was he about to lob a bomb? Make demands

she wouldn't accept? Because it was his child? 'What?' she demanded again in a higher pitch.

Draining the glass, he set it down with precision then lifted his gaze to her. 'My role as a father.'

Here we go. Tamara's stomach tightened, as though holding baby closer. As she waited to be slammed, her breath caught in her lungs.

'I want a part in my child's life.'

'I expected that, and want it too.'

'You sound wary.'

'Not at all,' she fibbed.

'Oh, hell, I'm worrying you sick, aren't I? You've warned me about your lack-of-trust issues and I'm walking all over them.' Conor leaned closer. 'I'm trying to start a discussion about how we're going to manage parenting from two different homes, and, if I stick to my plans, from two different countries, unless you come with me.'

That stalled breath limped across her lips as she accepted his explanation for what it appeared to be. 'I don't have to stay in Auckland.'

'I don't have to move to Sydney.' His head jerked back as though he'd just shocked himself. 'I haven't had my final interview yet. It's been put back for another two weeks as one of the doctors involved had to take an urgent trip to New York. I'm one of two they're considering so if I pull out they'll save time and expense.'

'If you really want the job, then go.' She hesitated, straightened her spine mentally and physically, and stepped into the abyss. 'I can join you over there. I'd get a job easily enough, I imagine.'

'You'd do that?'

Hadn't she just said so? 'I'm not suggesting we live together. I wouldn't ask that of you.'

Male pride flipped into his face. 'Why not? We get on okay. Or don't you agree?'

Embarrassment flooded her. 'I meant I wasn't proposing a couple-type relationship.'

Proposing? Tamara Washington, wash your mouth out. 'We could share accommodation and the baby.'

'She wounds so easily.' He hadn't quite banished the wounded-pride look but it was lifting.

The heat in her cheeks heightened to an inferno. 'This isn't easy for me,' Tamara muttered, wishing the floor would open beneath her.

'Seems to me you're doing great.' Conor refilled their glasses with iced water. 'You only said what I was getting around to in a haphazard kind of way. Sharing an apartment or house is a good solution to joint parenting. I don't mind if we share a bedroom too. I mean…' he shrugged '…we do get along in that department. Very well, in my view.'

Okay, floor, hold that opening for a moment. 'You want to live with me and our baby? As in a couple kind of relationship?' Was that what she wanted?

'Why the surprise?'

'It never occurred to me. You have a busy social life and I'm sure I wasn't the first woman you took back to your apartment after a night on the town. A baby. And me. We'd cramp your style.' What a good idea. The thought of Conor with another woman didn't sit comfortably.

He had the cheek to laugh. 'You think? You were the only woman in my apartment, in my bed, and before you suggest I've got a problem I probably have, just not the one you're thinking.'

She hadn't been thinking. It was too hard, and confusing. But tension backed off as his words hit home. She'd been the last woman he'd made love with. Yes! Slow down. It was too soon to be getting excited. She wasn't completely convinced she could trust her judgement yet.

He continued. 'We had a wonderful night together and it started me wondering if I was missing out on something. Then I'd remind myself of my pledge never to marry.'

'Is that why you left Ireland? There was someone you were serious about?' She'd walk away now if that was the case.

'I left because every time I was with my sisters and their families, the pain of what I couldn't have overwhelmed me. I wanted it so badly, yet asking someone to take that risk with me was impossible.'

'You chose not to marry because of what happened to your brother and dad. Why couldn't you have gone with no children and still married?'

'I couldn't ask a woman to give up having a family for me.' He even had a smile on that gorgeous mouth.

But since she'd got pregnant with *his* baby, he could ask her to join him because it was all too late. She was the soft option. He'd have the child he longed for and a woman who knew the score and couldn't walk away because of that child. Thanks a million. Tamara's heart sank. She definitely needed to delve further into what made Conor tick.

Conor was watching her as he forked up a mouthful of butter chicken and rice. 'One week at a time, Tamara.'

One week? One day was difficult enough. Tamara tried following his example with her meal but swallowing became impossible as she waited for what he'd say next.

Finally he put the fork down. 'That's seriously delicious.'

Her throat opened and her food went down—without

the enjoyment factor. What was going on? Was Conor toying with her? Or, 'Am I expecting too much of you?'

'What *do* you want from me, Tamara?' Conor's query stilled the questions in her mind.

'I didn't know what you'd do about—'

'The question is what do *you* want of me? When you knew you had to tell me about the baby, what were you expecting? A cash handout? A home? Me to walk away? To stay and support you? What?'

The truth and only the truth. Not that she'd worked everything out, but she would start as of now. 'Firstly, your support.' She drew a tick in the air. 'Got it in spades.'

'Yes, you have.'

'Secondly, that you'll always be there for your child, that he'd grow up knowing you, having you in his life for real and not a phone call or email away.'

'You even doubted that?' he growled.

'A little.' His face didn't lighten up. 'How was I to know? You were planning on moving to Australia, often commented about how settling down wasn't for you when others at work talked about buying a house or moving in with a partner. I didn't know why you move around. Now I wonder if you're aware of what you're getting into, how it's going to cramp your style.'

'I applied for that position in Sydney because I was starting to feel close to you. I had to put space between us, forget you.'

This guy was good at curve balls. She waited for her heart to stop the tap dance it was doing before saying, 'So you're open to settling down somewhere.' She wouldn't delve into what else he'd implied. Too tricky when she was trying to be level-headed.

'Yes. Believe me when I say I take this seriously and my son or daughter will always be a major part of my life, regardless of what you and I decide to do about a relationship.'

Her forefinger traced another tick. 'Thank you.'

Shifting his butt and draping his arm over the back of the chair, Conor nodded. 'Carry on.'

'I'd like the happy family scene if at all possible. I grew up safe and happy. Dad adored me, spoilt me rotten. Not so sure about my mum, though.'

Mum, you need to know I'm pregnant. There are so many things I want to tell you. Neither should you miss out on anything to do with your grandchild.

Conor nodded. 'Family is most important. Losing my dad was horrific, and I was a lost wee soul until the man who became my stepdad came along.'

'How do we make it work? It's not like we're in a relationship already.' They barely knew each other outside work and bed.

Now he locked his gaze on her. 'Look at how we're dealing with this. We know each other professionally, got on very well the night we spent at my apartment and the world didn't implode when you told me about the pregnancy. I reckon we're off to a better start than some.'

'You make it sound straightforward.' The warning bells were tolling. Was she being sucked in again?

'I don't mean to, and yet in a way I do.' He pushed his now empty plate aside, and reached for her hand. 'I want this, Tamara. More than anything. You, me and the baby. I've been given an opportunity I never believed I'd have, and I want to make certain we get it right. It's a chance for something special I don't want to stuff up or lose.'

Couldn't be more blunt than that. This was about the baby and how to jointly make it work. Not about them and love and any of those crazy things. Which was fine, considering she couldn't trust her heart either. 'Sydney or Auckland?' she asked.

Conor looked a little shocked. No doubt the enormity of what they'd agreed to was only beginning to sink in. 'Leave that to me for now.'

Those alarm bells clanged harder. 'A partnership, remember? You can't cut me out of any decisions that involve me or the baby.'

He winced. 'It's a work in progress, okay?'

'Not good enough.'

'You have to believe I'll do the right thing by all of us, Tamara.'

'The thing is…' Oh, grow up. Take responsibility. Give the guy a break. He hadn't put a foot wrong yet, but he also hadn't made it easy for her about everything. 'I do. Just don't exclude me from decisions, okay?'

CHAPTER EIGHT

CONOR BLINKED, THEN stared at the apparition walking into the department.

Tamara in fitted scrubs. Scrubs that showcased the perfect figure wearing them. Wow. She looked stunning.

Down, boyo. You're at work.

True. And if Tam knew what was in his mind she'd do the aloof thing all morning. But... A guy was allowed to dream, wasn't he? It was the end of the week, and who knew what they might get up to in the weekend? 'Morning, Tam.'

She didn't even bite. Just tightened her hands into fists as she walked towards him. 'Hi.'

Make-up. Her face was always beautiful. Today he was all out of words. Those deep brown eyes, accentuated with mascara and some other coloured goo, were bigger, brighter, more fall-into-them-looking. Her peaky cheeks had colour, her lips... How could he not have been aware they were so full? So luscious? It was going to be a very long day.

Tam came around the end of the counter and stood in front of him. 'You still on for four o'clock?'

Blink. 'Of course I am,' he snapped. 'Like I'd bail.'

'I was thinking more that you might have to stay back to do paperwork or something.'

At the end of most days he usually put in an hour behind his desk, trying to placate the paper gods upstairs.
'Not today. Our—'

She cut him off with a warning nod to the side. 'Morning, guys.'

The day crew had arrived all together. 'Later.' He gave
Tam a curt nod. Damn but she looked beyond beautiful.
Not even her permanent exhaustion was getting a look
in this morning.

A registrar from the previous shift filled them in on
patients before heading away.

Conor's nostrils received a hit of spring flowers. Tamara stood beside him. He breathed deeper, enjoyed the
scent, remembered her satin-like skin, and forced his
body to behave.

A gentle nudge from Tamara's elbow.

When he glanced sideways he fell into a huge smile.

An almost imperceptible shake of her head. She knew
what he was thinking?

Then Michael stood up. 'Hope everyone can join me
at the local after work. It's my birthday on Sunday so I'm
shouting a few rounds.'

'Sorry, but I've got an appointment at four.' One he
wouldn't miss for anything. Excitement fizzed in his
veins.

'You can't change it?' Michael asked. 'I know you
won't be drinking since you're running that race tomorrow but they sell water.'

'No can do.' Conor stared straight ahead, afraid
of looking at Tamara in case everyone could read his
thoughts.

'You're running in the morning?' Annoyance slapped
at him from the woman beside him.

'A ten k run on the North Shore.' It had never occurred to him to mention it.

Michael asked, 'What about you, Tamara?'

'I'm not running anywhere.'

'So you'll be there for drinks.' Michael laughed.

'Sorry, but I can't make it either.' She sounded as if she'd like to cancel their appointment.

'You both going to the same thing, by any chance?' asked one of the older nurses with a hint of laughter in her voice.

He looked at Tamara. *Shall we tell them?*

She glared at him, then just as abruptly sighed and lifted her head a notch to nod. 'I guess.'

Reaching for her hand, Conor gave it a little squeeze. He'd had a reprieve and from now on would try harder to include her in everything. 'Go on.'

Best Tamara told them. She had expressed doubts over this only last night when they'd talked on the phone, but if she was ready then she needed to put it out there, let go of some of the things holding her back.

Her fingers returned his squeeze. 'We're going to see a midwife and then I'm having a scan.'

Delighted gasps echoed around the department. Hugs ensued.

'Congratulations.' Michael shook his hand. 'You still should join us afterwards. We can have a double celebration.'

Not sure how Tam would feel about that.

'We'll be there,' she told Michael quickly.

Giving him a taste of his own medicine by not consulting with him before accepting? 'Seems that's a yes. Might as well have a meal at the same time.'

Tamara tugged her hand away and picked up a file from the counter, like she was dismissing him. Regretting that they'd told everyone? Or still assimilating the fact they weren't alone with this any more? Tam would struggle with having shared something so personal.

He leaned in to say, for her ears only, 'Yesterday I overheard two nurses commenting on your tiredness and how you're not eating as much as usual. By telling everyone, we've stopped the gossip before it gets out of hand.'

Troubled eyes met his gaze. 'Or started something bigger.'

The media. The ever-present monster. Maybe she'd been right to think it best to hide the fact she was pregnant. But that wouldn't work. Babies tended to become very obvious after a few months of incubating. 'Hey, guys, one more thing.' Probably huffing into the wind, but worth a try. 'We'd prefer it if our news could stay among the team, and not be broadcast over the city.'

'Fair enough.'

'Good idea.'

'Of course.'

They'd have to wait to know if everyone was completely with them on this. Or go to Sydney sooner rather than later.

The phone from Ambulance Headquarters rang and ended the chattering.

But not the questions buzzing in Conor's head as he picked up a patient's notes. Did he even want to move to Sydney now that the reason for going had disappeared? Would Tam be just as comfortable in Dublin? Or should they stay here and brazen it out? No. Not that. It would be unfair on the baby, and Tam.

Spring air floated before him. Soft fingers alighted on his forearm. 'Conor? Thanks.'

'What'd I do?'

'Made me see how much of a secret I've been living.

I don't tell people, friends even, much about what I'm up to and that's been stifling. For the last two years I've been in shut-down mode. Not the way I used to live and…' she drew a breath and lifted her shoulders '…not how I intend bringing up my child.' Her eyes were filled with surprise and something else. Relief.

To hell with being at work. Conor leapt to his feet and wrapped an arm around her shoulders, placed a soft kiss on her forehead. Okay, so not the kiss he wanted to give but, yes, they were in the middle of the emergency department. 'Go, girl. You will do just great. Never forget I've got your back.' Another sneaky kiss and he stepped back, still watching her. 'Hey, no tears, 'cos you're making my eyes well up and that is so not a good look when I'm the boss around here.'

Slipping the spring green floaty top over her head, Tamara peered into the ridiculously small mirror in the staff locker room. If that image didn't raise a smile on Conor's dial then she might as well go back to baggy tees.

Hugging herself, she laughed softly. In February she'd been walking past a shop that had once been her favourite go-to place for great clothes and had spied this blouse in the window. It had been one of those have-to-have moments that had cost far too much money even in the end-of-summer sale. Since then the blouse had languished at the back of her wardrobe. But today spring was in the air and in the colours of the blouse. Spring came filled with promise, exactly how she felt at the moment. The media wouldn't rule her life again. Neither would Peter get a look in. But Conor? Oh, yes. Bring him on, centre stage. And… Tamara did a little dance on the spot. And she was going to meet her baby in a little over an hour.

The door swung wide and Kelli strolled in. 'Hello? Has

anyone seen my friend? The one who hides in frumpy clothes and doesn't wear make-up? The one who doesn't own gorgeous, to-die-for blouses and tight capris. Seems you haven't forgotten how make-up works either.'

'I saw that woman leaving home early this morning,' Tamara gave straight back. 'You're stuck with me now.'

'I'm not even going to ask.'

Wait two minutes and I bet you do. I'll save you the bother.

'It's time, Kelli.'

Her friend nodded. 'I agree.'

'Way past it, if I'm honest. This baby's shaking me up something terrible. But it's also exciting. I want to do right by him or her, which means moving on, dropping the past.'

'Nothing to do with Conor, then? You're not trying to impress him?' A cheeky grin took any edge out of her words. 'Because you need to know baby has no idea what you're wearing, but Conor is going to melt on the spot when he sees you.'

Tamara smiled. 'Ninety percent to do with him. I've been a fashion nightmare far too long. It's surprising Conor took me to bed in the first place, don't you think?'

'No, I don't. You've always been more than your clothes, girlfriend. But I'm thrilled to see you all dressed up and looking like you own the world.'

'I'll pay you when I've been to the cash machine.' The excitement bubbled up again. Today she'd made inroads into getting on with this new life that made her feel proud. Strong, even. Stronger.

'I can't wait to hear about the scan. You will tell me everything, won't you?'

'I'll bore you to sleep with the details. Oh, Kells, it's true. I'm having a baby.' A little life was growing inside her and she was about to hear its heart beating and see it moving. A lone tear sneaked out from the corner of her eye.

'Yeah, you are.' A hint of wistfulness came through those three words.

'Kelli?'

'If you need a godmother for this baby, you've got my number.'

'The job's yours, as of now.' It was something she'd already decided on, had just been waiting to discuss it with Conor first. Oops. She needed to rectify that fast.

The stunned look on Conor's face when she walked into his office raised her self-awareness to a whole new level and made her realise how low she'd gone. 'I thought you looked beautiful before.' He came around his desk to kiss her. 'I had no idea.'

'Are you ready?' Time was moving too fast. 'Rush hour's started and I'd hate to be late for this appointment.'

He swung his car keys from his fingers. 'We're off.'

'Snails are passing us,' she muttered as the line of traffic stalled at lights for the umpteenth time.

'School's out. It's to be expected.'

'You're too calm.'

'One of us has to be.' Conor lifted her hand from her lap and kissed each finger in turn.

'Aren't you tearing apart with excitement? With the need to see our baby?' Her stomach was going to take days to recover from this, churning away like a washing machine stuck on fast.

'Oh, yeah.'

The car jerked forward, stopping an inch from the car in front. 'Come on, move,' Tamara yelled, and pounded her knees with her fists. 'This is ridiculous.' She turned on Conor. 'You can stop laughing and all.'

'We have forty minutes to cover less than a kilometre. I don't see the problem.'

Leaning back, she closed her eyes and counted to ten. 'Why are men so damned reasonable?' Opening her eyes, she fixed him with a glare. 'Or is it only you?'

He just laughed. Again.

'You are excited.' Yes. 'We're on the same page.'

'Better get used to it.' He grinned. 'This is how it should be for evermore.'

Her happiness tripped. Righted itself. She'd run with his easy talk. New day, new outlook. 'Um, just one thing. I was going to talk to you first but the words kind of slipped out. I told Kelli I'd like her to be baby's god-mother.'

'That's fine. She's a perfect choice.'

'You agree as easily as that?' Unbelievable. 'Even if we leave the country?'

'Yep. Gives me leeway for my stuff-ups.' Conor was tapping out a tune on the steering wheel as he waited for the lights to change. On the footpath two youngsters sped past on skateboards. 'Kids, eh? I can't believe we're going to see our child. *Ours.*'

'If we ever get there.'

'Is it a boy or a girl?'

'Does that matter?' She didn't mind one way or the other, though she had started calling the baby he or him. Probably because of the mental images her mind drew up on a regular basis of a much younger version of Conor. That black hair; those blue eyes that were more often than not filled with warmth and laughter; the smile to beat all smiles that turned her to putty.

Beside her Conor laughed. 'Not at all, but I want to know so I can call the baby her or him and be right. I want all the things I plan for our child to be in the right colour, the right head space, the right shape.'

'You want pink for a girl and blue for a boy?' Tamara spluttered.

'Old-fashioned, huh?'

'Very. Believe me, I won't be buying only pink if we have a girl. There'll be every colour of the rainbow in her clothes, her room, her toys.'

'Ah, but no pink anywhere if it's a boy.'

'Deal.' Another hand squeeze. 'Though what if he wants to be a ballerina?'

'Does he have to be a pink one?'

'His call.'

'Fair enough. Pick our battles is what you're really saying.' He turned to her and placed his hands on her shoulders. 'You're awesome, you know that?'

Her mouth dried. About to shake her head, she stopped. If Conor thought that she'd take the compliment, enjoy it. Accept it. 'I think we're a great pair of would-be parents. I'll make the rules and you follow them.' She held her breath while waiting to see how he dealt with her joke.

He laughed some more. 'Sounds like something my sisters would say.'

'So I'm in with a chance with the Irish gang, then?'

'I wouldn't put you in the bonkers league but, yeah, they'll adore you.' He gave an exaggerated sigh. 'And I'll be in deeper trouble.'

Tamara stared at the image on the screen beside her. A tiny human floated before her eyes as she listened to the gentle rhythm of her baby's heart. Her chest expanded, filling with love for this child. Her child. Hers and Conor's. Blindly scrabbling around, she found Conor's hand, grabbed it and held on tight, never taking her eyes off the baby. Words were beyond her. Probably just as well. She wouldn't make any sense.

'Will you look at that?' Conor's voice sounded all clogged up as he stared at the image. Their faces were reflected back at them from the screen as their baby moved in the fluid supporting it. 'That's my baby,' he choked around some obstacle no doubt in the back of his throat.

'Our baby,' Tamara admonished in an equally starstruck tone when speech was possible. 'Isn't he beautiful?'

Now it was Conor gripping her hand tight, holding on like he couldn't take in what he was seeing. 'To think I believed I could forego becoming a parent. I didn't have a clue. It wasn't an easy decision, I admit.' His free hand waved through the air. 'I don't know what to say.'

'Different from seeing your nieces and nephews after they were born, eh?'

'Doesn't come close. To think what I wanted to do to those condom manufacturers when you said you were pregnant. Now I could kiss them.'

Tamara continued watching the small movements on the screen as the sonographer pressed the wand deeper into her belly. 'Guess you get to hear all sorts of weird and wonderful conversations while you're doing scans,' Tamara said to her.

She grinned. 'You have no idea. You two are boringly normal.'

Normal was good. For them at any rate. So far not much else had been. 'Is everything as it should be?' Tamara asked with a hitch in her voice, her throat suddenly dry.

'Yes. Baby's the right length for twelve weeks. The heart rate is good.'

Tamara relaxed. 'That's the best news so far.'

'Do you want to know the baby's gender?'

'I do,' Tam answered quickly, then looked at Conor. 'Do you?'

'Absolutely,' Conor agreed. 'We can't keep calling the baby he or him without knowing for sure there's a wee lad in there.'

'You're just thinking of the paint pails.'

The sonographer rolled the wand across Tamara's stomach, staring at the screen as she found the view of the baby she required. 'There you go. You're having a boy.'

Wonder ripped through Tamara. A boy. Not he or it, but a boy. For real.

'A son.' Wonder deepened Conor's accent. 'Not that it would've mattered if we were having a girl.'

'An All Black in the making.' Except their son probably wouldn't be growing up in New Zealand. 'A soccer player or a rally driver.'

'Not a ballerina, then?' Conor grinned. Then he shivered and the excitement went out in his eyes, the colour faded from his face.

Tamara focused entirely on the man who was changing her life for the better. 'Conor?' Her hand gripped his tightly. She shook him when he wouldn't meet her gaze. 'Look at me.'

He shuddered.

Then she knew. He was afraid for his son. Leaning closer, she spoke quietly. 'Forewarned is forearmed, remember?' She turned to the sonographer now cleaning her gear. 'Could we have a few moments to ourselves, please?'

'Not a problem. I'll print some images for you and then the room is all yours.'

Tamara waited impatiently. Yes, she wanted those pictures. But right this moment she needed to talk to Conor, to help him past his fear. This time she had to be the strong one, had to ignore her own worries about baby's heart. For now anyway.

The door hadn't closed behind the technician when Tamara lifted Conor's cold hand to her lips and placed a kiss on each knuckle. 'You have every right to worry, Conor, but do you really want to spend the coming years going around in a cloud of doom and gloom when you could be enjoying so many things with your son?'

'A son whose life might be taken in an instant.'

'A son who will most likely annoy the hell out of you as he grows up and who will give you equally as much pleasure and joy and pride.'

'How can you believe that without being terrified something will go wrong?'

'I have to. I can't let fear dictate, otherwise our son's life will be a misery. I've lived that life recently, and it's a waste of valuable time. A complete waste.'

Winter was in the blue eyes that connected with hers. 'I wish I had half your strength.'

'You do.'

His eyes widened. 'I panic.'

'Sure you do. I go crazy if I see a spider. Not in the same league, but in the end just as pointless and just as uncontrollable.' As had been Peter. It wouldn't have mattered if she'd not done as he'd bidden, he'd have found a way to steal everything from her and her parents.

The tip of Conor's tongue slid along his lips. 'You're good for me, you know that?'

'Keep believing that and we'll get along fine.' She was learning to accept how good Conor was for her too. They were making progress.

CHAPTER NINE

'WANT TO GO to the mall in the morning?' Conor heard Kelli ask Tamara over the noise of their work friends at the pub. 'The shops are filled with new summer styles.'

He stared into his water glass as he waited for her reply. Not that he'd asked Tamara to do anything over the weekend yet. He'd been leaving that until they were alone. If they got to be alone tonight. Celebrating Michael's birthday and then the news about their baby had become a long haul even when drinking nothing more innocuous than water in deference to tomorrow's race. The night was taking its toll on Tamara. She looked exhausted, but also the happiest he'd seen her in a long time. If not ever.

'I thought I'd go and watch Conor run his race in the morning.'

'Are you serious?' Conor asked without thought.

'You don't want me there?' Tamara asked around that smile that hadn't slipped once since leaving Auckland Radiation Services.

And before it did he answered, 'It's more than all right, but be warned, you'll be bored most of the time.'

'I can stand with other bored onlookers.' That smile grew, filled with warmth and something else. Something more than affection? For him?

Hard to know. Tamara hid her feelings well. Like he did. But then he didn't know his feelings for her. Couldn't fathom them, knew he wanted to be with her always, but did that mean he loved her? There was this lurking sensation in his gut that once he admitted he might, she'd sense his change and withdraw when he'd only just got her onside. Plenty of time to think about this. 'You'd prefer that to a mall filled with shops and sales? You're nuts.'

'I get to spend time with you, don't I?' The smile softened further.

'I know when I'm not wanted.' Kelli rolled her eyes and headed to the bar.

'Something's up with her.' Tamara's eyes tracked her friend.

'Go with her tomorrow if you're worried.'

'As much as I'd like to, you and I have a lot to work through and for baby's sake that's more important at the moment.' Her hand lay on her tummy while her gaze was still on her friend. 'I'll see Kelli during the week. It's her grandfather's birthday on Sunday and I know everyone's worried about his health.'

'But you think there's something else?'

'It was the sadness in her eyes when I told her about our baby. Like she believes she'll never have the same opportunity.'

Conor leaned close, and kissed the corner of her mouth. 'You know what that's like.' Another kiss. 'And look how it's turned out for you.'

Tamara snuggled into him. 'Pretty darned good, huh, Dr Maguire?'

'More than,' he agreed. 'I want you to meet someone tomorrow.'

Sitting up, she locked her eyes on him. 'Who?'

'My mam. Thought we could have a call. I'd have to

check she's at home, otherwise we'll try on Sunday. But be warned, Sunday means the whole tribe will probably turn up at her house.'

He could see doubt warring with pleasure in her face. 'Is this to tell her about the baby?'

'Yes. She'll be thrilled.'

'But you're not married. Will that be okay?' Her voice trailed off.

Now was not the time to talk about marriage—not in a pub with too many sets of ears flapping. 'Mam will be more than happy we're having a baby. Trust me on this.'

'I wish my mother would listen long enough to hear my news.'

'Want to try again over the weekend?'

'I can, but I guarantee the result will be the same.' Now that smile had disappeared completely, tugging at his heartstrings.

He wanted to smother this woman with love and affection, give her all the things she'd missed out on for so long. There was that L word again. What was going on in his head? Patience. His new go-to word. Rushing either him or Tam was not the way to do things. 'Want another sparkling water? Or shall we head home?'

Her eyes widened. 'Home? Whose?'

As in we don't live together. Yep, he got it. 'My apartment's closer.' *And not filled with objects from your past.*

'I have nothing but the best memories of your apartment.' Her smile was slow, and teasing, and struck him right under his ribs.

'Up to making more?'

Tam stood and held her hand out to him. 'Show me.'

Memories. Tamara hugged herself as she waited at the finish line the next day for Conor to appear around the far corner. They'd made some amazing ones last night back at Conor's place. She was stacking up a load lately. All with one central figure.

Conor.

There. Running hard as he aimed for the end of the race, strangers and her cheering him on. His jaw was fixed in a determined way she'd not seen before. Those long athletic legs stretching out, eating up the metres, his strong arms pumping the air. Doing this to keep healthy, to stay alive. She could only hope he didn't go crazy and overdo the fitness thing now that he was becoming a father. Too much could be as dangerous as too little.

'Go, Conor,' she yelled, and jumped up and down. 'You can do it.'

He wasn't about to win the race—someone had already done that. He wasn't even in the first couple of hundred runners home, but he obviously wanted to keep the place he had, and therefore so did she.

As he passed her she waved and shouted, 'You're amazing, Conor Maguire.' She couldn't run one kilometre, let alone ten, in a good time.

His running shorts and singlet clung to his sweat-drenched skin, outlining every muscle, the wide chest and narrow hips she adored exploring. Not the perfect athlete's body, but perfect to her. The body that fitted hers, made hers hum. The man who was determined to be a part of her and their baby's life regardless of any argument she might put up. The man she wanted onside every step of the way with their child. With her. For life.

Memories. Those new ones felt good, right.

She walked towards him. He'd finished, was leaning over, hands on his knees as he took in great lungsful of air. She touched his shoulder, then his head. 'You're nuts. You know that, don't you?'

His eyes were that light blue she adored when he dragged his head up. 'I figured out halfway through that it would've been as energetic to have stayed in bed with you this morning, and a lot more enjoyable.'

'Good answer.' She dug into the day pack she'd carried slung over her shoulder all morning and pulled out his towel and water bottle. 'Here.'

'I was a bit short on energy today.' He grinned.

'That'll teach you for carrying that rubbish bin out to the roadside this morning.'

'Nothing to do with the midnight antics in my bedroom, you reckon?'

She stepped back, hands up. 'I'm not taking the blame for your poor performance. In the race, I mean,' she added with a laugh.

'Is that a compliment? Wonders will never cease.' He shrugged out of the singlet and pulled on a sweatshirt. 'Let's get out of here.'

'You don't want to stay for the speeches and prize-giving?' Not something that would excite her, but she hadn't been the one to put all the effort into running for the children's charity.

Conor shook his head. 'I'd prefer a shower, cold beer and food, and time with you—alone.'

Tenderness spread throughout her. This special treatment was—well, special. She was so not used to it. What if—? No. Conor meant what he'd said, showed her in actions as much as he put it in words. He cared. There was a soft tightening behind her breasts as she slipped her hand into his. 'Let's go.'

She was getting used to being this close to him. She felt safe. But her heart was still secure despite that achy nudge. The love factor was still on lock-down.

* * *

Tamara grabbed her phone to see who was calling. The band tightening around her heart relaxed. 'Morning, Conor.'

She'd missed him from the moment he'd climbed out of her bed midevening last night to go back to his apartment. At her insistence. They'd spent the afternoon doing weekend chores, grocery shopping for each of them, going to the farmers' market, doing their laundry, and getting on too well. Spooked at how well, Tamara had suggested Conor go back to his place after they'd made love. It was one thing to acknowledge to herself she was happy with the way they were progressing; it was quite another to be reminded of it at every turn, each glance. Too much too soon. She just wasn't as ready to have Conor full time in her day-to-day life as she'd thought.

'Hey, Tam, how are you?'

Back to calling her Tam. He can't have been too peeved at being kicked out of her bed. 'Couldn't be better.' Or was he using that to wind her in as he wished?

Stop it, Tamara Washington. Give the guy a break. He deserves so much better of you than this.

'What about you?'

'Bursting with energy.'

'After that ten k. Impressive.'

'You forgot to add the rest of my activities.' There was laughter in his voice. Was Conor happy? With her? To be with her?

'I haven't forgotten anything.' Scary. What really got to her was that it mattered. Conor in her life outside work was beginning to mean something special.

'Feel like catching the ferry across to Devonport for lunch? The day's perfect for being out on the water.'

'That'd be awesome.' The sky was blue for as far as she could see from her window. 'The harbour should be calm enough for my stomach.' It had done its morning ritual hours ago.

'You worry too much,' he admonished softly, that brogue tickling her in places best left alone unless he was standing right beside her. 'You're usually back to normal in no time at all.'

'What don't you notice?'

'Hard not to when you're usually scoffing a pastry by nine o'clock.'

'Stop talking and get around here.' She pressed 'off', feeling a hundred percent happier than before he'd phoned. So simple. One short call and her life was back on track. The new track that involved Conor and the baby and a life.

The one that had had her going through her wardrobe earlier to throw out all the shapeless clothes she'd accumulated. How had she let herself get so down that she hadn't cared about her looks? No one from her past would believe that. Right from when she'd been a toddler, clothes had been as important as being her father's special girl.

Today she sported another pair of capri pants and a blouse from a time when she had dressed well, the surprise being that they still fitted perfectly. But not for long. Her fingers splayed across her stomach. Did maternity wear come with style and flair? Must do, surely?

'I'm going on a date,' she sang as she applied eyeliner. A real dinky-die date with a real dinky-die hot man with a body dreams were made of.

Look what usually happened to her dreams.

She shivered, slapped the eyeliner pencil on the counter and tugged the mascara wand out of its tube.

Not the way to go, Tamara.

Ding-dong.

'Coming,' she sang. Since Conor's first visit here, on the day she'd told him she was pregnant, she'd grown to love the sound of her doorbell.

Even better was the kiss Conor gave her the moment she opened the door. His mouth claimed hers as though he would never leave her again. When he pushed his tongue across her lips she opened her mouth and let him in. Savoured his taste, the feel of him, his scent. Truly knew him, not as the father of her baby, the man she'd worked with for nearly a year, the guy who had sworn to stand by her, but as Conor Maguire—the whole package, the man who she could too easily fall in love with if she ever relaxed enough. Her body ached for him from her toes to her mouth. 'Have we got time?' she whispered through their kiss.

She was swung up against Conor's chest and carried towards her bedroom without his mouth shifting off hers. Guess that was a yes, then.

Some time later Conor stepped out of the bathroom, saying, 'Let's go and have us some fun. Have you got a jacket? There could be a sea breeze while we're on the ferry.'

Tamara snatched up the one she'd put on the table earlier. 'Yes, and sunscreen to protect my pasty winter skin.'

'It's me who'll need that. My Irish skin can't handle the Kiwi sun.'

The crossing was calm. Baby stomach hadn't objected. Bathed in sunshine, Devonport was busy with city dwellers out for a stroll and an alfresco lunch.

Walking slowly, her hand in Conor's, stopping to window-gaze at pottery, art and clothes, Tamara hadn't felt so relaxed in years. 'It's as though everything's coming together perfectly,' she spilled as they sat down at a small round table outside a lunch bar. Then the familiar dread crept in. Too perfectly. 'I shouldn't have said that.'

'Think you're tempting fate?' Conor asked.

'Over the last couple of years, whenever I've dared to think things might be looking up, something awful has happened.' And since they'd never looked up half as much as they were now, she might have a lot to fear.

'You're not on your own any more. We're a team. We're going to watch out for each other.'

'Aw, shucks. You say the loveliest of things sometimes.' *Sniff, sniff.*

'I wouldn't if I knew it was going to make you cry.' With the paper napkin from the plate at his elbow he gently dabbed her eyes.

Which only increased the volume of water oozing down her cheeks.

'Hey, steady. These napkins aren't made for waterfalls.' Conor's lips tipped upwards, sending her stomach into a riot of butterflies.

'I wish my dad could've met you. He'd have liked you.' Dad had dreamed of walking his daughter down the aisle since the first time he'd held her in his hands. Which had absolutely nothing to do with Conor. She wasn't marrying him, just setting up house to provide for their child.

'I'd have liked that too.' Conor screwed up the wet napkin and dropped it in the centre of the table. 'Want to order?'

They shared a large Hawaiian pizza and Conor had a beer while Tamara stuck to water. Leaning back in her chair, she glanced along the road to where the tide lapped at the edge of the promenade. 'I could stay here for ever.' There wasn't a driving need to fill gaps in conversation or to wonder what Conor might be thinking. 'Have you decided about following up on the Sydney interview?'

'How would you feel if I did? Would you be okay with joining me there? If you are and I get the position then I'll stay a few extra days to look for somewhere for us to live.' Caution lay between them, the cosy atmosphere gone.

'There's nothing to keep me here apart from my job, which I was going to give up at the end of the year to go to university. Kelli is my only friend and she would be the last person to want me not getting on with my life, and that's with you now. You and wee man.' Her hand circled her belly. Was it her imagination or had her stomach begun to pop out now that she'd accepted her pregnancy?

'You aren't agreeing to move just to keep me happy?'

'Not at all. I'm all for making changes in my life, and there are a lot coming up. Why not start our new life in a place neither of us has been before?'

'That job in Sydney's only for twelve months and then we get to repeat this conversation.'

'Done. Sydney it is. Because I know you'll be offered the position. They'd have to be crazy not to.' Something like excitement fizzed in her veins. 'I feel I'm starting to live again. My primary goal is no longer to keep my head down and avoid facing up to difficult people or decisions.'

'You were focused on going to university and med school.'

'I procrastinated for ever. All those "t"s and "i"s. If you hadn't kept telling me I could do anything if I wanted it badly enough, I'd probably still be dithering about applying.' Now the decision had been taken away from her it was surprising how little that hurt. How could it when she was going to become a mother?

'You could apply in Sydney.'

He'd just said he'd only be there a year. Anyway, 'I

don't want to become a doctor at the moment. Being a hands-on mum is what I'd like to be next. Does that make me sound flaky? Unreliable?' She didn't wait for an answer. He might say yes. 'Imagine all those hours I'd have to spend studying and later working and there'd be a wee man at home not getting my full attention. I don't think so. I'll get a part-time job nursing.'

'You can stay at home if you want. Be a full-time mother.'

'We'll see.' It was too early to accept his offer, if she could ever bring herself to do that. She was still getting her head around the fact she had agreed to leave Auckland. It felt right, but it was a huge leap in trust. What a difference a week made, unless she was back to her old tricks and handing over her heart too easily.

No, I refuse to believe that.

Until proved wrong, I will believe in Conor. Totally.

Because otherwise she'd do her head in, working it all out. Anyway, her heart still belonged to her, not Conor.

'We don't have to hurry back to the city.' Conor watched Tam across the table. 'Want to walk along the beach?' A relaxed Tamara was something to enjoy. She didn't do it often enough. Was he about to push too hard, too fast?

'That's a great idea.'

Placing some money under his plate, Conor rose and reached for her hand. 'I've never held a woman's hand so often.' He winced. 'Sorry, that wasn't exactly tactful.'

'We come with pasts. Not that I know anything about yours. Come on, spill. Any world-stopping affairs? Or a great love of your life that didn't work out?'

Now who was being tactless? But he rolled with it because it might help his cause by knocking down some more barriers. 'There was a girl I thought I'd love for ever, until the day she swiped my piece of birthday cake from my school bag and left me her mouldy scone. We were seven.'

'Silly girl. She might've got the whole cake if she'd played nice.'

He nudged her. 'Remember that.' He swung their hands between them. 'Next I fell hard for a student at med school until she turned up one day sporting a rock on her finger and her resignation in the other hand. She'd found the specialist she wanted to marry and live the good life with.'

'That must've hurt.'

'Only my pride. We weren't well suited. For a while I stuck to having fun without commitment, the only way to go when most hours were taken up with study.' The old demon rose. 'After my heart attack there was no way I was looking for a serious relationship.'

Her fingers jerked in his, but she didn't withdraw.

Conor stopped and took her into his arms to gaze into those deep eyes. 'Seems from the day I met you life took a bat and beat me over the skull, because everything I adhered to regarding relationships flew out the window. It has taken time for me to recognise what was going on.' Did she see where he was headed?

Her tongue worried at the centre of her top lip. 'You're okay with that? It's been a shock for both of us.'

'I'm not just talking about the baby, Tam.'

'Oh.' Worry, worry. Then she pulled away and continued walking along the beach.

They were still surrounded by kids and dogs, and couples, and elderly women chatting. Conor went with Tam, ready to wait a bit longer, despite the impatience sizzling in his veins.

Her fingers slipped into his again. 'That heart attack has a lot to answer for.'

'Yeah.' Too much. But not all bad. 'My mother struggled to come to terms with losing Dad and my brother. There was a while there when occasionally she'd go out to the store to get something and not come home.'

Tam gasped. 'Where were you?'

'The first time I was with a playmate and his mother went to find her. The second time it happened during the night and I woke up. My crying must've been loud because the neighbour rang the cops, who turned up real fast.'

'Were you taken away?'

'Fortunately, no. There's only so much a four-year-old could cope with.' That would've meant the start of welfare and strangers and he had already been broken-hearted. 'One of the cops was Dave and he'd known Mam for a long time so he stayed with me while his colleagues searched for her. It was Dave who spent hours with Mam, talking about whatever was important to her, and after that whenever she felt the urge to get away she'd ring him.'

'Is this the man who became your stepfather?' Warm brown eyes were turned on him.

'The one and only. If I couldn't have my dad, then he was the next best option. Not once did I feel different or not a part of the family that was to come.' He'd got lucky. Twice. 'I was better off than some kids at school who had their real fathers.'

'I'm glad. Guess that's why you're determined to be there for our young man.' Tamara stretched up to kiss him.

A gentle, sweet kiss that set his heart racing. They

were at the end of the promenade. Alone apart from one dog and a sky full of screeching seagulls.

With his hands on her shoulders he held her gently. 'Not the only reason.' His stomach lurched. *Too fast, man.* But waiting wasn't an option. There was so much to sort out and not a lot of time. 'Tam, will you marry me?'

Just as well his hands were holding her shoulders. He got the feeling she'd have dropped in a heap otherwise.

She was staring at him. 'Did you just propose? To *me*?'

Ouch. Not rushing to accept, then. 'Yes, Tam, you. I want to marry *you*. For us, and for our child.'

'For us?' The words were strangled.

He nodded as he smiled away his worry and gave her reassurance. 'Yes, us. We've practically agreed to live together, to raise our child jointly, to move around the world as a couple. Marriage would be the icing on the cake.'

Her shoulders sagged into his hands. Her mouth dropped. 'Oh.'

'I care about you, Tam. A lot. I want this. A family, you.' Conor spilled out the words in a rush of honesty. 'You've got under my skin and I can't ignore you. You make me hope for more, and believe anything's possible. I think we can have a wonderful future together.'

Her eyes widened and she straightened. 'Truly?' Doubt lurked on her mouth, in her face.

'This is not something I'd make up.' He wasn't her ex. He had no hidden agenda. He needed to remember that, and give her time. 'All I want is to make you happy. That'll make me happy too.'

'You care for me that much?' Her acceptance was sinking in. It was there in the softening of her mouth, the colour turning her cheeks pink, her hands spreading across his chest.

'Absolutely.' Was he falling in love with Tam? Yep, he

could be. 'I don't want you thinking I'm out to hurt you in some way. I'd never do that.'

'You don't think you're rushing things? It's only been a week since we found out we're joined together for ever by a baby.' She was stalling. Listening to her heart *and* her head?

'I tend to make up my mind and act on it immediately. But I can say that from that first night together you've been residing in my mind, taunting me, distracting me, making me sleep-deprived, and it has taken learning about baby to tease that wide open. That, and hearing about your past and why you are who you are.'

'That was important?'

'Absolutely. I like to understand what makes people tick, and with you it was becoming a full-time need. I could see you hurting at times, and how you hid a lot from everyone by putting up insurmountable barriers, and yet you came to me so willingly that night.' Conor's thumbs caressed her shoulders. 'I take that as a compliment.'

Her face softened as she studied him. 'Yes. Let's get married.' She blinked, stared at him. She hadn't thought this through. She'd be thinking she'd made the same rash decision as she had with her ex.

'Tamara?' He shook her gently, his heart heavy, knowing she needed space. 'You're sure? If you want a few days to think about it I'll understand.'

'You haven't spun false hope around me to suck me in. I don't want to live on the edge of something I might have, never knowing if I will actually get it or not. I need honesty and reality.' Rising up onto her toes, she whispered, 'This isn't how I envisioned accepting a proposal, but I will marry you, Conor Maguire.' And then she sealed her words with a kiss like no other she'd given him. It was full of hunger, and longing, and commitment, and caution.

He didn't recognise love in the mix.

Patience, man, patience. He hadn't exactly been brimming with love either. That was still working its way into his psyche, and could turn around and disappear before reaching its full potential. Those old gremlins were still in charge.

Conor was the one to break away, his chest rising and falling as he breathed fast, feeling out of sorts and not sure where they were headed. Other than bed some time later. 'What is it about you that turns me into a raging sex maniac? If we were anywhere but on a public beach with half of the city wandering past, I'd have you naked so fast it would be crazy.'

Tamara was swaying on her feet, and he caught her to him. She croaked in a heat-hazed voice, 'Let's go home. We're not crazy, not at all.'

But maybe they were. Nearly having sex on the promenade. Agreeing to marry with no lead-in time and no declarations of love. Having a baby after one night together. What the heck? Might as well go for broke. 'Tomorrow after work we'll visit a jeweller's shop so you can choose an engagement ring.'

'No.' Tamara whipped around to stare at him. 'Sorry, but I don't want an engagement ring.'

His mouth soured. She'd changed her mind already. Shortest engagement on the planet. 'Not now? Or not at all?'

'I didn't put that very well. What I mean is all I'd like is a wedding ring. A solid band with maybe one stone. A sapphire or ruby. Not a blazing big diamond.' She shuddered. 'I want this to be about you and me. We're not flashy, or false. We care about each other, about our baby. We're starting our joint life. You and me,' she repeated. Her eyes were pleading with him to understand.

'Got it in one.' He swung her up in his arms and held her close to kiss her. Got it in one. 'You and me and our son.'

CHAPTER TEN

—

TAMARA FOLDED THE dishcloth and hung it on the door of Conor's oven. 'Done.'

'Then it's time to call Mam and give her the good news.'

Her heart gave one hard kick. It had to happen, but tonight? When she was still getting her head around being engaged to Conor? Telling other people would make it more real.

It is real.

She swallowed down on her apprehension. 'Will anyone else be there?' Any one of those sisters he obviously adored.

'It's a family tradition to have brunch at Mam and Dave's house if you're anywhere near Dublin on Sundays. At least one of my sisters and her brood will be there.'

'Will your mother be happy about you marrying a Kiwi?' Nerves cranked up. Conor's mother might think she'd keep her son from returning to Ireland permanently.

'Why ever not? I suspect she might've been hoping I would meet someone while I was away.'

'That's okay, then.' She wished. And picked up the photo frame with the image of their baby in it. Her finger skimmed over the glass while her heart knocked on her ribs.

'Tam, I'd like you to talk to her. Everyone there for brunch will be lining up to say hello.'

She pushed her chin forward. Might as well leap in and get it over. 'Sure.'

'Get used to it. You're about to become part of a large, whacky family. They'll have a load of questions for us.' He laughed. 'Not that any one of them will wait for an answer before going on to the next question.'

'You look happy when you're talking about them. Have you ever been homesick since leaving Ireland?'

'I've had massive bouts at times, but I haven't been ready to hop on a plane and head home. The reason I left was still there.' Conor kissed her on the nose. 'You've turned my life around and now I'm ready for anything.'

Including marrying her. Was he certain about that? Or would he rethink his proposal when he'd had time to contemplate all the ramifications? Tamara returned the kiss, but on his stubbly chin, and then bit down on the flick of desire heating her low down. 'About all those questions…'

'The ones we don't have answers for yet? Don't worry. I'll tell everyone to stop being nosy and that we'll get back to them.'

But she did worry. 'They'll listen?'

Conor shrugged. 'Not at all.' He opened his laptop, booted it up. 'That's family for you. They know no boundaries.'

A knot of anxiety formed. 'We'll tell your family, but I'd like to keep our engagement from everyone else for a bit longer.' Everything was happening too fast, rushing at her from all directions. 'I need to take a breath, get used to being with you, our baby, getting married, possibly moving to Sydney. There'll be so many questions and…' she lifted her hands in the air '… I don't have all the answers.'

'And you can't function properly without answers. Fair enough. Your wish is my command.' He said it all through a gut-tightening, desire-expanding smile.

She threw herself against him. 'Thank you,' she murmured before kissing him, deep and hard.

'What for?' Conor grinned when he came up for air.

'Being you.' She smiled back before leaning in for another searing kiss.

The laptop needed rebooting by the time they were ready to make the connection with Dublin.

'Junior here…' Conor's hand splayed across her tummy '…will turn up thinking it normal to do lots of exercise at odd hours of the day and night.'

Tamara chuckled as she spread her hand on top of Conor's much larger one. 'We do give him plenty of workouts.'

Conor tapped the internet icon. 'Let's do this.'

Oh, boy. She parked her butt on a stool, fidgeted with the bracelet on her wrist. Not ready. So not ready. Was she rushing into this without checking out everything about Conor? But, then, how did she do that? And did she really want to? It seemed underhand. But last time she'd trusted a man she'd cared for deeply she'd overlooked so many signs.

'Hey, Mam, how are you?' Happiness radiated out of Conor's eyes as he talked to his mother for a few minutes. Then he shifted the laptop so she was in the picture too. 'I've got someone I want you to meet.'

A gazillion faces appeared before her, each person pushing someone else out of the way. The cacophony of excited, almost incomprehensible Irish voices was deafening and reminded Tamara of a visit to a bird sanctuary in Queensland many years ago. How did anyone in this family know what was going on when they were all talking at once?

Conor reached for her hand, held it firmly. 'Tamara is my fiancée.'

Her mouth fell open. Not going for a slow lead-in, then. 'Ah, um, hi, everyone.'

'Hello, Tamara. You look gorgeous.'

'What do you see in our lump of a brother?'

'Hey, Tamara, are you a Kiwi?'

'Conor,' his mother shrieked. 'How long have you been seeing her and not told me?'

He leaned close to Tamara and whispered, 'See? Another reason why I came Down Under.'

She shook her head at him. 'You have no idea how fortunate you are.' How could he have left Ireland? His family? She'd never have been able to do it.

'You're not saying much,' someone, female, said.

'I'm surprised any of you can hear a thing,' she quipped.

'Meet the family,' Conor's mum responded. 'It's like this all the time.'

Conor held his hand up. 'Okay, guys, shut up for a moment. Tamara and I have things to discuss with you and I only want to say them once.' Instant silence descended.

'Unbelievable.' Tamara smiled.

'Yep,' he mouthed in her direction, before leaping right in with the next load of news. 'We're having a baby in six months. We're also probably moving to Sydney.'

Conor continued yabbering to his family, and the level of voices coming back at him was rising fast. Back to normal, Maguire style. Warmth trickled through her. By carrying Conor's baby she'd become a part of this family. So far they hadn't pulled faces or called her names. It had never ceased to shock her how someone who only rec-

ognised her from camera shots or headlines in the paper
could come up and talk to her as though she was known
to them. Worse, they often had plenty of advice for her,
from how to get back on her feet to what she should do
to pay back all those millions Peter had stolen. And now
this. Amazing.

'Tamara, welcome to our family. You don't know how
thrilled I am about this news. And you must call me Judy.'
Conor's mother spoke directly to her. 'I guess we'd better go, but I'll talk to you again soon.'

'Th-thank y-you.' A tear sneaked down her cheek at
the simple kindness shown her by a stranger. Conor's
mother, until fifteen minutes ago unknown to her. Things
really were looking up. With such a wonderful family,
who appeared genuine, Conor must be the real deal,
surely?

Leaning her head against his shoulder, Tamara ran
her fingers over his chest. 'Your mother's lovely. So are
Dave and all those sisters and their families.'

'You should try contacting your mother again.'

She stiffened. 'What's the point? She'll only tell me
I've made yet another mistake and that I have to get on
with it. Without her.'

'When did you last talk? As in really talk?'

'The day after Dad's funeral.' A lifetime ago. 'The
fraud squad had just left the house with a vanload of car-
tons containing private papers from Dad's study.'

He started rubbing her back softly. 'You're beginning
to look pregnant.' Warmth stole through her as he cupped
her breast.

She placed a hand on her small baby bump. 'Mum's
sister came out from Australia for Dad's funeral. She
had plenty to say about me, blamed me for the fact that

Mum was no longer wealthy and would have to live in relative poverty.'

'Your mother didn't disagree?'

'That's the funny thing. She did at first. Stuck up for me, saying there was no way I could've known what had been going on. She even gave me hugs and talked about Dad as we'd known him before the dementia stole his mind. It was a sad yet funny morning. We looked through photos of the three of us on holidays, at functions, doing the things families do. Of course, we had no idea what would go down later.'

'When did it all change?'

'The next morning my aunt went to town to buy some clothes. That's when the reality struck, first her and then Mum. She came storming in and threw all the photos on the floor, jumped on them and screamed at me for losing everything. She'd never qualified at anything and bemoaned Mum's luck at finding a rich man. Dad had always kept them both in funds. That day the credit cards simply didn't work any more.'

'And it was all your fault.'

'Apparently. Mum didn't want to believe my aunt so they went out and tried to buy a bracelet at the local jewellers. Same result, and the end of my relationship with my mother. She went on a rampage, visiting fashion shops to try on clothes she could no longer afford, leaving them in piles on the shop floors. It was all there in the papers that night. They flew to Australia the next day and I've never heard from Mum since. I have rung her often, only to be hung up on.'

'She cut you off when you'd done nothing more than trust the wrong man, a man her husband had believed in enough to hand over the company's operations to.' Conor tightened his hold around Tam, and she leaned into him.

'Would you want your mother to know about the baby and take part in his life if she could get past what happened?'

'Yes.' Had he lost his mind? 'Of course I want Mum to be his grandmother in more than name.' She wasn't exactly the perfect role model for a mother, but she was her mother.

'Want to try another phone call?'

'And take another king hit? No, thanks.' But she would, just not tonight after that wonderful session talking with Conor's family.

'I've got a suggestion.'

She started to object.

'Hear me out. Write to her, tell her about us and the baby, and how we're moving to Sydney. Put it all on paper, including how you'd like her to be part of the family.'

'She'll tear it up.'

'Or she'll set it aside and keep going back to stare at the envelope with your writing on it until she can't resist it and gives in to curiosity.'

'She'll get rid of it the moment she sees my scribble.' Or would she?

'She might not. Or she might, but it would be worth the risk to get your mother back.'

A soft silence fell over them. Conor continued holding her close, and she continued soaking up the warmth he brought her. 'I'll think about it.'

Monday morning and bedlam. ED was overrun with year-three children from Parnell Primary. Parents were kept busy, trying to control the little getaways who seemed more intent on destroying the department than getting treated for bee stings.

'Tell me how so many kids were stung?' Conor shook

his head at the chaos before turning back to a harassed teacher who also had stings on her arms and face. 'I've never seen anything like it.'

'Me neither. We were out on the field, playing soccer, when a swarm came up the bank and straight into our midst. It's the first time I've seen bees swarming and it was scary.'

'I bet.' He'd never experienced a swarm. 'To have all those children out there, being attacked, would've been a nightmare.'

'I'm grateful only two had serious reactions. We did get most of the kids into the swimming pool quick smart.'

Hence all the wet clothes lying in piles around the department. Seemed most of the kids preferred being undressed than wet and cold.

Tamara approached with an amused expression lighting up her face. 'Remind me not to have more than one child, will you?' She tossed him a smile before picking up a book that had been dropped by one young patient.

Of course his gaze rested on her backside as she'd bent to retrieve the book. Of course. No problem with the chemistry between them. No difficulty with anything at this stage really. Not when he regularly felt light-headed and excited.

'How are the boys who had allergic reactions?' the teacher asked.

'One lad's doing well, but we've had to put the other on oxygen and morphine. He also reacted to the painkiller. His parents are with him, if you want to see them.'

The woman shook her head. 'They don't need me asking irritating questions. I saw them when they arrived.'

'We need to start moving some of these children out of here, preferably on their way home.' Conor glanced around the department. 'There are other patients waiting to be seen and none of these youngsters require our attention any longer.'

'Have you signed any of them out?' Tamara asked.

'Starting now.'

The teacher sighed. 'I'll get the parents together to explain that their children are ready to go.'

'That'll be a bag of laughs.' Tamara chuckled as she watched the woman begin rounding up her charges and their families.

'We didn't need to see most of the children,' Conor mused. 'But I don't mind admitting I've enjoyed the last hour.'

'You're a natural with kids. Our wee man is so lucky to be having you as his dad,' she murmured before heading over to a group of kids objecting to picking up wet clothes.

Down, chest, down. But, hey, any compliment Tam was handing out he'd happily accept. His gaze followed her and his heart clenched as the kids laughed at something she said.

Impatience gnawed. They had everything going for them and had coped well with the king hits over the past week, and, damn it, he wanted more than he should.

'Doctor.' A parent stood in front of him.

'What can I do for you?'

'Tell me again about this EpiPen my son will always have to carry. It seems extreme when he's had bee stings before with no side effects.'

Conor nodded. 'One sting, even two or three at a time, don't always cause problems, but your lad had more than fifty today. Those would've filled his system with toxin, which will eventually disappear, but his body now recognises the toxin and even a small sting will ring warning bells and start a response you don't want to take a chance on.'

'Better to be safe than sorry?' The man nodded.

'If it was my child I'd be doing it.'

I've got a son. A son in utero, but he's real. I'm going to be a dad.

And it felt wonderful. As long as he didn't think about hearts and stoppages. Funny, but those had been far from his mind the last couple of days.

The phone buzzed at his elbow. 'Call for Dr Maguire.' It was the director of emergency services at Sydney Hospital.

'Hold on and I'll transfer this to my office.' Conor punched some buttons and raced for his room.

'Hi, there, Conor. Hope I'm not interrupting anything serious.' The director's voice boomed over the airwaves.

'Perfect timing. How's things in Sydney?' What was this call about? He'd made arrangements to fly over for the interview on Friday.

'We're having a minor heatwave. The job? That's yours. The other contender has pulled out for family reasons.'

'I'm sorry to hear that. But I'm also stoked.' He and Tam could get serious about their plans for the future. 'Thank you. I'm thrilled.'

'So are we. We'd like it if you still come over at the end of the week so we can run through your contract and get to eyeball you before you start officially.'

'Not a problem. I want to look into accommodation anyway.' He'd got the job. Conor punched the air. Another tick in the going-well stakes. Where was Tam? He couldn't wait to tell her.

* * *

'Congratulations, Dr Maguire.' Tamara lifted her glass of sparkling water in a toast the following night. 'Watch out, Sydney Hospital.'

Conor tapped his glass against hers. 'We're on our way, Tam.' He glanced around the restaurant she'd chosen to celebrate his new job. 'I can't believe how everything's falling into place so easily.'

A flicker of doubt crossed her eyes but then she smiled. 'Don't tempt fate, whatever you do.'

'That first day I walked into Auckland Central's ED and set eyes on you, I had absolutely no idea how much my life would change.' If not for Tamara's pregnancy he'd still be avoiding the things that were now making him happy.

The sweetest pink coloured her cheeks under her make-up. 'Are all Irish men so charming?'

The off-the-shoulder little black dress she wore was sensational. 'You're like another Tamara Washington. Just as beautiful and lovely with an added dose of style thrown in.'

The pink darkened to red. 'I shudder when I think how I let myself go.'

Her hand was warm under his. 'Your shapely body and stunning looks weren't all that attracted me.' The words were coming too easily for a guy not used to putting his feelings out there.

'You're embarrassing me.' Tamara toyed with her glass. 'What I wouldn't do for a glass of wine right now. There's so much to celebrate and I'm stuck with water.' Her mouth was tipping into a big smile. One that didn't quite reach her eyes.

'For the best reason.'

'Totally agree.' No doubt in her eyes now.

* * *

'Thank goodness for nights,' Tamara muttered, as she dropped her bag on the kitchen table on Wednesday and pulled open the fridge to see what to have for dinner. 'Then again maybe not.'

One soft and spongy tomato, a piece of cheese growing a healthy dose of mould—or was that unhealthy in her condition? The solitary carrot on the middle shelf was so soft she could tie a knot in it. The groceries she'd bought last weekend were still at Conor's apartment.

Thank goodness for the café at work. Another supermarket trip was imperative, but would have to wait until the weekend. Her body ached with fatigue, as though it hadn't had any sleep in a month.

Flicking the kettle on, she leaned a hip against the bench and stared out into her tiny back yard. It was as if she'd been running forward at full tilt since the day she'd told Conor she was pregnant, with no stopping to take a breath and suss everything out in a reasoned fashion. No wonder she felt as though she was slowly unravelling. The excitement of seeing her baby for the first time had gone, replaced with lethargy. Conor's proposal hadn't banished all her doubts either. In the middle of the night the old fears rose to torment her. A fast proposal so he could carry on as he'd always intended? But she had agreed to go to Sydney with him anyway. What else did he want from her?

This should be the best time of her life and yet she couldn't drag up any enthusiasm. She was so damned tired. And still uncertain of relying on her judgement.

Ding-dong.

That darned doorbell. She never had got around to taking the batteries out. But, then, she enjoyed Conor drop-

ping in all the time. Still did, if only she could find some
energy. And complete belief that he wouldn't hurt her.

Ding-dong.

'Coming,' she called. *Please be Conor.* Conor without too many questions, not Conor wanting to sort out
dates for moving to Sydney, for getting married, for every
damned thing.

'Hey.' He stood on the step, looking good enough to
eat.

'Hey, yourself.' Pulling the door wide, she stepped
back, and breathed in his man scent as he walked in.
What a man. The man she wanted to trust implicitly,
but couldn't quite manage to yet. Getting close, but not
close enough. Following him into her kitchen, she said,
'I'm making a cup of tea. Want one?' How domestic was
that, then?

'I've got a six-pack in here.'

Only then did she notice the grocery bags swinging
from his hands. 'You've got more than beer there.'

'I'm on dinner. Hope you're okay with steak again?'
He placed the bags on the bench and began unpacking,
totally at home in her space.

'Grocery shopping was next on my to-do list. But I
wasn't getting excited about it.'

'Your excitement levels have been wavering most of
the week.' Conor leaned his butt against the bench and
locked a formidable gaze on her. 'Are you sure everything's all right? Not having second thoughts about anything?'

Since when had Conor become challenging? Was this
one of the reasons she was feeling at odds with herself?
'I'm pregnant, and that's taking everything out of me at
the moment,' she snapped, more forcefully than intended.

'Sure that's not an excuse for something else?'

'Like what?'

'If I knew I wouldn't have to ask. You don't tell me much of what's going on in your head.' Frustration was building in his voice, and those hands she loved on her body were tightening their grip on his hips.

'Until last week I always dealt with problems on my own.' Usually by ignoring them or hiding. 'I am still getting used to having you on my side, in my life.'

'Problems. Are you having doubts?' Conor demanded.

'No,' she shouted, too fast and too loud. 'No,' she repeated at lower decibels. At least she didn't think so.

He continued to look at her as though searching for something. She only hoped it was something good and that he found it. Finally he returned to unpacking the shopping. 'Guess we're still on for steak, then.'

Tamara's heart cracked. They'd had their first row. A very short one, but she felt terrible. This was Conor, the father of her baby, the man who'd stepped up to his responsibilities without a blink, including asking her to marry him. The man she could be falling in love with—if only she'd relax and believe in herself. Standing behind him, she slipped her arms around his waist and laid her face between his shoulder blades. 'I'm sorry.'

Turning in her arms, Conor wrapped her into a hug. 'Me, too, Tam. Me, too.' His chin rested on her head. 'It's all taking some getting used to, isn't it?'

She nodded. 'Yeah.'

'All I ask is don't shut me out, okay?'

'Okay.' She stared at him. 'You don't think you've rushed the proposal?'

'Definitely not. It's what I want. I've never been so happy,' he said gruffly. 'I'm hoping you are too.'

'It's time I gave you a key to this place.' That would

go some way to showing how much he meant to her. No one else had access to her home, not even Kelli.

'If you're sure?' A slow smile began creeping over his mouth, like a slow burn.

'Absolutely.' She trusted him with her inner sanctum. Just had to get the rest sorted out.

Conor flicked the cap off a beer. 'We haven't discussed names yet. Have you got any in mind?'

She had an idea, but hoped she wasn't opening up trouble. 'What was your brother's name?'

Whack. His hand landed on his chest. 'Sebastian.'

'And your dad's?' Might as well go for broke.

'Sebastian.'

That made it easy. As long as Conor agreed. 'Then our boy's called Sebastian.' She smiled at him, silently pleading he'd accept her idea. 'Or Sebastian Sebastian Maguire.'

The air whooshed across his lips and his eyes lit up with joy, then excess moisture swamped them and he was blinking rapidly. 'Thanks,' he managed before placing his lips on hers.

'No problem at all.' Now, that had been a lot easier than she'd expected, thinking Conor mightn't want a daily reminder of those he'd lost. She still needed to get to know him more thoroughly.

CHAPTER ELEVEN

A WOMAN'S SCREAM rent the air of the emergency department, lifting the hairs on Conor's skin. *Mam?* But of course it wasn't. Dad and Sebastian had died in another lifetime, another country.

Tamara appeared at the entrance to Resus One, gently leading a sobbing woman to a chair out of the way. She glanced across at him, her face so sad it hurt him before she refocused on the woman.

'Damn, but I love you, Tamara.'

What? His chair scraped the floor as he leapt to his feet. *I do?*

Yep, buster, you do. Lock, stock and every damned curve of her.

She couldn't have heard his whisper, but he was receiving another glance from those brown eyes and a small, intimate smile as she turned back to the patient she was with.

Conor sank back onto his chair, watching her. He'd gone and fallen in love despite doing his damnedest not to. Hard not to, considering how he couldn't get Tam out of his mind for a minute, day or night. And then she'd added a baby to the mix and bang. He was hooked.

Behind Tamara, Conor could see Michael and another emergency consultant working to resuscitate their patient, a forty-year-old man brought in after feeling unwell and noticing his mouth drooping. The man had a history of minor TIAs but today he'd hit the big mother. A stroke. And now heart failure.

Family history. It tore people apart, wrecked wonderful relationships, destroyed childhoods. Made a mockery of love. Love. He'd gone and fallen for Tamara. An oath tripped across his lips. He had made the biggest mistake of his life.

Conor needed to go help the medical team working on the stroke patient. Only then could he quieten his mind. But there were already more than enough highly skilled staff working on the guy. Instead, he tried to ignore the woman's deep, heart-wrenching sobs and began entering comments into the computer file of his last patient.

But as the woman's despair grew, there was no quietening his memories. Mam in the sitting room with two policemen. The spine-chilling screams and then the desperation in her bone-crushing hug as she'd clung to him. The tears that had lasted days. The hours when she hadn't talked, had barely known him.

The buzzer from the ambulance bay was sharp and very welcome. Now he had something solid to concentrate on, someone in need of his help who would banish these unsettling thoughts. Damned memories. To think people liked storing them up. If only they knew.

'Fractured bones at the elbow resulting in a torn artery and heavy loss of blood.' The advance paramedic handed over the patient work sheet to Conor.

A quick scan and he said to the thirty-four-year-old woman, 'I'm Conor, your doctor for the next little while. Can you tell me what happened?'

'I was painting my house and fell off the ladder.'

'Right, then let's get you into the department and

find out the extent of the damage.' He took one side of the stretcher and, together with the ambulance officer, pushed his patient towards Resus Two, where Kelli and another nurse were waiting.

'On the count of three.' And they shifted the woman across to the bed.

'Need Radiology and the lab here, and Orthopaedics on the phone,' Conor ordered as he began examining the right arm, which was lying at an abnormal angle. Carefully removing the cardboard cast the ambulance crew had put in place to save extra movement and pain, he gently probed the elbow joint.

And still that woman's sobs came through loud and clear from around the corner.

Ignore her.

Conor asked his patient, 'Did you hit your head when you fell?'

'Yes, on the back, but it can't have been too hard. I didn't black out,' she wheezed through gritted teeth as pain jarred her.

'We'll get an X-ray to be doubly sure.'

Someone handed him the phone. 'Orthopaedics on the line.'

He moved away, turning his back so his words wouldn't be heard by his patient. 'I'm waiting for Radiology to come and take pictures, but I suspect a fracture to the elbow ginglymus and others to the humerus and ulna at the point of the hinge. There's heavy blood loss from a torn artery.'

'I'll be down as soon as I've put Theatre on standby,' the specialist told him.

Returning to his patient, he informed her, 'You need surgery to put that elbow back together.'

She nodded. 'Figured as much. Can someone call my husband? Let him know what's going on?'

Another family whose day had been tipped sideways. But not as badly as the couple in the next unit. The sobs were quietening down now and Conor could hear his counterpart talking to the woman, explaining that her husband had been successfully revived.

'Until next time,' the woman cried.

Until next time. The words he'd carried around in his head since the day of his heart attack. *Until next time.* The reason for his panic attacks. That 'next time' hovered on the periphery of his mind. Most days it played nice. Occasionally, like last week, when life had been in turmoil, it had fired up, gripped his chest and sent him into a tailspin.

'Conor? This your patient?' The radiology technician had arrived.

He shook away the dark clouds in his head. 'Yes. I need as many angles as you can manage without further collateral damage.'

Conor put everything into focusing on his patient and not on the litany of doom banging around his head. But the moment the orderly wheeled her away the fears and memories were back, larger, louder than before.

He aimed for the counter and a computer to update the woman's notes. And locked eyes with Tamara as she stepped out of Resus One. Her face was drawn and that sadness in her eyes had grown heavier. His chest tightened. 'Tam?'

'We saved him, but he's got a long recovery ahead of him. His chances of walking and talking in the near future are remote.'

'How's his wife?'

'You heard her. Devastated. They've got three young

boys and at the moment she's not coping. But with help she'll get there.'

That could be Tamara with Sebastian. She was saying the woman would manage but, sorry, what the hell did she know? She hadn't lost her child as the result of a heart attack. Or her husband, who'd sworn to always support her and watch her back. Yet. His hand rammed through his hair. The screams, those sobs, they'd hit him deep, dried up the happiness that'd been fizzing along his veins for nearly two weeks. Brought him back to earth. 'I've been fooling myself.'

Spinning around, he strode quickly towards his office, almost running but managing to hold himself back.

'Conor, wait for me.' From directly behind him came the one voice he did not want to hear right this minute. Not until he'd sorted his head space.

'Carry on with the patients, Tamara.' His watch read two thirty-five. Nearly home time. Well, he wouldn't be going home to stare at his four walls, but he'd be out of here fast, away from the sounds of ED, which he usually enjoyed. But not today.

'Talk to me.' She didn't give up easily.

He spun around, stabbed the air between them with his forefinger. 'No. Not now. Leave me.'

She stumbled but kept walking towards him. Shock blazed at him, but didn't slow her down. 'We're in this together, Conor. You can't walk away from me as and when it suits you.'

I can when it's for your own good.

'I can't think clearly with you talking. Give me some space, Tamara.'

Tamara. Not Tam. He could see the hurt that inflicted and briefly contemplated pausing long enough to give her a hug and tell her not to worry. But she might have every reason to worry so he refrained.

'What's this about, Conor?' That doubt she carried everywhere was wide awake and glaring at him.

'Nothing to do with you, right?' he lied, then strode into his office and banged the door shut. Twisted the lock for good measure.

Guilt warred with the need to be alone. Now he was shutting Tamara out completely. *Snap*. The door was unlocked. But not open. He wasn't going to be able to undo that lie as easily.

At his desk he dropped onto the chair, hefted his feet on top of the desk and leaned back to stare at the ceiling, his hands clasped behind his head. His chest was pounding, his head starting to fill with haze.

'I am not having a panic attack.' He kept his elbows wide, refusing to let them fold in on his chest. He wasn't having an attack of any kind.

Except fear. Fear for Tamara and Sebastian. Fear that one day it would be her screaming in an emergency department as he left her to bring up their son alone. Fear that his little boy would spend years looking for him because he didn't understand what death meant.

The door opened and in walked Tamara, a mug in her hand and a wary smile on her face. 'Coffee.'

He wanted to say, 'Go away,' but the words refused to come.

She came around the desk to place the mug on the desk and stood there gazing down at him. 'Whatever you're thinking, Conor, it's too late. We are having a baby. The future may be an unknown on some levels but you're going to be a father and there's no changing that. Don't even contemplate becoming a remote parent. That would be far worse for Sebastian than the scenario I imagine is going on in your head right now.' Her kiss was soft on his cheek, her scent light. The bands around his chest loosened as she said, 'We're going to be fine.'

Then she left him to his thoughts, the door closing with a soft click behind her.

He went back to staring at the ceiling. 'You think?' How could Tamara be so positive? She'd been to hell and back, wore the scars from her own battles. Was strong because of them.

Could be a lesson here for you, boyo. Could be that Tamara is showing you a thing or two on how to grab life with both hands and enjoy it.

Could be he was wishing for the impossible. He did best by being alone.

Conor ran along the pavement circling the waterfront at Mission Bay, dodging around late-afternoon strollers enjoying the spring sunshine. His shoes slapped the concrete as he increased his pace, trying to outrun the torment in his head.

Tamara. She'd changed everything for him, given him hope, made him admit how much he wanted her and their baby. Yet he couldn't go through with it.

Stepping sideways onto the grass verge, he dodged around an elderly couple shuffling along arm in arm with smiles on their wrinkled faces. Beautiful. He wanted that. To do the whole lifetime-together thing with Tamara, to raise their child, or children, and be able to relax into old age and watch over everyone without getting too tied up in arguments and dilemmas. That's what he wanted. More than anything. But today reality had woken him up.

Increasing his pace until he was racing, not jogging at a sensible speed that'd last the distance, Conor sucked in abrupt breaths and ignored the occasional stabs of pain under his ribs. If he didn't leave the head stuff behind there'd be no peace. He ran and ran and ran until he could no longer put one foot in front of the other. Then he sank down onto a park bench and dropped his head into his hands, stared at the grass between his sports shoes.

The turmoil still pounded at him. Might as well have stayed at home. Or gone to the pub with Mac and sunk a few beers.

Might as well have visited Tamara and got this over and done with.

I don't want to hurt her.

I can't do what I'd planned on doing.

I can't live a lie.

I can't tip Tamara's world upside down again.

Conor's chest tightened. In a familiar, frightening way.

He jerked up straight, his hands fisted, his legs tense.

Not now. Go away. Breathe, damn it, long and slow, deep. Breathe.

Damn, but he was a useless piece of work. He would not have a panic attack now. Not when he had to front up to Tamara. That'd be like asking for sympathy when he should be thrown down the street on his face. It was time to deal with these stupid attacks once and for all.

Pain stabbed him behind his sternum. Swift, hard, intense.

So you're going to make it hard for me.

Gritting his teeth, Conor waited for it to pass. If it would go. If this wasn't a genuine heart attack. He had been running like he was being chased by a hungry tiger.

Stab. He gasped around the second burst of pain. Breathed in long and slow, relaxed his lungs to push the air out again. Stood up and walked slowly forward six paces, walked back to the bench. Yeah, that worked. The tightness was easing.

Do it again. And again.

'I got a parcel today.' Tamara forced a smile, despite the unease ping-ponging back and forth between her and Conor. He'd turned up at her flat just as she'd been pretending to cook dinner. An inedible chop and spud were now in the bin. And Conor wasn't happy about something.

'About today—'

'From Ireland.' She reached across to her dining table and held up the express package.

Conor's eyes widened. 'That's Mam's handwriting.'

'She must've held a gun to the courier company's representative to get it here this fast.'

'Knowing Mam, she probably fronted up to the pilot on the next flight coming down this way and begged him to bring it. What's in there anyway?'

'Your first booties.' Her heart expanded. 'She kept them all this time.'

'I'm not that old,' Conor choked out.

'Judy has plenty more to send later. I think she must've been so excited she had to send these straight away.' Tamara tipped the booties out of the courier package and into her hand. 'Blue, not pink.' So soft, and cute. Adorable.

'Mam's not thinking straight,' Conor snapped.

Here it comes.

'Are you?' She pulled a chair out from the table and plonked her butt down. Her elbows hit the table top too hard. Her head was whirling with wanting to know what Conor's next move would be. Everything had happened so fast it had only been a matter of time before he stalled, and proved her right not to give in to the love growing in her heart for him.

'I'm trying to.' He sat opposite her, like they were strangers.

Maybe they were. Deep down where it counted. She started the ball rolling. 'Today brought home the enormity of what it would be like if the same thing happened to you as it did to your father.' Her voice hitched. 'And Sebastian.'

'In spades. Those deep, anguish-filled sobs got to me in a way I've not felt before during my work in emergency departments.'

'I guess knowing we're having a baby makes it all the more real and worrisome. I understand that, Conor. I really do.' Tamara stood, went around to him and leaned in to kiss his mouth.

Conor's hands came between them, on her upper arms, holding her away. 'Tamara.'

Not Tam. *Thud, thud.* Her heart knew something was off. More than today's episode in ED. This tight, don't-be-hard-on-me feeling was familiar. She'd felt the apprehension before and knew it would lead to bad things. 'Tell me. Now.'

Conor's chest rose, and his gaze lifted to her eyes before his hands dropped away from her and he stood up. 'I'm sorry, Tamara, but I can't marry you.'

Why wasn't she in a heap on the floor? Her legs were like jelly and her heart had stopped. But standing she was, and in front of her was Conor, the man she'd believed in and come to accept wouldn't hurt her. All the moisture in her mouth dried up, and words were impossible as this rerun of her past unfolded before her. The man she'd foolishly fallen in love with when she'd known how dangerous that would be. Strange how the moment she learned he was leaving her she understood she really did love him.

'We'll still bring up Sebastian jointly. I'm not walking away from my son. Or my responsibilities.'

As the mother of your son, I'm one of your responsibilities.

No, she wasn't. Her life was her business, her problem. Not Conor's.

He looked pale and tense. But also determined. 'It might be easier if we have two homes in Sydney so that we're not tripping over each other all the time.'

Thought he'd enjoyed tripping over her, hauling her up against that divine body to kiss her whenever she got in the way. She sank back onto her chair. 'Why?'

'I've let you down. I'm sorry.' He stared out the window, his hands gripping his hips. What was he staring at? Seeing?

'Why?' she repeated over the clunking of her dreams breaking into tiny pieces. He'd never said he loved her, only proposed marriage to make it easier to raise their child together.

Conor leaned back against the windowsill. 'When I proposed I thought I could face anything with you at my side.'

'So what's changed?'

'I was fooling myself. I can't risk putting you through what my mother suffered.' Those dark eyes locked on her. 'I rushed into proposing before we'd talked through so many outstanding issues. I have been flying solo for so long, but for a few crazy days I let my guard down. I wanted to have the wonderful life you and our baby were offering.'

'You can. We can.'

'We can't.'

Anger began unfurling. He wasn't doing this to her. Not without a fight. 'You sure you're not using your medical history as an excuse?'

'I don't believe so.' Those lips were getting tighter by the word.

'So we're not getting married.' Her heart was curling in on itself, her stomach tightening defensively. Keep talking. 'We are having a baby, but we'll raise him in two homes, not one. We're moving to Sydney in the next couple of months.' Did he not see what she was saying? 'We, Conor. We, we, we.'

'I'll stay and apply for a permanent position in one of the hospitals in Auckland if you'd prefer.'

'Conor.' Her hands slapped her thighs. 'I don't want to change a thing.' She'd got it damned wrong. Again. Conor held her heart and he'd jumped on it. Unknowingly, sure, but it had happened.

She loved him through and through. Did that not count for anything? What if she told him how she felt? Just because she hadn't said those three little words it didn't mean they weren't real. She opened her mouth but the words would not come out. The last time she'd told a man she loved him he'd abused that love. And tonight wasn't going any better. How would saying it out loud help? Gulp. Swallow. She whispered, 'I do love you, you know.'

Conor jerked, like he'd been stabbed or something. 'Please, don't, Tamara.'

'Doesn't it mean anything to you?'

He stared at her, looking deep, as though absorbing her love. Then the shutters came down over those sad eyes, making them remote. 'All the more reason I let you go. Better to finish it now before we get too involved.'

Jamming her hands over her ears, she cut off that voice

that usually had her in a rush of hormones. No rush to-night. More of an Irish bog.

Tamara asked in a wobbly voice, 'But you intend being there for Sebastian for ever? Will go wherever I decide to go for his sake?' A recipe for heartache on a daily basis. Seeing him, hearing his voice, conferring over what was right for Sebastian. She couldn't do it.

'I'm sure we'll be able to make it work without too many problems.'

That kind of suggested he didn't love her in any way. She'd gone and done it again. Fallen for the wrong man. Only this time she'd looked hard, thought it all through before giving her heart. And had still got it wrong. 'You think?'

Uncertainty worked into his gaze. 'I don't see you making it difficult for me. You're not a vindictive person.'

'You're making it sound so black and white, no grey at all.' Her voice was rising. Too bad. 'Think about it. What'll happen when you meet another woman who gets under your skin? Will she follow me around too?'

'I doubt that'll happen. I managed to stay uninvolved for nearly fourteen years.' He turned away, turned back, said softly, 'I'm setting you free so it's you who can meet someone else. A man without my health issues. A guy who can be a part of our child's life too. In case,' he ground out through clenched teeth. 'But I am not desert-ing my son. I will be a part of his life.'

'Just not mine.'

His hands slammed through his hair, setting it awry. 'Everything happened too fast. I should've thought about everything before my proposal.'

'You're not getting any argument from me on that score.' Tamara sat rigid, her hands gripped together between her knees. She would not beg Conor to rethink. He wouldn't listen. His mind was made up. As hers needed to be. She had to accept his withdrawal and get on with organising a future for her child.

Lifting her shoulders, she eyeballed this man who'd devastated her, and told him the biggest lie she'd ever uttered. 'Other couples manage two-family parenting so I'm sure we can. Now, if you haven't got anything else pressing to say, I'd like you to go.'

Her voice broke. Tears threatened. This time her grief would be private, not played out in front of even one person. Certainly not Conor. She could not show him how much he'd hurt her. He might use that against her. An hour ago she wouldn't have believed it possible; now she knew anything was conceivable. Her heart was a ball of pain and her stomach was churning. So not good for the baby.

'Tam.' He swallowed hard.

'It's Tamara to you.' Gulp. 'We were working just fine,' she snapped. 'Then you changed everything.'

'Maybe I did.' Sadness dripped off his words. 'We still have a lot of things to sort out and plan, but they can wait.'

Just go. Now. 'Get out of my home.'

Before I fall into a sobbing heap. Before I make an idiot of myself in front of you. Because once I do that you'll know you've done the right thing, that you definitely don't want to be hooked up to me for ever.

She sank further into the chair and covered her face with her hands. 'Go away.'

Conor's hand touched her head, gentle and warm, and shaking. 'I'll leave my key on the hall table.'

And she'd thought she'd been hurting before. A throbbing set up behind her eyes, under her ribs, in her gut. The key to her flat she'd been so happy to give him only yesterday because it showed she trusted him. He was giving it back.

The end.

CHAPTER TWELVE

NEXT MORNING TAMARA called in sick. 'I've got stomach cramps and a head full of cotton wool.'

'You're not going to Sydney for the weekend with Conor, are you?' Michael asked with a chuckle.

I wish. 'I could send you a selfie of me tucked up in bed, looking paler than a bottle of milk, but that'd be gross.'

Michael coughed. 'Didn't mean to sound uncaring. Maybe you should see your midwife if you're having stomach ache.'

Now, that would be the solution to all Conor's problems. Except she knew he'd be gutted if she miscarried. She'd be breaking down the midwife's door if there was any chance she was having a miscarriage. Her tummy wasn't too bad. Just showing its usual disgust at breakfast, probably made worse by anguish over Conor's desertion, and with lack of sleep thrown in. 'I think it's more what I ate for dinner than anything.'

'Keep vigilant and make an appointment if you think you're wrong. We'll see you on Monday.' Michael hung up.

All that was wrong with her was she'd been dumped by the man she really and truly wanted to spend the rest of her life with, and she couldn't face him today.

Her phone rang. 'Conor?' *Nope.* The screen showed Kelli.

'Are you all right, girlfriend?'

Tamara stifled the threatening tears. 'I'm wagging work.'

'Now I know there's something wrong. You don't take time off for anything.'

Calming breaths. 'I'm fine. A bit jaded. Think the pregnancy is taking its toll and what with everything else that's gone down these past days I'm exhausted. A day off is about the baby and looking out for him.'

'You're sure? I can come around at the end of shift.'

Sniff. 'Don't you dare. Come three o'clock you're on a week's leave, and I'm not going to be responsible for you missing that flight to Queenstown.'

'Okay, if you promise you're okay.'

'Promise.' Hopefully Kelli hadn't heard the crack in her voice. But in case she had, Tamara said goodbye and hung up. Now she'd lied to her best friend, but for all the right reasons. She wasn't subjecting Kelli to another round of her heartbreak.

Shuffling down the bed, Tamara pulled the sheet over her head and pretended to sleep.

Monday took for ever to arrive. Not that Tamara wanted to show up at work with the shadows highlighting her cheekbones and the shine gone from her eyes. Everyone would guess something was up between her and Conor. But working with patients to distract her was way better than hiding in her flat. There was only so much washing and dusting she could do and she'd done it all by midday Friday.

'Ambulance bringing in an elderly lady from Ponsonby. Found unconscious on her floor by a neighbour,' Michael told her. 'Can you take this one?'

'Cubicle three,' she acknowledged. 'How was your birthday?'

The morning dragged by, barely faster than the weekend had. Every turn she made, she fully expected to see Conor with a patient or reading patient notes or typing details into a patient's file or smiling at her. Every single time her gaze came up blank and her heart rolled over to belt her ribs. He was in Sydney and she missed him so much it was a permanent ache.

While she'd been in the shower yesterday, Conor had left a message on her answering machine that had quickly become her addiction. Hearing his voice was her only solace while at the same time it brought its own brand of agony. That Irish brogue stirred her deeply, tormented her and reduced her to tears every time she replayed the message. Not that she needed to hit replay.

'Hey, Tamara, heard you were off work on Friday. Hope you're not ill. I've made appointments to look at rental properties near the hospital next week. Will keep you posted. Oh, and you won't have a problem getting work at Sydney Hospital. Catch you.'

The actual words did nothing to comfort her. He sounded as though nothing was wrong between them. Unfortunately she couldn't stop listening to his voice.

Conor had left her. Sure, they'd get together over Sebastian, but that wasn't the same. That wouldn't satisfy her hormones, feed her desire, make her happy.

'Tamara, your patient's arrived in the ambulance bay.' A nurse nudged her.

Cripes. *Concentrate*. 'On my way.' Leaping up from

the computer, her head spun and she had to grab the counter.

'Are you sure you should be back at work?'

'Didn't eat much over the weekend.' Stale bread was so not appetising. Neither was three-day-old salad. Hitting the supermarket was top of her to-do list after work today. The only thing on the list.

'Nearly three o'clock and home time,' a nurse eventually told her with sympathy in her tone.

'Great.' Home. Alone.

At home with a bag of heat-and-eat meals that didn't excite her taste buds but should keep baby happy, she made a cup of raspberry and pomegranate tea and sat with her feet up on the couch and the TV filling the empty space with background noise.

On her lap lay a courier parcel with Judy's handwriting scrawled over the address section. A bigger package than the last one, it had been sitting on her doorstep when she'd staggered up the path.

Should she even open it, considering she and Conor were no longer together? But Judy was still Sebastian's grandmother-in-waiting. As was her mum.

Putting the parcel aside, Tamara picked up her phone and hit 'Mum'. Listening to the endless ringing, she kept up a line of *Please, please, please.*

Finally, 'Hello?'

'Don't hang up. This is important.'

Click.

Write to her. Let her hold your letter, see your writing. Conor's advice wove around her, making her sit up straighter.

Did he have a point? Before she could overthink what she was doing, she scrawled two pages of news to her mother about her baby and moving to Sydney and sealed them in an envelope.

Then she picked up Judy's parcel and used her teeth to tear a hole big enough to push her finger through and rip it wide open. A teddy bear with one ear reattached with black thread and a leather patch stitched onto its front landed in her lap. Pressing it against her face, Tamara took a deep breath and smelled childhood and possibly Conor.

Soon the fake fur was saturated with tears, and still she clung to the bear. A letter had fallen out of the packet too.

Dear Tamara,

I hope you don't mind me sending you some of Conor's baby things, but I've waited so long for this day I can't hold back. Tell me to stop if you don't want any more parcels.

I know I'm being sentimental, but I love my son and know you'll be wonderful for him.

The page became a ball in her fist.

No pressure, Judy.

At least by now Conor's mother would know the score and was probably regretting sending the teddy. Lifting the bear, she stared at it, unable to toss it aside. It had been Conor's, would be Sebastian's.

Flattening the letter with her hand, she reread Judy's kind words, and through more tears felt her heart slow. Reaching behind her, she lifted her copy of the image of Sebastian taken during her scan. 'Sebastian, this is your teddy now. It used to be your daddy's. What do you think? Isn't he cute?'

Where was Conor? Swanning around Sydney like he

hadn't gone and broken her heart? Chatting up his new colleagues, making himself popular?

Preparing for his son? And finding somewhere for her to live?

Damn it. She could find her own place. Didn't need his help. Certainly didn't want his input if he wasn't going to be a part of her life.

'Conor, I am missing you so much it's unbearable.'

Saturday afternoon Tamara listened to Conor's message one last time and hit delete.

For the hundredth time since he'd left, her heart broke all over again. He really had gone. Time to accept it and start planning the future.

If only Conor loved her then he wouldn't have left her. But he hadn't wanted to fall in love at all.

Just like she hadn't.

Ding-dong.

Her heart picked up its pace.

Conor? You've come back to spend the weekend with me, to make plans for our living arrangements and talk through your parting speech and maybe find a way out of this abyss.

Excitement rushed through her as she tugged the door open and swiped at the tears on her cheeks. She had another chance. He'd returned to try again.

'Oh, girlfriend, you look terrible.' Kelli was inside and hugging her before it completely hit home that Conor hadn't come back for her.

Her earlier tears had nothing on the flood now hosing out of her eyes, deep sobs racking her body.

Kelli held her until the storm abated. 'Conor?'

'H-he's g-gone,' Tamara hiccupped.

'That was the plan. To go sort out his new job and set up a place for you both to live.'

'He doesn't want to get married.' She started for the kitchen to put the kettle on. That'd give her something to do with her hands if nothing else.

'When did he tell you that?' Kelli demanded. 'I'm going to knock his block off for hurting you.'

'Thursday night last week.'

'That explains why you weren't at work last Friday. Why doesn't Conor want to get married? Changed his mind about loving you, has he?' There was an angry glint in Kelli's eyes that spoke of danger to Conor if he came anywhere close.

Water splashed over the front of her shirt when she turned the tap on too hard. 'He never said he loved me.'

'Has he got cold feet about becoming a father? Because leaving you doesn't change a thing about that. The baby is still going to arrive.'

'No, Conor would never shirk responsibilities. Anyway, he wants to be a part of Sebastian's life.' She nibbled her bottom lip.

'Then what's the problem?'

'He says he's protecting me from getting hurt if he has another heart attack.'

'What?' Kelli's question ricocheted off the walls.

Now she'd gone and spilled the beans. 'No one's meant to know but he had one fourteen years ago. He's terrified it'll happen again.'

Kelli sank onto a stool. 'Never saw that coming. But are you sure that's all? I mean, people have health problems all the time. Doesn't mean they don't get married and have families.'

'You don't think I didn't tell him that?' Tamara growled. 'I love him so much, it's crazy.' How was it so easy to admit that to Kelli when she'd struggled to tell the one person who mattered? The man who needed to hear it?

'There's not a person at work who doesn't know that. Same goes for Conor. He is totally smitten. I want to bang some sense into that skull of his.'

If only it was that easy. 'Tea?'

'You got anything stronger? Even if you're not drinking, with baby on board, I need something with more punch than tea. And it's wine o'clock somewhere.' Kelli grinned.

Opening the fridge, Tamara found a half-full bottle of wine Conor had left there. 'This do?'

'Yep.' Kelli got a glass from the cupboard and filled it to the brim. Bringing the stool to the bench, she perched on it and studied Tamara like she didn't know her.

'What?' Tamara demanded.

'You haven't told Conor how you feel, have you?'

'Yeah, I did. But it was like a last-minute confession, as though I was using my love to keep him here.' She looked away, ashamed at the censure in her friend's eyes. 'It wasn't easy to come right out with it, you know?'

'Sure it is. Don't let him get away, Tamara.'

Her head tipped up. 'That's what I've done, isn't it? Let him go without a fight. Wrecked everything for me and the baby.'

'Phone him, put your heart on the line. But don't beg, whatever you do.' Kelli's voice softened. 'He's nothing like Peter. Conor adores you and would never do a thing to hurt you.'

'He left for Sydney on last Friday without coming round to say goodbye, or—or anything.' Tamara hesitated. 'Sounds like I'm laying all the blame at Conor's feet, doesn't it?' Why hadn't she told him how hard it was to put her feelings into words? 'Is telling him I love him often enough going to make him shelve his fears? Or is there something else I can do?'

'There's only one way to find out. Put your heart on the line. You'll get an honest answer. He's not going to take advantage of you.'

'He talked me into writing to Mum.'

Kelli looked stunned. 'And you let him get away?'

Suddenly Tamara laughed. Where that had come from she had no idea, except that it felt as though a huge weight had lifted off her. 'I must be mad.' Or was that bonkers? Seemed she could fit right into Conor's family.

'I'd say so, but then you'd probably want to kill me.'

Another laugh. Slightly hysterical, but filled with relief. 'Just remember this advice you've been throwing at me. I can see a time coming when I'm going to give it all back.'

Kelli's smiled dipped. 'Not happening, girlfriend.'

We'll see. But not now, not today. Today—

'I'm going online to book a flight.'

'It had better be to Sydney.'

'Where else?' The laptop was already booting up.

'Want me to start packing some clothes for you?'

'What are my chances of a flight tonight?' Tamara stared at the screen, trying to hurry it up. Remembered to ask, 'How was your week in Queenstown?'

'Went mountain-climbing for three days. Awesome.' Kelli leaned over her shoulder. 'Looks like you're going to have to pay big money to go tonight.'

'Don't care. That seat's got my name on it.' Now she'd made up her mind to go to Conor, a shortage of cattle-class seats wasn't going to stop her. She clicked on the flight and filled in her details. Booked a seat. Business class no less.

Ding-dong.

'Get that for me, will you?' Tamara was entering her credit card number into the airline's booking page.

'Yes, Your Highness.' Kelli saluted. 'Do I get to drive you to the airport as well?'

'You don't think I can afford a taxi after paying top price for my ticket, do you?' There—number in…expiry date too. She pressed 'pay now' and watched the little circle go round and round and round. What was taking so long for the airline to grab the money?

'Tam?'

Her hand wobbled over the keyboard. She'd have sworn she'd just heard an Irish lilt saying her name but that was impossible. Lack of sleep did strange things to her mind. Better get Kelli to check her booking to make sure she wasn't flying to Brazil next week.

'Tam.'

Don't do this, mind.

But she looked around anyway. And froze. 'Conor?'

Really? Truly? She closed her eyes. Opened them. *Yeah, really. Truly.*

'Conor,' she squealed, and leapt at him, wrapped her arms around that amazing body she loved and held on like she'd never let go again.

'Hey, Tam. You okay?'

The hesitancy in his voice changed her mind and forced her back, away from him. Just because he'd turned up here when he was supposed to be in another country, it didn't mean anything had been resolved.

'I'm fine,' she muttered.

Then she glanced at the table where the screen of her laptop showed her payment had been accepted. She was leaving for Sydney in four hours.

'No, I'm not. I'm all over the place.' Leaning across,

she stabbed the 'continue' key on the screen and up came a ticket.

'What's that?' Conor asked, sounding confused. His eyes were fixed on the image.

'Take a closer look.'

He did. 'You were coming to see me.'

'Yes.'

'Why?'

Just do it.

'To tell you I love you. Tell you with all my heart this time. To ask you to reconsider about not being with me.' There. It hadn't hurt a bit. Conor hadn't started running for the hills. In fact, he looked stunned even as a smile began breaking out across his face. She said it again. 'I love you, Conor.' Dang, but that felt good. 'And I don't accept your reasons for calling off our marriage. I'm perfectly capable of coping with whatever happens. It might be messy but I'd pull through.'

'I know.'

'What do you know?'

'That you won't let me dictate what we're going to do in the future—about Sebastian and about us.' The smile widened, soft and warm and, oh, so sexy. 'I know you love me. You showed me countless times how much you cared about me. It was there in how you wanted to wait for me to go with you to that first scan. In how easily you chose Sebastian as the name for our son because it meant so much to me. I can't walk away from that.'

'What about your fears of another heart attack?'

The smile faded. 'They're always going to be there, and I'd worry about how Sebastian and you would manage even if I didn't live with you as my wife.'

'Conor Maguire, I would rather live with you than have to watch you from afar, no matter what the future brings us.' Tamara stepped up to him. 'Now, can we kiss and make up? It's been too long without you.'

Kissing Conor had always been her favourite pastime but this one surpassed them all.

'So you're back here and I'm flying out to Sydney shortly,' she teased.

His arms tightened around her. 'No, you're not, sweetheart. You're not going anywhere yet.'

'Oh, and what am I doing this afternoon, then?' Hang on. 'Kelli?' she called. 'Where are you?'

'She's gone. Just opened the door, saw me and kept on walking down the path with a great big grin on her dial.'

'That sounds like my friend.' She knew when she wasn't wanted.

'One in a million, I reckon.'

Tamara felt all her muscles melt as that Irish brogue washed over her. 'I've missed you.' She stretched up to kiss him but was stopped by two big hands on her upper arms.

'Wait.' Conor's expression turned serious.

Strange how that didn't worry her at all. He wouldn't have come back only to hand her another load of grief.

He took her hands in his. 'Tam, will you marry me?'

Damn, she was crying a lot today. 'Yes…' she choked. Then she shouted, 'Yes!'

His lips touched her cheek, oh, so gently. 'Can we set a date this time?'

'We could apply for a licence on Monday.'

'Could?'

'We're moving to Sydney, right? A new start for both of us. Why don't we wait and get married over there? It would give your family time to come out for the wedding too. If they want to.'

'Try keeping them away. You have no idea what you're letting yourself in for.'

'Yes, I think I do.' There was a teddy on the couch that explained a lot about how Conor's family loved each other. 'Can you kiss me again? There's been a drought this past week.'

Not only did Conor kiss her, he kissed her until she didn't know which way was up. And then he carried her down to her bedroom and followed through on the promise of that kiss.

EPILOGUE

THE SKY WAS bright blue and Tamara swore there was glitter in the air as she and Kelli walked along the promenade of Sydney's Darling Harbour towards to the restaurant she and Conor had chosen for their wedding. There were certainly bubbles every time she drew in a breath.

The bunch of daffodils she carried gave off a poignant spring smell and their colour was vibrant against the cream of her simple but stylish wedding dress that draped softly over her baby bump.

'Well, girlfriend, you're really marrying that gorgeous Irish hunk. You know every female back home in ED is so jealous?'

'Yes. And do I care?' She grinned at Kelli. 'This is the best day of my life.'

'I'd be worried if it wasn't,' Kelli retorted. 'I'm so happy for you.'

Along with a few special people, a small Irish crowd was attending her wedding and she couldn't be happier. All those bonkers sisters and their husbands and children had insisted they were coming out for the wedding with Judy and Dave. Tamara had fallen in love with each and every one of them the moment they'd walked through the arrivals doors at Sydney International Airport and drew her into their midst. When the end of Conor's stint in Australia came round she'd be pushing to move to Dublin.

At the entrance to the restaurant Tamara stopped and turned to hug her friend. 'Thank you for always being there for me. I'd never have got this far without you.'

'Shut up or my make-up will be wrecked when I start crying.'

'Too late.' Tamara made a discreet wipe at her own cheeks. 'Right, here we go.' And she stepped inside. Stopped, agape. Her heart thumped—hard. Her tummy squeezed. 'Conor...?'

From now on he was going to have to wear a suit twenty-four seven. The navy-blue fabric outlined his body to perfection, hugging his pecs, emphasising his wide chest and narrow hips. The crisp cream shirt highlighted his blue eyes and black hair.

'I'm going to faint.'

'No, you're not. Go get him, girlfriend.'

She took a step and he was there, reaching for her, taking her hand. 'You look more than beautiful,' he said.

Tamara locked eyes with her soon-to-be husband and sucked in a breath. Forget the suit. The look of pure love radiating out from those eyes just melted her. Completely. 'I love you.' Those words came so easily now that she couldn't believe how difficult uttering them had once been.

'And I you. Shall we do this?' Conor smiled and if her heart hadn't already melted it would've done so right then.

She nodded. 'Yes.'

Together they turned to walk up to the marriage celebrant. Conor's best man, Mac, stood on one side, dressed in nearly as amazing a suit. Glancing at Kelli, Tamara found her as awestruck as she'd been over Conor. Good.

Maybe these two would finally get over what ailed them and learn to love each other.

'Tamara, darling, you look wonderful.'

She turned to face her mother, her poor overworked heart now beating against her ribs. 'Mum.'

Hard to believe that her mother had phoned out of the blue to ask when and where the wedding was happening. She didn't know it nearly hadn't happened, but the moment Tamara had told her it would be in Sydney in a month's time she'd been on her way to meet her grandson and take charge of planning the perfect wedding, with Tamara's aunt in tow. Tamara had happily given in. She was over not having her crazy mother in her life.

'I'm so glad you're here.'

'Oh, pish—as if I'd miss my own daughter's wedding.'

The words were cheap but the sentiment was strong. Typical Mum.

'You know that's not what I meant.'

Mum's smile said it all. 'Your father will be kicking up a storm, wherever he is.'

Conor was still holding her hand. 'Ready?'

'Absolutely.' They faced the celebrant, both smiling widely.

The woman cleared her throat and began. 'Tamara and Conor, today is very special for you both. Today is the beginning of a new life, and it's made more special with your families here to witness your vows.'

Tamara squeezed Conor's hand. Focused as she was on the celebrant's words, there was no not being aware of the man standing beside her. The man she loved more than she'd have believed possible. The father of her baby. The caring doctor. The good friend to Mac. Conor. Her about-to-be husband. The light in her heart.

'Tamara Washington, do you take this man to be your

lawful wedded husband, and to love and cherish him for as long as you both shall live?'

'Oh, yes.'

'Conor Maguire, do you take this woman to be your lawful wedded wife, and to love and cherish her for as long as you both shall live?'

'Damn right I do.'

'Then you may place the ring on her finger.'

Conor dug into his pocket, apparently not willing to trust the ring to Mac. As he slid the wide gold band with an elegant emerald set perfectly in the centre onto her finger he whispered, 'Love you more than ever, Tam.'

The marriage celebrant had the last word. 'I declare you husband and wife. Conor, you may kiss the bride.'

Conor's kisses just kept getting better and better.

* * * * *

If you enjoyed this story, check out these other great reads from Sue MacKay

RESISTING HER ARMY DOC RIVAL
THE ARMY DOC'S BABY BOMBSHELL
DR WHITE'S BABY WISH
BREAKING ALL THEIR RULES

All available now!

REUNITED WITH
HIS RUNAWAY DOC

BY
LUCY CLARK

MILLS
BOON

Published in Great Britain 2017
By Mills & Boon, an imprint of HarperCollins*Publishers*
1 London Bridge Street, London, SE1 9GF

© 2017 Anne Clark

ISBN: 978-0-263-92653-8

Our policy is to use papers that are natural, renewable and recyclable
products and made from wood grown in sustainable forests. The logging
and manufacturing processes conform to the legal environmental
regulations of the country of origin.

Printed and bound in Spain
by CPI, Barcelona

Dear Reader,

The world is full of trials and tribulations—and if you're a *Star Trek* fan, like me, sometimes it's full of Tribbles… But I digress. There are times when it feels as if the world is throwing curveball after curveball in our direction. But although we get knocked down again and again it's the getting up part which is the most important.

Throughout the many versions of this story I found a new level of normality—especially after the death of my beloved father, moving house and having my marriage end. There are so many of those curveballs we just don't see coming, and when they all come at once it can be very difficult to remain standing! That's when it's vitally important to reach out for those you can rely on.

Maybelle Freebourne and I went through a lot of adventures together. She was broken, just as I was broken, but with the help of wonderful people—and in Maybelle's case an incredibly handsome hero by the name of Arthur Lewis—we were both able to find our new 'normal'.

I do hope you find Maybelle and Arthur's story of being brave, of taking a step into the unknown, a story that inspires you to also be brave when those darn curveballs make you a little unsteady on your feet.

With warmest regards,

Lucy

For the people who are *always* there to hold my hand when I doubt myself—Melanie, Austin, Cassie and Kate.

Thank you for your support this past year.

Proverbs 19:1

Books by Lucy Clark

Mills & Boon Medical Romance

Outback Surgeons

English Rose in the Outback
A Family for Chloe

The Secret Between Them
Her Mistletoe Wish
His Diamond Like No Other
Dr Perfect on Her Doorstep
A Child to Bind Them
Still Married to Her Ex!

Visit the Author Profile page
at millsandboon.co.uk for more titles.

PROLOGUE

MAY FLEMING STOOD at the top of the stairs, fear starting to grip her as she listened to her parents speak in muted tones with the two men who had arrived only twenty minutes ago. Closing her eyes, she listened to try and grasp the gist of the conversation but all she could hear were words like 'leave', 'danger', 'tonight'.

What was going on? Was this anything to do with the break-in they'd had at their house a month ago? Her father had played down the incident, saying there had been a spate of robberies in the neighbourhood of late and as nothing had been taken it was of little consequence, but who broke into a house and didn't take anything? She knew he'd been trying not to worry her and when she'd questioned her friend Clara, who lived next door, Clara hadn't heard anything about robberies in the neighbourhood.

Add to that fact that since that attempted robbery, both of her parents had been acting more weirdly than usual lately. Sometimes they didn't come home for dinner, telling her to eat next door at Clara's house, and when they were home they were locked away in either her mother's or father's study, their voices sometimes rising to hysteria. 'Shh. You'll wake May,' her father had said to her mother just three nights ago. It had been too late for that warning. May had been woken fifteen minutes earlier by her mother's loud sobbing.

The door to the lounge room started to open and May fled from the top of the stairs to her bedroom, quickly closing the door behind her and leaning against it. Had they heard her? Was she going to be in trouble? Her parents weren't the usual type of parent. They didn't care if she stayed up all night, watching television, as long as her grades were good. If she wanted to shower at three o'clock in the morning, they were fine with that, as long as she wasn't late heading out to school in the morning.

Education was vitally important to them and, whilst May knew they loved her, they both loved their scientific researching careers more. She was OK with that because it did afford her a lot of freedom. Tonight she'd had a shower and washed her hair, hearing the doorbell ring just after she'd turned off the hairdryer.

Unsure whether she'd be required to head downstairs to meet whoever was dropping around at ten o'clock at night, she'd dressed in three-quarter-length jeans and a T-shirt, choosing not to be introduced to her parents' friends whilst wearing her pyjamas.

But she hadn't been asked to come downstairs and the firmly closed lounge room door, plus the panic in her mother's voice, had helped May to decide to stay well out of sight. Had she succeeded?

She listened, hearing the lounge room door close again, and when she ventured back out to peek downstairs, it was to see the hallway was dark and the deep-toned discussion had continued. Straining to hear, she heard the words 'tonight' being used again and again. 'It isn't safe', 'security must be maintained', 'act now'. Those were some of the other phrases and all of it was enough to cause the knot of apprehension and fear in May's stomach to expand.

She headed back to her room but the four walls started to close in around her as she tried to figure out what was going on downstairs. Shaking her head, she headed to her balcony, needing to be anywhere but here. Her parents had given her the room upstairs with the balcony, the room that would usually be considered the main room of the house, whilst their bedroom was sandwiched between their two studies so they could work long hours into the night and not disturb her. As a young girl, she'd felt like a princess in a tower, waiting for her prince to come and rescue her. As she'd entered her teens, she'd decided not to wait for anyone to rescue her but to learn how to rescue herself.

She and Clara had figured out how to shimmy up and down the poles of the balcony and now, after May had pulled on her sandshoes, she slung a leg over the railing and retraced the path she'd used so many times before.

Over the rail, down the pole, keeping to the shadows of the back garden so she didn't trigger the light sensors of the security lights her parents had installed after the break-in. She climbed the shoulder-high wire fence that marked the border between the houses and quickly ran across to the large gum tree in the Lewises' yard, the cool breeze soothing her skin, helping her to gain some sort of clarity. The old gum had nice long branches, thick enough for her to carefully make her way across, then with one large step she made it to the ledge that was next to the open window of Arthur's room.

'May!' He placed his hand over his heart and she wasn't sure whether it was because she'd startled him or the fact that his heart belonged to her. She desperately wanted to think it was the latter. Here he was. Her Arthur. Her knight. He made her feel so needed, so desirable and so precious. She'd never known a feeling like that before, and even though she'd had a crush on him for the past few years, she'd never, in her wildest dreams, thought he'd ever like her back.

But on her sixteenth birthday, just a few short months ago, Arthur had let her kiss him. Not only that but he'd kissed her back, as though something inside him had snapped and he'd finally given in to the sensations of desire. Since then, they'd been sneaking around, not wanting to tell people—even Clara—about their relationship just yet. May hadn't wanted the fact that she was dating Clara's older brother to ruin her friendship with Clara.

Now, as she looked at him, *her Arthur*, time seeming to stand still for that split second, she drank in everything about him. How could this relationship go wrong? They were perfect for each other.

He was dressed in an old pair of shorts with rips and holes in them, ones his mother had forbidden him to wear outside the house. The T-shirt he wore was equally as comfortable and, given it had been a stinking hot summer in Victoria that year, it wasn't surprising he was dressed like that. His legs were long, his feet were bare, the desk in his room was littered with papers and the bed sheets were rumpled with more study notes on them. She knew he had an exam tomorrow and that he'd told her he needed to study, but right now she didn't care about anything except being with him.

When she was in Arthur's arms, everything in her world made sense. With the way her parents had been jittery and argumentative lately, it was little wonder she wanted to feel protected. Usually, her scientist parents spent a good portion of their time at their research labs, meaning that May, instead of staying in the large two-storey house all on her own, spent most of her time next door with the Lewis family.

Being with them, with Clara and Arthur and their parents, always welcomed and included in everything they did, from outings during the holidays to eating dinner in the evening, made May feel like she was living in a normal family, rather than with scatterbrained parents who often forgot to go to the grocery store.

Spending time with the Lewis family, and in particular with Arthur, made her feel wanted and loved, and as he stood there, staring at her, she wanted nothing more than to feel his comforting arms around her, to feel the touch of his hair with her fingertips and to have his lips pressed firmly to her own in a reassuring kiss.

Having overheard words such as 'danger', 'leave', 'tonight', from the conversation in her parents' lounge room, was it any wonder May wanted to feel secure? She covered the distance between them and wrapped her hands around his neck, urging his head down so their lips could meet.

The instant she felt the pressure of his lips on hers, May began to relax. This was where she belonged. In his arms, with his mouth on hers. Her teenage heart sang for joy when he immediately kissed her back, his arms coming around her, holding her close as though he, too, was desperate to be with her. Her heart soared with love and she deepened the kiss, wanting to know everything, wanting to experience everything, wanting to feel everything.

Something big was going on next door at her house, her parents behaving crazily, but here with Arthur she was lost in the bubble of belonging and she never wanted it to end. On and on she kissed him, edging him backwards, closer to his bed so they could lie down together, could *be* together because surely doing something like that for the very first time would help her to forget everything else.

'What…?' He eased away from her, staring into her face as though he couldn't quite believe she was here and kissing him in such a way. Never, in the few months they'd been sneaking kisses and sharing touches, had she ever been this forward. As she was a few years younger than him, she'd always let him guide her, but tonight she needed to take charge, to let him see just how much she loved him, how much she wanted him. That's what all guys wanted, right?

'What's going on? What are you doing here?'

'I want you, Arthur.' She went to kiss him again but he stopped her. She closed her eyes, not wanting him to stop her. She didn't want to think things through, she didn't want to be rational and reasonable. She simply wanted to feel, to lose herself in him, in the sensations that being with him evoked throughout her entire being.

'Whoa. Wait a second.'

She let him talk and she answered him and all the while she needed to keep her thoughts focused on him, on the here and now. The words 'danger', 'leave', 'tonight' were trying to force their way to the surface and even though she didn't understand what it all meant, her intuition told her it wasn't good. She had no idea how she could explain any of this to Arthur, how she could let him know what was going on at her house, because she had no real idea herself.

She didn't want him to tell her she was overreacting, that she was allowing her imagination to get the better of her, that she should go back home and they could talk about it more in the morning. He kept glancing at his bedroom door and she knew he was skittish about having her here this late in the evening. Although his parents had no real cause to come into their son's bedroom at this hour of the night, no doubt presuming he was studying for his coming exams, there was still the possibility they might and it was clearly making Arthur more than a little nervous.

All she wanted was to lose herself in him and when the opportunity presented itself she managed to kiss him once more, letting him know through her actions, rather than her words, just how determined she was.

She loved the way his fingers tangled in her hair, the way his mouth felt on hers, the way he kissed her with such hunger and passion. He felt the same way she did. She was certain of it. Although he'd never told her exactly how he felt, the fact that he hadn't put a stop to them sneaking around and spending time together showed her just how much he really did like her.

They were so caught up with each other, her mind focusing on nothing but the way he was making her feel, that when he touched the waistband of her three-quarter-length jeans she froze for a split second, a new thrumming starting to pulse through her mind. *This was really happening!* She was going to lose her virginity here—*tonight...right now*!

Arthur paused. 'What's wrong?' He stared at her and she tried as hard as she could to let him see that she wanted this, that she wanted to be with him, to forget about everything else in the world except for the two of them and the way they made each other feel. 'We don't have to do this.'

But she wanted to. Why couldn't he realise that? It was just that it was so...so...grown-up and scary, in a good way. She tried to reassure him but even then she stammered over her words. If only she hadn't overheard what was being said in her parents' lounge room…'danger', 'leave', 'tonight'… If only she and Arthur had more time, to let their relationship develop into an even deeper sensation of passion and love, but the fear that things were going to change drastically was something she couldn't shake.

'Honey, you don't need to do anything. I'm not going to force you.'

'Oh, I know you would never do that. Never.' Her words were clear and to the point. He brushed her hair back from her face and bent to kiss her mouth once more.

'Then why? Why come here and say what you did when you clearly have reservations?'

'Because I don't want to die a virgin!' she blurted out.

'Die? Who said anything about you dying? I'm not going to let anything bad happen to you and, besides, where you and I are concerned, we have plenty of time. Things will take their natural course when we're *both* ready.' Arthur's lips quirked a little at the corners and instead of getting cross at him for finding what she'd said amusing, she relaxed, his humour showing her she was probably overreacting.

'I know.' She extracted herself from his arms and shifted so she could lie on his bed, her head on his pillow. She absent-mindedly wound her hair around her finger, something she often did when she was confused or agitated. 'It's just that…my parents have been acting strange lately.' At Arthur's raised eyebrow, she amended, 'Stranger than usual.'

'Stranger than spending more time at their research lab than with their daughter?'

'Hey, I don't mind. It means I get to hang out here and your parents treat me like another daughter, and Clara and I can have fun together, and you and I…' she winked at him '…get to have fun together, too.'

'Don't tease,' he growled as he came to lie down next to her, slipping his arm under her head. The intense moment had passed and now, as they lay there, the atmosphere was one of friendship and support between a boyfriend and girlfriend. 'It's the way they don't seem to take much of an interest in you, as though you're always the afterthought, that I don't like. Apart from that, I think your parents are both incredibly intelligent people who will one day find a cure for cancer.'

'Perhaps they already have,' May murmured. Was that the reason her parents had been so closed off lately? Installing extra security around the house? Huddling together whilst having wildly gesticulating conversations? Had they found a cure for cancer and someone didn't want them to share it?

'Really?'

'I don't want to talk about them,' she told him. 'Tell me about your exam. Are you supposed to be studying now?'

'Yes. I was timing myself with the answers.' He pulled his watch from his pocket and May immediately put it onto her wrist.

'What subject?'

'Biology.'

'Ah. That's my speciality. I'll help you study. Where are your papers?'

'I think you're lying on them.'

'Oh.' She shifted around and pulled them out from beneath her, making sure they didn't rip. 'All right. Question number one,' she said in her best gameshow-host voice and the two of them laughed.

'Shh. We don't want my parents coming in.' He kissed her nose and she snuggled closer to him, breathing him in.

'You smell good.'

'I don't think that information is included in my revision notes.'

'I'll soon fix that.' May pulled a small pink pen from the pocket of her three-quarter-length pants, having left it in there from school that day, and wrote, 'Arthur smells delicious' in pink ink at the top of the page. 'All fixed,' she said, and handed him the pen so she could hold the papers more easily. 'OK, future Dr Lewis. Time to study.'

'I'd rather spend more time kissing you,' he returned.

'And that will be your reward because I'm not having you fail this exam because of me.' She scanned his notes. 'OK. Answer this.' She chose a question and waited for him to answer. Whenever he got it right, she kissed him. Several times she asked him questions that weren't contained within his notes, making him think even harder on the subject.

'How do you know all this stuff?' Arthur chuckled as he kissed her once more.

'Are you kidding me? With one parent researching the human genome and the other an expert in synthetic compounds, is it little wonder this stuff runs through my veins?'

'You should study medicine.'

'And become a doctor like you're going to be?'

'I'll be a couple of years ahead of you at medical school so we could study together.'

'Like you help me study for my school exams?' May giggled, remembering how their last study session had ended with the two of them making out on the couch. 'I'd never pass!'

'Sure you would. You're smart.'

May eased back and looked him. 'You think I'm smart?'

He seemed surprised by her question. 'May, you're the smartest girl I know. Why else would I be with you?'

'Because I'm pretty?'

'Honey, you're beautiful. My belle.' He kissed her. 'And yes, there's no denying we're attracted to each other, but one of the main things I love about you is your intelligence.'

'Love?' Her eyes widened at the word. 'You love me?' May's voice broke on the last word but she didn't care. Inside, her heart was soaring as high as the highest bird on a cloudless day.

'Yes.' His grey eyes were intense, his words quiet and sincere. 'Problem?'

'No. No.' She shook her head, a wide, silly grin pulling on her lips before he kissed her. She kissed him back, deciding that this was most definitely the best night of her life. Arthur loved her. Arthur *loved* her and she loved him back. It was as though her life was finally starting to make sense—as if she'd found the one place where she belonged.

'You know I love everything about you,' she said a moment later, the two of them a little breathless. 'Except for the fact that your knee is digging into my leg.' She tried to shift a little, to get comfortable so she could take his weight on top of her, but as she did so he shifted as well, almost tumbling off the bed. In order to stop himself, he reached out a hand to his bedside table for support but in the process accidentally knocked his clock off.

The clattering noise as it fell onto the polished floorboards made them both freeze. Holding their breaths, they stared at each other, waited to see if his parents had heard the noise. With the sound of a door being opened and footsteps heading towards Arthur's room, they both scrambled like wildfire, moving fast. May headed towards the window, whilst Arthur righted the clock and picked up the scattered biology papers they'd previously knocked to the floor.

May just made it out the window and over to the branch of the tree, completely out of sight, when his father opened the bedroom door.

'You all right?' his dad asked.

'Yeah, yeah. Just dozed off while trying to cram this information into my brain,' Arthur remarked, shaking the biology papers with his hand. 'The sooner this exam is over, the better.'

His father laughed then said goodnight to his son, closing the door behind him. May waited, almost willing Arthur to come over to the window. He did just that and she edged off the branch to meet him there. He kissed her through the open frame. 'You'd better go.'

'I know.' She kissed him again, putting all her love and heart into the action. 'I love you, Arthur Lewis.'

'And I love you, May Fleming. Now go. Get to bed and I'll see you tomorrow.'

With a giddiness of epic proportions, May shimmed down the tree, climbed the fence and was soon scaling her balcony as though her feet had wings. The instant she stepped inside her bedroom she froze, her giddiness turning to ice as she saw both her parents were standing in her room. The light was on, her mother's face was ashen and her father's jaw was clenched more tightly than she'd ever seen before. She was in trouble now!

'May. Oh, my goodness. There you are.' Her mother dragged her close and hugged her so tightly May thought she might pass out.

'We thought they'd got you already.' Her father wrapped his arms around his two girls. 'Don't ever scare us like that again.'

May wasn't sure what was going on except she was positive this wasn't the way normal parents disciplined their child for sneaking out of the house. A moment later she realised her mother was crying and her father was shaking.

'What's…?' She stopped, not sure she wanted to ask what was going on because she wasn't sure she wanted to hear the answer. Instead she said, 'Why are you crying?'

'Oh, May.' Her mother kissed her head. 'I'm so sorry.'

'We need to get things organised,' a deep voice said from the doorway, and that was when May realised they weren't alone. The dread that had caused her to run to Arthur in the first place returned with full force as she eased back from her parents and stared at the dark-suited figure.

'Pack only what's necessary for now. The agency will pack the rest once you're safe.'

'Safe?' May swallowed, trying to control her rising panic.

'You're all in *danger*. You need to *leave* here. *Tonight*.'

CHAPTER ONE

MAYBELLE FREEBOURNE ALL but strutted into Victory Hospital in one of Melbourne's outer suburbs. She had finally returned to the last place she could remember being truly happy. She grinned to herself at the thought. It wasn't necessarily the *hospital* that made her feel happy but rather the memories of the suburb where the hospital was located.

She stood in the middle of the new and improved hospital lobby and looked around. Victory Hospital was a medium-sized teaching hospital with all the required medical and surgical departments, but it was nowhere as big as the Royal Melbourne Hospital situated in the heart of Melbourne City about an hour away. It would do her just fine.

Maybelle wanted to get lost in the crowd but not swallowed by it. She already knew how to blend in, how to adapt her looks and personality to be accepted by her colleagues. When you'd lived a life where you were forced to relocate every two to three years, you became good at it. There was a determination about her, a determination she hadn't felt in a long time, and it felt good. Her life was finally her own. That was a good thing…right?

She wasn't going to focus on just how she'd achieved such freedom. If she did that, she risked her thoughts spiralling down a black hole it was almost impossible to get out of. *Almost* impossible. The psychologist had said she was doing exceptionally well, given everything she'd been through.

Focusing her attention on the hospital walls, noting the renovations that had vastly upgraded and improved the overall aesthetics of the building, her mind compared it to how it had looked when she'd been eight years old. She'd been rushed into the emergency department in the wee hours of the morning with appendicitis, her scientist parents beside themselves with worry. They'd been smart people when it came to the human genome and synthetic molecules but actually seeing their daughter sick had made them both feel ill.

Nevertheless, that stay in hospital had highlighted many things for young Maybelle, the main one being that she loved the way the hospital seemed to function like its own little world, from the cleaners all the way up to the surgeons and everyone in between. While both her parents had encouraged Maybelle from her very first Christmas to be a scientist, especially as they'd given her a plastic Petri dish as a gift, her mother had been astounded when Maybelle had declared she'd wanted to be a doctor.

'But there's a lot of blood with medicine and during your medical training you'll be working on cadavers.' Her mother had paused for effect. 'A cadaver is a dead person, sweetie. You don't want to be around dead people.'

'She can make up her own mind, Samantha,' her father had chimed in, looking up from the scientific journal he'd been reading. 'Just because you and I don't like dealing with people and would rather spend time with a microscope, there's no reason why she can't be a doctor. Besides…' he'd fixed her with an indulgent look

'…you're only eight, sweetie. You might change your mind when you're older.' Then he'd given her mother a look that said it was best to drop the subject and her mother had done just that.

Of course, when Maybelle had finally graduated from medical school, her parents had been incredibly proud of her.

'I don't know how you do it, sweetie,' her mother had stated one night when Maybelle had returned from a long night in Emergency. 'But I like it that you're helping people, saving lives.' She met her daughter's gaze. 'Especially after everything we've put you through.'

Maybelle had hugged her mother close. Ever since they'd been put into witness protection, it had forced the three of them to spend a lot more time together, and in some ways the close family Maybelle had always wanted was what she'd finally received.

'Silver linings,' her father had often declared. 'We need to look for the silver linings in our day-to-day lives, especially if we've had a bad day.'

As it turned out, her parents hadn't discovered a cure for cancer. Instead, they'd discovered something that could cause death and devastation on a mass scale if it fell into the wrong hands. The break-in at their house had been because the thieves had been looking for her parents' research. Maybelle had found out many years later that there had also been several break-ins at their laboratory. The government had offered to protect her family, if her parents continued to work for them, creating antidotes and staying out of sight.

'Our work may never be published under our own names but we're alive,' her father would continue when he was on one of his silver-lining speeches.

'And May was able to get through medical school with

only two relocations,' her mother would add. 'One day she'll be free of all this and able to start her own life—her *real* life.'

'That day has come, Mum,' Maybelle whispered to Victory Hospital's walls before she headed towards the bustling emergency department, which was located on the other side of the lobby. Sure, things had changed but she'd changed a lot, too. It was the perfect mix.

She swiped her new pass card through the security lock and pushed the door open. On the other side, her excitement waned as she glanced around the very non-bustling ED. She was pumped, ready for action, and yet there were several medical staff at the desk, which was located in the middle of the treatment bays, chatting and laughing together. No action. No franticness. No calls of 'Grab the crash cart', or 'Get the doctor here, *stat*'. Several of the treatment bays were indeed full but with patients who were now stable and being monitored.

With a deflated sigh, she headed towards the desk. She hated quiet and controlled environments. She liked busyness and movement and being rushed off her feet. None of the staff looked her way as she approached. Instead it appeared they were all listening intently to someone who was telling what must be an enthralling story.

'And then,' she heard a deep male voice say, 'she stepped on the ball!'

At the delivery of the line, everyone laughed and the spell was broken. It was then that one of the staff turned and saw her standing there. The woman jumped and placed a hand over her heart.

'Good heavens, you scared me. You must walk very quietly.'

Maybelle paused for a second, remembering how she'd been taught to sneak around places, to be inconspicuous, to make herself unnoticeable, but this time she hadn't been doing it on purpose. She held up her identification badge. 'New doctor. Officially start work in…' Maybelle glanced at the clock on the wall '…about thirty seconds' time.'

'Oh, you must be Dr Freebourne. Uh… May, is it?'

'Maybelle,' she instantly corrected, and held out her hand.

'I'm Gemma, the ED ward clerk, and I have your paperwork…somewhere here.' Gemma quickly shook Maybelle's hand, then started shuffling papers around on the desk. 'Ah. Here it is.'

'Did you say you were starting work?' one of the nearby nurses questioned. 'Fantastic. We've been so short-staffed of late.'

'Hospitals are always short-staffed,' another nurse mumbled in a matter-of-fact tone.

Gemma gathered the different pieces of paper together and held them out to the man who, Maybelle belatedly realised, had been the one enthralling the staff with his stories. 'Here you go, Arthur.'

Upon hearing the name—Arthur—something clicked in Maybelle's long-term memory. *Arthur?* It wasn't a very common name nowadays—in fact, it was still considered rather old-fashioned—but the only Arthur she'd ever known had been named after a beloved family grandfather and, as such, he'd worn the name with pride.

Her Arthur. Her King Arthur. The first boy she'd ever loved. She smiled at the memory the name brought to mind but schooled her thoughts as her new colleagues started asking her questions.

'What did you say your name was?' one of the nurses asked.

'This here,' Gemma interrupted before Maybelle could

get a word out, 'is Dr Maybelle Freebourne. She joins us from a very busy and hectic teaching hospital in the heart of Sydney.' Several of the staff, who were a mix of doctors, nurses and interns, listened to Gemma's introduction before shaking hands with Maybelle and introducing themselves. This was just the sort of thing Maybelle wasn't used to—this intimate attention. It made her feel as though she were under a microscope, that they'd want to know everything about her, and she most certainly didn't want to tell anyone *everything* about her. However, it couldn't be helped. She'd made her choice and was determined to make her life work.

'Maybelle?' The deep voice that had spoken her name made her look at the man who had spoken it. He was tall, about six feet four inches. He wore navy-blue scrubs with a white coat over the top, and a stethoscope around his neck. His hair, which had once been blond, was now a light brown, peppered at the sides with a hint of distinguished grey. His nose was slightly bent, indicating a break in the past, but it was his grey eyes that caused her mouth to go dry and her heart to momentarily skip a beat. There was no way she would ever forget those eyes. How could she when they'd once looked at her with such tenderness?

'That's a very old-fashioned name,' Arthur stated.

'Like you can talk,' Gemma interjected, as Maybelle continued to stare at the man before her. 'Arthur's an old-fashioned name, too. You two will fit perfectly together. Maybelle and Arthur.'

'Old-fashioned names are making a comeback,' one of the nurses said, and began talking about how her friend was pregnant and quite a few of the baby books had many of those old-fashioned names in them and… Maybelle wasn't listening to a word.

Instead, all she could hear was the thrumming of blood pumping wildly throughout her system, reverberating in her ears, causing her heart rate to increase. It *was* the same Arthur. This was the same boy who had lived next door to her so many years ago but now…he was even more devastatingly handsome. She couldn't help but drink her fill of the man before her.

Why, oh why, hadn't she questioned her government case worker more closely? When the paperwork had been prepared for the transfer to Victory Hospital, to her new life, Maybelle had only enquired about the CEO, not the director of the ED! However, it was too late to back out now and as his warm hand enveloped hers in the normal way of greeting, sparks spread up her arm, flooding throughout her body. If she'd had any doubt whether this Arthur was the same man who had been her first crush so many years ago, it fled with that one simple touch.

'I'm Arthur. Arthur Lewis. Director of the ED.'

Arthur Lewis and his sister Clara. What fantastic times they'd had together. She and Clara had been soul sisters and for a long while Arthur had been the big brother she'd never had…that was until she'd started to see him as something *more* than a surrogate big brother.

Maybelle cleared her throat and forced her mind back to the present, extracting her hand from his as though the touch had slightly burnt her. She quickly pushed her fingers through her short blonde curls and tried hard not to fidget. Fidgeting had always been a sure-fire sign she was uncomfortable in a situation, unsure how to proceed. *Not* a good first impression to make when starting a new job.

'Pleased to meet you, Arthur.' She took a small step back, needing to put some distance between them. She dragged in a deep breath in an effort to try to calm her senses, belatedly realising it was the wrong thing to do.

Her senses were treated to the spicy, hypnotic scent she'd always equated with him. Any time she'd smelt that particular type of aftershave, she'd always thought of Arthur. Darn her smell receptors!

'Ready to start work?' He turned and gathered a few sets of case notes from the desk. 'Come into my office and we can have a chat.' He smiled at her then, an impersonal, polite smile that indicated he had no idea of her true identity. Good. This was a new beginning for her but what she hadn't expected was to be immediately confronted with her past.

Maybelle followed Arthur to his office, the name plate on his door confirming his full name—Arthur Lewis— and that he was indeed the director of the ED. Now that she'd overcome her initial shock, a part of her was secretly delighted to see what twenty years had done to him.

He offered her a seat then sat behind the well-organised desk and put on a pair of wire-rimmed glasses. Maybelle couldn't help the smile that touched her lips at seeing him wearing glasses. It made him look like his father.

'Something funny?' he asked, and it was then she realised he was watching her.

'No. No. I like your glasses,' she proffered.

'Uh…thank you.' His brow puckered a little as though he wasn't quite sure how to respond. 'Anyway, let me have a quick look over the paperwork, make sure everything is signed in the right places and that your security clearance is up to date.'

'I used my identity badge to gain access to the ED so I'd say that's a "yes".'

'Good.' He finished looking over her papers, added his own signature to two pieces of paper and then took off his glasses. 'We've had an issue with some of the staff having problems with their passes. The CEO is looking into the situation but between you and me the system does need an upgrade. However, if you have an issue where you can't gain access or get stuck somewhere, just let me know.'

'OK. Thanks for the heads-up.'

Arthur folded his hands together and looked at her intently. Maybelle tried to remain calm, tried not to do anything that might give away her true identity. Could he see it? Could he find some resemblance to the sixteen-year-old girl he'd once known?

She waited for Arthur to speak but instead he simply sat there, staring at her as though he really was seeing a ghost—and well he might be.

'Have we met?' The words seem to tumble out of his mouth before he could stop them.

Maybelle slowly shook her head. 'I—uh—'

'You just seem oddly familiar.'

She shrugged and forced a polite smile. 'I guess I have one of those faces.'

He stared at her for another long moment, as though desperately trying to place her, before leaning back in his chair. 'Anyway, do you have any questions about the ED? I'm presuming you've familiarised yourself with the hospital and departmental protocols?'

'Absolutely, and everything seems straightforward.'

'Good. Well, until you learn your way around, don't be afraid to ask for help.'

'Will do.' She wasn't sure whether to stand, whether to keep sitting until she was dismissed or whether he wanted to talk to her some more. Maybelle played with one of the curls by her ear, winding it around her ear, then realised what she was doing and forced her hands into her lap, clenching them tightly together.

The phone on Arthur's desk rang and he quickly answered it. 'Yes, Gemma.' He paused then nodded once. 'We'll be right there.' He put the phone down and stood in one swift motion.

'Three ambulances on their way, re-routed here from the Royal Melbourne. They're inundated and we're empty.' Maybelle stood and watched him walk to his office door and open it. 'Well, Dr Freebourne, there's nothing like throwing you in at the deep end. Let's see how well you swim.'

'You'll be watching me closely, I take it?' she asked as she preceded him through the door. Why had her voice sounded so intimate and soft as she'd spoken the words? 'I mean with regard to how I handle the situation,' she amended.

His answer was a small, deep chuckle that made goosebumps tingle up and down her spine. The same laugh...but richer. This new Arthur was already proving to be a distraction and right now she didn't need any of those, especially if he was going to be monitoring the way she performed her job.

'I knew what you meant, Maybelle, but you can take it any way you like,' he remarked as they strode to the nurses' station, then he looked at her over his shoulder and winked before turning his attention to Gemma. 'What's going on?' he asked the ward clerk. As Gemma spoke, Maybelle's mind tried to decipher why he'd done that.

Why had he winked at her? What did it mean? Had he simply been teasing? He'd always been one to joke around but never to the point where it caused anyone pain. Given the way he'd been joking with his staff when she'd arrived, and the way everyone in the department seemed to be relaxed with each other, it seemed that Arthur Lewis was still the type of man to put people at ease with a touch of humour. Was that what the wink had meant? Did it mean that he'd be watching her from a professional point of view, evaluating her skills as an emergency specialist, or did it mean he was more than willing to watch her from a non-professional point of view?

Even the thought made her body warm with anticipation as her mind dredged up the memory of exactly what it had been like to be kissed by those luscious lips of his. She also couldn't deny the effect that the wink had had on her. Arthur Lewis…winking at her in that easygoing manner of his, of teasing her, laughing with her. It hadn't been the first time he'd ever winked at her and the action was having the same devastating effect on her equilibrium as it had in the past. Darn the man for being so incredibly handsome and making her feel all feminine. She needed to concentrate on her work, not on how he could still ignite her senses with one simple action.

When Arthur started briefing the staff on the present situation, Maybelle was relieved when her mind clicked over into professional mode. Concentrating on the impending arrival of the patients, of what was expected of her, of who she would be working with, was definitely a welcome diversion from reflecting on how Arthur Lewis made her *feel*.

'There's been a bad accident on the freeway where a semi-trailer jack-knifed across the road, collecting several cars in its wake. From the reports, there are still several people trapped in their cars and the emergency service teams are doing their best to get them out. The Royal Melbourne ED is backed up with patients from other accidents from the morning commute, hence why we're getting the overload.'

'Do we know what the semi-trailer was carrying?'

Maybelle interjected. 'What cargo? Was it a tanker with chemicals or fuel inside, or was it transporting animals?' She spread her hands wide. Arthur looked over at Gemma, who quickly flicked through the notes she'd taken.

'It was a tanker. Petrol tanker.'

'Good question, Maybelle,' Arthur pointed out, and she could have sworn there was an impressed quirk to his eyebrow. 'This means the possibility of burn injuries as well as the general car-related injuries such as whiplash, fractures, bruises and concussion.'

Arthur continued with his briefing, breaking people up into treatment teams and giving specific instructions.

'Maybelle, as you're fully trained in emergency medicine, you take treatment room two. I'll be in treatment room one. We'll work tag team. Larissa, you take triage. Kate, you organise the non-life-threatening patients as they arrive,' he went on, indicating to two of the nurses who had been part of the enthralled group when Maybelle had arrived. 'Gemma's called through to Emergency Theatres to have them prepare and the wards are making room. Surgical staff are being called in and registrars from the various departments are about to be notified of the situation.'

The sound of ambulance sirens could be heard in the distance and Arthur nodded to his team, his gaze focusing on Maybelle last of all. 'Let's treat these patients.' The phone on the desk started ringing and Gemma quickly answered it. With the briefing done and patients needing their attention, everyone started to go about their assigned tasks.

'Maybelle,' Arthur said. 'You're with me. Ambulance bays, *stat*.' With that, he took off his white coat and grabbed a disposable protective gown from a box, handing another one to Maybelle.

She had the tapes tied in place over her practical trousers and light knit jumper as the first ambulance pulled into the bay. Arthur opened the rear doors as the orderlies helped the paramedics get the stretcher. 'Your patient, Maybelle. Do the Victory proud,' he stated, and she could feel him watching her intently as she turned her attention to the paramedic, ready for the handover.

If there was one thing Maybelle had become good at over the years, it was compartmentalising her thoughts and emotions, and right now, whether Arthur was assessing her or not, she had a life to save.

CHAPTER TWO

EACH OF THE three ambulances had two patients in them and so where the Victory ED had previously been vacant, it was now bustling with activity. The nurses were doing their jobs, Larissa doing triage and Kate taking care of the non-life-threatening cases. Maybelle could hear Arthur in treatment room one speaking clearly and directly to the staff members who were assisting him. His voice was deep, melodic and calming. Even though she didn't know her way around the Victory's ED, she certainly knew her way around procedure.

'Patient is a Mr Houston Bird, sixty-two years old,' the paramedic stated as Mr Bird was wheeled into treatment room two. Maybelle and the nursing staff hooked Mr Bird up to their equipment, taking his blood pressure and measuring his oxygen saturation.

'He was trapped in his car, both legs crushed beneath the steering wheel. Firefighters cut him out. Right foot is worse than the left. BP was dropping in the ambulance but after a plasma infusion it stabilised. Wound to the head, signs of whiplash and a bruise from the seatbelt.'

'Analgesics?'

'Only the green whistle.'

'Methoxyflurane?'

'No, mythelallium. It's a new compound that does the same as methoxyflurane but costs the government less.'

'Thanks. Hello, Mr Bird,' Maybelle said firmly to the man lying before her. A large bruise was forming on his forehead where he'd obviously hit it. 'I'm Dr Maybelle Freebourne. Can you hear me?'

'Of course I can, you silly woman. You're standing right next to me. I hit my head. I'm not deaf.'

At Mr Bird's clear response, Maybelle couldn't help but smile. 'That's good news.' Having not only a response but a response with chastisement was a good sign, especially when dealing with a patient who could have a possible concussion. She'd be ordering scans of his head to ensure there was no internal bleeding and as she used her penlight torch to check his pupils, Maybelle was pleased to note they were equal and reacting to light.

The nurse, whose badge indicated her name was Cici, was cutting the clothes off Mr Bird whilst an intern was removing the temporary bandages the paramedics had put around Mr Bird's feet. From the look of them, the fourth and fifth metatarsals on the right foot would require amputation. The left foot wasn't as bad but might possibly require amputation of the little toe.

'Clean and debride the wounds,' she told the intern. 'And can we get an orthopaedic registrar here to assess Mr Bird, please?' she added as the paramedics left the room, the handover complete. 'Cross, type and match.' Another nurse entered the room to help Cici and Maybelle address her patient. 'Mr Bird, have you ever been to Victory Hospital before?'

'No. No. Never before. No. I'm never sick. I'm OK. I don't know what all the fuss is about.' Mr Bird tried to shake his head as he spoke but his neck was supported by a brace, which made his efforts more cumbersome.

'Try and keep your head still until we can get some X-rays of your spine to check you haven't done any damage. Are you taking any medications you didn't tell the paramedic about?'

'What?' Mr Bird looked at her as though she was crazy. 'It's nine-thirty in the morning. The only medication I've had is my fish-oil tablet and a cup of coffee with my breakfast. How long is this going to take? I have to get to work.'

Maybelle looked across at the staff opposite her, all of them sharing a concerned look.

'Mr Bird, do you remember the accident?'

'Of course I do.' Mr Bird closed his eyes as though trying to think. 'I was driving to work—I own the company so it's imperative I get there—' He broke off, his body starting to shake and twitch.

'Mr Bird?' Maybelle looked at the read-outs from the equipment. She took the oximeter clip off Mr Bird's finger just in case he started to thrash around. The last thing they wanted when a patient was twitching in such a way was for the patient to hurt themselves so it was best they weren't connected to machinery.

'Seizure?' Cici asked. No sooner had the nurse said the word than the shaking stopped. Maybelle clipped the oximeter back and noted the change in readings.

'Push fluids. We don't want him going into shock.'

'That I get there before the rest of my staff,' Mr Bird continued as though there had been nothing wrong. It appeared he was completely unaware he'd even had a seizure. Maybelle once again checked his pupils. They were still equal and reacting to light.

'Do you remember the emergency services crews being at the accident site?' she asked her patient. There was clearly something not right. Did Mr Bird have an internal injury? She checked his reflexes and palpated his stomach. At the touch, he moaned with pain. She'd thought his seizure might have been caused by shock but with the whack to his head she couldn't rule out something more sinister.

'They were…' Mr Bird stopped and frowned as though it was increasingly difficult for him to remember. He moaned again but this time the sound was more guttural.

'It's OK. You don't need to remember right now,' she told him gently. She needed to get him some more analgesics as well as adding a few more scans and tests to the list. 'Are you allergic to anything?'

'No.' Thought seemed difficult for him. Cici was monitoring him closely, listening to his heart and checking his blood pressure. She reported the findings. Something was definitely not right.

'Mr Bird? Can you hear me?'

'Of course I can,' he growled, his answer laced with repressed pain.

'Are you sure you're not allergic to anything?' As she asked the question, Maybelle thought back to the report from the paramedic. Mr Bird had been given a plasma infusion and the green whistle. That was it as far as medications went.

'Ugh.' He clenched his teeth. 'Uh…yes. I'm allergic to garlic but you're hardly going to serve me a meal right now.' Again his frustration was coming out in his tone and she didn't blame him.

'He's sweating,' Cici told her as she grabbed a piece of paper towel and wetted it before placing it on Mr Bird's head.

'He might vomit,' Maybelle stated. 'Do his vitals again. I need to go and check something.' While Cici took Mr Bird's vital signs once more, noting the differences, the intern finished cleaning Mr Bird's feet and placing another temporary bandage on them.

Maybelle rushed out to Gemma's desk, wanting the ward clerk to look something up on the computer, but the other woman wasn't there. She needed the computer but as there had been no time to log her into the system, she wasn't quite sure what to do next.

'Something wrong?' It was Arthur who spoke from just behind her.

'I need the computer.' There was agitation in her tone. 'I need to look up the new medicine in the green whistle.'

'Mythelallium?'

'Yes. They still use methoxyflurane in Sydney so I was unfamiliar with the new green whistle drug and I don't know…' As she spoke, Arthur sat down in the chair and quickly logged into the computer, typing the name of the drug into the system. 'Something isn't right. My patient had a small seizure and then moaned when I palpated his abdomen.'

'Any known allergies?'

'Garlic.'

Arthur raised his eyebrows as the compound breakdown of mythelallium came up on screen. 'The breakdown for mythelallium is…'

Maybelle leaned towards the computer, her shoulder touching his, but it was the words on the screen that interested her more. Arthur was rattling off a list of drugs and the second to last one was *allium sativum*.'

'Otherwise known as garlic?' she queried, and a moment later, after he'd opened another screen to check the information, they had their answer. There was a garlic synthesised compound in mythelallium.

'He's vomiting,' she heard Cici call from the treatment room.

'I need to get him an antiemetic.'

'I'll get it,' Arthur said as Maybelle rushed back to her patient.

'Mr Bird,' she said as Cici helped Mr Bird to get cleaned up. 'Mr Bird, can you hear me?'

'Yes, yes.' His voice was much weaker than before and when Maybelle looked at the readings of his pulse, heart rate and oxygen sats, she noted they'd spiked.

'Mr Bird, the medication you were given in the ambulance contains a synthesised garlic compound, which means you're having an allergic reaction to the drug.' Arthur came into the room with the antiemetic and double-checked it with Maybelle before administering it. 'This medication should help counteract the reaction and help us to stabilise you.'

Thankfully, it didn't take long for the medication to work and by the time the orthopaedic registrar arrived for the review, Mr Bird was in a much better position to receive treatment for the injuries he'd sustained during the accident.

'That was quite something,' Arthur stated, clearly impressed with the newest member of the Victory Hospital ED. Maybelle didn't want any accolades.

'Just doing my job, boss.' She returned to the nurses' desk in order to write up her notes and was thankful that Gemma was back and able to help with the computer log-in.

'How did you know?' Arthur asked, leaning against the desk next to where Maybelle was sitting.

She shrugged a shoulder and continued to input the information into the computer. There was no way she was going to mention the fact that her mother had been an expert in synthetic compounds and that Maybelle had been raised listening to her parents discussing the various ways synthetic compounds could cause reactions.

Hearing Arthur's tone should make her pleased that she'd passed the test, but instead it made her a little uneasy about having his undivided attention focused solely on her. Any time anyone gave her their undivided attention, watching her closely, intrigued by her, Maybelle's automatic response was to pull away, to put up walls, to withdraw. It was what she'd been taught to do, to remain as inconspicuous as possible… But now there was no need to hide, no need to keep such a strong distance from interacting with other people. Arthur was paying her a compliment and she needed to learn to accept them.

Drawing in a deep breath, she glanced at him and offered a small smile. 'Process of elimination. Mr Bird's reaction to the trauma already inflicted on his body wasn't within normal parameters so I simply looked for the abnormal.'

'Have you come across another patient who was allergic to garlic before?'

'No.'

'So it was a lucky guess?'

She stopped typing then and raised an eyebrow at him. 'It was a *calculated deduction*, thank you very much,' she pointed out, and received one of his delicious, rich chuckles as a reward.

'As I said, lucky guess.'

Maybelle sighed, unable to believe how happy it made her feel to be there with him, to interact with him in such a normal way. She absent-mindedly twirled her hair around one finger. 'Don't you have any more patients to attend to, Dr Lewis?'

Arthur didn't immediately answer but instead watched her closely, his brows drawing together in a frown. He paused a moment before saying quietly, 'Are you sure we haven't met before? You really do seem oddly familiar.' His voice was quiet, as though he was trying to put the pieces of the puzzle together but couldn't remember where he'd left the jigsaw.

Maybelle instantly dropped her hand and turned her attention from him. She wished he wouldn't look at her in such a way, one that said he was intrigued by her. She didn't want to be intriguing to anyone—man, woman or child—and especially not to Arthur Lewis.

If she told him the truth, if she confessed that they really did know each other, it would only bring a plethora of questions and most of them were ones she either couldn't answer or chose not to. The past twenty years of her life had been crazy, insane and by no means normal. This meant that people who had lived a very normal, very mundane life found it nigh on impossible to understand exactly what she'd been through.

It was the reason she'd been given a new identity, a new name, a new hairstyle and even new contact lenses. What would Arthur say if she took them out? Would he recognise her more easily with blue eyes rather than the brown contacts she wore? Would he know that her name had been May Fleming rather than Maybelle Freebourne?

Even the way he was looking at her brought back memories of another time when he'd looked at her with such intensity. Back then she'd had butterflies in her stomach, sweaty palms and jelly knees. This time, though, the sensations seemed magnified as she was no longer a teenager in the throes of a silly high school crush. How was it possible she still felt a smouldering attraction to a man she hadn't seen in such a long time?

Thankfully, she was saved any further thought on the matter by the sounds of ambulance sirens in the distance as the next wave of patients was brought to their door. However, as he gave her one last quizzical look before walking away, Maybelle realised she'd probably just given herself away by not immediately answering him, by not immediately denying any claims to his questions.

'As I told you, I have one of those faces,' was what she should have said. Or she could have followed with, 'It's the haircut. It reminds people of Marilyn Monroe,' which was one she'd been planning to use, but instead all she'd done was drop her hand from the tell-tale fidget of winding her hair around her finger and look at him with an expression of trepidation lest he figured out exactly who she was.

Gritting her teeth and closing her eyes for a moment, Maybelle dragged in a deep breath, pulling her professionalism around her. She could do this. She could start a new life even with part of her old life lurking around the edges. All she had to do was to keep her personal distance from Arthur Lewis and she would be fine. It was a good plan and one she was intent on keeping.

By the end of her first shift, apart from the 'Arthur' problem, Maybelle was pleased she'd made the decision to move back to the area where she'd grown up. The staff at Victory Hospital were great and she'd managed to find an apartment only five blocks from the suburb she'd lived in all those years ago. The apartment block was close to the hospital, which meant she could walk to and from work until she managed to find time to organise a car.

Walking into her building, which housed four apartments, two upstairs and two downstairs, Maybelle knew she should be exhausted but there was still a spring in her step. All in all, today had been a good day and she'd made a point, so many years ago, to always acknowledge the good days when they came along because all too often her days hadn't been that happy.

Unlocking her front door, Maybelle headed into the furnished apartment. Yes, it was sparse, yes, there were quite a few boxes waiting for her to unpack, but she could still call it 'home'. The furniture was utilitarian but served its purpose, and she'd more than likely be spending most of her time at the hospital, rather than lounging around here, watching movies on television… At least, that was how her life had been in the past. Work, sleep. Work, sleep. Don't get involved with people. Don't be too friendly with people. Don't leave a lasting, memorable impression on people. Work, sleep. That had been her life.

However, now that she was technically free from the constraints that had governed her life, she'd come to realise she had no idea *how* to be free. Her world had been ordered, direct and absolute in so many ways with little room for deviation. The last thing her government case worker had said to her was, 'Go. Live a normal life.' The problem was, she had no idea how to do that.

Heading to the kitchen, she opened the fridge, looked at the shelves, empty except for half a container of milk, then closed it again. It was then she remembered the one thing she'd been planning to do after finishing work—go to the grocery store.

Although there were several twenty-four-hour grocery stores in the area, all of them would require her to take a taxi there and then another one back, laden with shopping bags, and she simply didn't have the energy for that. Where the ED had been quiet when she'd arrived at work that morning, it had remained at a steadily hectic pace until Arthur had ordered her to go home and let the next shift take over.

'Looks as though it's take-out time,' she told her

empty apartment, but even then she wasn't sure who to
call or who delivered. She could use the internet on her
phone to check restaurants in the area but not only did
that not guarantee a decent meal, it was also the antisocial
thing to do. The only other thing she could do was to see
if one of her neighbours was home, to see if they could
provide some intelligence to good nearby food places or
take-out menus. 'That's what a "normal" person would
do,' she told herself as she headed back out of her apartment. 'They'd interact with neighbours and be friendly.'
However, the apartment on the upstairs landing next to
hers yielded no response to her knock.

Down the stairs she went and again received no answer from the first door she knocked on. One more door
to try and if she was the only person in this building it
looked as though she might be having milk for her evening meal.

Maybelle knocked on the door, whispering to herself
what she was planning to say. 'Sorry to bother you. I'm
your new neighbour, Maybelle Freebourne. I live upstairs
and—' The door opened before she could complete her
preparation and the polite smile she'd pasted onto her
lips died a sudden death as she stared into the grey eyes
of Arthur Lewis.

'What are you doing here?' she demanded as they
stood staring at each other.

'Me?' He laughed at her question. 'I think you're forgetting that you're the one who knocked on my door,
Maybelle.'

'Your door? *Your door*?'

'Yes.' Arthur pointed to the door he'd just opened.

'You *live* here?'

'I do.' It was his turn to frown. 'How did you find me?'

'I didn't. I didn't find you.' She closed her eyes and

rubbed one hand over her forehead before pinching the bridge of her nose as though trying to stave off a headache. 'I can't believe *you*, of all people, live here.'

'What does that mean?' He laughed, the delightful sound filled with utter confusion. 'Why did you knock on my door?'

She dropped her hand and opened her eyes. 'Food.' She spread her arms wide as though her answer made perfect sense.

'You want food?' He laughed again and she wished he wouldn't because the more gorgeous he sounded and the more breath-taking he looked, the harder it was for her to shut him out of her mind. 'Maybelle, I don't understand what's going on. Are you all right?'

'I'm hungry.'

'And you're just knocking on random doors, hoping someone will give you food?'

'No.' She pointed up the stairs. 'I only moved in yesterday and with the emergencies today, I didn't get around to going to the grocery store.'

'Oh, *you're* the new tenant in the building.' He stepped back from the doorway, no longer confused but still looking incredibly handsome with that sexy smile touching his lips. 'I was notified there was someone moving in but I didn't realise it was you. Well, as you're looking for food and as I'm just dishing up my dinner, please, come on in...*neighbour.*'

CHAPTER THREE

'Uh…' Maybelle faltered as she stood on the threshold. Not only was she trying to wrap her head around the fact that the one man she'd wanted to keep at a distance lived downstairs but now he was inviting her to dinner! 'I…uh…don't want to intrude. I just wanted to know the phone number of a place that delivers food.'

'I understood the request, Maybelle.'

There it was again—that infuriating quirk of his lips and that twinkling brightness in his eyes that displayed his amusement at the present situation. 'Good. Well, if you wouldn't mind giving me some phone numbers or menus, I'll get out of your hair.'

Arthur stepped forward and leaned in close to her. 'What if I don't want you to get out of my hair? Ever think of that?'

At that moment, Maybelle couldn't think of *anything* due to his closeness. There it was. That glorious scent of his that made him smell like he'd come fresh from a shower, that he was a strong and confident man, that he could cope with any situation life threw at him. How she managed to get such a strong image from just the scent, she had no idea! Chances were it also had a lot to do with his own personal pheromones, his charm and his incredibly toned body, which, presently, wasn't far from her own. If she were to lean in just a touch and angle her head a little to the left then...

'Uh...' Great. She was back to faltering again. What on earth was wrong with her? Usually, she had a thousand quips, all designed to keep people at arm's length but Arthur Lewis wasn't 'people'. He was *Arthur*, and he was only trying to be neighbourly. If she made a big deal out of the situation, then it might bring more questions. Besides, doing something was better than standing here, staring at him, remembering with perfect clarity what it had been like to feel those lips against her own.

Maybelle cleared her throat. 'OK.'

'OK...what?' It was only when he spoke that she realised he'd been looking at her just as much as she'd been looking at him. A thread of panic wove through her. Had he recognised her? For one split second she couldn't remember whether she was still wearing her brown contact lenses or not. Had she taken them out when she'd arrived home? She blinked her eyes a few times then glanced down at the floor. The contacts were also prescription and as she could see things quite clearly, that tended to indicate they were still in place.

Whew! Forcing herself to think logically rather than with emotional irrationality helped calm the rising panic that Arthur had recognised her. The new persona was still firmly in place and she should stop dithering and make the decision to either stay or go. What would a new neighbour do when invited to dinner?

'OK, I'll come inside.' She glanced up at him and forced a smile.

'Oh. Good.' With that, he seemed to recover his equilibrium and stepped back to welcome her into his apartment. 'As I said, I was just about to dish up.'

Maybelle breathed in and immediately felt her stomach gurgle. Arthur heard it too and chuckled. 'I'm going to take that as a compliment, Maybelle.' He headed into the kitchen where the delicious spicy scent increased.

'What is that?' She pointed to the slow cooker sitting on the bench top. 'It smells delicious.'

'Hungarian goulash,' he told her.

'You made it?'

'Of course.' He glanced at her over his shoulder as he pulled another plate out of the cupboard. 'Cutlery's in the drawer.' He indicated the drawer in question. 'Why don't you set the table while I dish up?'

'Yes, boss,' she replied, all awkwardness fleeing in the light of having something warm and delicious to eat on such a wintry night. It was strange to be in someone else's kitchen, going through the drawers and following his instructions regarding where to find other things such as place mats and wine glasses.

'I'm hardly your boss here, Maybelle.'

'Sorry. I meant, yes, chef.'

She was rewarded with another one of his delicious chuckles. 'Better.' It didn't take him long to dish up and by the time he'd done that, Maybelle had managed to find everything she needed to set two places at the table.

'Bon appetit,' Arthur remarked as he placed a plate in front of her. Not only was there Hungarian goulash on the plate but mashed potatoes and vegetables, and everything smelled delicious.

'Thank you, Arthur. This is…this is very kind of you,' she replied, anxious to let him know that this hadn't been her plan. She was trying desperately not to think about the last time they'd been alone together…that night in his room. In some ways it felt completely right to be here alone with him, and in other ways she half expected his parents to walk in, much as his father had interrupted them so very long ago.

'Ah…my mother would be proud.' He raised his glass of wine and held it out to her.

'Your mother?'

'Yes. She done raised me good and proper like.' He clinked his wine glass to hers then chuckled at his incorrect English. Then, as though he had no idea of her turbulent emotions, he sipped his wine and started to eat his dinner.

Seeing Arthur again was one surprise she'd managed to deal with, but to hear him talk of his mother made her want to ask questions about his family. How were his parents? Were they still alive? Doing well? How was Clara? Oh, her dear, sweet friend Clara. How she'd missed Clara those first few years.

As they ate, Arthur asked very general questions about her last job in Sydney, asking her if she knew certain people. She did her best to keep her answers vague because at that last hospital she'd had a different identity. There, she'd been Margaret Adamson, working in the paediatric emergency department.

That was one thing with being in the witness protection programme organised by the government—you were able to have all sorts of papers and passports provided in the new identity they created for you. Every time she and her parents had been forced to move, another set of papers had been created and the old ones destroyed.

This last time around, with the threat to her life deemed to be over, she'd asked if she could go back to her real name, to finally become May Fleming again. Her case worker had denied the request, telling her that when they'd first been put into witness protection their true identities had been listed as void.

'There's no going back. Only moving forward. Why not choose a name that is similar to your own?'

And hence Dr Maybelle Freebourne had been created, and whilst May Fleming's experience in medicine was indeed at an exceptional level, the qualifications for Dr Maybelle Freebourne had been adjusted and printed up on new parchment paper by her case worker. There was no way she could tell Arthur any of that, so tried to change the subject, turning her attention back to the delicious food.

'There's a specific spice in your goulash that I'm having trouble pinpointing.' She took another mouthful and closed her eyes, trying to figure out what it might be. 'Hmm…cardamom?' Maybelle licked her lips and opened her eyes to find him staring at her with such intensity that her stomach flipped with nervous knots.

'Garam masala,' he stated bluntly, clearly having other topics he wanted to discuss rather than the 'secret' ingredient in the food. 'Maybelle, I know you say we haven't met before but there's something about you that is…' He stopped and shook his head. 'You're familiar to me. So much so that it felt completely natural to invite you to share a meal with me, especially when we've only just met.'

'You…ah…don't usually…' She stopped, realising her breathing was starting to increase and that she didn't want him to question why his words had flustered her. Clearing her throat, she worked hard to get her heart rate back to normal because when Arthur looked at her the way he was now, with that intriguing gorgeousness, it was almost impossible for her to not blurt out the truth.

She had to confess that she'd felt that same tug of awareness he was talking about, but she had the advantage over him as she knew exactly why she was feeling that way. Surely if she told Arthur the truth, he would understand. Yes, her case workers had assured her she was out of danger, so what would be the harm in telling him? She didn't have to lie about her true identity in order to protect him, but after years of keeping herself to herself, it was difficult for her to open up and share such an intimate confession…even with someone like Arthur, the first boy she'd ever trusted.

Her main problem now was that he was still staring at her, and very soon it was possible she'd forget all rational thought and throw herself across the table into his arms. The thrumming of her heart reverberated around her body and she found it nigh on impossible to look away from his compelling stare.

'Arthur… I…' An unexpected yapping at her heels startled her and she quickly shifted in her chair to see a gorgeous Pomeranian dog sniffing around her feet. 'Hello!' Maybelle glanced at Arthur but rested her gaze somewhere around his throat, unable to completely meet his eyes after such an intense moment. Her heart rate started to settle as she looked down at the pooch. 'I didn't realise you had a dog.'

'I don't.'

'Uh…' Maybelle put a hand down so the dog could sniff her and when the cute little thing nudged and licked her hand, Maybelle patted the soft fur. 'Then I'm clearly imagining things.' She smiled as the dog continued to lick her hand. 'What's your name, sweetie?' she asked the dog, unable to believe the complete delight she felt at the total acceptance from the animal. There was no judgement here, no need to worry about what her name used to be or what it was now. The adorable dog just accepted her and Maybelle's heart swelled with delight.

'That's Fuzzy-Juzzy. Technically, she belongs to my sister.'

'Your sister? Your sister lives here?' Maybelle's eyes widened in astonishment, her gaze meeting Arthur's. Clara was here? Her mouth went dry at the thought. She was sixty-five percent sure she could convince Arthur they'd never met but Clara was a different story. Clara had been Maybelle's first and only best friend. Their mothers had been pregnant at the same time, with Clara being born two days before Maybelle. They'd been as close to twins as two girls could be, even to pricking their fingers and mixing their blood, proclaiming themselves to be soul sisters.

'No. She's overseas. She told me she'd be gone for six months and would I mind her dog.' As he spoke, he stood and came around the table and picked up Fuzzy-Juzzy, who was eyeing Maybelle's unfinished dinner with relish. 'That was two and a half years ago, so I guess in some ways Juzzy is mine as well.' He patted the dog. 'And you've had your dinner, Ms Juzzy.' He carried the dog from the room, giving Maybelle a moment to close her eyes and find some level of composure.

'That was close,' she whispered. Hearing that Clara was out of the country allowed Maybelle to breathe more easily. At least she didn't have to face that hurdle straight away. She opened her eyes, knowing the best thing she could do right now was to leave Arthur's apartment and return to her own. Tomorrow she would buy groceries and find out the best take-away places in the area so there would be no need for her to bother her neighbour again. She ate two more mouthfuls of the yummy food before carrying both plates to the kitchen.

It was there she found Arthur, scooping another spoonful of the goulash into Juzzy's food bowl and putting it down in the laundry, which was where the dog had obviously been eating when Maybelle had arrived.

She chuckled at the sight. 'Clearly Juzzy's used her feminine wiles on you. Clever dog. I guess it shows you really are a big softy at heart, aren't you, Dr Lewis.' The question was rhetorical but seeing the way he obviously cared for the dog warmed her. It appeared Arthur Lewis was the same in essentials as he'd been all those years ago. Thoughtful, caring and giving. It was a comforting thought.

He straightened as though he didn't like being caught in the act. 'She was whining.' His tone was a little gruff.

Maybelle laughed. 'I think it was more like she looked at you with those big brown puppy eyes of hers and you capitulated.'

He looked at the dog for a split second then shrugged his shoulders, conceding defeat on the matter. 'Or that.' Arthur put the kettle on. 'Coffee? Tea? Another glass of wine?' He wished she hadn't laughed like that. The tinkling sound had filled his apartment with vibrant colour, something he hadn't realised had been missing until that very moment. What was it about this woman that seemed so natural, so normal, so incredibly familiar?

Why did he find Maybelle Freebourne so compelling? Was it her blonde curls? Her rich brown eyes? The gorgeous smile that was still hovering on her perfectly shaped lips? Lips that, for some odd reason, he suddenly wanted to taste. He swallowed over the thought and dismissed it. They were colleagues and although he was intrigued, he also needed to keep things professional.

There was no doubt she was an excellent doctor, which she had proved most readily today with her patient, Mr

Bird, but he'd also noted that she'd held herself aloof from other members of staff. Of course, with it being her first day on the job, she might want to find her feet when it came to social interaction with colleagues but the ED team was a close-knit one and he didn't want her disrupting that camaraderie with her reticence at joining in.

That close-knit atmosphere was something he'd taken time to nurture since his appointment to Director eleven months ago. The team was often called upon to work in excessively stressful situations, and knowing there was a level of trust in those types of situations was vitally important.

'Thanks but I'd better go. Dinner was absolutely delicious but I think I've imposed on you enough for one night.' She jerked a thumb towards his front door as she spoke.

Arthur wasn't sure why but he didn't want her to go. He'd enjoyed her company during dinner—a meal he either ate alone or with a heap of journal articles in front of him so he could catch up on his reading whilst eating.

'Actually, there's something I wanted to show you first.' Thinking about the journal articles had reminded him that he'd read one a few nights ago on food allergies and how to identify them in an emergency situation.

'Can you…uh…show me at work tomorrow?'

Didn't she want to stay? Why was it she seemed cagey and eager to leave? In fact, there had been several times when he'd noted his new neighbour to be a little jittery. Was that normal for her? Was she trying to leave his apartment because she found him boring? If that was the case, why on earth was he trying so hard to get her to stay?

'Is my company that bad?' The words burst from his

mouth before he could stop them. She raised an eyebrow, clearly surprised.

'No. No. Not at all. I've enjoyed a lovely, home-cooked meal with *good* company.' Her words were almost over-polite. 'I simply didn't want to impose any further.' Maybelle stood with her back close to the wall, as though she didn't trust him.

'It's no imposition, Maybelle.' He watched her for another moment, noticing how she was starting to edge towards the hallway. If she didn't want to stay, he couldn't make her. 'I was reading an article about food allergies. I'd like your opinion on it.'

'Thinking of writing up Mr Bird's condition for a publication?' she queried as he headed into his bedroom. Arthur tried to quickly locate the article from the stack of medical journals on his bedside table.

'That's a possibility,' he returned, raising his voice so she could hear him. 'Perhaps we could co-author the paper, given that you were the one to discover Mr Bird's allergy in the first place.'

'And as you're the director of the ED, would that mean you'd take lead on the article?' she called back.

He paused for a second and analysed her words. Had that happened to her before? She'd done all the work and someone else had taken the credit? 'If *I* did more research and provided more information for the paper, then it would follow that my name would be lead on the article.' Where was that journal he wanted? He had the feeling that if he took too long, Maybelle would simply let herself out of his apartment and right now, he had to admit, it was great to be able to discuss a mutual topic of interest after dinner.

There was also the possibility he wanted her to stay and chat for a while so he could figure out just where he'd met her before. The few times he'd been caught staring at her, it had been as though his subconscious had been incredibly close to unlocking the memory. Perhaps they'd met years ago at a medical conference overseas. Or sat next to each other at a fundraising dinner...although if that had been the case, he was sure he would have remembered such a stunningly beautiful woman as Maybelle Freebourne.

'Do you read the *Journal*?' he called as he threw the stack of journals onto the messy bed in an effort to expedite his search. He didn't receive a reply to his question. 'Or do you prefer a different medical publication?' Still silence. He flicked through another copy of the *Journal* and finally found the article. There was no answer to his question and he half expected to find her gone when he returned to the lounge room. That, however, wasn't the case.

Instead, he found Maybelle standing at the mantelpiece next to the unlit fireplace. In her hand was a photograph of Arthur's sister Clara and her best friend. The photo had been taken at the joint sixteenth birthday party for the two girls.

'That's my sister, Clara.' Clearly Maybelle hadn't heard him walk back into the room and she spun around, her face so white it was as though she'd seen a ghost. Did Maybelle think he was mad at her for touching the pictures? 'That's not how she looks now, of course. She's a grown-up...or so she tells me, but she has such a crazy sense of humour that oftentimes I do tend to wonder.'

Arthur put the *Journal* onto the arm of the lounge and went to stand next to Maybelle. Was it his imagination or did she take a slight step away from him? 'This photograph,' he continued as he took another one off the mantel, 'was taken not long after Clara graduated from

medical school. That's my parents and myself and Clara.'
He held it out for her to look at and belatedly realised,
when Maybelle lifted her gaze away from the picture of
the two girls, that her eyes were brimming with tears.

'Maybelle? What's wrong?' Arthur put out a hand on
her shoulder but she immediately flinched and backed
away.

'Uh…' She sniffed and blindly shoved the photograph
she'd been holding in his direction. He didn't grab it in
time before she let it go, the frame falling to land on the
soft carpet. 'I can't.' She was breathing fast and shaking her head as she continued to back away. There was
a mixture of emotion in her eyes—surprise, trepidation,
confusion mixed with a large dose of fear. 'I can't do this.'
The words were barely audible before she turned and almost sprinted to the front door. Within another moment
she was out and gone.

Arthur headed to the door after her, absolutely stunned
at what had just transpired. What was going on? There
was so much about Maybelle Freebourne that made no
sense. He looked out the open front door, only to hear
the door to the apartment above him close.

He shut his own door then looked down at the photograph he still held in his hand. His parents, his sister
and himself, standing in front of their old family home.
What had spooked her about that photo? Returning to the
lounge room, he picked up the photograph she'd dropped
and sat down on the lounge to study it further.

Where he'd previously thought his new colleague was
something of an enigma, he now realised he didn't know
the half of it. What on earth had upset her? She'd been
staring at the photograph of his sister and her friend,
and she'd been crying. Why? And why had she said she
couldn't do this? What on earth was that supposed to

mean? She couldn't socialise with her neighbours? She couldn't be friends with him outside the hospital? Perhaps looking at his family photographs had made her realise she was standing in her work colleague's apartment and that the lines of personal and professional shouldn't be crossed? What? What had happened? What had she been thinking? His mind whirred in a never-ending circle as he stared at the photographs before him.

There was the one of his family and then one of Clara and her childhood friend, May Fleming. Clara had dark brown curly hair, the curls bouncing on her shoulders in a haphazard mess, her brown eyes smiling happily. May, on the other hand, had long, straight strawberry-blonde hair with pale blue eyes. Like chalk and cheese. The two girls had been friends all their lives then, about two months after that photo had been taken, May and her parents had left the neighbourhood without a word to anyone. The house next door where they'd lived had been sold and they'd never heard from them again.

None of this reflection gave him any indication as to why Maybelle had been so distraught over the photograph. Perhaps she knew May Fleming? Had she recognised Clara's friend who had disappeared without a trace? That had to be it, or something like it, and from the way Maybelle had reacted when she'd seen the photograph, things hadn't ended well for young May.

That thought alone made him feel sick to his stomach. Poor May. Being only two years older than Clara, he'd grown up with May around all the time. She'd been like another little annoying sister to him...until the evening that photograph had been taken.

Arthur put his head back and closed his eyes. May. Young, gorgeous and quietly sassy. He'd known she'd had a crush on him and that night, with everyone else enjoying the outdoor sweet-sixteen party in his parents' backyard, he'd gone against his better judgement and let her kiss him. Pushing a hand through his hair, he exhaled harshly and closed the door on the memory because not only had he let her kiss him…he'd kissed her back.

Although it wasn't too late, he had an early start in the morning and decided to get a bit of reading done after he'd tucked Fuzzy-Juzzy in her bed. It wouldn't be too much longer until Clara was back to claim her pooch but after living with the dog, Arthur had to admit he liked having Juzzy around for company. To come home to an apartment where there was no one to greet him seemed foreign now yet when Clara had begged him to take the dog all those years ago, it had been difficult to adjust to having someone around.

Sitting in his bed, he settled down to re-read the article about food allergies he'd been wanting to show Maybelle. Now, having experienced first-hand how an allergy to garlic could have drastic consequences for a patient, he read the piece with new interest. Perhaps he and Maybelle *could* investigate this further and write a paper together. He smiled at the thought. It would definitely give him time to figure out just where he knew her from. She'd obviously made an impression on him but clearly the same couldn't be said for her as she kept stating she didn't know him.

Still, he couldn't shake the feeling that she was hiding something. He made a mental note to review her job application in the morning, hoping to find some clue as to why she tended to be jittery and emotional.

I can't do this. The words she'd uttered before she'd bolted from his apartment reverberated around his mind. He closed his eyes, recalling the fear in her eyes, as though she was positive he'd already stumbled onto her secret. What secret? What was she trying to hide?

The ringing of his phone startled him from his deep thoughts and after checking the caller ID, he breathed a sigh of relief and connected the call. 'Hi, sis. How's life in the northern hemisphere?'

'Fair to middling,' Clara stated. 'Have you spoken to Mum today?'

'Not today. I spoke to Dad on the weekend.'

'Off to Italy for a holiday! Oh, the life of the retired.'

'They deserve it.'

They chatted about Clara's week before his sister asked after her dog. 'How's Juzzy? I miss her so much.'

'Then come home.' Arthur missed his sister. As it had been only the two of them growing up, whilst they'd most definitely fought and had their moments where they'd hated each other, as adults they were actually good friends. 'You said six months!'

'Yeah, I know. Sorry about that, bro.'

Arthur could hear the sadness in his sister's voice. He knew why she'd left in such a hurry and he'd hoped she was now over her broken heart. He'd sworn that if he ever saw the man who had caused Clara such distress, he'd punch him in the nose—and he was not a man prone to violence. Not only that but shortly after the relationship had ended, Clara had been in a terrible accident. Once her physical injuries had healed, she'd headed overseas with the hope of escaping her past and making new, happy memories. He needed to keep their conversation light so he chatted more about the dog. 'At any rate, Juzzy certainly likes my beef goulash.'

'You're going to make her fat, Arthur.' Clara's tone lightened as she laughed.

'So how's the life of a hectic country GP this week?'

'Hectic,' Clara replied. 'Clinics, emergencies and absolutely no respect for office hours. I'm the county doctor, which means my time and my life are not my own, they clearly belong to the village and surrounding districts.'

'So come home.'

'I said I was going to and I will.' There was still hesitation there. 'I got the email you sent about that new specialist centre opening up as part of Victory Hospital. Do you really think I'm right for the position of GP in such a busy practice?'

'Most definitely. There will be state-of-the-art equipment and the practice will be intimate yet busy enough for a workaholic like you and the fact that you did your training at the Victory and know a lot of the staff is definitely a bonus.'

'Do you know, I was just saying to my friend Imogen the other day that…' As he listened to his sister talk, Arthur's thoughts once more turned to the way Maybelle had reacted to the photographs. One of him and his family, one of Clara and May. It didn't matter how many times he'd told himself *not* to think about it, he didn't seem able to stop.

'What's wrong, Arthur?'

'Huh?'

'You're ignoring me. You only ignore me when you're completely preoccupied by something else.'

'That's not the *only* time I ignore you,' he joked.

'Very funny,' she replied drolly. 'Spit it out.'

'I don't know.' He paused, knowing this was going to sound completely strange to his sister. 'I was, uh… I was thinking about May Fleming this evening.'

'May? Wow. That's a blast from the past. Why were you thinking about her?' Clara's tone indicated she was genuinely interested, so he told his sister everything about his new colleague and neighbour, and how he'd asked her in for dinner. He told her about Maybelle's reaction to the photograph on the mantel. When he'd finished, there was silence on the other end.

'Clara? What do you think?'

'It *is* odd. Why would she drop the photo like that? And be so upset?'

'Right.' He was glad his sister thought the same way as him.

'Do you think she knew May?'

'That's the only thing that makes any sense. Do you remember anyone called Maybelle Freebourne?'

'Name doesn't ring a bell but perhaps she knew May after we did.'

Arthur paused for a moment and frowned. 'Doesn't it strike you as odd the way the Flemings just upped and left like that? Never to be heard from again?'

'I heard from May,' Clara stated.

His sister's words completely stunned him. 'What? When?'

'She wrote to me. About a month after they left. She said that her father had received a promotion overseas with his work and it had started immediately.'

'She wrote to you! You never told me that.'

'Yeah. She also sent me birthday cards for a few years but then they stopped.'

'Was there ever a return address?'

'No.'

'So you had no way of contacting her?'

'No, but in the last birthday card she sent she wrote that she hoped one day we could meet again and that I would forgive her.'

'For what?'

'For leaving, I guess.'

'Why didn't I know any of this?'

'Because every time I even mentioned May's name in passing you'd bite my head off, just like you are now!'

Arthur leaned his head back on the pillows and closed his eyes, slowly exhaling. 'Sorry, sis.'

'Go to sleep, bro. It sounds like you need it. Clear your head and tackle the problem fresh tomorrow.'

'Can you at least try to remember if you know someone called Maybelle Freebourne?'

'This woman's really got you in a spin, hasn't she?' Clara chuckled. 'You like her.'

'Stop it.'

'It's about time you got back in the game, bro.'

'You can talk.' There was no way he was discussing his love life, or lack thereof, with his sister. But she did have a point.

'Yeah, we're both hopeless cases. Anyway, I've got to go. Patients are starting to arrive for clinic. I'll talk to you soon.'

Arthur said goodbye to his sister then tried to control his thoughts by reading, but after reading the same sentence fifteen times he closed the publication and shook his head. He simply couldn't stop thinking about Maybelle's reaction to that photo. Something very odd was going on and he didn't like unsolved mysteries.

May's disappearance was an unsolved mystery. He could see it all so clearly in his mind, himself and May, standing beneath the foliage at the end of the garden, twinkle lights creating a festive environment. There had been so many people there—a joint sixteenth birthday party—that May had assured him no one would miss them.

'I just need to talk to you for a minute or two,' she'd told him, taking his hand and leading him to the end of the garden. Arthur had looked around to see who might be watching them but they'd escaped unseen.

'I'm not sure we should be—' he'd begun, but she'd pulled him further into the foliage and then pressed a finger to his lips to silence him.

'I have a very special birthday wish, Arthur, one only you can fulfil.' And before he'd been able to say anything else, she'd stood on tiptoe and replaced her finger with her mouth. Her lips had been trembling, tasting of sugary desire with a hint of sweet desperation. He'd known she'd had a crush on him and he'd been flattered. Then she'd kissed him, and he should have put his hands on her shoulders and gently eased her back...but he hadn't.

In that one moment, he'd become intoxicated by her... and had kissed her back. He'd had to force himself to take his time, to be gentle and not rush into a hard and hungry kiss, which was exactly what he'd wanted to do. He'd cupped her face with his hands and cherished her mouth, delighting in every response she gave him. When he'd pulled back, both of them breathless, he'd looked into her eyes and would never forget the mixture of surprise, trepidation, confusion and the smallest hint of fear he'd seen there.

Surprise. Trepidation. Confusion.

Surprise, trepidation, confusion...and fear! That was exactly how Maybelle had looked at him that evening.

Arthur sat bolt upright in bed, belatedly realising he'd been dreaming. His heart was thumping erratically against his chest as he held onto that last thought.

Surprise, trepidation, confusion and fear. Maybelle had looked at him in exactly the same way May had looked at him all those years ago, although Maybelle's ratio of fear had been much greater. It didn't matter that her eye colour was different—it was the *look*.

His eyes widened as his brain seemed to be reaching far-fetched connections. May and Maybelle. Maybelle and May. May*belle*. His beautiful May!

He'd known there was something familiar about Maybelle Freebourne…but was it possible? Was it true? Were Maybelle and May one and the same?

CHAPTER FOUR

MAYBELLE WAS AT work early the following morning. What was the point of lying in her bed, marking time, when she could be doing something useful? As it turned out, when she arrived just after five o'clock, the ED was packed and the night staff were grateful for her help.

She'd spent half the night with her thoughts tumbling one over the other as she'd tried to figure out what she should do. Should she cut and run right now? Leave Victory Hospital and get a job somewhere else? Or work at the hospital but find a new place to live? That was the problem with being in witness protection, she was so used to change it was second nature to her, yet she wasn't used to settling down. There was no permanence, no ability to remain in one place because as soon as a threat came, their entire family had been uprooted and moved yet again.

The big question was, if she stayed, would she be able to work alongside Arthur and still maintain her equilibrium? She'd certainly failed last night but if she kept her professional mask in place whilst at work and avoided him when at home, then surely she'd be able to see out her twelve-month contract. Besides, she really wanted to work at this hospital. It was nostalgic and with the recent death of her father it was helping her to focus on

happier times. Should she let a little thing like a past relationship with the man who had been like a big brother
to her get in the way?

Arthur was far more than a big brother, her heart
stated, but she pushed the thought away. She couldn't
think of him in such a way because if she did, it would
derail everything she was trying to do. Romantic entanglements were the last thing she needed when trying to
carve a new life for herself.

With new determination, she continued on with her
work, treating her patients and saving lives. When the
handover from the night shift to the day shift had finished, Maybelle could feel her anxiety starting to rise.
Arthur would be here soon. He'd probably want to talk
to her, demand an explanation, and she wasn't sure she
wanted to give him one. Lying to people wasn't something she enjoyed and in the past she'd had to lie in order
to protect herself and her parents.

'Except the threat is over,' she reminded herself softly.
That only made things worse because now she was lying
to protect herself only. Maybelle eased back and looked
at the ceiling, trying to figure out how her life had become so incredibly complicated in such a short space of
time. She heard a sound behind her and spun around so
fast in her chair she almost gave herself whiplash. Was
it Arthur? She held her breath as she came face to face
with Gemma.

'Morning.' Gemma looked bleary-eyed and half-
asleep. 'Need coffee,' she mumbled and headed off to
the kitchenette. Maybelle continued with her work until
the next little noise startled her. It was ridiculous because
with every little sound her heart rate would increase and
then decrease when she discovered it wasn't him. Where
was he? Wasn't he rostered on today? She'd simply pre-

sumed that, as Director, he'd be around during the day but she didn't see him until the afternoon.

Eight-year-old twin girls had been brought in by ambulance, one suffering from abdominal pains and the other having sympathy pains.

'It's worse for me,' Evie told her twin, who was clutching her abdomen in pain. 'There's nothing wrong with you, Lizzy.'

'But it hurts!' Lizzy's tone was filled with anguish.

'Lizzy does have a temperature,' Cici reported as she finished doing Lizzy's observations.

'Evie's abdomen is excessively tender,' Maybelle said after she'd palpated the girl's stomach. The anxious parents were waiting in the corner of the room, both looking whiter than their girls.

'They were premature,' their mother stated. 'They were in the children's hospital in Melbourne for the first three months of their lives and any time either one of them is sick, I tend to crumble.'

'When both of them are sick, like this, it takes us back to that time when they were so small and unwell,' their father added, doing his best to reassure his wife.

'I'd like to scan the abdominal area of both girls, as pain can manifest itself in different ways. We'll give them both some pain relief because even psychological pain can be quite debilitating,' Maybelle told the parents.

'This isn't the first time something like this has happened,' their father added. 'When Lizzy was four, she sprained her wrist and Evie was the one in pain.'

'We just like doing things together,' Evie clarified, listening to the entire conversation while her sister sweated and moaned with pain. Cici was trying to sponge the girl down, needing to break the temperature.

'Let's get some analgesics into them and then we can

run some tests.' Maybelle wrote up the notes for the required medication.

'What could it be?' The mother's anxiety was starting to rise. 'What's wrong with them?'

'I won't be one hundred percent sure until I have the results from the ultrasound,' Maybelle said. 'But possibly appendicitis.'

Lizzy moaned at this news. 'Appendix. Is that scary?'

Maybelle smiled and headed to Lizzy's side while Cici did Evie's observations again. 'A lot of things are scary when you come to hospital,' she told a very concerned Lizzy. 'In fact, when I was about your age, I was admitted to this same emergency department with appendicitis.'

'Were you?' The question came from a deep voice behind her. Maybelle knew that voice far too well and she quickly looked over her shoulder to see Arthur standing just inside the curtain, listening to what was going on. 'You came to Victory Hospital to have your appendix out?' he continued, shaking hands with both the parents and quickly introducing himself. He scanned Evie's and Lizzy's charts just as quickly and as thoroughly as he scanned Maybelle's face. Did he think she was lying? That she was offering a false story in order to keep the girls nice and calm?

'That's a coincidence. I had a friend who had her appendix out at this hospital when she was eight years old as well,' he said, then waggled his eyebrows at Evie. 'Clearly you've come to the right hospital because we know how to deal with appendicitis.' He checked both girls and confirmed the assessment. After Maybelle had administered the analgesics, the girls were wheeled to Radiology for their ultrasounds.

How could he have remembered she'd had appendicitis as a child? He hadn't even visited her in hospital, although Clara had been there every day after school. Perhaps it wasn't her he was talking about. Perhaps he'd had another friend who'd had their appendix out when they were eight. That was a definite possibility. Wasn't it?

Now all she needed to do was to keep her distance from Arthur. He was at the nurses' station, chatting with Gemma about something, but she could have sworn he'd glanced in her direction several times. It was odd how she could almost feel his gaze on her, checking to see where she was, as though he was about to confront her, about to reveal her secret in front of everyone, to strip her defences bare.

When he'd finished talking to Gemma he headed down the corridor to his office and Maybelle breathed a sigh of relief. Given how she'd left his apartment last night, she was feeling more jittery than normal and tried hard to control her rising anxiety.

'Any more patients I need to see?' she asked Gemma. She needed to be doing something, anything.

'I think we're good right at the moment. Why don't you go and have a cuppa?'

Maybelle shook her head. The prospect of bumping into Arthur in the kitchenette was too high. 'I'm good. Is there anything else I can help you with?'

Gemma gave her a quizzical look, but then shrugged and handed her an inventory list on a clipboard. 'Some of the treatment rooms are running low on stock. I was going to go and get it later—'

Before Gemma had finished speaking Maybelle had taken the clipboard from her.

'Glad to help.'

'OK.' Gemma was clearly surprised at a doctor volunteering to do a task usually performed by orderlies, nursing or clerical staff. 'There's a stock trolley just over there. If you can get everything on the list, then I'll get Cici to re-stock the rooms when she has a moment.'

Maybelle nodded before heading off to collect the stock trolley. The stockroom was most definitely a good place to hide from Arthur, plus she'd be helping Gemma.

'You just need to keep out of his way,' she mumbled to herself as she tried three times to swipe her pass card through the sensor. Finally, the door opened and she headed into the small room with the stock trolley and list of required items. The door clicked shut behind her and she breathed a sigh of relief. A reprieve…for now, but she couldn't spend the next twelve months running away and hiding from Arthur.

As she started to find the contents of the list and arrange them on the stock trolley, Maybelle's thoughts began to churn. How on earth was she supposed to keep her distance from him when he seemed to be near her at every turn? At work. At home. Perhaps finding somewhere different to live would be the best option. That seemed good. At least then she'd be able to have some time to relax and not be on constant 'Arthur' alert.

She didn't want to leave the hospital as she felt in her heart that this was where she was meant to be. Surely she could work alongside Arthur without him discovering the truth? If she simply kept denying they knew each other, he'd let the subject drop…wouldn't he? And, besides, what was the worst that could happen? What if he *did* discover who she really was? It wasn't as though her life was still in danger.

'Work through the scenario,' she told herself as she continued pulling supplies off the shelves and adding them to the trolley. 'If he finds out, then you simply tell him the basic details of the matter and notify the case worker that Arthur knows the truth.' She continued to take calm, reassuring breaths.

Besides, even though she'd made a bit of a mess of things last night, Arthur probably thought she was some sort of crazy woman and hadn't given it another thought. Perhaps all he cared about was her doing her job so he could keep the ED running smoothly. Wasn't that what was important?

When she'd finished filling the trolley, she tried to open the door but found it locked. There was a swipe access panel next to the door and she belatedly realised she needed to swipe her card to get in and out of the room. She swiped her pass card but the door didn't open. She tried again several times but the door remained firmly locked.

'Seriously?' she grumbled as she pulled her cellphone from her pocket but after a moment realised there was no cellphone reception in the small room. Frustrated and annoyed, Maybelle accepted there was nothing else she could do except wait. At least Gemma knew where she was and when someone finally said, 'Where's Maybelle?' they would come looking for her.

While she waited, Maybelle tidied the already tidy shelves simply because she needed something to do. She wasn't the type of person who was good at sitting and waiting, but once the shelves were as neat as they could possibly be there was nothing else for her to do except wait and try swiping her access card every thirty seconds.

She was almost at the point of complete and utter boredom when the sound of the door clicking open made her heart jump for joy. It then skipped a beat altogether when Arthur came into the room.

'Sorry it took me so long to realise you were missing,' he remarked.

'It's only been…' She checked her watch, more for something to do than actually checking the time because in actual fact she knew exactly how long she'd been waiting to be rescued. 'Twenty-two minutes.' Maybelle grabbed the end of the supply trolley and went to wheel it out, only then realising that Arthur had shut the door behind him, effectively locking them both in.

'Why did you shut the—?'

'I didn't mean just now,' he interrupted.

There was something in his tone that forced her to lift her gaze to meet his, rising anxiety starting to pulse through her veins.

'Er…well…erm…what do you mean?'

'You've been missing for twenty years…May.'

'Uh…' She forced a tight-lipped smile and shook her head. He'd figured it out and there was nowhere for her to run and hide. How had he figured it out? What should she say to him? She decided the best course of action was to maintain her cover story. 'It's Maybelle.'

'Why did you run out of my apartment last night?' Straight to the point. That was so like him.

'I don't think this is the right place to discuss such a topic,' she said, standing opposite him, both of them with their backs to supply shelves. He was dressed in trousers, white shirt, college tie and his usual white doctor's coat. His hair was a little mussed, as though he'd been raking his hands through the soft locks in frustration or agitation. His grey eyes were looking at her with such intensity that she was positive her heart skipped a beat. Good heavens, did the man realise just how utterly gorgeous he was?

'I think it's the perfect place because there's no escaping.' He paused for a moment as though trying to collect his thoughts. 'Even if I've got this wrong, I just need you to hear me out. Please?'

At her hesitant nod, he began. 'Ever since you walked into the ED yesterday morning, there's been something niggling in the back of my mind. You're so incredibly familiar to me, Maybelle, and then last night…watching you eat and the way you smiled when you cuddled Juzzy and how your eyes widened when I spoke about Clara and then seeing you so upset when you were looking at that photograph…' Arthur raked both hands through his hair, an action she'd seen him do several times when he'd been exasperated. 'Who are you?'

'Maybelle Freebourne.' Her words were soft.

'Why did you cry when you saw that photo? If you're not May Fleming then you at least must know her. What happened to her?'

'What makes you think—?'

'Just stop.' He held up both hands. 'I'm not going crazy. You know something, and for some far-fetched reason you can't tell me. Are you being threatened? Are you unsafe?'

'Arthur…' She paused, trying to think of what to say next.

'Even the way you say my name, especially like that, is familiar. I know you…and I also know there's only one way to prove my hypothesis.'

With that, he took a step towards her. What was he doing? Was he going to…to kiss her?

Maybelle immediately put up her hands to protect herself but all that did was make them come into contact with his shirt-covered chest. Her fingers tingled with heat, a heat that spread up her arms and flooded her entire body. How was it that this man could affect her in such a way? That he could make her heart race, take her breath away? Cause her to be filled with need and desire and all with a simple glance?

When he raised a hand to cup her cheek she gasped with repressed need. 'Wait.' The word was a whisper. 'Wh-what are you doing?' Her tongue came out to lick her dry lips and she watched as he watched the action, his Adam's apple sliding up and down his smooth throat as he swallowed.

'I'm going to kiss you.'

At the soft, deep words Maybelle's entire body was ignited into a frenzy of longing, one she hadn't felt in a very long time.

'Why?'

He was very close now, his head already starting to dip towards her own, his gaze flicking between her eyes and her lips but lingering on the latter as though he needed this just as much as she did. 'Because it's the only way to be completely sure you are who I think you are.'

She opened her mouth to ask another question but instead had her lips captured by his, her breath catching in the moment. There was definitely no denying anything now because, as her eyes closed, it was as though she was transported back to the moment of their first kiss…in the backyard of his parents' house at her sixteenth birthday party. Back then, she'd been determined to seize the moment, to let Arthur know that she didn't think of him as a big brother any more but rather as someone who had stolen her teenage heart.

To her utter astonishment and complete delight, he had kissed her back. Kissed her tenderly, testing and teasing, just as he was doing now. How was it possible that his scent was still so intoxicating? Or that the taste of him was exactly the same, except with more knowledge and experience in the background?

When he eased back, they both exhaled, their breaths mingling. She stood with her eyes closed, trying to grasp the magnitude of what had just happened. Not only was it now impossible to deny exactly who she was, but worse than that was the realisation that whatever had been brewing between herself and Arthur two decades ago still lingered in the far recesses of their minds and bodies.

He slid his fingers down from her cheek to cup her chin, his thumb brushing lightly over her still-parted lips. 'May?' Her real name was a question on his lips. 'It's you.'

Maybelle looked at him from beneath hooded lids. 'Yeah.'

'What…? How?' He dropped his hand and took a step back, shoving both his hands into his trouser pockets. 'Why are you called Maybelle?'

She exhaled slowly, trying to get her breathing to return to normal so she could make some sort of attempt to explain the past two decades in the simplest way possible. Even then, she had no doubt he'd want to know the ins and outs of exactly what had transpired. She knew she would, if the positions were reversed.

'When we left—'

'When you and your parents vanished without even a simple goodbye,' he interrupted, a hint of old annoyance in his tone.

'We were put into witness protection.' The words seemed to tumble out of her mouth in a rush.

He was silent for a moment as he processed this information. 'OK.'

'OK?'

'OK.' He shrugged. 'Clearly something bad had happened and it was necessary to protect your family from harm and it explains your sudden disappearance without a word of warning.' He nodded again. 'OK.'

'Just like that? You accept what I'm saying?'

'After that kiss, there's no reason for you to lie to me.'

'I…guess not.'

'So your name is Maybelle now?'

She was still trying to process the fact that Arthur had simply accepted her explanation with no other questions or repercussions. Where were the twenty questions? The need to understand the details of exactly what had happened with her parents, of the threat they'd all lived under for far too long? 'Yes. It's as close as I could get to my real name.'

'And Freebourne?'

'I chose Freebourne because, technically, I'm free from the threat.'

'You've been reborn?'

She smiled as he pulled out his pass card and swiped it through the access panel, the door clicking open on the first try.

'Something like that.' He was holding the door open and grabbing hold of the stocked trolley before Maybelle held up her hand to stop him. 'Wait a second.'

'What?'

'That's it? That's the extent of the explanation you need to let you know that you're not crazy? That I'm the same person you grew up with? The person who vanished from your life without a trace?' Especially after what had happened between them the final night before she'd left?

'A lot of things finally make sense,' he said with a shrug of his shoulders. 'May…belle.' This time when he spoke her name his gaze rested momentarily on her lips before he smiled. 'It suits you. A sort of grown-up version of May…and you've definitely grown up.' He winked at her then, just like he had in the past, just like he had yesterday when he'd been teasing her, but this time, the wink was filled with a double entendre. Then he turned on his heel and wheeled the trolley from the supply room, leaving a stunned Maybelle to follow him.

She'd been so used to playing her cards close to her chest, not confiding anything about her true identity to anyone, and now that she had, Maybelle couldn't help but experience a sense of anticlimactic confusion. She was happy Arthur had believed her so readily, that after their shared kiss he knew there was no way she could lie to him.

Perhaps this new life of hers wasn't going to be as difficult as she'd originally thought…except, of course, for the fact that her attraction to Arthur was most definitely still there after all these years. What she was going to do about that, she had no clue. No clue whatsoever.

CHAPTER FIVE

NOW THAT SHE wasn't hiding the truth from Arthur, Maybelle couldn't believe how free and giddy she felt. It was almost as though she were happily intoxicated because she didn't need to lie to him any more. Free. She felt free and freedom had been the one thing she'd been craving for years.

When the twins, Evie and Lizzy, returned from having their scans, Maybelle looked at the results on the computer screen. 'Evie definitely does have appendicitis,' she confirmed, explaining to the girls' parents what would happen next. Arthur was standing beside her as she spoke, which made her feel a little self-conscious. Yes, he was her boss and he had every right to monitor her when she spoke to parents and patients. However, this didn't feel like a test but more like a 'let's work together' type of thing...and Maybelle liked it.

'We've called the surgical registrars, who will be down very soon to take Evie to Theatre. They'll be the ones to go over the consent forms with you.'

'And Lizzy?' their mother asked.

'Lizzy is fine, just sympathy pains.'

'She's not faking it, you know.' The protective maternal tone was insistent.

'Oh, no. I completely agree and to that end I'll be prescribing some fast-acting analgesics to help take away Lizzy's pain until Evie's out of Theatre and on the mend. There have been a lot of research papers written about emotional pain transference with twins and sometimes with close siblings who aren't twins. I'd also like to admit Lizzy tonight because once Evie's out of Theatre, it will aid in Evie's recovery if Lizzy is close.'

'If everything progresses well,' Arthur added, 'the girls should be able to go home tomorrow afternoon or early the following morning.'

'That's right. Our ED clerk is organising beds for the girls in the ward but with the advances in technology and the means of removing the appendix via laparoscope, the surgery is much easier nowadays.'

'Better than when you had your appendix out?' the dozing Evie asked, rousing for a moment.

Maybelle smiled and placed a hand on Evie's forehead, brushing a few strands of hair out of the way. 'Much better,' she confirmed.

'And here's Felicity. She'll be the doctor looking after you,' Arthur said, introducing the surgical registrar to the girls and their parents. Once the handover was complete, the girls were transferred to the surgical ward, where their treatment would continue.

'Another satisfied customer,' Maybelle said, as she sat at the desk and started typing her notes onto the computer. Arthur looked at the list of patients waiting to be seen but kept glancing over at Maybelle. 'What is it?' she finally asked.

'Huh?'

'You keep looking at me as though you're—'

'Seeing a ghost?' he interrupted.

Maybelle glared at him. 'You said you didn't need any

explanations.' Her words were quiet and she looked around to make sure no one could overhear their conversation.

'It's not an explanation I'm after, per se, but...' Arthur leaned in closer and stared into her eyes. 'Why are your eyes brown? You used to have the bluest of blue eyes.'

'Contact lenses.' Maybelle tried to ease away because when he'd leaned closer to her she'd caught a breath of his hypnotic scent and found it difficult to look away from his own sexy eyes. He'd grown into an extremely handsome man and she was stunned he wasn't yet married. No sooner had the thought come than she voiced it. 'Why aren't you married?'

'I was. Now I'm divorced. Didn't work out and right now I'm more than happy to do the work and career thing.'

'Oh. I'm sorry it didn't work out for you.'

The corner of his lips twitched. 'Are you?'

Her heart skipped a beat when he looked at her like that and with his sexy scent still winding its way through her senses, causing a flood of awareness and desire, Maybelle slowly shook her head from side to side. 'As long as you're happy.'

'You, too.'

'I hope the two of you are discussing a patient.' Gemma's words interrupted their *tête-à-tête*. 'Because if you're not, there's some serious sexy stuff going on between you.'

Arthur's answer was to laugh, turning to face the clerk. 'You think there's serious sexy stuff going on between everyone.'

Gemma joined in the laughter. 'It's true. I do. What can I say?' She sighed longingly. 'I'm a hopeful romantic.'

Arthur left to go and see a patient and Maybelle

watched, confused by what had just happened. She had definitely been drawn in by him, staring intently into his eyes as he'd stared into hers. Like Gemma, she'd thought there'd been some serious sexy stuff going on but apparently not. Did Arthur flirt like that with all women? Was this just part of his natural charm? Something she'd misinterpreted? He had kissed her, though. Had she misinterpreted that? Had he been interested in kissing *her* or had it simply been a way for him to prove he wasn't going insane?

Was that why he wasn't that curious as to what had happened to her? Hadn't he just stated he was more focused on his career than romantic entanglements? She shook her head, more cross with herself than with him. She'd been so worried about him finding out about who she really was that she hadn't considered how he would treat her once his curiosity had been satisfied.

This was why she did her best not to get personally involved with the people she worked with. She didn't need to be contemplating such questions when she was at work. It was unprofessional and, more importantly, she didn't like herself for being weak and letting Arthur get under her skin so easily. They'd known each other in the past— so what? They'd shared some kisses and highly intimate moments—so what? They'd kissed, less than two hours ago, in the supply room and it had been…breath-taking, mind-boggling and heart-stopping—so what?

Gritting her teeth, she shoved all personal thoughts of Arthur Lewis to the back of her mind and concentrated on her job: treating patients and writing up her notes.

When her shift was over, Maybelle walked the five blocks back to her apartment, rugged up against Melbourne's cold weather but pleased it wasn't raining.

As she showered her day away, she resolved to only think of Arthur as an old family friend and a new colleague. Nothing more. Once she was dressed in her pyjamas, she sat down and made a list of all the things she still needed to purchase. At the moment she had the basics when it came to furniture, such as a table and four chairs, a bed, a wardrobe and a lounge suite. She would, however, like a microwave and a blender.

She also needed to lease a car. It was the most direct way of getting transport because right now she didn't have the time it took to purchase a good car. Maybelle was just looking up the number for a car leasing company when she heard a dog yapping outside her door. Intrigued, she opened her apartment door and, sure enough, there was Fuzzy-Juzzy sitting proudly. Behind her stood Arthur with a bag of take-away food in one hand and a bottle of wine in the other.

'Dinner?' he asked with a smile, and before she could reply, Juzzy ran past her into the apartment.

'Juzzy!' Maybelle called, and quickly chased after the dog. Spending another evening with Arthur hadn't been on her agenda so if she could quickly catch the dog, she could politely refuse him. 'Juzzy, come here.' The dog was sniffing her way around the apartment and just when Maybelle thought she had the pooch cornered, the dog would dart to another location.

Finally, Maybelle was able to pick the dog up but by the time she'd done that Arthur was in her kitchen, already dishing up the food. The dog was licking her and nuzzling with delight, clearly happy to be with her. So, it appeared, was Arthur.

'I'm starving. I hope you like Italian cuisine.' He placed the plates on the table with cutlery then hunted around the kitchen for a pair of wine glasses. Eventually, he pulled out two coffee mugs. 'No wine glasses, eh? Looks like you need to go shopping.' He tapped the list she'd made. 'I'm free on Saturday and so are you.'

'How do you know when I'm free?'

'Because I draw up the rosters. I'll come by around ten o'clock. It's always good to have a sleep-in when you can.'

Maybelle stood, still holding Juzzy and patting the dog, who was snuggling into her as though they were the oldest of friends. She shook her head. 'What are you doing, Arthur?'

'Pouring wine into coffee mugs,' he replied, before carrying the wine-filled mugs to the table.

'I mean what are you doing here, providing me with dinner—again?'

He looked at her for a long minute before shrugging. 'You need to eat and so do I. We've had a long day—'

'You have questions.' It was a statement and for some reason Maybelle was disappointed.

'Don't you? We've got twenty years of catching up to do.' Arthur pulled a clean dog bowl from one of the bags he'd brought in and opened a can of dog food for Juzzy. Sniffing, the dog scrambled to be free of Maybelle's arms and headed into the kitchen, where Arthur was most definitely making himself at home.

Once Juzzy was eating her dinner, Arthur walked behind Maybelle and held a chair for her, indicating she should sit down. Realising it was easier to accept than refuse his nice gesture, Maybelle sat down and waited until Arthur was seated.

'Thank you. For dinner, I mean.'

'Welcome.' He peered at her. 'You haven't taken your contacts out.'

'I don't usually do that until I go to bed. Besides, the contacts are also prescription so taking them out means finding my glasses and at the moment I think they're at the bottom of a packed box.'

'What happens when you wear the glasses out and people see that you have blue eyes instead of brown?'

'Simple. I don't wear my glasses out of the house. In fact, it's very rare I wear them at all.'

'But what if friends drop by unannounced?'

'And bring dinner and their dog with them?' Her words were pointed.

'Exactly.'

'I don't have friends who drop by.'

'Never?' Arthur started eating the delicious spaghetti Bolognese he'd brought.

'When you're in witness protection it's best if you don't make friends, at least not ones who feel comfortable enough to drop around unannounced.' She twirled a forkful of pasta before raising it to her lips and chewing, belatedly realising just how hungry she was. 'Mmm... This is delicious.'

'Good.' He was looking at her with a slight frown creasing his forehead, a hint of sadness in his eyes. To have spent years keeping herself distant from others, from not making any real friends...he couldn't fathom it. 'I've also brought you one of their take-away menus.'

'Thank you. That's so kind.' She gestured to the food. 'This is kind, too. You're still a kind man, Arthur.'

'Thank you. However, I think I've changed quite a bit in twenty years, as, clearly, have you.' He put down his fork and raised his coffee mug to her. 'A toast.' He waited while she followed suit. 'To learning more about who we are today.'

'Why? Why would you want to do that?' When she made no move to bring her cup towards his, he clinked his cup to hers and then drank, sealing the toast.

'Why would I want to get to know you?' Arthur seemed surprised at the question. 'Because you're family,' he stated, as though it was the only logical answer.

'Family?' She quickly lowered her cup to the table as a lump formed in her throat, the emotions of sadness and loss surprising her with their sudden appearance. 'I don't have family any more.' The words were out before she could stop them.

Arthur put his fork down and reached out to place his hand over hers. 'Your parents?'

The warmth of his touch, combined with the caring compassion in his tone, caused her to feel vulnerable. She shook her head, biting her lip in order to get the surge of sadness under control. 'Mum's been gone just over ten years now and Dad died four months ago.'

'Oh, Maybelle.' He shifted his chair around the small round table so he could be nearer to her. The next thing he did was to envelop her in his arms, drawing her closer. 'You're on your own? Is that why you've come back to this district? To a place where you felt comfortable?'

'Yes, exactly.' She'd forgotten what it was like to have someone comfort her and while she wanted to accept that comfort more than anything in the world, the ingrained training to keep her distance rose to the fore. She stiffened her spine, hoping to send the signal that she didn't like being touched in such a way, but either Arthur didn't pick up on it or ignored it completely. More than likely it was the latter. It reminded her that being in his arms, resting her head against his chest, feeling the heat from his body infuse into her own had made her feel so safe and secure. 'How could you possibly know that?'

'Because that's exactly what I would have done in your place.' Arthur watched as Maybelle tried to contain her emotions. It only took a minute and she was back under control. He couldn't imagine what she'd been through but the difference from the young teenage girl to this deeply controlled woman was vast. He dropped his arms and returned his attention to his food.

It was clear she didn't want to talk about things too much and he was fine with listening to whatever she wanted to share and curbing his curiosity about what she didn't want to say. Besides, his instinct to draw her into his arms, to offer comfort had been a huge mistake because now her fresh scent was lodged in his senses, enticing him to want more. The kiss they'd shared in the stockroom still lingered on his lips, begging him to repeat the action again and again.

Even at the nurses' station, when he'd been looking deeply into her brown eyes, the need to kiss her had been intense and he'd forced himself to walk away, to put some distance between himself and this woman... this woman who could turn his world upside down with one simple smile.

Maybelle Freebourne was even more dangerous to his thoughts than May Fleming had been. Back then, he'd been an adolescent intrigued and bewitched by her. Now he was a grown man with more life experience and more willpower, yet here she was, bewitching him all over again. She was as dangerous to his thoughts as ever. Since he'd kissed her, he hadn't been able to get her out of his mind. Like a moth to a flame, he'd ordered them dinner, using poor Juzzy as a diversion to gain access to her apartment. Desperate measures. That's what he'd employed. Desperate measures in order to spend more time with her, to be with her, to breathe her in, to see if that spark he'd felt when he'd kissed her in the stockroom had been real or residual.

'What *can* you tell me, about the witness protection, I

mean?' The question was necessary. He wanted to know and secretly hoped that she wanted to tell him, to open up to him, to share with him.

Maybelle ate another mouthful, chewing slowly as she considered his question. When she spoke, it was as though she was choosing her words very carefully. 'My parents were scientists,' she started.

'Yes. I remember them working long hours in the lab and often forgetting they even had a daughter. Wasn't that why you spent so much time at our house? Some weeks you were there for dinner every night.'

She smiled at the memory. 'Yes. They were a little absent-minded and back then it did bother me that we weren't a "normal" family.' She laughed without humour at the words. 'Anyway, remember how we sort of wondered if they'd cured cancer?'

'You mean they did?' Arthur was astonished. If that was what had happened, why wasn't her parents' discovery celebrated? Why had they needed to go into witness protection?

'No, or not that I know of. My dad's speciality was the human genome and my mother—'

'Was into synthetic compounds,' he finished.

'You remember?'

He fixed her with a look, one that said that she shouldn't underestimate his intelligence. 'I spent a lot of time with you over the years and especially in those last few months, May…belle.' She smiled at the way he'd connected her old name with her new name, and the action almost made him lose his train of thought, such was the power her smile still seemed to have over him. 'I remember what your parents did.'

'OK, then. Well, even though their individual research was in two different fields, they often used each other as sounding boards. Eventually that meant that their research…' she linked her hands together '…combined, in probably the most scientifically interesting and yet earth-shattering way.'

'What was it? I remember you saying, just before you vanished, that your parents had been arguing more than usual.'

'And that was because they knew what they'd stumbled on.'

'Can you tell me what it was?'

'I can tell you the gist of it. As a safety measure, I wasn't allowed to be privy to their work, even after I'd obtained my medical degree.'

'So…in a nutshell?'

Maybelle sighed and actually leaned forward, closer to him, her voice dropping to a level just above a whisper. 'They developed a synthetic compound that was originally supposed to attack the genetic mutation for bowel cancer but ended up becoming a silent killer.'

Arthur's eyes widened at her words. 'In what form?'

'An injection of a minute amount could cause human death within seconds, leaving no trace of the synthetic compound upon autopsy.'

Arthur was stunned. It took a moment for him to wrap his head around what she was saying—and not saying. 'Nothing?'

'Nothing, and, believe me, even after we went into witness protection their work continued, but this time, instead of being funded by a pharmaceutical company with connections to underground cell organisations, they were funded by the government. As long as they continued to work for the government, we could remain in witness protection.'

'So it was still a restricted life.'

'A very restricted life—for them.'

'And for you?'

'I was able to get a medical degree, even though I had to change medical schools twice.'

'It was that bad?'

Maybelle closed her eyes for a moment, the food before her forgotten. 'Yes.' There was deep-seated pain in the word and when she opened her eyes he saw despair and hopelessness before they were quickly veiled. Anyone who had just met Maybelle Freebourne wouldn't think twice about such a look but he hadn't just met her. In fact, he knew her far better than she probably realised. He remembered everything about those few wonderful months they'd spent together, cuddling and kissing and talking. It was as though their souls had entwined in a way that even time and desperation could not separate. The realisation left him feeling a little shaken, especially as after his divorce he'd sworn off permanent relationships.

'We don't have to talk about it any more, Maybelle,' he offered. He didn't want her to feel despair and hopelessness any more. 'The last time I saw you, your hair was flying into the breeze as you raced from my house to yours.'

'You watched me?'

He nodded. 'From my window, through the branches of the tree. Once you'd climbed the fence into your yard you disappeared from view, but then…just as you reached the top of your balcony, I caught the most fleeting glimpse of you as you went over the railing and into your bedroom.' He put his thumbs and forefingers together, making a sort of rectangle shape. 'It was only the slightest glimpse and back then I had no idea that would be the last time I would see you—until yesterday.'

'I wanted to contact you, but… I didn't know what to say.'

'Clara told me that you sent her birthday cards.'

Maybelle nodded. 'It was easier to lie to Clara. I didn't want to but I could say to her that my dad had been transferred and she wouldn't have asked any questions.' She slipped her hand across the table and, to his surprise, laced her fingers with his. 'I didn't know what to write to you. I started several drafts but after what I said to you that night…' She paused, almost waiting for him to say something, and when he didn't she continued. 'You *do* remember what I said?'

'Uh…yeah. It's a little difficult to forget.'

She smiled at his words but then the smile slowly slipped from her face. 'That was the day the government entered our lives. The agents were downstairs, talking to my parents, when I came to see you.'

'What? Why didn't you tell me?'

'I didn't know what was going to happen next.' Maybelle slipped her hand from his. She could hear the confusion in his tone, the slight hint of censure because she hadn't told him *why* she'd behaved the way she had. 'All I wanted right then and there was to escape from my life.' She stood from the table and started to pace the room, agitated from talking about it. 'The way I felt about you was so…encompassing and I thought if I could lose myself in you, even for a short while, I'd find some level of happiness, of contentment. I don't know if I've ever been content.'

She paused, then angled her head to the side. 'Except for when I was in your arms. That was when I could dream, when I could imagine myself a different sort of life, a life where my parents were normal, where we could tell our families we were together and not have to sneak about.' Where they were grown-ups, in love with each other and wanting to spend the rest of their lives together. She bit back those last words because that clearly hadn't happened.

Arthur was silent for a moment, clearly processing her words. 'So I guess that explains why you demanded I make love to you.'

'I'm sorry, Arthur. It was an adolescent mistake to put you on the spot like that but—'

'Maybelle.' He stood and walked to her side, hearing the break in her voice, seeing the tears shimmering beneath the surface.

'I never meant to hurt you and I never meant to hurt me either because, believe me, I was hurting.' The words were a whisper and Arthur gazed into her upturned face for what seemed an eternity before drawing her closer, their foreheads resting together as they absorbed the truth of that lost night all those years ago.

'If only I'd realised…'

'Would you have said yes?' As she spoke the words, they were peppered with small hiccups as she tried to choke her emotions back where they belonged. It was only with this man that her vulnerabilities rose to the surface. Usually, she prided herself on staying in control.

'I would have held onto you and never let you go.' His voice was laced with a strong possessive streak and her heart leapt at the thought of just how much she'd meant to him back then. But what did she mean to him now? Was this…this thing between them simply residual? She pushed the question aside.

'We were just kids, Arthur. We'd been secretly dating for all of nine weeks.'

'Ten, actually.'

She was pleased to find his memory so precise. 'What could you have possibly done?'

'I don't know, but I would have at least *tried*.'

'Besides, even if I'd stayed, I'm not sure things would have lasted. You would have left home, gone to medical school. I still had two years left at high school and goodness knows what Clara would have thought of our relationship.'

'She was happy about it.'

'She knew?' Maybelle pulled back to look at him, delighted at the small twitch at the corner of his mouth as he smiled.

'She figured it out.'

'How? We were so careful.'

'So we thought.' He rested his hands at her waist, needing to keep her close. 'For the first four weeks after you left…well, let's just say I was a little dark.' He knew it had been longer than four weeks that he'd been angry at her but she didn't need to know that.

'A little dark, eh?'

'Or, as Clara termed it, in a permanent black mood.'

'Oh.'

'When she pressed me on the matter, I sort of blurted out that we'd been seeing each other. She gloated and kept saying over and over that she knew it, until I threw her out of my room.' He chuckled as he spoke, the sound floating over her like a welcome safety blanket. She liked it when he was happy. She liked his smile, the way his eyes twinkled, the way his lips twitched with mirth. Oh, those lips. Those lips had kissed her time and time again and she'd loved every moment of it. His thumbs were moving in tiny circles, rubbing at her waist, each stroke causing sparkles of desire to flood throughout her entire body.

Being this close to his delicious scent was making her want to breathe it in for ever, to resurrect the easygoing plans she'd had for her life all those years ago. At sixteen, she'd planned to finish high school, go to medical school and to marry Arthur. That's all she'd ever wanted.

'I wanted to say yes.' At his soft words, she raised her gaze from staring at his mouth to meet his eyes. 'That night. I wanted to say yes more than anything but I didn't want you to have regrets.' He lifted his head so he could look into her eyes, his clever fingers still creating havoc with her senses. '*I* didn't want to have regrets. Now we *both* have regrets.' It was his turn to stare at her mouth, indicating they were both on the same wavelength. 'I can't imagine what you've been through.' He wrapped his arms about her waist, drawing her closer against his body. 'I wish I could have saved you.'

And those words were her undoing. For years, that was all she'd wanted. She'd wanted Arthur to track her down, to come riding towards her on a white horse, her knight in shining armour, her King Arthur. In the end she'd had to learn how to save herself, but at what cost?

'Arthur…' She closed her eyes, unable to look at him any longer, unable to see the certainty reflected in his gaze. She swallowed, her throat thick with repressed tears.

'Hmm…?'

'Don't.'

'Don't what?'

'Be nice. Caring. Compassionate.' She bit her lip in an effort to bite back the rising tide of emotions she'd kept locked away for far too many years. Only with Arthur was she ever this vulnerable and it appeared time and experience hadn't changed a thing.

'Why not?' There was confusion in his tone as he tenderly brushed the backs of his fingers across her cheek, tucking a stray curl behind her ear. 'If there's one person in the world who deserves my compassion and understanding, it's *you*.'

And those were the words that broke the dam of emotion she'd been holding at bay for far too long, and before she knew it she'd burst into tears.

CHAPTER SIX

SHE WAS CRYING. She was crying and Arthur was comforting her. He was holding her close as she leaned her head against his shoulder and cried. She never cried. She'd become as hard as nails and she never cried…at least, not in front of anyone.

'We need you to be brave,' her mother had told her a lot during that first year in witness protection.

'She's strong. Far stronger than we realise,' her father had countered. 'Our girl understands the gravity of the situation.' He'd tapped the side of his head twice to indicate his daughter had intelligence. 'You won't catch this one breaking down at the drop of a hat.'

And she hadn't. She'd been able to control her emotions, to quash her fears, to hide her feelings. Maybelle had found herself in some terrible situations over the years and she'd coped with them all…and now, with one small modicum of compassion from Arthur, she was a mess.

Why was it that when someone did something nice, especially if the intention was genuine, it was so difficult to accept? And how incredibly wonderful did it feel to lean on him, even if it was just for a moment. In that one split second, all the wishes and dreams she'd had as a young girl came flooding back. All she'd ever wanted had been for someone to look out for her. Not in a protective detail kind of way but rather in an emotional 'I care about you' way. Her parents hadn't been able to provide her with that sort of care, as they'd been too busy providing it for each other. Then, after her mother's death, she'd had to be the one to care for her father as he hadn't known how to go on without the love of his life. How Maybelle had longed for such a love, for a man to be devoted to her in such a way... And with the way Arthur was holding her right now, it felt as though that sort of love might be possible, might one day become a reality.

The thought both frightened and filled her with questions. Was the person she'd become too different from the young woman Arthur had known? Was he still infatuated with the idea of them together or could he see the reality of their present situation—two people drawn together through the emotions of a mutual past love?

'Everything's going to be all right, Maybelle,' Arthur murmured, bringing her thoughts back to the present. The tears were starting to diminish and she became more conscious of the way Arthur was rubbing a hand up and down her back, soothing her.

'Is it?' She sniffed and eased back. He didn't try to hold her close to keep her captive and she was grateful. If he'd been anyone else, if he was a man she'd recently met, she'd be suspicious about his actions, but not with Arthur.

Free from his arms, she dragged in several breaths, trying to get her mind out of mush mode and back into logical mode. 'Is everything going to be all right?' She started pacing around the apartment, shaking her head. 'Because I have no idea if it is or if it isn't. Besides, isn't that just a token statement? "It'll be all right."' She used air quotes as she spoke. 'When people say that, what do they really mean?'

Arthur watched as she stopped moving and planted her hands on her hips. Her eyes were flashing with determination, her tone was laced with stubbornness and her body language indicated she was spoiling for a fight. Good heavens, the woman was stunning!

'*Is* everything going to be all right, Arthur? Define *everything*. Do you mean politics? World peace? Are you talking about sport, wondering if your football team is going to win? Or perhaps you're referring to a patient, hoping they'll make it through their treatment?' She spread her arms wide, staring at him as though daring him to answer. She was toned, fit and healthy. That was all he could think about as she started pacing again, once more jumping up onto her soap box to continue her rant. All the while, all he could think about was how he desperately wanted to kiss her, and not just any kiss but a *real* kiss.

Yes, he'd kissed her at the hospital in the stockroom, but that had been to prove a point, to confirm he wasn't going crazy. What he hadn't expected was to discover in that stockroom that the attraction which had existed between them all those years ago appeared to have been on a low simmer, the fire never really having gone out. It was still there, still very much alive, and after that kiss it had been re-ignited with a vengeance. At least, it had been for him.

How did she feel about it? He'd already lived through a one-sided relationship, with his ex-wife deciding that monogamy wasn't for her. Yvette's affairs and her blasé attitude to her marriage vows had made him wary of other women. Yvette had loved him, had been interested in him, in sharing a life with him. She just hadn't understood why she also couldn't share a life with other men, be interested in other men and love other men.

His fiery red-headed defence attorney had plunged her hand into his body and ripped his heart out. Then she'd crushed it into tiny pieces and left it to rot. It had taken him almost eight years to piece his life back together, to try not to fixate on a woman's ulterior motive when they started dating.

And here he was, wondering how Maybelle had felt about that kiss in the stockroom? About how she'd felt when he'd held her close just now? About why she was ranting and raving the way she was? Was it all designed to put him off? To make him realise that she was a woman with a lot of baggage to sort out? The real question was, did he want to stick around and help her, especially when he wasn't sure he'd ever understand what it was she'd been through?

As she continued to pace and talk, he couldn't help but become aware of her fluid movements, how she seemed to glide with ease yet every muscle in her body was taut and on red alert. Was that how she'd lived her life these past years? On red alert? Never being able to fully relax?

He could hear his mother's words as she'd given him some advice he'd often employed. 'Sometimes, Arthur, you'll have to accept that you can't understand everything in life. Much like men and childbirth. They can empathise but they'll never truly know what it's like to give birth.'

He was facing that situation now. He could never understand but he didn't need to. What he needed was to find a way to ease Maybelle's constant pacing, her nervousness, her anxiety. Instead of getting lost in his own thoughts, he focused more closely on what she was saying.

'Yes, the threat is over. That's what I've been told ever since Dad passed away. With the death of my parents, the major threat has been removed. Now I've been "released back into society", whatever that's supposed to mean, and I'm meant to just lead a normal life?' Her voice choked slightly at the end and his heart turned over with sympathy. Arthur also knew that was the last emotion she'd want from him.

Maybelle stopped pacing. 'It's like a war hero coming back from being on tour, having witnessed distressing events, then being told to get back to the life they'd left behind. It's not that easy, especially when the last time I had a normal life I was sixteen years old.'

Listening to her, watching her movements, sensing her frustration, Arthur's need to help and protect her increased. He wanted to do all he could to help her settle into the normal life it appeared she was looking for. And yet the memory of the kiss they'd shared was still fresh in his mind and that brought another set of problems to the fore.

Could he open himself up to sharing his life with a woman? There was already the high probability that she'd hurt him again. Heavens, the last time she'd left, it had been as though she *had* ripped out his heart and taken it to wherever it was she'd disappeared to.

So just how far was he willing to go to help Maybelle find her new level of normal? He was attracted to her, yes, but was he emotionally capable of opening himself up to the possibility of getting hurt again?

'I don't know how to make sense of this new life, Arthur.' He looked across at her, meeting her gaze and noticing how emotionally helpless she looked. She *was* emotionally helpless and he was emotionally cautious. Not a wise combination. Could they find a safe combination? Could they go back to being friends and ignoring the effects of the re-ignited fire that surrounded them?

'I guess that's what I'm trying to say,' she continued

when he didn't say anything. 'My life has been structured one way for so long—a life with strict rules and regulations because those rules and regulations were designed to save my life, which they did on several occasions.' Maybelle fluffed her curly blonde hair with her fingers and he had to admit the style really did suit her. Yes. He was definitely attracted to her. There was no doubt about that but could he be her friend? She didn't need any more complications in life and neither did he.

'But can I live my new life with rules that aren't as strict? Or rules that I have to make up myself? I need to put parameters in place but first I need to figure out what those parameters are.' She frowned and spread her arms wide. 'Am I making any sense?'

'Uh-huh.'

She fixed him with a glare. 'Have you even been listening to me, Arthur?'

'Yes. I've heard every word.'

'And yet with the way you're staring at me now, it's as though you'd like to sweep me off my feet and head towards the bedroom.'

Damn. Was he that obvious? Even hearing her say those words out loud caused a wave of desire to surge through him. He closed his eyes for a brief moment, trying to school his features into an impassive mask. Meeting her again had definitely disrupted his life and destroyed a lot of the preconceived ideas and theories he'd had regarding her disappearance. She was alive. She was healthy—emotionally scarred, but healthy. These were good things, given the alternatives, but what she needed from him now, and also what he needed from her, was some time to let the dust settle as they reconnected.

'I won't deny I find you attractive.' He kept his eyes closed as he spoke those words out loud, knowing if he looked at her it would make them all the more difficult to say. 'However…' Arthur dragged in a calming breath and finally opened his eyes. 'I want to help you, Maybelle.'

'How?' The question was quiet.

'By being your friend. I'm still processing the fact you're alive, and you're still figuring out your life. Any romantic entanglements are only going to complicate things and, quite frankly, I've had my fair share of complicated.'

'Friends?' She sounded sceptical.

'We've been friends before.' He smiled at her. 'Surely we can do it again.' It would require a lot of self-restraint from him but the choice was simple. If he pushed for a romantic entanglement, it might fizzle out within a month and then they'd start avoiding each other. As they worked together, and now lived very close to each other, that would cause more tension than he was willing to endure.

Besides, by a stroke of luck, she was back in his life once more. His old childhood friend. Wasn't that more important than any desire-filled tryst that would cause them both more pain? Maybelle was back in his life and he wanted her to stay there. The decision was cut and dried, so why did he feel as though he was lying to himself?

'Friends.' She sighed with relief. What did that sigh mean? That she didn't want a physical relationship with him? That she, too, had had enough of relationships that only brought stress and confusion? He halted his thoughts and watched as a lovely smile lit her features. 'Yes. We can be friends. Friends is good.'

'Excellent.' After resolving what had clearly been an undercurrent both of them had been avoiding, Maybelle sat down on the carpet, as though her body had no more energy to keep her standing upright. She crossed her legs and her head sank forward, only to be disturbed a moment later when a cute Fuzzy-Juzzy came over to her and started licking her hand.

Maybelle's unreserved laughter caused his gut to tighten. Good heavens, that was a glorious sound and as he watched her play with the dog, a smile of utter delight on her face, he wondered if he hadn't made a mistake. Just friends? It was going to take a lot of self-control for him to keep his promise.

For the next few days, Arthur made sure he kept to his promise of being friends with Maybelle. He helped her to lease a car—she'd refused to buy, saying she wasn't ready for that level of permanence yet—and provided her with a plethora of menus from take-away places that delivered.

'We could even do something completely wild and go grocery shopping so you have actual food in your apartment,' he'd suggested when he'd found her eating breakfast at the hospital cafeteria on Friday morning. He'd taken his coffee to her table and sat down, enjoying the surprise of spending some one-on-one time with her. The ED had been hectic during the day and he'd forced himself to keep his distance in the evenings. Surprisingly, he'd missed her. Missed seeing that smile that lit her features, or that little frown that crinkled her forehead, or the way she twirled her hair around her finger.

'Perhaps on the weekend,' she'd offered as she'd finished off her scrambled eggs, toast and coffee.

'You do realise the weekend is tomorrow?'

She paused for a moment. 'Huh. So it is.'

'Are you still planning to buy some extra bits and pieces for your apartment?'

'Yes. I need a microwave and a proper coffee machine.'

'And some throw cushions for your lounge and a few

pictures to hang on the walls. Plus, didn't you say that your doona wasn't warm enough?'

'Yes—yes, I did. Right. I'll add doona to the list, but I don't think the other things are necessary.'

'Why not?'

'They're not practical, Arthur.'

'I beg to differ. Your lounge is incredibly uncomfortable, and a throw cushion might just make all the difference.'

'It is not uncomfortable.'

'Then why do you sit on the floor so much?' When she opened her mouth to protest, he leaned forward and pressed a finger to her lips. 'You asked me to help you find a normal life, Maybelle. Normal people have…'

He faltered as the warmth of her breath caressed his fingertip, the sensation travelling up his arm and engulfing him with desire. He swallowed and jerked his hand back, forcing the rest of his sentence out and hopefully covering over his slip-up.

'They have throw cushions and pictures on the walls.' Why had he touched her? Touching her provoked sensations he was desperately trying to keep under control and made them rise up to the surface.

'If…if normal people do it, then I guess I have to as well.' The sigh she gave was an exaggerated one but he hadn't missed the slight stumble over her words, indicating she'd felt that same natural chemistry that seemed to flow through them no matter how much they tried to deny it.

'We could definitely go shopping tomorrow.' As he said the words, the hospital cellphone on his belt started ringing. 'Uh-oh.'

'The phone of doom is ringing.' She started to pack up

her dishes onto a tray so she could stack it on the dirty dishes trolley on the way out of the cafeteria.

He smiled at her words and was glad they'd worked their way past the dangerous moment. As he answered the phone, he made a mental note not to touch her again because it seemed the instant they made contact both of them lost all resolve over their self-control. At least, that was the way it was for him. He wasn't quite sure how Maybelle felt about it.

They headed back to the ED, Arthur talking to Gemma on the phone.

'Let me guess,' Maybelle remarked once he'd ended the conversation. 'Emergency? Ambulances on their way?' Her words were laced with an easygoing sarcasm as she stated the obvious. Light-hearted banter. He could definitely cope better with this light-hearted banter than being in close proximity where her sunshine-and-roses scent infiltrated his senses and made his need for her increase.

He laughed. 'See? This is why we only employ the best doctors in the ED. They're so switched on.' They worked together in Emergency, treating their patients and stabilising them so they could be transferred to either the ward, the emergency theatres or back home. That evening, Arthur decided it was time he tackled the mound of paperwork that was starting to swamp his desk. He gathered the new stack of papers Gemma had handed him and started towards his office.

'Are you working on those at home tonight?' Maybelle asked as she fell into step beside him.

'That was the plan.'

'Need any help? I could order pizza. Halve the work-load.'

It was a tempting offer. To sit and talk about boring

work stuff with someone who completely understood what he was on about, both of them eating pizza and making the mundane chore less of a chore, would be wonderful and it was for that very reason why he had to decline her offer.

'Thanks, but it shouldn't take me too long.' He went to use the pass card for his office door but it failed twice. He was balancing a mound of papers in a rather precarious fashion and if his stupid door didn't open soon, he was going to end up dropping everything. Add to that the fact that Maybelle's delightful summery scent was winding itself around him, driving him crazy, and it was little wonder he was starting to get a tad impatient.

'Here. Let me,' she said as she took the pass card off him and swiped it through the sensor at a different angle. The door clicked and Arthur immediately entered his office, almost tripping over his own feet in the rush to put a bit more distance between them.

He dumped the papers onto his desk and shook his head. 'And they said we'd be living in a paperless office by now. Sheesh!'

'So is that a yes to help and pizza?'

'Actually, I think I might just knuckle down here and get it done. You can, however, help me by feeding Juzzy.'

'Oh. Uh…sure.'

He could see she was disappointed. Did she want to spend time with him because she liked being with him? Or perhaps she simply didn't want to be alone? Or worse yet—she liked doing paperwork? 'Great. I'll get my spare keys for you.' He opened the small safe that was located in a cupboard under his desk and took out a set of keys.

'You keep spare keys at your office?'

'Where else would I keep them if I accidentally locked myself out?'

'Huh.' She accepted the keys. 'So that's what normal people do.' She tapped the side of her head as though making a mental note.

'What would you have done if you'd been locked out of your apartment? You know, in the "not so normal" world of witness protection?'

'I would have asked my bodyguard if I could borrow their key, or get them to break down the door,' she stated, then shrugged when he stared at her. 'There's not a lot of immediate privacy when it comes to witness protection. Someone always has to know your whereabouts.'

'Was it always that way?' He couldn't help the question. He didn't want to dwell on the past or bring up bad memories for her but at times his curiosity got the better of him.

'For the first year, definitely. Then things settled down for a bit.' She paused, looking off into the distance. 'It changed again when my mum died, that's when I had a bodyguard for a while, but...' Maybelle drew in a breath and forced a polite smile. 'All over now.' She jingled his keys and repeated his instructions for Juzzy to make sure she had them correct. The last thing she wanted to do was to overfeed his dog.

After she'd left, Arthur sat down in his chair and reflected on the newest snippet he'd learned about Maybelle. He really couldn't comprehend what she'd been through in any way, shape or form and yet here she was, trying to make a new life for herself...on her own. She really was...the most amazing woman he'd ever met.

Maybelle felt very strange walking into Arthur's apartment without him being there. Then again, the only other time she'd been here she'd felt just as strange. She turned on the light and quickly closed the door behind her as

Fuzzy-Juzzy started barking and running in her direction. The dog almost stopped short when she realised it
wasn't Arthur walking through the door but after a moment seemed to be pleased someone had come to feed her.

She trotted to the laundry where her food bowl stood
empty. She even tapped the bowl with her nose as though
to give clear direction of exactly what she was wanting. Maybelle couldn't help but laugh at the dog's antics
and dutifully gave her food as per Arthur's instructions.
When the dog started eating, Maybelle crouched down
and stroked the soft fur.

'You really are gorgeous,' she told the dog, who didn't
miss a bite. It only increased the longing for a pet of her
own but she wasn't sure if she was ready for *that* level
of normal. What if there was another threat? What if she
needed to move? She wouldn't be able to take the animal
with her and that sort of heartbreak was one that could be
avoided. For now, though, she could spend a bit of time
with Juzzy and let herself dream.

She sat down on the floor and waited until the dog had
finished eating, delighting in watching the Pomeranian's
every move with her curly little tail and twitchy little
nose. What stunned her further was when the dog decided to climb onto Maybelle's lap and seat herself there.

'This isn't your bed,' Maybelle told the dog, but she
didn't seem to care.

She raised her head to look at Maybelle as if to say, *I'll
sleep where I want, thank you very much, and I choose
here.*

Maybelle stroked the soft fur and rested her head back
against the cupboard, her legs stretched out in front of
her. She could get used to this, having someone accept
her and love her unconditionally, just as Juzzy was. There
were no questions, no censure, no recommendations on

what she should do with her life. There was just…love, and Maybelle absorbed it.

She continued to rhythmically stroke the dog, the action proving far more relaxing than she'd anticipated. Given she was sitting in Arthur's apartment, stroking Arthur's dog, she couldn't help but ponder whether Arthur would be like Juzzy, able to accept her unconditionally. She knew she was broken, damaged and even a little shell-shocked, and that she had a long way to go before she could really let herself relax, but it was possible, wasn't it? She *would* get to her goal in the end, wouldn't she?

For so many years she'd told herself that happy endings weren't for everyone and she was one of the people who was missing out. Sitting here, stroking Juzzy's fur and relaxing—far more than she could ever remember before—Maybelle began to let the faintest glimmer of hope start to ignite. It *was* possible. Why shouldn't she have a happily-ever-after ending? Hadn't she been through enough already?

Not only had her life been uprooted at the age of sixteen, she'd had to watch her mother die in the most horrific way possible. Then, recently, her heart had broken as she'd seen the utter despair and regret in her father's eyes not long before he'd given up the fight.

Although she'd felt alone for so many years, she now was truly alone. Being in witness protection had bonded her family together even more, which only made the loss of her parents even greater.

Closing her eyes, Maybelle continued to draw comfort from Juzzy's warmth as she stroked the dog. For so long she'd wanted nothing more than to be out of witness protection but now that she was, it was incredibly scary. She was facing her future all alone, and it was that loneliness that made a few tears slide down her cheeks. Sniffing, she wiped them away, annoyed at herself for not controlling her thoughts better.

These past few days with Arthur had been wonderful. Yes, the beginning had been a bit rocky but now that he knew her true identity, and seemed happy she was back in his life, the two of them had managed to rekindle their friendship. Naturally, it was different from how it had been all those years ago as they'd both had different experiences that had moulded them into who they were today, but the essentials of their friendship seemed to have remained. Arthur had told her that she was like family to him and even early today he'd mentioned the possibility of taking her to see his parents.

'They'd be delighted to see you again.'

'But…how do I tell them who I really am?'

'You just tell them, Maybelle.' He'd shrugged as though he wasn't sure what her problem was.

'It's not that easy, Arthur. For far too long I've had to hide who I really was. I had to change my name, my hair, my eye colour.'

'Was the threat really that bad?'

'That *bad*?' Tears had welled in her eyes and she'd been far too aware that they had been at the nurses' station, in the middle of the ED. Shaking her head and doing her best to get her emotions under control, she'd swallowed and said in a vehement whisper, 'My mother was murdered. In front of me.' With that, she'd excused herself and headed to the women's changing rooms in an attempt to get herself under control.

The next time she'd seen him had been just before she'd left work, when he'd been carrying all those files to his office. Her offer of help had been rejected and she couldn't help but feel that Arthur was already putting distance between them. If she hadn't told him about her mother, they might well be sitting here now, enjoying pizza, laughing together as they managed to sort out the ridiculous amount of paperwork that was attached to the administration of a department.

Arthur had wanted time away from her. Away from her because she was far from a normal woman. She was emotionally scarred—and she hadn't even told him that the instant her mother had been killed she'd been drugged and held to ransom for the next two and a half days. Although it had happened ten years ago, she still had nightmares about it, often waking up thinking someone was after her, trying to kidnap her again.

'That's all in the past. That's all in the past. That's all in the past.' She spoke the words over and over again, trying to calm her mind, forcing herself to focus on the rhythmic movements of stroking the dog, concentrating on how the soft fur felt against her fingers, of how she seemed to be patting Juzzy in a pattern. Two strokes one way, a touch under first one ear, then the other, then several long strokes down Juzzy's body.

As though Juzzy wanted to reassure her, the little tongue licked Maybelle's hand, tickling her and making her smile. It helped the constriction in her chest to ease and her breathing to even out. Juzzy's body became heavier, the licks now few and far between as the dog settled into a secure and comfortable sleep.

She followed suit, her hand slowing in its movements, but the dog didn't seem to mind. Finally, she rested her hand on the dog's back, both of them content within the long moment that seemed to stretch into an eternity.

'Maybelle?' Her name was like a caress on Arthur's lips and she could have sworn she felt his hand on her shoulder. She tried to open her eyes but they were just too heavy. Her hand automatically started to stroke the dog's soft coat again but stopped after two short strokes, exhaustion claiming her.

'Hmm?' She felt herself warmly enveloped in his big strong arms, being held firmly as he picked her up and carried her. Then she was placed on a comfortable bed, one with a nice warm doona that seemed to cocoon her, locking out the bad dreams, the fear and trepidation that had hounded her life in the past. 'Safe,' she whispered, then turned her head into the pillow and slept.

CHAPTER SEVEN

ARTHUR WENT INTO the kitchen and checked on Juzzy, unsure how he felt at having Maybelle so close. Where he hadn't wanted to spend time with her, doing paperwork and eating pizza, because he simply hadn't been able to trust himself not to grab her and kiss her, he now had to fight the way she'd felt in his arms, the way her scent seemed to be permanently swirling around him, confusing his logical thought process.

Since she'd made a reappearance in his life, his thoughts had been continually drifting back to the past, pleased he now had some answers to the questions that had sat at the back of his mind for far too long. They may not have been the answers he'd been expecting, especially the bombshell she'd dropped earlier today, telling him that her mother had been murdered.

He'd always had mixed feelings about Maybelle's parents but most of them were from an adolescent perspective. He'd thought they should have paid more attention to their daughter, that they should have spent more time with her, but now, as an adult and as a medical professional, he could understand their dedication to their profession. Add to that everything Maybelle had told him about their work and he had a new appreciation for Samantha and Hank Fleming. To think of Samantha being

killed and then to think of Maybelle witnessing that incident—his heart ached for them both.

In fact, it had made it almost impossible for him to
concentrate on his paperwork and in the end he'd given
up and left the hospital early, wondering if he could drop
by Maybelle's apartment and offer her a hug. He wanted
her to know he was there for her, as a friend, as a sounding board, as a guide in finally obtaining the normal life
she wanted. He doubted, given what she'd told him, that
her life would ever be completely normal, but then a lot
of people in the world managed to make it through very
traumatic experiences to achieve a *new* level of normal.
That was what he wanted to help Maybelle to achieve.
After all, deep down inside she was still his May and she
was still most definitely beautiful.

What Arthur hadn't expected was to find Maybelle sitting on his laundry floor, the dog on her lap, both of them
asleep. How long had she been there, sleeping in such an
awkward position? When he'd moved the dog from her
lap, he'd expected Maybelle to stir, but she hadn't. That
was when he'd realised just how exhausted she must be.
Had she been sleeping at all since moving to town? She'd
said that her father had died a few months ago, so had
she managed to have a decent night's sleep since then?
This entire week she'd been at the hospital long before
her shift began, which usually indicated the inability to
sleep or settle.

With Juzzy all tucked up in her little bed and sleeping soundly—just like Maybelle—he made himself a cup
of tea and took it to his bedroom, pausing momentarily
outside the door where Maybelle slept. Should he check
on her again? Was that creepy? What if she woke up and
didn't know where she was? Perhaps he should leave her
a little note, telling her not to panic?

He closed his eyes and shook his head, continuing on to his own bedroom and shutting the door firmly behind him. Even the sight of her cocooned beneath the doona, snuggled deep and murmuring the word 'safe', had been enough of an undoing for him for one night. The need to hold her close, just as he used to, to talk quietly with her, just as they used to, to offer his support and to listen to what she had to say, was becoming more intense with each passing second he spent in her company.

Instead, Arthur forced himself to get ready for bed, deciding that tonight it might be advantageous for him to sleep in pyjama bottoms and an old T-shirt…just in case of an emergency or in case Maybelle sleepwalked or—

His thoughts stalled on the fact that she might very well sleepwalk. Sleepwalking was often attributed to stress and anxiety, the subconscious attempting to deal with what the conscious found difficult, and Maybelle had definitely had her fair share of anxiety and stress. What would he do if she sleepwalked right into his bedroom? He swallowed at that thought and sat back on his bed, resting against the headboard. He could well remember the last time she'd been in his bedroom, although that time she'd come through the half-open window rather than using the door. He'd been studying for an exam and although it had been late, he'd only managed to get through half of his notes. Then she'd appeared.

The memories that he'd locked away so many years ago came flooding back as he recalled the events of that night. The window had been right next to a large tree, one he'd climbed up and down several times over the years. The screen from his window had long since been removed to make covert access to his room easy when he'd arrived home past curfew.

The cool summer breeze had brought welcome relief

from the oppressive heat they'd been enduring, but the last thing he'd expected to come through his window that night had been the girl who had been constantly in his thoughts for the past few months. Ever since they'd kissed at her birthday party, Arthur had found it difficult not to think about her, not to want to kiss her again and again and again…and to his dismay he had. They'd shared inviting looks across the dinner table while the rest of his family had been eating dinner; they'd allowed their fingers to touch when doing the dishes together; they'd sneaked kisses when no one had been around. And then she'd appeared in his bedroom.

Drawing in a long, deep breath, it was as though the smells of that night were re-creating themselves around him now. She'd been dressed in light sandshoes, three-quarter-length summer jeans and a light blue T-shirt. Her hair had been loose, the long strawberry-blonde locks floating around her shoulders, enticing him to reach out and run his fingers through them. It was her eyes, though, her bright blue eyes that had reflected her emotions of eager, wild, urgent desire.

'May!' He'd placed a hand over his heart at her sudden appearance, although even now he wasn't sure if he'd been startled by her or desperate with desire for her. 'What are you doing?' He'd stood from his desk and drunk his fill of her.

She hadn't given him an answer, except to walk purposefully towards him, wrap her hands around his neck and pull his head down so their lips could meet. The action had been done as one fluid movement and the grip she'd had on his neck had been tight, as though she was never going to let him go. Her lips had been demanding, insistent, desperate.

For a brief second he'd kissed her back, because how

could he not? She was warm and inviting and tasted like strawberries mixed with pure sunshine. Intoxicating and addictive, he'd wanted more, he'd wanted everything she could give, to greedily have his fill of her. The hunger inside him had been met and matched by her, something she'd never done before, and a part of him had been delighted at this turn of events…but the reasonable part of his brain had begun to make itself known, begun to question why she was there, why she was kissing him in such a fashion and why she was manoeuvring them towards the bed.

Finally, he'd come to his senses and put his hands on her shoulders and eased her firmly from him. 'What…?' He'd swallowed, slightly breathless and captivated by the sight of her. 'What's going on? What are you doing here?' He'd glanced towards the door, afraid that his parents or his sister might walk into his room and find her here. Yes, it had been late. Yes, his parents had retired to bed, but still, the fact that he'd had a girl in his room at such an hour had been something that had made him feel skittish.

'I want you, Arthur.' Her words had been firm, with no hint of hesitation, and as she'd spoken she'd made a move to kiss him once again.

'Whoa. Wait a second.' He'd dropped his hands from her shoulders and taken a few steps away, needing to put some distance between them. 'What's going on?' He'd tried again, hoping this time to get some sort of sensible answer from her.

She'd shrugged her perfectly sculpted shoulders and had started to twirl one finger in her hair, a sure sign that she'd been nervous. 'We've been sneaking around for a while now, stealing kisses here and there, talking on the phone and having some very unsuccessful tutoring sessions.' She'd smiled at him then and he couldn't help but return her smile as he'd recalled the two of them sitting at the kitchen table while he'd tutored her in mathematics. His father had been at work and his mother had taken Clara to her violin lesson, which had left the two of them alone for twenty minutes. They'd made good use of the time, enjoying a make-out session rather than an algebra session.

'That still doesn't explain why you've sneaked out of your house and into my room.'

'And here I thought the words "I want you, Arthur" would be all the explanation you required.' With that, she'd made her way to his side and started kissing him again, her sweet lips enticing him to give in to the powerful urges he'd been desperately trying to fight. This time, though, they had been much closer to the bed than before and when she'd eased herself down to sit on the mattress, he'd been too captivated to resist following.

His fingers had tangled in her hair and his mouth had matched the intensity of hers. She'd smelled so good, as though she'd just had a shower and blow-dried her hair. The strands had been as soft as silk and touching them had only added fuel to the fire already raging inside him. He'd wanted her. There had been no question of that. For the past two and a half months he'd become increasingly infatuated with her, so much so that he'd been considering throwing all caution to the wind and suggesting they tell his sister and their parents they were dating.

It had been her idea to keep their burgeoning relationship a secret from everyone. Initially he'd understood her reticence with their parents, but Clara had been her best friend and he hadn't wanted to be the person to splinter that long-standing friendship. Having May in his room, in his arms, on his bed had meant that things had become far more serious much quicker than he'd anticipated and if anyone—family, friends, strangers—had asked him if he'd had strong, romantic feelings for her, there was no way he'd ever be able to deny it. In fact, he'd been positive that what he'd felt for her could also be defined as being in love.

He'd been so caught up in the heat, in the pheromones, in the realisation that this was really happening, that she was really in his room, really wanting him to make love with him, that he'd almost missed the slight hesitation as his hands had slipped to the waistband of her jeans. Almost.

'What's wrong?' he'd asked, breaking his mouth from hers and staring into her eyes. There, the hesitation had been confirmed and he'd quickly removed his hands, placing them back on her shoulders. 'We don't have to do this.'

'Yes. Yes, we do. I… I want to do this.'

'Honey, you don't need to do anything. I'm not going to force you.' He'd wanted to make that absolutely clear.

'Oh, I know you would never do that. Never.' The words had been adamant and he'd breathed a sigh of relief that she'd known he would never take advantage of her.

'Then why? Why come here and say what you did when you clearly have reservations?'

'Because I don't want to die a virgin!'

A loud crack, followed by a thud reverberated around him and Arthur sat up with a jolt. Had that sound come from his memories? He remembered being completely floored by her words back then, as though his entire world had ripped apart at the seams. Why did she think she was going to die? Why the sudden urgency? Yes, his thoughts had been turbulent at the time but right now he was unsettled. His gut told him something wasn't right and he always followed his gut instincts.

Arthur crept from his bed over to the door, opening it slowly before staring at the closed door to the spare room. Everything seemed quiet but the fact that Maybelle was here meant he was on edge. Was she all right? Should he check on her? Deciding it couldn't hurt to check, he walked from his room and reached out for the door handle. Before he could touch it, the door was wrenched open and he was whacked on the head with something hard.

'Ugh.' He instinctively raised a hand to ward off the next attack. The next thwack hit his arm and he realised her weapon of choice was a large hard-back dictionary. 'Maybelle. Maybelle. It's me.' His words were punctuated by a few more swipes of the book, which he managed to dodge. 'May!'

When he spoke her real name she paused, her breathing erratic, and from what he could see of her in the darkened room her eyes were wide and filled with confusion. The book was raised in her arms, ready for another strike. It didn't matter that his head hurt, it didn't matter that something had caused her to completely freak out. All that mattered was getting through to her that she was safe, that she wasn't in any danger—at least, not from him.

'It's Arthur.' He tried once more to calm her down and when she lowered the book, letting it drop to the floor, he stepped forward and placed his hands on her shoulders. 'You're safe, May. You're safe.'

'Arthur?' She looked up at him with utter confusion and the urge to resist her was lost as he gathered her close into his arms. She went willingly, wrapping her arms around his waist and resting her head against his chest. Arthur held her trembling body, doing everything he could to let her know she was safe.

He breathed in the scent of her hair, allowing the

present-day reality to combine with his past memories. He'd held her like this on several occasions, especially that last evening. They'd been lying on his bed, above the covers, fully dressed, his arms around her, holding her, talking quietly with her.

'I love the sound of your heartbeat.' It was a few minutes later that she mumbled the words against his chest. 'I would often think of lying there in your arms, listening to the soothing *lub-dub* of your heart as you stroked my hair and spoke reassuringly in your deep, modulated tones.'

He smiled at that. 'Deep modulated tones?' He tried to ease away but she only tightened her grip around his waist, clearly not ready to break the hold.

'Your voice has a certain…cadence to it and I've always equated that with safety.' Only now did she slowly lift her head from his chest and look up at him. 'There were times in my life when things weren't safe, when we'd been discovered and had to leave everything in the middle of the night and try to start our lives again.'

'Oh, sweetheart.'

'And when my life was so uncertain, when I had no idea from one day to the next what was happening, where we were going to live, what my name was going to be… then I would remember that night. That special night… with you.'

'Nothing happened.' He wanted to make sure she was remembering it the right way.

'Everything happened, Arthur.'

He eased back and this time she let go. 'That's not the way I remember it.' He bent to pick up the book, wanting to put some distance between her and the item that had connected with his skull. Returning it to the shelf, he took her hand and led her from the room.

'Where are we going?' she asked, but thankfully didn't fight him.

'I'm making us some tea. You're clearly delusional.'

'A strong shot of whisky would probably help more but I'll take the tea.' And there it was, that wonderful, teasing sense of humour he'd missed so much. He glanced at her over his shoulder and smiled.

'I've missed you.' The words were out of his mouth before he could stop them and Maybelle squeezed his hand and nodded.

'I missed you, too.'

They stood and stared at each other for a long moment, the air around them almost starting to crackle with electric tension. It had always been this way, ever since that first kiss so very long ago. He glanced at her mouth— that perfectly sculpted mouth that had always fitted so perfectly with his own. Swallowing, he met her eyes and only now that they were in the artificially lit kitchen did he realise she'd removed the contacts.

Bright blue eyes, the colour of the sky on a cloudless summer's day, gazed back at him, repressed desire visible in their depths. She bit her lower lip and he realised she was nervous. He didn't blame her. He was nervous, too. He knew it was possible for the physical attraction he'd felt all those years ago to return with a forceful thump but the emotional connection, the one that years apart should have wrecked, was still very much alive.

Then, before he could think anything else, she'd moved towards him in one fluid motion, wrapped her hands around his neck and pulled his mouth down to meet hers. It was exactly that way she'd approached him all those years ago, as if she had to follow through on her desire before she lost her nerve.

Memories of the last time she'd done this and the fresh

sensations of the present blurred together to make one almighty, powerful aphrodisiac. Where years ago the kiss had been testing and hesitant, this time it was filled with heat, experience and adult appreciation for the possible outcome such a kiss could evoke. Gone were the questions about whether or not they should consummate these feelings because this time there was no doubt that she wanted him and definitely no doubt that he wanted her. There was no hesitation, no hesitation at all.

How was it possible after all this time that the sweetness of her mouth was just as intoxicating? The woman was in his blood. That was the only explanation he could garner. She'd left an imprint that hadn't faded and now it was time to bring their story to the full conclusion.

'This needs to happen,' she whispered against his mouth. 'I've dreamt about it for so long.'

'You have?' The words were mumbled between them as he spread kisses across her cheek and down to her neck. She'd always liked it when he'd kissed her neck and now was no exception. Tilting her head to the side and allowing him access to her smooth, delicious skin, she moaned with delight before sliding her fingers into his hair and momentarily massaging his scalp. He liked that. He liked that she knew him and he knew her. When she tightened her grip on his hair and pulled his head up, he knew she was ready for the next onslaught of emotions, the heat between them now at a dangerous level.

This time when their mouths met there were no more questions, no more hesitation, no more confusion. Hot and hungry, they devoured each other, her hands sliding beneath the T-shirt he wore and making short work of removing it. The tantalising touch of her fingertips on his skin left a trail of desire-filled fire that only fuelled him on. She broke free from his mouth to smother his chest with kisses that nearly sent him over the edge. He groaned with longing, with need, with desire as she continued to create havoc with his senses.

'Do you have...*any* idea, what you...do to me?' he ground out, his hands at her waist, holding her body close to his.

'I think...you do the same to me,' she returned as she lifted her own knit top over her head, revealing a lilac-coloured bra beneath. Before he had time to drink his fill, she'd pressed her almost naked chest against his and captured his lips with hers. 'I want you, Arthur,' she murmured against his mouth. 'Even more than I did back then.' She kissed him again and again and he accepted those kisses, but there was a pinging noise at the back of his mind that was gradually getting louder and louder.

'You do know we didn't...' He gasped as she nipped at his lower lip. 'We didn't do anything.'

'Not in my world.' Her words were fast and impatient as though she wanted things to continue on their natural course of progression. She eased back ever so slightly and grabbed both his hands in hers, urging him from the kitchen and back towards the bedroom. Arthur was too dazed, too stunned to believe this was actually happening, that they were going to rewrite history and actually—

'Wait.' He stopped her in the hallway just next to his open bedroom door. 'What do you mean, "not in my world"? We didn't have sex that night, Maybelle.'

'We should have.'

'We couldn't!'

'What does it matter now?' she said as she backed into his bedroom, beckoning him closer.

'It matters that whatever you're doing now, you're doing it for the right reasons, that you're not simply trying to live out a fantasy of a life you weren't able to have.'

'You're overthinking this.' She perched herself on the end of his bed and gazed at him with such devotion he almost capitulated.

'Am I?' If this was going to happen, he didn't want either of them to have regrets.

'I want you, Arthur. Isn't that reason enough?'

'And what about tomorrow? What about working together? Trying to be friends? Don't you think having sex will change all that?' He stayed in the hallway, trying to keep his logical thoughts in place, even though his libido was telling him otherwise.

She frowned at him for a moment, as though she was trying to process what it was he was actually saying. 'Are you turning me down *again*?' Maybelle spread her arms wide, glaring at him with those incredible eyes of hers. He had no idea what had happened to her brown contacts and he didn't care. All he cared about right now was the pain in her eyes and the fact that he'd been the one to cause it.

'I'm not saying we *shouldn't*, I'm just saying we should perhaps take things a little slower.'

Her grin turned wolfish. 'Slow is good.'

'Maybelle.' There was a slight warning in his tone and he leaned against the doorjamb. 'Is this what you really want?'

'Arthur, it's all I've wanted since I was sixteen. I want to know what it's like to be with you, to have you as close to me as humanly possible. I want to know what it's like to sleep in your arms all night long, to wake up with you in the morning, to sit together at the breakfast table and read the paper.'

He raised his eyebrows in surprise. 'You want marriage?'

'Marriage!' Her surprise echoed his. 'What? No. That's not what I meant.'

'So you *don't* want marriage?'

'Arthur...' She glanced around his room and spied an ironed shirt in the closet. She took it off the hanger and put it on, clearly feeling self-conscious standing in the middle of his room wearing only her trousers and bra. The problem was she looked even sexier wearing his too-large shirt. 'I don't know what I want. I don't know what's going on in my life. I don't even know who I am yet. The last thing I need is to drag anyone else into my upside-down world.'

'Yet you're clearly willing to drag me in...to a point.'

'You're different.'

'So you *do* want to drag me in?'

Maybelle sighed with impatience before closing her eyes and shaking her head. 'I'm saying I don't know what I want. No one ever knows what they want.'

'But you just told me that you wanted *me*.'

She opened her eyes and glared at him. 'That's not what I meant. Stop taking everything I say out of context. Yes, I want you—*physically*—but long term...?' She shrugged, her shoulders rising and falling in his too-big shirt. 'Do you? Do you know what you want?'

'Yes.'

She rolled her eyes. 'Of course you do. You're Arthur. You plan everything.' She paced around his room for a moment then fixed him with a glare. 'I've often wondered, back then, if it had been your idea to have a romantic tryst, then it would have happened. You would have pulled out all the stops in order to seduce me but the fact that *I* was the one who came to you, asking you to make love to me, well…there was simply no dice.'

'What? Maybelle, you were confused and young and—'

'Desperately in love with you,' she pointed out. 'And you were in love with me, or so you said.'

They'd been two very confused teenagers back then. He full of general teenage hormones and angst, and she full of confusion and fear. 'I couldn't take advantage of you, Maybelle. What if having sex had hurt you—physically? What if you'd become accidentally pregnant? What if you'd hated me for taking advantage?'

She sat down on his bed, twirling her hair absently with her finger as she pondered his words. The action only made her look more appealing and the fact that she was doing it unconsciously made his heart lurch for her. How was it that even after all these years, after everything they'd been through, she still looked innocent? 'I hadn't thought of it like that,' she said after a moment. 'I just presumed all teenage boys wanted to have sex.'

'They do. I did. I *really* did.' He wanted to venture into the room, to sit beside her, to put his arms around her, to hold her close, but he was shirtless and she was…well, she was adorably sexy and incredibly inviting. 'However, that night we had together was one of the best nights I've ever had. Sex is one thing but we had a connection. We bonded that night.' Arthur couldn't keep the passion from his tone. 'It was an amazing night.'

'It was.' She dropped her hand to her side and stared unseeingly at the room before her. 'I thought about that night often, usually when I was melancholy or upset. Memories of that night would cheer me up, would give me hope.' Hope that one day she'd bump into him again but, given her circumstances, she'd known it to be impossible. A small smile touched her lips. If only her past self could see her now, sitting on Arthur's bed, wearing one of Arthur's shirts, her lips still tingling from Arthur's kisses.

'A lot has happened in our lives since then,' he pointed out.

'Hence why you're suggesting we stick to being just friends?' Maybelle covered her face with her hands and he could tell she was feeling foolish. 'Yet I kept pushing, kept insisting, kept throwing myself at you in an effort to satisfy my own desires.'

Arthur gave in and crossed to her side, crouching down in front of her, pulling her hands from her face. 'I have those same desires, Maybelle.'

'Yet you clearly have more self-control than I do.'

'Perhaps that's because I know where I want my life to lead.'

'And where's that?'

'My career. My research. I put two grants in for funding and one was accepted last week.'

'Your *research*?' The way she said the word it was almost as though he'd just told her he wanted to stick a needle in her eye. 'That's all that's important to you? What, wouldn't you want to get married again? Have children?'

He shook his head and stood, walking away from her, unable to see that look in her eyes, the one that was silently calling him a traitor. 'Research is important. It can change people's lives, it can change the way surgeons perform various operations, and without research there would be no further advances in medical science.' He was on the defensive and he knew it.

'You're darned right when you say that research

can change people's lives.' She shook her head and he couldn't blame her for feeling that way. With her parents being married to their research and, in the end, having that research affect her life in such a dramatic way, it was little wonder she was looking at him as though he was out of his mind.

'And with regard to marriage, it didn't work for me. I tried the house in the suburbs.'

'And children?'

'My ex-wife didn't want any.'

'And how about you?'

Arthur spread his arms wide. 'Of course I wanted to have children but it didn't happen.'

'What *did* happen, Arthur? Because, while you're very much the same as you ever were, this…' she pointed in the direction of his heart '…this part of you has always wanted children. You told me so, remember? We were sitting on the couch, making out instead of studying, and when we both came up for air, you sat with me in your arms and we talked about what we wanted for our future and you told me you wanted to become a doctor, get married, live in a house like the one we were in and raise children just the way you and Clara were raised. You told me that, Arthur.'

It was true and he knew there was also no point in lying to her because he'd nearly made the Freudian slip of saying *their* house in the suburbs, *their* life together, *their* children, because back then all he'd wanted was to be with May Fleming for the rest of his life. That hadn't happened. 'That was then.'

'What happened, Arthur? What happened with your marriage?' Maybelle's words were filled with sadness and regret for him. At least her disdain for his proposed research projects had decreased…for the moment. He sat down on the floor beside the bed and shook his head.

'Yvette was an attorney—well, she still is. She practises in both Sydney and Los Angeles and is now a junior partner in the firm.'

'Impressive. How did you meet?'

'I was being sued.' He shrugged his shoulders. 'A wrongful action against the hospital I was working at.'

'In Melbourne?'

'Sydney,' he offered.

'You moved to Sydney.' She smiled with surprise and shook her head. 'It's a wonder we didn't run into each other sooner. I spent several years at Sydney General Hospital and several in the outer suburbs.'

'Wasn't meant to be.'

'And you were married to Yvette the attorney. I'm guessing it was good in the beginning?'

'As all marriages are.' He stretched his legs out in front of him and leaned back on his hands. Maybelle shifted up the bed and rested her head on a few pillows, watching him, listening to him, her heart aching for the pain he'd endured. 'Yvette was dynamic and funny.'

'And beautiful.'

Arthur smiled at that. 'Naturally. She wasn't afraid to go after what she wanted—and at the time she wanted me. I was a doctor. For her, whenever she had to network with clients and other firms, having a doctor for a husband, being the epitome of a professional couple, was important to her.'

'But not for you.'

'No. I was more interested in spending time with *her*, getting to know *her*, wanting to be with *her*.'

'And she…'

'Wanted to spend time with her senior partner, in his

bed. And with her colleagues, in their beds, and with other attorneys from other law firms, in their beds.'

'Oh, Arthur. I'm so sorry.'

He scoffed. 'She wasn't. She couldn't understand why I thought that *marriage* meant we couldn't see other people. She thought we had a great professional relationship. She never complained about how often I was at the hospital, about my dedication to my work, about my career plans. In fact, she told me she applauded them and that if we stayed married, she'd be able to assist me with the rise in my career, with networking, with playing the dutiful wife and hostess at business functions and conferences.'

'She *sounds* like an attorney.'

'She's a good lawyer. We had a house in the suburbs. She didn't want to buy it. I did and she ended up getting it in the divorce. We had two cars, mine was a normal sedan and hers was a sports car, and yet she ended up with both in the divorce.'

'But she was the one who'd committed adultery.' Maybelle lifted one hand as though completely confused by what he was saying.

'I just wanted it to be over. I agreed to most things just so I could end it as painlessly as possible.'

'And yet it's left a lasting scar on your heart.'

'It has.'

'We all have our pain.'

'But mine is nothing compared to yours.' He sat up and shifted towards the bed, still remaining on the floor as though it was safer. It felt incredible to be talking to her again, to be sharing with her, to know that she was actually interested in what he had to say, even if she didn't always agree with it.

'Your pain is *your* pain. Don't compare it to mine.' She yawned as she spoke and closed her eyes.

'I want to stroke your hair,' he murmured, and she opened one eye to look at him. 'I'm only saying this out loud because I don't want to touch you when your eyes are closed and have you freak out on me again, breaking my hand because I've frightened you.'

Maybelle started to laugh as she recalled how she'd thumped him with that dictionary. 'I'm so sorry, Arthur, about hitting you with the book, I mean.'

'Where did you think you were?' He asked the question softly as he gently reached out to touch her blonde curls. He sifted his hands through the silken strands, knowing it was a mistake, that doing such a thing was not putting distance between them, but right now he didn't know how to stop himself.

'Locked in a room.'

'Why were you locked in?'

She closed her eyes. 'Because I'd been kidnapped.'

'You were kidnapped?'

Maybelle bit her tongue to try and get control over her rising emotions. Talking about the experience had never been easy and she usually avoided it as much as possible, but Arthur was asking and if she was going to tell anyone about the ordeal it was him. Her Arthur. Her protector. Her knight in shining armour.

'Uh... Mum and I had decided to go to a conference in Sydney. We were living in Broken Hill at the time, all three of us working at the base hospital there. I was just finishing up my internship and my parents were secluded in one of the research labs.'

'Still working for the government?'

'Yes, but in secret. They would work on their pet projects, my father still researching the human genome and my mother doing her work with synthetic compounds. That was the reason she'd wanted to go to the conference in Sydney. Part of her research had been handed on to a different scientist, who had taken it to the next level.'

'I take it your parents were never credited for their work?'

'No. That had been one of the conditions of witness protection. There were to be no unauthorised trips, no unauthorised research and no ownership of the research. At times it was difficult, more for my mother than my father, as she'd worked so hard, made so much progress and then, when the research was at a certain level, it was taken from her and handed on to another researcher, one who could work on it and publish the findings.'

'That would have been difficult.'

'And that was why she and I went on an unauthorised trip to Sydney. We thought we'd taken precautions, that we'd registered under pseudonyms, changed our hair and eye colour, everything we usually did, but this time we had no bodyguards, no one looking over our shoulders, no one telling us what to do.'

'And your dad?'

'He was against it at first but my mum was always able to talk him around and in the end he covered for us with the government.' Maybelle sighed, a small smile on her lips. 'We had a great time. Driving over to Sydney was fantastic. It was as though the veil of secrecy that had shrouded our lives for almost ten years was lifted and we could be ourselves. Samantha and her daughter May, taking a road trip together. Mother and daughter time.' She opened her eyes for a moment and looked at Arthur. 'That road trip to Sydney contains some of my favourite memories and I felt as though I was really getting to know my mum. Not as my mother—'

'But as a person in her own right,' he finished for her.

'Exactly.' The smile slowly slid from Maybelle's lips.

'The trip back, however, contains the worst memories of my life. You see, somehow Mum had been recognised at the conference. Even though we'd sat in the middle of the crowd, even though we didn't speak to anyone, even though we'd gone through all checks and precautions as we'd been taught. I don't know how they figured out who she was but it wasn't until we were between Cobar and Wilcannia—'

'Which means you were in the middle of nowhere,' he added.

'They…they started shooting at our car.' She paused, her heart starting to pound wildly against her chest, the images of what had happened flashing through her mind like snapshots. She clenched her eyes tightly shut, wanting to shut them out but unable to. 'We hadn't even realised we were being tailed. We were…we were having fun, laughing together, and then there was a loud bang and Mum found it difficult to control the car as it started swerving all over the place. Then the next thing I knew the car was rolling. Over and over.' She remembered screaming, of putting out her hands in order to try and brace herself, but the screams were muted, as though she was watching the picture unfold without sound. She'd caught a glimpse of her mother's face and noticed the terror.

'We…we came to a stop. The car was on its side and I managed to undo my seatbelt and climb out. I was about to go around to Mum's side of the car—she was lying with her head against the steering wheel, at such an odd angle—and then I felt arms clamp around me. I hadn't even realised there was anyone else there. They held me. Really tight. I tried to struggle against them, to remember everything I'd been taught by my case worker, but that all stopped as I saw them drag my mother's body from the car. She was still breathing. She was alive but unconscious.' Maybelle shook her head and sniffed. 'Then they put a cloth over my mouth and nose and…as things started to go black…as I began to slip into unconsciousness, I heard a gunshot.' Her words were broken and she sniffed again, trying to draw breath into her aching lungs.

She flinched back as Arthur's hand touched her face. Maybelle opened her eyes and glared at him.

'You're crying,' he murmured softly, and it was then she realised he was wiping away her tears with his thumb.

'I am?' She sniffed once more and immediately sat up. Arthur shifted back to give her some space, offering her a tissue. 'I'd better go.'

'No. Stay. I don't want you to be alone after reliving such a memory. Stay with me. I'll hold you. I'll make you feel safe. Nothing else will happen, I promise. Just…rest in my arms, Maybelle.'

She stood and took two steps towards the door. 'I would like nothing more than to do that, but… I can't. I can't. I can't do this.'

And for the second time in a week Maybelle rushed from his apartment…and he simply let her go.

CHAPTER EIGHT

THE PICTURE OF him holding out his hand to her, offering support, to make her feel safe, especially with those hypnotic eyes of his, was difficult to get out of her head. Ever since she'd left his place in a rush, that picture had refused to disappear.

There was no doubt that a huge part of her had wanted to stay. Maybelle shifted on the lounge, resting her head back and closing her eyes tight. How was she supposed to get that image out of her mind? Arthur looking at her with devotion. Arthur looking at her as though he wanted nothing more than to really try and protect her for the rest of her life.

Was it possible? Would she be able to really put the past behind her and move forward? She shifted again, lying down on the lounge and wishing for a cushion to bury her face in as she remembered what she'd done to him. Shaking her head in embarrassment, she recalled attacking poor Arthur with a very heavy book. The terror, the panic, the fear—all had been present the instant she'd opened her eyes and gazed at the unfamiliar surroundings. And what had increased her agitation had been that she'd had no memory of getting to her present location.

Then the pounding in her eyes had taken over as she'd realised she'd fallen asleep with her contacts in. Trying to get out of the bed, her feet had become tangled in the blanket, which had been placed over her by...well, she presumed by Arthur, and she'd fallen from the bed, landing on the floor with a thud. The sound had only increased her own anxiety and she'd quickly removed the disposable lenses and looked around for a weapon. Her vision may have been fuzzy but the large book had felt solid in her hands.

At no point had she recollected coming to Arthur's apartment to feed Juzzy. At no point had she remembered closing her eyes as she'd sat on the floor with Juzzy on her lap, the two of them snoozing together. At no point had she even contemplated she hadn't been somewhere safe because she'd been acting on instinct, on pure adrenaline. That had dissipated after she'd whacked Arthur with the book and he'd called her name.

Hearing him say her name—her *real* name—had been the only thing to break through her crazed thoughts. She'd instantly felt remorse for hurting him and embarrassment for having him see the side of her life she wanted to keep hidden. To his credit, he'd behaved in exactly the way she'd hoped he would, by listening to her talk and offering his support. He was quite a man.

Yes, she could have stayed tonight, she could have felt secure and comfortable in his arms, just as she had many times before, but what if she'd fallen asleep and woken up thrashing about? What if she'd hurt him again, hit him with an even harder object? And if she'd given in and stayed with him tonight, then she'd want to stay with him the next night and the next night and the one after that. If she was able to sleep soundly with him holding her, she'd never want to let him go.

Was that what he wanted? For her to become dependent on him? Was that what she wanted? Not only that,

Arthur had come straight out and told her that he wasn't looking to do the marriage thing again. He'd been hurt once—and badly from the sound of it—and he wasn't about to embark on another adventure that might turn out to be just as disastrous. It was true that should she and Arthur start dating, there was no way in the world she would ever cheat on him. She most definitely believed in monogamy.

But Arthur had also told her that he wanted to focus on his career, on his research, and especially as he'd already obtained funding, which, in a highly competitive field, was a triumph in itself. The problem was that she had already lived a life where she'd often been considered second to a Petri dish. If Arthur really wanted to pursue that level of research, it would require all his attention and she didn't want to be in a relationship where once again she was playing second fiddle.

'Good things don't happen to you,' she told herself. 'Accept it as fact.' So it was a good thing she had left his apartment, that she'd hightailed it upstairs into her new sanctuary. Perhaps friendship was their only answer. There was too much water under the bridge for the two of them. They'd missed their opportunity and now the only avenue left open to them was that of very good friends.

Could she do that? Surely the weakness she felt in her knees every time he looked at her, or the way her heart raced whenever he smiled, or the tingles that enveloped her entire body when he spoke, would one day become a thing of the past? Right?

Maybelle sighed in exasperation and shifted on the lounge yet again, grudgingly agreeing Arthur had been right about the lounge needing some cushions. She needed pictures on the walls, too. She needed to put her own identity into this apartment. After all, she didn't have to move if she didn't want to.

She didn't have to move! The realisation was like being hit by a truck. The government had decreed the threat null and void. She was free and it wasn't until that moment that the truth of her situation started to sink in.

She'd told Arthur she wanted to find normalcy, to have a life like everyone else. She'd striven for years to find a level of normal but getting comfortable had often meant complacency and letting down her guard. Whenever she'd done that, bad things had happened. Being vigilant for so long had taken its toll on her but surely it wasn't going to stop her from really trying to make a go of a normal life.

Arthur had previously suggested taking her shopping for cushions and pictures and normal things, and as she glanced around the apartment she compared it to Arthur's. He had shelves filled with books, photographs on the mantelpiece and pictures on the walls. Yes, she had the necessities in life but it was sparse and bland. Would letting some colour into her life bring her happiness?

Was that really what her life was like? Sparse and bland? Would spending time with Arthur help her to get some colour into her world? She wanted to spend time with him, to be friends. Could they be just friends and avoid the frighteningly natural chemistry that existed between them from taking centre stage?

Rising from the lounge, she headed into the back bedroom, which still had several boxes waiting for her to unpack. She reached into one of them, pulling out various items until she found what she was looking for. Her old jewellery box. It was the one item she'd been adamant about holding onto, no matter how many times they moved. Carefully she opened it up, the tinny music starting to play.

She carried the box out to the lounge room and sat down, winding the box up when the music stopped. Inside the box, mixed in amongst her mother's jewellery, was something she had treasured ever since that night. She picked the item up and rubbed a finger over the face of the watch. Arthur's watch. The one she'd been timing him with when he'd been studying that night, the watch she'd put onto her wrist and then, when his father had come into the room and she had fled, it hadn't been until much later that she'd remembered she was still wearing it. As they'd been forced to leave their home that night, she'd kept the watch, secretly delighted she had something of his, something that could bind her to him.

If only things had turned out differently. If only…

When Arthur knocked on her door the next day, Maybelle was ready. They hadn't confirmed whether or not he was still taking her shopping but she was delighted he'd turned up. Earlier that morning she'd ignored the sensual dreams she'd had of him—the one where she'd woken with the memory of his kisses on her lips—and donned her armour of friendship. She was wearing denim jeans, running shoes, a T-shirt and an old baggy sweatshirt. If her hair had been long enough to pull back into pigtails she would have done that, but instead she fluffed the unruly curls and added a baseball cap. She was the exact opposite of sexy and the epitome of friendship.

'Wow. Don't you look like fun?'

Maybelle stared at Arthur with stunned surprise when those words came out of his mouth. What did she have to do to get him *not* to notice her? Wear a garbage bag?

'Fun?' She adjusted the hot pink baseball cap on her

head and ran her finger around the rim of the brim. 'I'll have you know I take my shopping trips very seriously.'

'I stand corrected,' he remarked. He didn't venture into her apartment and instead waited on the threshold as though kept there by an invisible force field. Could he feel that tug? She could. Could he feel that spark that seemed to sizzle beneath the surface? She could. Could he stop glancing at her lips as though he wanted nothing more than to kiss her hello?

Maybelle jerked a thumb over her shoulder. 'I'll just grab my bag.' She walked off but called back to him, 'Are we taking your car?'

'Seems reasonable, given I know the way to the store.'

'Right. Right.' She returned with her bag and made sure she had her keys before closing the apartment door behind her. Arthur stepped back to allow her room but didn't venture towards the stairs. 'Something wrong?'

'You have the brown contacts in again.'

'Of course.' She walked towards the staircase, needing to keep things moving, needing to keep things on an even keel because when Arthur was around her, especially after the heat they'd generated together last night, she most definitely lost all focus—contacts or no contacts.

'Huh.' He followed her down the stairs. 'Short-sighted or long?'

'Short.' She cleared her throat as she reached for the front door to their apartment block. 'How's Juzzy this morning?' Maybelle was determined to keep the conversation nice and light, on general topics, and it seemed Arthur was only too willing to oblige. Perhaps he'd had second thoughts after what had happened last night? Perhaps he'd regretted telling her what it was he wanted out of life? Perhaps he, too, thought it was wise to put some emotional distance between them?

As he chatted about the dog's antics that morning, Maybelle took the time to peruse him more thoroughly. He, too, was dressed comfortably in a dark pair of denims and a black jumper. Casual but not dressy. He could walk into a casino or a fast-food restaurant and seem completely at ease in both. He looked good, though, really good, and she bit her lip in an effort to distract her mind from the memories that were starting to rise to the surface.

Arthur drove to the district where several homeware and furniture stores were located. Maybelle couldn't believe how different the area was from when she'd lived here. 'So much has changed,' she murmured, not realising she'd spoken out loud until Arthur chuckled.

'What did you expect? Twenty years is a long time, Maybelle. Progress does tend to happen.'

'Oh, no, look. There. That restaurant. I remember that restaurant. It was an Italian restaurant with awesome food.'

'Still is.'

'Ha! Something stayed the same.' She sighed with happiness, then glared at Arthur when he laughed at her again. 'What's so funny?'

'You. You're such a juxtaposition unto yourself.'

Maybelle rolled her eyes. 'Whatever, mate. I just know what I know and like what I like and you can take that anyway *you* like.'

'That type of attitude should make picking houseware a real treat. Next you'll tell me that you're not really sure what you want but when you see it, you'll know.'

'You know me too well.' They were the wrong words to say as it brought back just how well he did know her. She glanced at him and he glanced at her, before they both returned their gazes to the front windscreen.

'Let's have some music.' Arthur quickly turned on the radio, needing to break the awkward tension that was starting to swirl around them. Thankfully, it wasn't too much longer before they arrived at the store and when they entered, Maybelle clasped her hands tightly together. Not because she was excited to be here but because there were just so many people around.

The store was huge, a wide open-plan store that was set out in departments. There were dining-room tables and chairs on one side and sofas on the other. In the far right corner were beds of all shapes and sizes and to the left was a different section, which had pillows, curtains and household linen.

In the rear part of the store was another large area where she could see kitchen appliances, cameras and computers. Streamers and balloons were everywhere, brightly coloured and moving slightly with the breeze from the heaters, which were working overtime trying to keep the people in the store warm against the outside weather.

Parents, children, babies, prams, pregnant ladies, pensioners and couples of all ages seemed to have congregated in this one large store all at the same time. The sales staff were easily distinguished in bright red blazers and several were walking the floor, offering their assistance to the patrons.

The noise. The heat. The lights. The decorations. Everything blurred into one big headache and Maybelle breathed out slowly in order to try and calm her rising panic.

'Are you all right?'

She looked at Arthur, surprised to see a worried look on his face. 'Why?'

'Because every muscle in your body is tense. Your

jaw is clenched. You're squeezing your fingers so tightly together, your knuckles are turning white. What is it?'

'It's nothing.'

'Rubbish.' He placed a hand beneath her elbow and steered her carefully to the corner of the store, where he sat her down on a small sofa. Arthur sat next to her and placed a hand over hers. 'Tell me what's happening, Maybelle. Let me help you. Please?'

'It's just very…busy.'

'In the store? Do you want to leave?'

Maybelle stopped looking around at everything and focused her attention on Arthur. He was concerned. She could see it in his eyes and hear it in his voice. He was concerned…for her. How was she supposed to resist him when he cared about her so much?

'Talk to me, Maybelle. Don't shut me out. Tell me what's going through your head. Let me help you find that new normal you're so desperately seeking.'

She dragged in a breath, held it for a moment, and then slowly exhaled. 'Large places like this,' she began quietly, 'can be dangerous. When you're trying to hide from someone, they're good. You can blend in with the crowd but at the same time it means there are more people around to keep your eye on, to ensure you don't accidentally bump into the person you're trying to get away from.'

Arthur slowly shook his head, compassion and concern etched in his expression. He didn't say anything but his thumb was rubbing her hand gently, as though urging her to continue.

'The instant we entered this building I scanned the place for the exits. I do it everywhere I go. It's become part of my normal routine. In here, apart from the main doors where we came in, there are eight. Some are nor-

mal entry and exit ways, but the others—over there behind the linen department and the one next to the kitchen
appliances—are for the staff and no doubt lead to the
stockrooms. There are thirteen desks where people can
sit with staff and discuss their purchases and in the bed-
ding section there's a small side room hidden behind the
large plastic plant.'

'How did you do that?' Arthur turned his head to
check out the areas she was mentioning, his jaw momentarily hanging open in surprise.

'When I was rescued after the first kidnapping, the
government decided I needed some training in martial
arts and espionage techniques. I didn't turn them down
and the next time someone tried to kidnap me, that training kicked in. I had those kidnappers disarmed and on
the ground with broken bones like a pro, then I escaped.'

'Uh…right.' She could hear the shock in Arthur's tone
at her matter-of-fact words.

'That training has become ingrained. I can also tell
you where the restrooms are, the disability ramps and
how much this sofa costs. This is how my brain is wired.
This is what I have to endure every time I walk into a new
place. My mind seems to slip into covert mode and scans
the room for possible threats and exits. I can't help it.'

'What about the hospital? The ED? Do you do the
scanning thing every time you walk in?'

'Not so much now, but the first time, yes. The staff
were captivated by some anecdote you were sharing.'

The side of his lips quirked upwards. 'I like to ensure
we can laugh together. I find it helps the teamwork to be
more cohesive.'

'That's the sign of a good leader.' She smiled at him
and dragged in a calming breath, immediately feeling
better. 'Thank you for listening.'

'Thank you for sharing. I know it must be difficult for you sometimes—'

'Like waking up in a strange bed and attacking you with a book?'

Arthur chuckled and rubbed his head. 'Certainly gets the adrenaline pumping.' He stared at her, the smile slowly fading from his lips. How was it that his eyes could change from joviality to seriousness within a split second? 'Whatever you need, Maybelle, I'm right here. Support, friendship, a shoulder to cry on.'

And she was right where she'd told herself not to be... gazing once more into Arthur's eyes and wanting him, so desperately, to kiss her.

CHAPTER NINE

'THIS ISN'T GOOD,' Arthur murmured, his words barely audible, but even if he hadn't spoken out loud, Maybelle was sure she would have heard him as the connection between them seemed to transcend the normal parameters of the world. Her heart was beating perfectly in time with his. How she knew this, she had no clue. She just knew. Their attraction was only magnifying their connection, their need for each other, and once again she had the urge to just go for it, to take their relationship to the ultimate consummation, and then she would have him out of her system. She could let go of the man who had been a large part of her world and she could move on.

He was looking at her lips as though he could kiss her with his caress and when she angled in closer to him, wanting the same thing, he slipped his arm further around her shoulders, gathering her near. When his gaze met hers once more, the fire, heat and desire was exactly what she'd been expecting to see…needing to see because she knew it matched her own.

'Why are we fighting this?' Again his words were so quiet but they reverberated loudly within Maybelle's heart and she placed a hand on his thigh and moved in even more, a hair's breadth from what it was they both so desperately wanted. 'I need you.'

'I know.' And with that, she pressed her mouth to his in the softest, most tantalising kiss she was sure they'd ever had. Such a feather-light touch, which caused a riot of fireworks to explode within her. Whether they were hot and hungry or as gentle as the beat of a butterfly's wings, the tension between them was always intense and she doubted that would ever change.

'I see the love seat is working its magic once again.'

The rude words were like a stylus scratching across the surface of an old vinyl record and they both turned to see a red-blazered sales assistant regarding them as though they were cute little cherubs. Her hands were clutched to her chest and the smile on her face was one of encouragement.

Arthur cleared his throat and eased away from Maybelle. 'Pardon?'

'The love seat.' The sales lady gestured to the sofa they were sitting on. 'We often have couples come and try it out. It's very comfortable and very…encompassing.' She spread her hands wide, then brought them together, her fingers linking as though to illustrate her point. 'Perfect for that wintry night, snuggled up by the heater, watching a movie.'

Feeling closed in with the woman hovering over them, Maybelle started to feel her earlier anxiety—the anxiety Arthur had been more than effective in quashing—begin to return. She didn't like feeling closed in, or patronised by pushy salespeople. Maybelle stood, pleased she was slightly taller than the other woman, and pulled her baseball cap down a little further. 'Excuse me.' She sidestepped the woman and walked towards the restrooms. She knew she was leaving Arthur to deal with the situation but he was more than capable of fending off a fawning piranha.

Her heart was pounding against her chest and she knew it was more from the way Arthur made her feel than anxiety. Chalk one up to sensual desire, she mused. A good cure for anxiety. In fact, she would be more than happy to have Arthur help her deal with her anxiety in such a way in the future and she knew he'd be willing to assist her with that research project. A small smile touched her lips and she felt her earlier dread begin to disappear.

She was doing normal things in the normal world. No one was here to kidnap her, there was no threat to her life any more. She would splash some water on her face, take five calming deep breaths, and go out and buy some throw pillows and pictures to brighten up her apartment. She could do this. She could.

Entering the restroom, she was immediately distracted by the sound of a woman in one of the stalls crying out in pain. Maybelle's professional persona was immediately on alert. She waited. Perhaps someone had a bad case of gastroenteritis. A moment later the sound came again.

'Are you all right?' Maybelle asked. The only reply she received was a panting and grunting sort of sound. 'Please? I'm a doctor. I can help.'

The next answer she received was another loud grunt, a cry and a yell all combined. 'I know that sound,' Maybelle muttered. She immediately bent down to check beneath the stalls, remembering seeing a heavily pregnant woman wandering around the store when they'd first entered and the woman had been heading towards the restrooms. 'Are you in labour? If so, are you able to unlock the stall so I can get to you?'

'Wasn't…supposed to be happening…yet,' a woman panted as Maybelle heard the sound of a locked latch being undone. She went into the cubicle, seeing a woman bend-ing forward, half sitting, half trying to get off the toilet.

'How many weeks' gestation are you?' Maybelle asked as she helped the woman to manoeuvre out of the stall and onto the floor of the bathroom.

'Twenty-eight.'

Maybelle was surprised as the woman looked much bigger. 'Twins?'

'Yes. Girls.'

'I'm Maybelle, by the way,' she said as she pulled her cellphone from her pocket and called Arthur.

'Jenna.' She slowly let out a long breath, then leaned back against the wall as the contraction passed. 'I think it's all right now.'

'I disagree,' Maybelle replied, then turned her atten-tion to the phone as Arthur answered. 'Can you come into the women's bathroom, please? I have a woman in labour.'

'Who are you calling?' Jenna demanded as Maybelle disconnected the call.

'The director of the emergency department at Vic-tory Hospital. He's right outside.' She smiled at Jenna.

'Are you an obstetrician?'

'No, we're both emergency specialists—and this most definitely classifies as an emergency.'

'I'd just said to Sean that something didn't feel right and that we should leave here and go to the hospital but I needed to go to the—' Jenna stopped talking, wrinkled her nose and opened her mouth as another contraction started to make itself known. Jenna clearly wasn't back-wards in letting her discomfort out, and as Arthur came into the bathroom he was greeted with a full-on yell of pain and anguish as only a woman in labour could make.

'You weren't kidding.'

'Is there a first-aid kit nearby? And can you get some towels or sheets or both so I can at least make a sterilised area?'

'Being in a store that sells all those things shouldn't make that request too difficult,' he replied, and headed out again. Maybelle stood and took off her hat before thoroughly washing her hands, coaching Jenna through her breathing. When the contraction started to subside, Jenna tried to lever herself from the floor.

'What are you doing?' Maybelle asked as she finished drying her hands with the hand-dryer.

'I'm standing up.' Jenna glared at her as though she was insane. 'I need to get to hospital and get this labour stopped. My girls aren't done yet. I still have twelve weeks left of my pregnancy and—' Jenna's words were cut short as her abdomen contracted once more and she immediately slumped back against the wall, wrinkling her nose and crying out in pain.

'That was less than a minute between the two contractions,' Maybelle stated as she knelt down, being careful not to touch her hands against anything. 'Jenna. I need to check to see how far dilated you are.' The woman's underwear was still around her ankles and her shoes had somehow come off but thankfully she was wearing a skirt, which Maybelle lifted up with her elbows. As Jenna continued with the contraction, concentrating on her breathing but screaming in pain every now and then, Maybelle was extremely surprised to see a tiny hand presenting first—as though waving hello and letting everyone know that no matter how much they may wish to stop this labour, it wasn't going to happen.

'Your waters must have broken because things are definitely progressing fast,' Maybelle told her just as Arthur came back into the room with a first-aid kit. Behind him was the store manager, carrying a bundle of fresh towels and sheets, along with a pillow and blanket for the labouring woman, which he quickly placed on the floor and then rushed out, telling them he would ensure they had privacy.

As Maybelle pulled on a pair of gloves, Arthur pulled the clean sheets from the packets and spread them around the area where Jenna now slouched.

'I found some paper straws, which we can use in place of suction, and also some bag clips to clamp the cord if the ambulance doesn't get here in time.'

'It won't,' she told him softly, and indicated the little hand.

'Ah...'

'Scissors?'

'Should be some in the first-aid kit.'

'Good.' Maybelle nodded and went back to coaching Jenna as the contraction started to ease once more. This time Jenna didn't even bother to move, except when Arthur needed her to lift her bottom so they could get the clean sheet and a comfortable towel beneath her.

'And look...the sheets are nice and pink. Perfect for two little girls.'

'Ambulances are on their way.'

'Ambulances? More than one?' Jenna asked, a little dazed and light-headed. Before Arthur could answer, there was a ruckus at the closed bathroom door with raised male voices.

'I'm sorry, sir,' came the store manager's voice. 'There's an emergency in progress.'

'Where's my wife? My wife was in there! She's pregnant. Jenna! Jenna?'

'Sean?' Jenna called back, and within the next moment a man came bursting into the women's restroom and rushed over to his wife's side. 'Where were you?' She burst into tears as he crouched down by her head and hugged her close, kissing her.

'I was still looking at the cribs. I'm here now.'

'So are our girls,' Jenna managed to get out as another contraction came. Maybelle supported the little hand, which was up beside the baby's head, as she talked Jenna through the contraction. Sean's eyes widened as he looked at what was happening.

'Is that a hand?'

'Yes,' Arthur answered. 'Sometimes babies are born with an arm above their head and given there are two babies in there, things may have been getting a little cramped.'

'Who are you?' Sean demanded.

'Shut up, Sean,' Jenna yelled between breaths.

'That's it. The head's almost out…now pant, Jenna. Pant. I just need to check that the cord isn't around the baby's neck.' Maybelle's tone was calm and controlled, as were her actions as she confirmed the tiny little neck was clear of the cord. 'Arthur?'

'Ready,' he told her.

'OK, Jenna. With the next contraction, I want you to focus all your energy on pushing down. That's it. Good. Good. Grit your teeth and… That's it! Baby girl number one is out.'

Maybelle expertly handled the tiny twenty-eight-week-old baby and held her out so Arthur could wrap her in a towel. The fluffy new towel almost engulfed the baby, which Maybelle guessed to be less than one kilogram in weight.

Arthur was rubbing the baby with the towel, trying to stimulate blood flow and breathing. Maybelle grabbed the box of paper straws Arthur had brought in and pulled one out, sucking the mucus and gunk from the baby's mouth then nose, spitting the contents onto the sheet surrounding the area.

'Why isn't she crying?' Jenna's voice was tremulous, worried and extremely concerned.

'They're working on it,' Sean soothed, as he watched what was going on. Once Maybelle had finished sucking out the nose, the little one dragged in a fighting breath, gasping a little as Arthur continued to rub the vernix off and stimulate blood flow.

'New towel,' he stated, and Maybelle reached for another one and accepted the baby from him.

'Nostrils are flaring a bit and there's sternal recession.'

'Wh-what does that mean?' Jenna's tone was almost hysterical and with good reason.

'Baby's having a bit of trouble breathing,' Maybelle told the new parents. 'But she's a fighter.' Maybelle was about to pass Arthur two of the bag clamps so they could clamp off and then cut the umbilical cord when Jenna's body tensed with another contraction and she started to yell once more from the pain.

'Give me the one-minute Apgar,' Maybelle told him as she returned her attention to delivering the next baby. Arthur was more than capable of clamping and cutting the cord. Ordinarily, they'd get the father to do it but right now there was no time for formalities. These little girls needed expert attention and it was up to them to provide it. 'All right, Jenna. Here we go again.'

'Isn't the ambulance here yet?' she panted as she tried to breathe her way through the pain racking her body.

'One-minute Apgar is six and a half,' Arthur stated and Maybelle nodded.

'You're doing great, Jenna. Let's just focus on what's going on here. I can see the baby's head. It's bigger than the other twin.' She paused and checked, feeling around. 'Quite a bit bigger.' Maybelle glanced over at Arthur, her look indicating that something wasn't completely right with this whole situation. It would be wonderful if they had a baby heart monitor, or a stethoscope or even an old Pinard horn so she could check the other baby's heart rate because what she was thinking meant that the baby who was still to be born wasn't about to have an easy ride.

'When was your last check-up?' she asked Jenna as the contraction eased. Jenna closed her eyes and rested her head against her husband's shoulder. 'Sean?' Jenna needed to rest and if she didn't feel up to answering questions then her husband could do it for her. 'When was the last check-up?'

'Last week. Our obstetrician wanted Jenna to have a scan on Monday because she had some concerns.'

'Did she happen to say what those concerns might be?'

'She told us one baby was bigger than the other but that it should settle down. She wanted it monitored closely, though. Why? What's wrong? Is there something wrong with our little girls?'

'Sean!' Jenna growled at him. 'You're freaking me out. Just let me get through this delivery.'

'This next baby is quite a bit bigger than the other.' Maybelle spoke softly to ensure Jenna remained calm and focused.

'That's OK, right? Our doctor said that neither of the twins were the same size as a normal baby...you know... if we weren't having twins.'

'Yes, that's right, but one big twin and one small twin can sometimes mean one has been greedier than the other in the womb.'

'Fighting already?' Jenna groaned, before gritting her teeth as another contraction began. Once more, Maybelle looked at Arthur and he nodded as though he received the silent message she was sending.

'Are the babies identical?' Arthur asked as he continued to care for the tiny baby rugged up in the fresh towel.

'Yes. They share a placenta.' Sean answered immediately, proud that he knew and understood that much.

'Oh. Did your doctor talk to you about the possibility of twin-to-twin transfusion?'

'She said a lot of things,' Sean answered when Jenna seemed more focused on getting the job done, rather than answering questions. As Jenna started to push, Maybelle focused her attention on delivering the baby's head and while this one was bigger than the first twin, it was still quite tiny compared to a baby carried to full gestation. 'Just checking there is no cord around the neck…and we're good. Excellent panting, Jenna. Almost there. Almost there now.'

The store manager opened the door for a moment and announced that the ambulances were pulling into the car park.

'There you go. Good news. Keep pushing, keep pushing,' Maybelle encouraged as Jenna continued to deliver her second daughter. Arthur announced the five-minute Apgar for the first baby to be eight.

'Good,' was Maybelle's reply.

'Sean. I need you to come and hold your daughter,' Arthur told him, and beckoned him over. 'Open your shirt and we'll put her on your chest.'

'My chest?' Sean's eyes were already wide at what was happening but they grew even wider at this.

'Body heat. It's the best way to keep her warm.'

The bemused Sean opened his shirt and Arthur placed the baby on his chest. 'Hold her firmly and watch her in the mirror—that way you can report any breathing difficulties or change of colour. It's imperative we keep her warm. See how she's breathing a bit better than she was before? Now you need to keep her in this position. We need to be able to see her breathing. See her sternal area?' Arthur indicated the area where the baby's chest was rising and falling as she breathed. 'Keep her at this angle because it helps get air into her lungs. We also need to make sure we support her head and not move her around too much.'

'Are you sure I should be holding her?' Sean asked, clearly freaked out by holding his extremely tiny baby girl.

'Yes. I need to help with your other daughter and, as you're her father, who better qualified?'

'Father!' Sean's eyes suddenly registered the truth of the word.

Arthur smiled but left the tiny baby girl in her father's more than capable arms before preparing to accept the second daughter from Maybelle. Towels at the ready, it wasn't long before the little girl was out of the womb and into his waiting hands.

He wrapped her up and started to stimulate the blood flow, the poor little thing grunting for air. Maybelle used the straws once again to suck out as much mucus and gunk as she could from the mouth then the nose, in order to clear the airways, but still the baby grunted, the breaths shallow.

'What's happening?' Jenna asked as she lay back, eyes closed, but the concern in her tone was evident.

'This one's having difficulty breathing.'

'But she's really red and a good colour,' Sean interjected.

'She's too red,' Maybelle said as she readied another towel after Arthur had finished wiping all the vernix off. 'What are you going to call the girls?' She pressed her fingers to the baby's umbilical cord in order to take a pulse.

'The first one is Poppie and the other one is Lillie,' Jenna said, trying to open her eyes to see what was going on, but exhaustion was kicking in and they still had to deliver the placenta.

'Well, Lillie is red because she has too many blood cells. It appears that although the girls were sharing a placenta, they weren't getting equal shares of the nutrients.'

'One-minute Apgar for Lillie is four.' Arthur continued to stimulate blood flow but they really needed to get her into the hospital and sort her out sooner rather than later.

'Is that bad?' Sean asked. 'Poppie's score was six and a half and—'

Before he could finish his sentence, the door to the restroom burst open and the paramedics came in, carrying their medical bags.

'Good timing,' Arthur said as they finished clamping and cutting Lillie's cord. 'Twin-to-twin transfer. Placenta still to be delivered,' he stated, as the paramedics knelt down to assist them. 'Maybelle, you and I need to get the girls to the hospital, *stat*.'

'The ambulance with the incubator is in the parking lot.'

'Excellent.'

'We'll take care of the mother,' the other paramedic told them as Maybelle and Arthur wrapped Lillie in another towel to keep her body temperature up. 'Oh, and by the way, the media's here. TV crew pulled up just after us.'

'Media!' Maybelle was the one who reacted and she quickly shook her head repeatedly. Not the media. She just couldn't deal with that. Not now. She'd already been emotionally exhausted from dealing with the crowds, fighting her attraction to Arthur and having to deliver sick babies! She'd been raised to keep herself hidden, to never appear on any sort of media, most of all on television.

'The store manager must have called them,' she heard someone say, but their words seemed far away, echoing around her. All she was conscious of was fear and panic beginning to grip her. The media…cameras…reporters… everything she'd been avoiding for years was right outside those doors. Her mouth went dry and her breathing increased as she tried to figure out a way she could escape without being photographed by any cameras.

'Someone clearly did,' Arthur replied as he handed Lillie to Maybelle, before retrieving Poppie from Sean. 'We'll take good care of your girls.' As she accepted the baby from him, she briefly met his gaze and tried to swallow over the dryness in her throat. Arthur's eyes widened imperceptibly as he recognised the panic in hers.

'Dr Maybelle here is going to give Lillie her undivided attention.' His words were pointed and Maybelle acknowledged them with a slight nod of her head. Yes. She had to concentrate on Lillie, on ensuring the little girl could breathe properly. Then Arthur picked up her baseball cap and placed it on her head, pulling it down so it obscured a lot of her face from the view of prying cameras. The action was so considerate, so nice, so thoughtful.

'They couldn't be in better hands,' the paramedic agreed, trying to fill both Jenna and Sean with confidence as their newborn twins were being taken away from them.

'Focus on the babies.' Arthur's words were warm and

caring. He was standing just behind her, his warmth seeming to encompass her, calming her previously frazzled nerves. How was it possible that one reassuring look from him could instantly settle the anxiety she'd spent years trying to control?

'Because he's Arthur!' she whispered to Lillie as together they walked out of the store.

CHAPTER TEN

As THEY ENTERED the ambulance, Arthur and Maybelle were solely focused on the babies.

'That wasn't so bad, was it?' Arthur asked softly as they placed the babies in a shared incubator. The paramedics shut the door, stopping the prying eyes of the media from watching them any further. As they'd exited the women's restroom and walked through the store, the media cameras had been rolling, reporters trying to ask them questions as they'd carried the babies through to the waiting ambulances. The store manager had been trying to clear a path for them, as well as getting himself in every photograph being taken, either by the media or others in the store.

Maybelle had kept her head down, focusing on Lillie's breathing, still stimulating blood flow, hoping it wouldn't take too long to settle down, but poor Lillie was still grunting and gasping for air.

'It went as well as could be expected,' Maybelle replied, as they made sure the babies were on their backs, their heads up. Thankfully, this ambulance was equipped for treating small babies and children. She found the smallest-sized mouth and nose mask in one of the drawers and attached it to the Laerdal bag before assisting Lillie with her breathing.

'Five-minute Apgar is around seven, which is a definite improvement,' Arthur added a moment later after he'd attached an oximeter to Lillie. 'How's Poppie?'

'Oh, she's a fighter. Look at her colour. Nice and pink.'

They continued on to the hospital, their attention solely on the girls, and when they arrived, finally able to get some tests started for both girls, Maybelle checked Lillie's umbilical pulse and was pleased to find it improved.

They were met at the doors to the emergency department by one of the ED nurses and one of the neonate nurses.

'Twenty-eight weeks gestation monochorionic twins: Poppie and Lillie,' Maybelle stated, giving the staff the information they needed. 'Twin-to-twin transfusion with Lillie being the recipient, as you can see. Lillie's Apgar scores were four, then seven; Poppie's were six and a half, then eight.'

'Chest X-ray, cranial ultrasound, full blood count, blood gas and electrolyte levels,' Arthur added as they finished transferring the girls to their individual incubators. The nurses performed their observations and reported their findings.

'So tiny.' Maybelle checked Poppie's blood pressure reading, which was being monitored via the umbilical arterial line. She put her sterilised hand into the crib through the arm porthole and gently placed her hand on the girl's chest.

'Just as well we were out shopping.' Arthur's words were quiet as he visually assessed Lillie, the cardiac monitor letting them know her beats per minute had progressed to one hundred and ten. She was under the lights, the jaundice starting to appear.

Gemma came over to let them know that both Jenna and Sean were at the desk, wanting to see their girls.

When Maybelle walked over to greet them, pleased that Jenna was in a wheelchair as she would be exhausted after her ordeal, she was astonished when Jenna grabbed her hands and pulled her down for a fierce hug.

'Thank you, thank you, thank you.' There were tears in the new mother's eyes. 'I hated it when you took my babies away but I knew you had to.'

Maybelle managed to murmur all the right responses as she slowly pulled back from the anxious woman.

'You saved my girls. You saved me. So many things could have gone wrong and yet—'

'We're not going to think about that,' Sean interjected as he placed both hands on the wheelchair handles and started to edge the chair forward.

'I was only in the maternity ward for a matter of minutes before they said it was OK to come and see our girls,' Jenna continued, as though Sean hadn't spoken, her desperation for her daughters mounting with each passing second. 'Can we see them? Can we?'

'Of course. They've both stabilised and we're getting ready to transfer them to the NICU.'

'What's that?' Sean asked, concern in his tone, and Maybelle smiled.

'Neonatal Intensive Care Unit. Let me introduce you to Iris. She's one of the NICU nurses.' Maybelle headed over to where Lillie and Poppie were lying, so tiny but so very much alive.

'Can we hold them?' Jenna's eyes greedily drank in the sight of her baby girls.

'Not for a few days but you can definitely touch them. No stroking, just putting your hand through to touch them.' Maybelle waited while they washed their hands, then took them over to their babies, the twins lying side by side in their incubators.

'What's wrong with Lillie?' Jenna shook her head as she looked at her daughter hooked up to tubes and monitors. 'She's so much bigger than Poppie, but I thought Poppie would have been the one who was struggling.'

'In a twin-to-twin transfer, which is what's been happening here with your girls,' Arthur explained as he finished adjusting one of Lillie's monitors, 'Lillie's been getting the lion's share of the nutrients provided by their shared placenta. This means that Poppie has always been used to fighting.'

'You mentioned something like that when Lillie was born,' Sean added as he stared in wonder at his girls.

'Lillie, on the other hand,' Arthur continued, 'isn't used to fighting and hence why she's the one now needing more attention, but she's picking up. Her breathing has settled, her oxygen saturations are much better and her blood gases are improving.'

'They're improving.' Jenna sighed as she spoke, relief in her tone. Arthur and Maybelle stayed with Jenna and Sean until after the babies had been transferred to the NICU and once their obligations were done, they headed out of the hospital.

'That wasn't how I thought the day would go,' Maybelle commented as they walked towards the car park.

'Part and parcel of the job, eh?' he asked rhetorically.

'They're just so…tiny…so innocent. They have no idea how bad this world can be.'

'Or how good,' Arthur countered.

Maybelle glanced at him. 'There's more bad in this world than good, Arthur.'

'I beg to differ.'

'That's because all you've seen *are* the good bits. You got the good parents, the stable life, living in one house, doing the things that every normal person does.'

'And you got the bad,' Arthur stated. 'Not living in one house, seeing the dark side of life and learning how to live in it, but, Maybelle…' He placed a hand on her arm to stop her movements and when she turned to face him, he spoke earnestly. 'You survived. You conquered. With everything that's been thrown at you, everything you've gone through, you won, honey. You won!'

'Did I?' She lifted the cap off her head and ran her free hand through her curls. 'I'm so confused, Arthur. Those twins…they've…confused me. They're so tiny and innocent and if I was their mother, I would want to wrap them in cotton wool and never let them out into the world.' She shook her head and returned the cap, needing the shield the brim provided. 'Why do people even *have* children? Why would they put them through the pain this world can bring?'

'Because, in normal circumstances, the good outweighs the bad.' Usually, she could keep her emotions under control and locked away but ever since Arthur had come back into her life, it was as though he'd brought her vulnerabilities out of the darkness and into the light. It was annoying because part of her wanted to keep everything locked away and hidden from sight, to keep her distance from Arthur and the dreams of a future together.

However, having seen those gorgeous little babies, so incredibly tiny and fighting for life with every breath, something deep inside Maybelle had burst forth and she found she *wanted* to tell Arthur about her past, to share her insecurities with him, to shine light on the darkness, because that was the only way it was going to disappear for ever. She now had firm images in her mind of what Arthur would look like holding a newborn babe and in her mind it was *their* newborn babe he was holding.

'Maybelle, you don't realise how gifted you are. Your

trials and tribulations have given you such a unique perspective on all sorts of alternative medical situations. Take Mr Bird, for example. If your life, your experiences had been different, you wouldn't have even thought to check the synthetic compounds in the anaesthetic.'

'Huh. I hadn't thought of it like that before.' She frowned for a moment. 'I guess that can be said of all of us working here. Our unique, personal experiences provide us with unique perspectives on the injuries and ailments we treat in the ED.'

'Exactly.' Arthur smiled and couldn't help caressing her cheek. 'You're unique, Maybelle, in *so* many ways, and regardless of what happens in your future, whether you have children…' his voice dipped slightly at the word and his gaze momentarily encompassed her lips '…or not, you'll still be able to bring your unique perspective to everything you do.' He shifted closer to her, his gaze flicking between her mouth and her eyes, the tension surrounding them beginning to thicken with repressed desire and need. 'For the record, I think you'd make an incredible mother. Fierce and protective but still able to enjoy those moments of pure happiness.'

'Do you think so?' The uncertainty in her voice was his undoing and he began to lower his head towards hers.

'I have no doubt.' His words barely a whisper, he brushed his lips across hers in one of those insides-melting, heart-thumping, teasing butterfly kisses.

'Arthur?'

'Yes, honey?'

'You confuse me more than anyone else.'

'How so?'

'Because I… I…' She stopped, biting her tongue. She was exposing herself, making herself vulnerable. They were in a public place, anyone could see them kissing, whispering, staring at each other with pure lust and desire in their eyes.

'I really want to be friends with you, Maybelle,' he remarked softly. 'I keep telling myself that over and over but then you look at me and I get all twisted up inside.'

'I'm sorry.'

'No. Do not apologise. I like getting twisted up by you.' He ventured another butterfly kiss and she almost melted into his arms, momentarily not caring who saw them. 'Is this thing we both clearly feel a residual from all those years ago? That because our relationship was cut short—'

'We never got to see how it really ends?' she asked, finishing his sentence.

'There has never been anyone who has made me feel the way you do.'

'Not even your ex-wife?'

'No. Only you make me this crazy, this determined, this afraid.'

'Afraid? You're afraid of me? I promise I won't slug you with any books ever again.'

He chuckled and shook his head slowly from side to side, caressing her cheek before dropping his hand and stepping back. 'That's not what I meant. I mean…how I feel about you, how I feel when I'm with you, how I feel when I'm without you.'

She nodded. 'Me, too. That's exactly how I feel. I'm confused and I'm happy and I'm scared and…and I don't know which way is up.'

'Then…' He paused for a moment and exhaled slowly. 'What if we…cautiously…research this attraction? Instead of trying to deny it, we explore it.'

'To see if it *is* just residual?'

'Exactly.'

'And what if it is? What if we try this and it fizzles out?'

'Then we can go back to being friends because that's the one part I don't want to lose. I don't want to lose your friendship, Maybelle.'

'So we do some *research* into exactly what this is we're both feeling.' Even saying the word 'research' made her feel nauseous. She gritted her teeth and momentarily closed her eyes. It was just a word…a word, that was all, and yet it made her stomach churn.

'What's wrong?' he asked cautiously when she looked at him again.

'Nothing.' He fixed her with a look that indicated he knew she wasn't being completely honest with him. 'It's just that…' She felt stupid even telling him this.

'What?'

'The word *research*—it…it makes my stomach churn.'

'But it's just a word.'

And now he was looking at her as though she was insane. 'Don't you think I know that and I also know that not all…scientific investigations…' she paused, using the alternative for the word '…are bad? And in this case, it's only right that we figure out what it is we feel for each other.'

'But hearing the actual word makes you feel ill?'

'Yes.'

'However, you're willing to do some…scientific investigation into how we feel about each other?'

She nodded, pleased he'd listened to her. Even if he hadn't completely comprehended what it was she was saying, it was nice of him to avoid the word on her account. She relaxed for a split second before tensing her shoulders once more as a new thought occurred to her. 'But wait a second, what if one of us feels it's great and the other one doesn't?'

Arthur frowned. 'Huh. I hadn't thought that far. I'd always assumed we'd both be unanimous in our decision.'

'Something still to consider, then.'

'Yes.' His frown deepened. 'Should we go for it, then? Embark upon this new re— Er…new project?'

Maybelle considered it for a long moment. Research. Her parents had researched things together and apart but each time it had drawn them closer together. Perhaps that had been the formula all along where she and Arthur were concerned. They needed to do their investigations, to discover exactly what it was that existed between them, so she nodded. 'Yes. We embark on this new project.'

'OK.' The frown instantly disappeared, to be replaced by one of his glorious smiles. 'OK. This is good.'

'It is.' She smiled back at him, a slight awkwardness starting to surround them. 'So now what?'

'That's a good question.' He chuckled and the sound broke the tension. 'Dinner? Tonight?'

'Sounds great. Your place or mine?'

'How about we actually venture out to a restaurant? That Italian one we spotted earlier today.'

'A real date?' Why did the notion instantly fill her with dread? But, she rationalised, it was what normal people did. They would go out to dinner, enjoy a meal, talk and laugh and generally have a good time.

'Seems as good a place as any to begin our…investigation.'

'I'll pick you up at seven-thirty,' she offered.

Arthur leaned forward and pressed a kiss to her lips, sealing the deal. 'It's a date.'

When Arthur arrived home, he was still reeling from the fact he and Maybelle were actually going out on a date.

Even all those years ago, they'd never been out on a real date so tonight would definitely be a first for them.

He couldn't believe how happy he felt, how right this felt, and with that realisation came a load of questions.

'All good research projects come with questions,' he told Juzzy as he fed her. 'Right? I mean, if we didn't ask questions, what would we research?'

The most prominent question was that after his disastrous marriage to Yvette he'd promised himself not to become embroiled in a serious relationship again and here he was, not only embarking on a date but a date with the first girl he'd ever given his love to.

'She's not just any woman,' he told Juzzy. 'And that's what scares me.' She was an amazing woman, one who made him contemplate life in a different way, one who challenged him at work to research further and look deeper into patient problems, one who made his heart miss a beat every time she smiled at him.

He walked into his bedroom and reached far back on the top shelf of his cupboard and pulled out an old shoe box. Inside were two photos of himself and Maybelle. One had been taken at her sixteenth birthday party before they'd kissed. He had his arm around her in a brotherly sort of fashion and she was looking at him, smiling that secret smile of hers. Now, at least, he knew what that smile meant!

The other photo had been taken by Clara about five weeks later when the three of them had gone to Melbourne City for the day. There had been a parade on and both the girls had wanted to go. Arthur's mother had asked him to tag along to make sure the girls were safe. Arthur hadn't needed to be asked twice. This time they were sitting next to each other eating ice creams, both of them grinning brightly at the camera, and she had some-

how managed to get ice cream on the end of her nose.
She had been so carefree, so innocent back then. So different from the woman she was today…and he cared deeply for them both.

The other thing in the shoe box was a small pink pen with a top. She'd used that pen on the last night they'd had together, writing *Arthur smells delicious* on his revision notes. He'd thrown the piece of paper out after she'd vanished from his life, but for some silly reason he'd kept the pen.

He took the box out to the lounge room as his cellphone rang. He immediately hoped it wasn't Maybelle calling to cancel their date but rather that she was calling to say she wanted to start the date earlier…as in right *now*. But it wasn't Maybelle, it was his sister.

'Hey, sis,' he said after connecting the call.

'Hey, bro,' she returned, following through on the usual way they greeted each other over the phone.

'What's happening?'

'I could ask you the same question.' There was a tone to Clara's voice that made him wary.

'What are you talking about?'

'Maybelle Freebourne? The woman you haven't been able to stop mentioning in your emails and text messages? Remember her?'

'Sure. What about her?' Did Clara know? He hadn't said anything about Maybelle's true identity to his sister simply because it wasn't his secret to tell. Until Maybelle told him that Clara knew, he had to keep silent.

'Do you remember what you wrote in your last email? About how you like spending time with her and that she makes you laugh and how Juzzy thinks she's amazing?'

'Juzzy *does* think Maybelle is amazing.' He sank

down into the lounge and stared at the pictures on his mantelpiece, especially the one with Clara and Maybelle at their birthday party.

'Are you crazy? You're falling in love with this woman!'

Clara had a valid point, although Arthur had to wonder whether he'd ever really fallen out of love with Maybelle.

'Why would it be crazy if I was in love with someone?'

'Because of what Yvette did to you! Because of what Virgil did to me! We made a pact, remember? We said we'd give up on love and focus on our careers and then that way we'd spare ourselves from ever feeling as though our lives were worthless, meaningless and downright depressing.'

He sighed. 'We did say that, didn't we?'

'On your last visit to see me.' Clara sounded crushed.

'I'm sorry, sis. I'm sorry Virgil broke your heart but at the moment I'm not sorry that Yvette broke mine.'

'What? How can you say that? She cheated on you with any man who looked twice at her and then blamed you for not being progressive enough to want an "open marriage".'

'If Yvette hadn't broken my heart, it never would have mended again.'

Clara paused. 'You really are in love with this May-belle Freebourne woman, aren't you?' His sister's tone was softer now, more calm.

'I don't know for sure but one thing I have realised is that I need to try. If she breaks my heart, *then* I'll give up on love for ever.'

'Promise?'

Arthur chuckled. 'Promise.'

'Well, I'm now really looking forward to meeting this woman in four weeks' time.'

'Four weeks, eh? You're coming home? For real this time?'

'Yes. For real this time. I've booked my flight and I'll send you the details so you can pick me up from the airport.'

'Oh, thanks.' While Clara talked about her plans for the next month, Arthur kept a close eye on the clock. Only four more hours until Maybelle was due to knock on his door…and he couldn't wait.

CHAPTER ELEVEN

WHEN MAYBELLE ARRIVED home from the hospital, she lay down on her bed, trying to get rid of the headache that had started not long after she'd suggested going on a real date with Arthur. Why should she be so concerned about it? Yes, they were going out to a public restaurant—something she hadn't done in…well, she couldn't remember the last time she'd gone out for a nice meal. Yes, she had trouble feeling so exposed in such a place but she had to keep reminding herself that the threat to her life was over, that she was free.

One of the last things her father had said to her before he'd passed away had been that he was sorry for her missed opportunities.

'I'm sorry you never got to date like a normal girl. That you never got to have your heart broken as a young woman because even getting your heart broken can build such strength of character.' He'd smiled at her, a small, sad smile that had pierced her soul. 'I'm sorry you never get to go out to dinner with a man, to have him send you flowers, to be courted in the way I courted your mother.'

'Dad, it's not as though I haven't dated over the years—' She'd tried to interject but her father had hushed her.

'I mean a real and long-lasting relationship,' he'd

added. 'The kind your mother and I had.' Then he'd fallen silent for a long while, his eyes closed, his voice hoarse and barely audible. His breathing had been uneven and a few times Maybelle had checked his pulse to make sure he'd still been breathing. 'I'm sorry for everything we put you through but at the time we thought we were making a difference in the world, that we were making it a better place for you to live in, for our grandchildren and great-grandchildren.'

'So that's the main reason why you want me to find a fellow? You want grandchildren,' she'd teased, and had been rewarded with a small smile from her father.

'I love you, May, and I'm proud of you. Find someone. Find someone who loves you in the way you deserve to be loved. An unconditional love. A love that will stay with you for ever and never let you go, no matter what the consequences. Promise me.'

'I promise, Dad.' She'd spoken the words back then, promising him the world if she'd thought it would put his mind at ease. Now she spoke the words softly into the silence of her apartment. 'I promise, Dad, and I think I've found him. I think I found him long ago and I hope… I really hope that this works out because if it doesn't, well, perhaps I'll have to make do with living for my career, of making a difference in this world for future generations.'

At seven-thirty, Maybelle knocked on Arthur's door. Her hand was still raised when he opened it, as though he'd been standing on the other side, just waiting for her knock. 'Hi.'

'Hi.' He gazed at her, taking in the black trousers, red lace top with undershirt and big red coat. 'You look lovely.'

'So do you.' She appreciated his suit and chambray

shirt. 'I wasn't quite sure what sort of attire the restaurant required so went with something I'd usually wear to work. Sorry.'

'Don't apologise.' Why were they both talking this way? So stilted? So formal? 'Uh…you ready to go?'

'Yes. Yes.' She stepped back from the threshold as he exited the apartment. 'Juzzy asleep?'

'She's eaten her dinner and is tucked up in her doggy bed.' He locked his door and then turned to face her. 'Would you like to take your car or mine? Because I'm more than happy to drive.'

'I'm fine to drive, too,' she stated, and then they both stood there, staring at each other for a long moment. Never before had Maybelle felt this uncomfortable with him. What was wrong with them? Now that they'd decided to actually pursue their relationship, to give it a try, were they both trying too hard?

When he didn't say anything else, she turned and headed towards the parking garage. Arthur followed behind and as soon as she drove out into the street, he turned the radio on. Discomfort reigned the entire journey to the restaurant and Maybelle kept trying to think of a decent topic of conversation that could keep them going for a while but her mind was too busy focusing on the uncomfortable tension.

It wasn't until they were seated in the restaurant, with large menus to hide behind, that Arthur cracked.

'This is ridiculous.' He put his menu onto the table and stared across at her. 'We shouldn't be this uncomfortable going out on our first date.'

'I think it's because we've both realised it *is* our first date that it *is* uncomfortable.'

'Then let's not call it a first date,' he ventured with a

shrug. 'Let's call it a discussion, with food, about our... mutually beneficial scientific investigation.'

Even though he wasn't using the word *research*, which she appreciated, there was no other way to really disguise that what they were planning to embark on was, in fact, a research project. She sighed at the words.

'What's wrong?'

'It's nothing.' She looked at her menu. 'I think I'll have the gnocchi.'

'It's not "nothing". Tell me. What's wrong?' He reached across the table and touched her hand but the touch felt wrong, clinical and very...*researchy*. She tried not to recoil because deep down inside she really did want this to work. She wanted to be with Arthur. He was her knight in shining armour but right now he felt more like her lab partner.

'My parents were scientists.'

'I know.'

'Researchers.'

'I know.' He nodded, a small confused smile on his lips.

'They spent more time in their labs, studying the contents of microscope slides, mass-spectrometers and Petri dishes than they did with me.'

'I know.'

'As parents, they were married to their work, and as a child I could accept that.'

'What's your point?'

She shook her head. 'I don't want this...' she gestured to the invisible air between them '...to become an experiment. I don't want to be analysing every little thing, to be taking notes, comparing data.'

'I'm not saying that's exactly what we'll be doing.'

'But you said we should cautiously investigate the possibility of the attraction we feel.'

'Maybelle, what is it you're trying to say?'

'I don't know.' She closed her eyes for a moment and shook her head. 'Perhaps we're trying too hard. Perhaps coming out to dinner was a mistake.' She glanced around them, feeling highly exposed and self-conscious. 'I'm not good in open spaces. I'm not good at making small talk. I'm not good at these normal things.'

'You agreed to come to the restaurant. We could have stayed home.' He spread his arms wide.

'I know, Arthur. I'm trying to do the normal things but the more I try the more I realise that I'm not good at the normal things. I'm good at the abnormal things and—'

'May I take your order?'

At the sudden appearance of the white-aproned waiter Maybelle almost jumped through the roof, he'd startled her so much. Her knee hit the underneath of the table, causing the glassware to clink and the silverware to rattle. She had a fork clenched in her hand, ready to use it as a weapon if she needed to.

'I'm s-sorry...' the waiter stammered.

'You startled her,' Arthur remarked, smiling at the surprised man. At the same time Arthur leaned over and placed his hand over Maybelle's clenched fist, almost willing her to relax. 'Perhaps you could give us a few more minutes, please?'

'Of course, sir.' The waiter disappeared and Arthur tried to meet Maybelle's gaze. When he did, he realised she'd shut down. She wasn't going to open up and talk to him, not here, not now, not tonight.

'We can leave, if you'd like,' he said.

'We can?' She seemed surprised at that, unsure of the social parameters of dining in a restaurant. 'OK, then.'

Without another word, she dropped the fork, collected her bag and coat, and walked quickly towards the door.

Arthur didn't want to delay too long in the restaurant, quickly apologising to the waiter and seating hostess, in case Maybelle left and drove home without him. On the drive back to their apartments she was silent. It wasn't until she was at the foot of the stairs, ready to head up to her apartment, that she ventured to say anything.

'I'm sorry, Arthur. I thought I could do this.'

'That's OK. Perhaps we should have eaten at home, at least until you get the hang of being out in public spaces and—'

'I meant you and I. I thought I could do this—that I could be impartial, try to see whether the feelings we have are residual or something more…but I can't.' She started up the stairs.

'Maybelle, wait. It's just a trial run. Remember we'd agreed that if we both feel it isn't going to work, we'll go back to being just friends.'

'I'm sorry, Arthur. I can't do this.' She continued up the stairs.

'That seems to be your answer for anything you don't like, Maybelle,' he called. '"I can't do this". Well, I have a question for you. What *can* you do? Huh? Let me tell you what you *can* do. You *can* tie a man up in knots and make him question his previous rational decisions. You *can* confuse a man so he doesn't know which way is up and you *can* break his heart if you continue to walk away.'

Maybelle tried not to listen, tried not to hear the pain in his voice, but his words pierced her heart. She leaned over the balcony and looked at him. '"I can't do this" means… I'm empty, Arthur. I have nothing to give you and the last thing I want to do is to infect you with my emptiness. All my life, every step and decision I've made has been analysed, first by my parents and then by the government. And the one time—the *one time* I allowed myself to throw caution to the wind, my mother died.' Maybelle choked back tears.

'I was held to ransom for two and a half days, locked in a dark room with dirty water offered as my only means of sustenance, while my father went through the hell of being blackmailed. Finally, I was rescued with government operatives shooting dead my captors. I saw all that and once I was free I had to deal with the task of burying my mother. After that, I had to care for my father because he didn't know how to live without my mother.'

She shook her head. 'Relationships are hard. I know this and when I say I can't do this, I mean that I can't...' She stopped, her voice breaking along with her heart. 'I can't open myself up to you in case I lose you, too.

'The government's told me that the threat to my life is over but what if it isn't? That might just be paranoia talking but what if they come after me again, thinking I know the magic formula to give them their undetectable serum? What if they come after me...through you? I can't let that happen. I can't and I won't.'

With that, she turned and headed into her apartment, closing the door firmly on any relationship between herself and Arthur.

It was almost impossible for Maybelle to sleep at all that night, tossing and turning in her bed as visions of the life she'd always dreamed she'd have with Arthur floated around her. Part of her wanted to accept what he was offering with both hands, to run to him and wrap her arms around him and never let him go. The other part of her saw the two of them running from people who were chasing them in big black cars. Arthur was holding their daughter in his arms and she held their baby son as they ran.

Finally she managed to get them to safety, where they were no longer being followed, and Arthur looked at her with anger and hatred in his eyes, telling her this was all her fault, that he was taking the children from her so they could be kept safe. That he didn't want her or the trouble she'd brought into his life any more, that he didn't love her.

'Arthur! Arthur! No! No!'

Waking with a start, she sat bolt upright in bed, her face wet with tears. Her heart was thumping wildly against her chest as though she'd just run a marathon. It took a good five minutes for her to even move her head, her eyes still wide with fear as she looked at the clock. Four o'clock in the morning. That couldn't be right. She felt as though she hadn't slept at all. As she tried to untangle herself from the bedsheets, she realised she was covered in sweat.

It wasn't the terror of things that had happened to her that was causing her to feel so incredibly empty but the realisation that her life without Arthur would be worse than anything she had experienced.

'I love him,' she whispered as she walked slowly out to the kitchen, the coolness of the morning soothing her over-warm skin. 'I honestly love that man and I will never love another the way I love him.' Speaking the words out loud as she poured herself a glass of water only made her accept the depth of her feelings for Arthur. He was her other half. He was the man she'd measured all others against and she'd ruined it.

How she was supposed to keep working alongside him when she felt this way, she had no idea. She'd faced some difficult things in her life, hiding, changing her name, kidnappings, her mother's death and watching her father fade away to nothing. She'd been taught how to survive in a dark and sinister world but nothing had prepared her for the world of light and happiness. How was she supposed to survive?

Sitting on her lounge, she sipped the water and contemplated her dream. Bad things had happened and Arthur had blamed her. The look in his eyes, the look of hatred had been enough to scare her far more than anything else in her life ever had. She knew it had been a dream but dreams could come true, especially bad dreams.

Shaking her head, she tried hard to clear her thoughts, to push the panic of never having a life with Arthur out of her mind, and headed to the shower. She was up and awake, so she may as well get ready and head to the hospital. At least there she could bury her thoughts about Arthur in work...unless she saw him there...unless she was called to work alongside him.

'What am I going to do?' she wailed as she stepped beneath the water, the soothing droplets doing nothing to ease the tension in her shoulders. After her shower, she dressed and contemplated eating something, but when her stomach churned at the thought she grabbed her bag and keys and headed out the door.

She was halfway down the stairs when Arthur's front door opened. Reacting on instinct, Maybelle immediately turned and sprinted up the stairs back to her apartment, hoping he hadn't seen her.

'Maybelle?'

The sound of her name being called made her speed up, made her want to hide inside her apartment for the rest of her life. She managed to make it to the door but was fumbling for her keys when he took the stairs two at a time, coming to stand next to her just as she fitted the key into the lock.

'Maybelle, you can't start avoiding me.'

'Yes, I can.' She unlocked her door and went to go inside, but dropped her bag as she struggled to pull the key out of the lock. Arthur, being the incredible man he was, graciously stepped inside her open door, holding it for her while she picked up her bag and removed her key from the lock.

'Can't sleep either, eh?'

'I can sleep.' Her answer was defiant as she walked back into her apartment, knowing there was no way of avoiding him now. The conversation she didn't want to have was about to happen and she tried to steel her nerves by walking into the kitchen and switching the kettle on. Why couldn't they just go on living their separate lives, finding a sort of weird level of friendship so they could at least work together without things being awkward?

'I know you can sleep. I carried you to my spare bed, remember. You were *out* of it.'

Maybelle pointed her finger at him. 'Don't be cute.'

'That's a little difficult given my natural charm and charisma but for you…I'll try.' He leaned against the kitchen bench, watching as she moved around the kitchen. She wasn't sure what she was doing. She was trying to be busy, to make them tea or coffee or something, because she didn't want to talk about things, didn't want to face the truth of the situation.

'Maybelle.' He paused. She knew he was waiting for her to look at him but she couldn't. 'Honey—'

'Don't call me that.' Maybelle picked up the cloth and started wiping down the bench, completely avoiding the area where he stood. She was being a complete coward and that wasn't like her but when it came to facing the truth about how she felt about him, a coward she was. Putting the cloth aside, she clasped her hands together and turned her back to him. Closing her eyes, she counted to ten but still her heart continued to race and her brain refused to acknowledge any sort of rational thought apart from the tattooed rhythm of the words, *I love you. I love you, I love you*.

'Maybelle. I just have one question for you.'

'Hmm?' She opened her eyes and forced herself to look at him.

'Did you mean it when you said you couldn't lose me again?'

Maybelle thought for a moment, trying desperately to remember exactly what she'd said to him last night. She'd been distraught and over-emotional. Regardless, she knew the words were true. She would be devastated if something were to happen to Arthur, especially on her account.

'Yes.'

'And you can't enter into a relationship with me in case you let me down or hurt me, is that right?'

'Uh…' She went to pick up the cloth, to try and clean something again, but with her heart continuing to thump out that *I love you* tattoo, making her breathless with longing, wiping the bench seemed so incredibly meaningless. In fact, everything in life seemed incredibly meaningless…without Arthur. 'Uh…yes.' She nodded for emphasis.

'Oh, honey.' He took a step towards her and she immediately took one back. 'Will you just stand still for a second?' He took another step towards her and she remained where she was, her mouth dry, her knees turning to jelly and her every nerve ending in her body zinging to life as he slipped his hands around her waist. 'You're far more messed up in the head than I thought.' He brushed a kiss across her lips. 'But I love you, Maybelle. I don't think I've ever stopped loving you and I don't think I ever will. It's for ever, this love. For ever. I offer it to you, with all my heart and with no conditions. My love is yours. Unconditionally.'

'Unconditional love?' she breathed the words, unable to believe that what her father had told her to find, she'd actually succeeded in doing. 'You love me? *Really* love me?'

'I'll prove it to you.' Arthur drew her closer and pressed his lips to hers. The way he kissed her, the way his lips held firm to hers for a long and powerful moment, the way he made her realise he wasn't going to let her go was also a promise. It was as though he was promising to always be there for her and Maybelle was having a difficult time wrapping her mind around that concept.

'But…' she managed when he eased back for a moment. 'But what about your career? Your research projects? You already have funding for one of them. That, combined with your work in the ED and running the ED and researching and career-ladder climbing and…when are you going to have time for a relationship?'

'I thought long and hard last night about everything you'd said, and I realised that what you were trying to say in the restaurant was that you didn't want to take second place to my work.'

'I spent all my life being way down the list of my parents' priorities.' Her voice was soft.

'I know, honey.'

'I can't live the rest of my adult life being way down on *your* priority list. I can't do it.' She shook her head as though to emphasise her words.

'You won't be. The re—the scientific investigation

projects are each only six months in duration. Both of them will be conducted one day a week in the research laboratories attached to the hospital…and I'll be needing specialised staff to assist me with the investigations.' He looked deeply into her eyes. 'I know you've been through hell and all because of scientific research, honey, but the areas I'm looking into are *nothing* like the research your parents were conducting.'

'I know that. Don't you think I know that? Don't you think I know that not all research is bad? That the majority of research projects don't lead to life-threatening situations? The rational side of me understands that. However, the irrational side of me, the one that has been fed through surviving in such difficult circumstances… the side that makes my stomach churn at the mere thought of entering into any sort of research, tends to become predominant, causing me to behave like a crazy lady.'

He couldn't help but chuckle softly at her words. 'You might be a crazy lady, honey, but you're *my* crazy lady.'

'I am?' He clearly wasn't put off by what she was saying and that astonished and delighted her.

'You're also the smartest girl I know. I told you that years ago and it hasn't changed now, which is why I would be honoured if, for that one day a week at the hospital labs, you'll work alongside me, taking part in the scientific investigation and applying your incredible intelligence to it.' He brushed his hand across her cheek, gazing into her eyes. 'I want you near me. I want you with me…all the time. I lost you for twenty years and I couldn't possibly put anything in my life first…except you. I was in a marriage where I was most definitely not first in her eyes, and when that marriage ended I told myself it was easier to be married to my career. My career wouldn't let me down, it would always be there. There's always re—scientific investigations that need doing. But then you came back into my life and... Maybelle, honey, you changed everything. *Everything*. Yes, I want to help people by being a doctor but if I had to choose to be with you or to practise medicine, I'd choose you.'

'I don't want you to choose. I want to—'

He pressed his finger to her lips to silence her. 'I know you're not asking me to choose. I know you respect my work, not only as a doctor but as an emergency specialist. You get that and I know, once you read my research proposals, you'll become as passionate about the projects as I am...because I know you. You give and you give and you give, and again that's just another thing that I love about you.'

Tears had started to well in Maybelle's eyes at the way he was speaking so passionately, not only about her, and the way he thought she was intelligent, but about his work, and in that one moment Maybelle finally understood the relationship her parents had shared. It had been one of mutual love and respect but also an equal meeting of intelligence.

She couldn't help herself any longer and threw her arms around his neck and drew his head close to hers until her lips met his in a powerful kiss. She poured all her love into that kiss, and to let him know that she wanted to be with him, to share every aspect of his life.

'So you love me?' he asked a while later, and she was astonished to hear the slight hesitation in his tone.

'Yes. I do.' She felt rather than heard his sigh of relief.

'And I love you.' The words were spoken without hesitation.

'And we're going to work together at the hospital in the ED and in the labs...' She kissed him again.

'And on building a life together.'

Maybelle paused in her elation for a second as a thread of fear passed through her at his words. 'A life together... Arthur, what if...what if bad people *do* come after me again?' She shook her head. 'I had a terrible dream where they came after you and our children and...and...'

'I'll learn all the martial arts and protective measures and whatever else I need to, to ensure my family's safety,' he told her firmly.

'Family? Are you sure?'

He laughed and kissed her. 'Oh, Maybelle. You really are so perfect for me. I swore I'd never enter into marriage again but you were right. My heart wants to have a family, to have a house in the suburbs and to be with the woman I love for the rest of my life...and that woman is you.'

'Are you asking me to marry you?' She moved back and smiled at him.

'I believe I am. What do you say?'

She stood on tiptoe and kissed him before easing from his arms. 'I say, wait here a second.'

'That's not a yes!' he called after her as she rushed into her bedroom then quickly returned. She held out her hand and he opened his to accept whatever it was she was giving him. So trusting. She liked that.

Into his hand, she placed his watch. 'I've had this ever since that night. I've kept it safe. Kept it close. Kept it as a bond, linking us together.'

He shook his head with incredulity. 'You kept my watch.' He reached into the pocket of his trousers and pulled something out. He followed suit and held his hand out, waiting until she opened hers so he could place something on it.

'My pink pen? You kept my pink pen?'

'I think the ink's dried up, though.'

'You kept my pen.'

'You kept my watch.'

'We've stayed connected all these years.'

'It was meant to be.' He drew her close once more.

'We belong together.'

'We do.'

'Marry me?'

'Yes.' Then she pressed her lips to his, hoping to convey her heartfelt love to the man who had always been her knight in shining armour…her King Arthur.

EPILOGUE

FOUR WEEKS LATER Clara Lewis arrived back in Australia and was met at the airport by her big brother and his fiancée, Maybelle Freebourne.

'May! It's really you?'

Maybelle laughed as Clara completely ignored her brother and embraced May as though the past twenty years hadn't existed at all. Maybelle had had a similar reaction from Arthur's parents, the Lewises welcoming her into their family in the same way they had all those years ago.

Although Clara and Maybelle had spoken on the phone several times during the past four weeks, seeing each other face to face was very emotional.

She was glad Clara had returned to Australia when she had, because in another three weeks Clara would be her maid of honour, and Mr and Mrs Lewis would both walk her down the aisle so Maybelle could marry Arthur and officially become a member of the Lewis family.

'It's what I'd always hoped,' Clara whispered in Maybelle's ear as they continued their hug. 'You're really going to be my sister.'

'OK, you two. Break it up,' Arthur remarked as he put an arm around each of them, his beloved sister on one side and his incredible future wife on the other.

'You're just jealous,' Clara sniffed.

'Completely. I've been used to having Maybelle all to myself. Now I have to share her and I don't like it one little bit.'

'Possessive, much?' Clara teased her brother as they headed off to the luggage carousel.

'Happy?' Arthur asked Maybelle later that evening as they sat on the lounge, Juzzy snuggled up between them.

'Beyond my wildest dreams. I've gone from being all alone to having parents, a sister and a dog.'

'What about me?'

'Oh, yeah. And an incredible man who loves me… unconditionally.'

* * * * *

If you enjoyed this story, check out these other great reads from Lucy Clark:

A FAMILY FOR CHLOE
ENGLISH ROSE IN THE OUTBACK
STILL MARRIED TO HER EX!
A CHILD TO BIND THEM

All available now!

THE ULTIMATE IN ROMANTIC MEDICAL DRAMA

A sneak peek at next month's titles...

In stores from 29th June 2017:

- **The Surrogate's Unexpected Miracle** – Alison Roberts
  and **Convenient Marriage, Surprise Twins** – Amy Ruttan

- **The Doctor's Secret Son** – Janice Lynn
  and **Reforming the Playboy** – Karin Baine

- **Their Double Baby Gift** – Louisa Heaton
  and **Saving Baby Amy** – Annie Claydon

617/03

MILLS & BOON®

EXCLUSIVE EXTRACT

Lana Haole and the all-too tempting Dr Andrew
Tremblay agreed to a marriage of convenience... But
suddenly their convenient arrangement has become a
whole lot more!

Read on for a sneak preview of
CONVENIENT MARRIAGE, SURPRISE TWINS

Lana's request had caught him off guard, but he wasn't
displeased by it. Not at all. It was just that he couldn't.
He'd just never expected it from her. She was always so
careful, guarded, but the more time he was spending with
her, the more he realized a hot fiery passion burned beneath
the surface.

And that was something he wanted to explore, but he
had a sneaking suspicion that if he tasted this once, he
was going to want more and more. So, even though it
killed him, he left the room. Walked the beach, far away
from the wedding, to calm his senses, but it didn't work
because all he could think about was Lana's lips pressed
against his.

The feeling of her in his arms.

And her begging him to make love to her.

You can't.

Although he wanted to.

After what seemed like an eternity he returned to the
room. Hoping that everything had blown over, that she
might be already asleep even, but instead he saw her sitting
on the couch, a flute of champagne in her hand. She turned
to look at him when he shut the door and he could see the
tearstains on her cheeks.

Pain hit him hard.

He'd hurt her.

"Oh, I didn't expect you to come back," she said quietly and she wiped the tears from her face.

"I just needed a moment to myself."

"I see," she said quietly. Then she sighed. "Well, I think I'm going to turn in."

"Lana, I think we need to talk," he said.

"What is there to talk about?" She frowned. "You didn't want me and you have nothing to apologize about. I'm the one that wanted to step out of the boundaries we set. Not you."

"No, that's not it."

"What do you mean?" she asked, confused.

"I want you too, Lana. It's not for lack of desiring you. I want you. More than anything." And, though he knew that he shouldn't, he closed the distance between them and kissed her, fully expecting her to pull back from him the way that he had pulled from her, but she didn't. Instead she melted into his arms and he knew that he was a lost man.

Don't miss
CONVENIENT MARRIAGE, SURPRISE TWINS
by Amy Ruttan

Available July 2017
www.millsandboon.co.uk